# One December

### Kyle Hunter

P. O. Box 30981
Raleigh, NC 27622
www.Kyle-Hunter.com

Cover design by Designography, LLC.

ISBN 978-0-9906246-7-7

*One December*

*More novels by Kyle Hunter*

**Circle Back Around**
**One December**

*Provence Series*

**Prodigals in Provence**
**A Promise in Provence**

*The Second Chance Series*

**Marissa Rewritten** *(A Novella)*
**Julia Redesigned**
**Sydney Rewound**
**Eden Redefined**

*The Brenner Falls Series*

**Good Gifts**
**Custom Made**

*One December*

# Chapter One

Nikki Mancini couldn't stop herself from humming as the holiday tune filled the kitchen from her phone perched on the table. "Merry little Christmas. . ." The familiar words slipped out as she rolled a soft mound of dough on the wooden cutting board.

"This crust is almost ready, Mom," Nikki said. "It's for lemon meringue, right? Hint, hint. . ." She raised her eyebrows and grinned.

Her mother leaned over the pot simmering on the stove and took a deep sniff. She held the lid and gave the bubbling sauce a stir with a wooden spoon. Long shafts of winter sunlight, cloudy with swirls of flour dust, spilled through the kitchen window.

Nikki's Aunt Trudie answered, "This one's mincemeat." Trudie leaned over the counter and poised her knife over a pile of nuts. She had the same thick, black hair and laughing eyes as her twin brother, Nikki's father. "Not very Italian, but it's one of your dad's favorites." She turned a smile toward Nikki. "My kids like it too."

"Are they coming for the holidays this year?" Nikki blew a stray hair away from her cheek, then glanced at her aunt. The phone launched into an orchestral version of "Silver Bells."

"Just Drew and his girlfriend for Christmas Day. Shelby is spending the day with her boyfriend's family this year." She sighed. "Can't have everybody at once, I guess, especially as the kids grow up."

Nikki frowned and pressed the dough with more force than necessary into the glass pan. She fluted the edges with her thumbprints, still frowning. Though she was only twenty-four, she'd probably be at this very table in thirty years doing the same thing. The single daughter, making piecrusts at Christmas.

"We'll still have a crowd." Her mother's tone showed she clearly enjoyed her tasks. "Not that I mind, of course."

Nikki rolled her aching shoulders backward, then forward. She too loved the annual tradition of helping her mother cook on holidays. From October on, she looked forward to the holiday season. Basking in the festivity, surrounded by tantalizing smells and traditional music. . .

That year, there would be twenty around the table. Ample motivation for Nikki, her mother, and her Aunt Trudie to work with the unflinching focus of a military campaign two days in advance.

Living only a town away enabled Nikki to drop by her parents' house easily and often anytime throughout the year. The Big House, as her parents' home was called by family members, was the official gathering place for the Mancini clan. *This* Christmas stood apart from other holidays. The very thought of one particular guest due to arrive later that day stoked a flutter like a flock of birds deep inside her.

"Are Danny and Cheryl coming tomorrow, Marie?" Aunt Trudie nudged her glasses up on her nose.

"Yes, they'll get here tomorrow afternoon. Danny couldn't get away from the dealership any earlier. I guess lots of people are buying cars for Christmas gifts this year." Nikki's mother moved briskly to the refrigerator and back to the stove, a wedge of fresh parmesan in one hand. "I wish my Danny lived closer, like Nikki and Laura. Once the new baby comes, I'll probably have to go out to them more often."

"And isn't Mike coming this year too?" Trudie asked. Something inside Nikki's stomach jolted. She tried to look nonchalant, unsure if she'd succeeded.

"Yes, it's his year." Nikki's mother chuckled. "He knows he'd be disowned by the family if he didn't come for Christmas at *least* every three years. Jim and Catherine are on their way to the airport now to pick him up. They should all be here by dinner."

Nikki glanced down at her watch.

"I guess Mike has made his own life out in San Francisco," Trudie said. "It'll be so nice to see him again, after all this time. Remember, Nikki, when you were young and had a crush on him?" She chuckled.

"Please, Aunt Trudie." Nikki took a jocular tone to hide her mortification and the hot flush creeping up her neck. "I took a lot of teasing for that. For years."

"Said you wanted to marry him. It was so cute. You were only, what, six or seven?"

"Something like that." Nikki sighed, and her mind groped for options to change the subject. Snow that evening? Flu outbreak? She'd have to think of something.

"I'm surprised he's not married yet," her mother said. "So handsome and smart."

Nikki shrugged with feigned indifference. *Let it go already.*

"He was engaged, or almost, to that girl who dumped him. Stephanie, or something?" Trudie shook her head. "He's almost a member of the family, but I know so little about his life."

Marie swiped her hands on her apron. "We'll put those pies in the freezer and thaw them on Christmas morning." She turned to her youngest daughter, her dark eyes smiling through rimless glasses. "Thanks for all your help."

"Bet you're glad to have some vacation time, Nikki." Trudie rinsed her hands. "Teaching high school must be challenging."

"Try it in a foreign language." Nikki pictured her students and smiled. "I love 'em, though. Every year there's a problem kid or two. This year it's Torrie the Terror, in French Two. I'm always on the fence between wanting to be her friend and wanting to smack her."

Trudie and Marie laughed. Nikki was grateful that the conversation had moved on from Mike and her childhood infatuation. "I've finished these crusts, so I'm going to go out to cut

7

some greenery for the mantle." And escape any more awkward conversations.

She pushed back the chair with an abrupt scrape, washed her hands, and escaped to the hall. After stealing another glance at her watch, she slipped into her fleece jacket. Just a few more hours.

Ginger, the aging orange and white cocker spaniel, gazed up at her with watery black eyes. Nikki bent down and rubbed her ears. "My good old girl." At least Ginger wouldn't remind her of childhood embarrassments. Ginger would keep Nikki's secret.

She went out the front door. The chill of December, refreshing after the hot kitchen, immersed her, stinging her cheeks. The pine scent from the wreaths affixed to the huge double doors wove a slight tang into the winter air. She headed to the bushy white pine tree in the backyard, clippers in hand.

After college, Nikki hadn't been very adventurous. Instead, she returned to Adams Bridge, where she'd grown up. There was something decidedly reassuring about being able to drop by the Big House anytime she wanted to. And it felt good to be part of a large, close family. Especially at Christmas.

Nikki pushed her glove away from her wrist to glance once more at her watch, trapping the pine boughs in the crook of her elbow. Mike's plane was due to touch down in about one hour.

Three years had passed since she'd seen Mike. Would things be any different this time? If only she could feel nothing but friendship for Mike Branagan, finally free from the chronic, aching chasm of unreturned love. She'd try to get through the holidays with their friendship intact as well as keep her heart in one piece.

Once back inside, she arranged the pine on the mantle near the couch where her older sister, Laura, sat with her boyfriend, Trey. Nikki's eyes frequently roved to her watch, like a hummingbird to nectar.

At six-thirty, car doors slammed outside, and a clatter of voices approached the front porch. Nikki swallowed. *It's just Mike. You've known him your whole life.*

That was part of the problem.

There was a loud knock, then the muffled "Ho, ho, ho." Her grandfather's voice on the front porch. Her mother dashed into the foyer, still aproned, and eagerly yanked open the front door. Grandpa Jim's navy blue down parka doubled his body volume, the collar nearly hiding his whiskered jaw and wide grin.

Mike materialized behind him like a long-awaited mirage in a tan bomber jacket. He looked weary, his chin smudged with a five o'clock shadow. Thick dark hair swung across his forehead and deep brown eyes lit his slightly rounded face. Nikki's heart tugged inside her.

Lastly, Catherine, Nikki's step-grandmother, shuffled in, carrying a covered dish. She pulled the door behind her with a clack and placed her casserole into Marie's waiting hands. "Whew, it's cold!" She shivered and unwound her frizzy, red scarf. "Traffic wasn't as bad as we expected on a holiday. We made good time."

Immediately, the family enfolded Mike in hugs. "Frank, Laura, great to see you," he said to Nikki's father and sister. "Marie, you look good." He gave Nikki's mother a tight hug, then shook hands with Trey. When he saw Nikki, his face widened into a warm smile, dimples lengthening. Her insides seemed to liquefy.

"Hey, Nikki." Mike's arms encircled her, and he lifted her a few inches off the ground.

"You look just the same," she whispered against his ear as she breathed in the faded scent of his cologne.

"And you keep getting better." He pulled back, his hands still on her shoulders. Was he simply glad to see her, or might there be more? She pulled her tunic sweater down further, in case he noticed the five pounds she'd gained since his last visit.

"You must be tired and hungry, Mike." Nikki's mother pulled his jacket away from his outstretched arms and piled it atop Jim's and Catherine's. "Dinner's ready, so we can eat now."

Everyone filed into the dining room, chattering as they went. Nikki and her mother brought platters of roast beef, potatoes, vegetables, steaming biscuits, and gravy into the dining room. Nikki relaxed, since the moment which she'd obsessed about for weeks was finally past. At least Mike seemed glad to see her.

Colored Christmas lights blinked around the picture window. A steady glow shimmered out from the red tapered candles Marie had spaced down the long table. The clink of cutlery against china plates broke into the hum of conversation. Muted strains of Christmas music floated in from the den. Mike was the center of everyone's curiosity, having given little news over the past three years.

"What do you do in San Francisco?" Trey broke his usual silence and leaned forward on his elbows.

"I work as a graphic designer for a software company," Mike said. "I also have a few rental houses I fixed up and rent to low-income families." He glanced at Nikki, holding her gaze for a second, just before a new volley of questions came from her mother.

Mike answered Marie. Appearing eager to turn attention away from himself, he turned to Nikki's father. "How's the car business doing, Frank? Has the economy affected it very much?"

Nikki's father preened. "Last year we opened a new dealership, so that makes four. The one Danny manages has been doing well. In all, I'd say it's very good. I should start thinking about retirement." His impish smile belied the sincerity of his words.

"I don't know what I'd do with him underfoot." Marie grinned as she reached for the gravy boat. "I'd have to work full-time instead of part time."

The rest of the meal passed in a blur as the noise level rose and the food kept flowing from the kitchen. Nikki stayed quiet, observing and listening. She longed to fill her eyes with the sight of Mike, after years of what felt like starvation, but didn't dare. She'd be mortified if anyone guessed her feelings, those she'd carefully hidden for so long. When everyone had finished dessert, Nikki stood to help clear the dishes.

"Nikki, sit awhile," her mother said gently. "Then we'll do it together." To no one in particular, she added, "Nikki's been an enormous help during the holidays."

"It's okay, Mom. I don't mind." Nikki gathered a few plates into a pile, doing what she did so easily, fading away into practical work. Catherine rose to help her as the conversation around the table continued.

After sponging off the last counter, Nikki was alone in the kitchen. She rummaged under the sink for dishwashing powder, then stood to find Mike leaning against the counter. "You disappeared," he said. "Not tired of me already, are you?"

"Hardly!" She met his eyes, which sparkled with amusement and warmth. "There were too many people talking all at once. And just wait till Christmas when that number will triple." She grinned to let him know she didn't mind.

He crossed his arms and smiled back at her, the same relaxed warmth she remembered, had imagined so many times. He was really *here*. In the flesh.

"I have an idea." His eyes engaged hers. "To get you away from the noisy crowd. Why don't we meet for breakfast tomorrow so we can catch up? Jerry's Deli for lox and bagels, hot coffee, fried eggs? Tempted?"

"Hmm. Might be noisy there too. How about Pancake Palace?"

"Ten o'clock?"

"You're on. Do you remember how to get there?"

"Pancake Palace? That was my second home in high school. All-nighters at the Palace, remember?"

"No, I guess I was out of your life by that time," Nikki said quietly. Instantly she regretted her words, fearing he'd hear an accusation.

His expression softened and his voice dropped almost to a whisper. "My loss. We'll catch up tomorrow at ten, okay?"

He stepped toward her for a hug goodbye. It was only a brotherly hug, but Nikki felt carried away by a dream, buried in his arms for just a moment. With difficulty, she released him. "See you tomorrow."

CR   CR   CR

At the old farmhouse where he'd spent his high school years, Mike sank wearily onto the foot of the bed in his old room. It smelled of decades-old furniture and musty books. Following a quick cup of hot chocolate with Jim and Catherine, he'd begged for sleep and trudged up the creaky stairs. His body sagged with fatigue, but his thoughts were in freefall as the present collided with the past.

His gaze found all the evidence of familiarity, vestiges of a life left behind. High school wrestling and basketball trophies, faded team photos, and school banners lined knotty pine shelves along one wall. Several sketches of animals and landscapes that he'd drawn as a teenager, yellowed with curled up edges, were still thumb tacked to the wood paneling.

He should really clean all this up one day. It had little bearing on his current life and provoked a truckload of negative memories when he visited. He felt like a completely different person than he had been then. Or had he ever been that person?

His new life in San Francisco was uncluttered, carefully sealed off from shadowy memories of grief and loss. There, he could pretend he didn't have a past.

He leaned toward the shelf to peer at a photo of himself with Danny, standing in soccer uniforms, feet spread apart, grins reaching wide. They must have been eight or nine, shortly after they had become best friends.

Absent from the shelf was a photo of his parents. At first, it had been too painful to have their faces staring at him every day. After that, he just never bothered to put their picture with the others. Back when life was normal, his parents' work absorbed their days. He'd spent a lot of time hanging around with Danny, Nikki, and Laura at the Big House, in the above-ground pool or in the neighborhood. After the accident, he was there even more, at Marie's insistence. Every holiday, for dinner, all the time.

Maybe Marie had felt sorry for him. At any rate, the Mancinis had always treated him like a member of the family, especially Jim and Catherine, who'd taken him in when his parents were suddenly ripped out of his life.

Only Frank had been distant and communicated disapproval without words. Mike wasn't a Mancini. No, he would always be Mike Branagan, and he was alone, despite his borrowed family.

He missed San Francisco already.

Mike toed off his shoes, leaned back, and stretched full length on the bed. He hooked his arms behind his head and stared up at the ceiling, letting fatigue flow over him like shallow waves. A month ago, he started wondering whether he should taper off his visits to New York. They were few already. He made the trip at Christmas every three years, mostly for Jim and Catherine. He owed it to them, especially after some of the rough patches he'd put them through during his adolescence. But these trips blocked his full recovery, sucking him back into the past each time he came east. Sure, he'd miss them all, but in time they'd fade from one another's memories, like a mild case of amnesia.

Mike let out a sigh. So much for *those* plans. Ely's phone call last week changed everything. His father's friend had kept sporadic contact with Mike over the years. That gesture had threaded comfort and continuity into his life, brushing the surface of his aloneness.

As the executor of his parents' estate, Ely had completed all the necessary financial requirements following the accident. But the previous week, he'd called out of the blue and claimed to have new information about Mikes' parents' deaths. After thirteen years. An unwelcome jolt splintered Mike's fragile healing.

Mike had no choice but to wait for Ely's return to town after Christmas to hear the news. In the meantime, he'd attempt to enjoy the holidays and the people who, despite everything, still seemed to care about him.

And Nikki. A different emotion rushed in unbidden when he thought of her. How she looked tonight, her gray eyes sober, her olive skin set off against a bright red sweater. There it was again, a tug of attraction. It had begun three years earlier during his last visit.

He smiled, picturing her following him around, love-struck, when she was only seven. Tonight was a different story. She looked even more grown-up than she had three years ago. And how amazing that they'd both found faith about a year apart. Who could have ever guessed that would happen?

She puzzled him, though. She'd been quiet at dinner, almost avoiding his eyes, though he'd tried several times to snag her gaze and send her a smile. At least tomorrow they'd talk over breakfast and catch up on the last few years, hopefully renewing the friendship they'd had as kids. The friendship he'd been guilty of letting slip away, and just when he'd so *needed* a friend.

Despite the emotional turmoil these Christmas visits provoked, seeing Nikki again might add a much-needed bright spot. He'd ignore his attraction to her. Soon enough, he'd be back in his own world on the West Coast.

# Chapter Two

The parking lot of the Pancake Palace was packed. Nikki spied an available space as someone backed out and wedged her Honda between two SUVs. She cut the motor, then checked her appearance in the rear-view mirror. Despite a turbulent night's sleep, she looked alert, hopefully even cute, in a black cable-knit sweater and fleece vest. Silver hoop earrings glistened through her wavy, dark hair and a silver braid necklace that had belonged to her grandmother, hung around her neck.

She pushed the chilled glass door and breathed in the smell of fried hash browns. Along one wall a wide opening gaped toward the noisy kitchen where cooks slammed prepared plates upon a metal counter.

After a quick scan of the dining room, Nikki spotted Mike already seated in a booth. She took a breath, crossed the room, and slid into the vinyl seat opposite him.

His eyes, hooded with fatigue, lifted to hers and he smiled. He already cradled a steaming mug of coffee in both hands. He lifted it toward her. "Hope you don't mind. I started without you. I forgot that you can still get jet lag with only a three-hour time difference." A fleece sweatshirt covered his broad, sloping shoulders. The sleeves were pushed up to mid-forearm, revealing thick, manly wrists and a brown woven bracelet.

"Your body still thinks it's seven in the morning." Nikki looked down at the menus sitting on the vinyl tablecloth and suddenly felt awkward. "Have you decided what to order?" Even if she wasn't distracted by the hammering in her rib cage, how could they catch up after so many years?

15

"I always order the same thing. Special Number Nine, Eggs Benedict with orange juice." He leaned back and stared at her. "I don't know where to start, Nikki." An apology laced his voice. "I haven't kept in touch very well."

"How long will you be in New York?"

"Till the twenty-eighth."

Nikki's shoulders dropped and she pressed her lips together. "Not very long, then."

Mike lifted his head when a flushed waitress with a graying ponytail appeared. She took their order and poured coffee for them. After she left, Mike and Nikki looked at each other in silence then laughed. "Okay, you first," he said. "Tell me about your job, your life. Bring me up to date."

"Okay, that's easy." Nikki reached for her coffee mug. "I'm in my second year teaching high school English and French. I share an apartment with Elaine, my best friend from college."

"French, huh? All I know is 'je ne sais pas' and 'je t'aimez', or something like that."

Nikki laughed. She began to relax. "That won't get you very far, but it could get you into trouble."

Mike grinned back at her. "Do you enjoy teaching high school? And is it true that teaching teenagers is a hard job? And why English and French instead of just one? Sorry, too many questions."

"Ah, a press conference. First of all, I love teaching. Once you get to know the students, they're really great. I'm not much older than they are, so I have to be firm in the beginning of the year."

She settled against the seat, glad that her nerves were calming down. They were friends, after all. Friends catching up after a long, long time. She took a deep gulp of tepid coffee. "And I teach English *and* French because I love both subjects. I minored in French. Then there was this perfect opening at the high school for teaching both. That's one reason I came back here."

"I wondered why you came back to Adams Bridge."

Nikki swallowed. What a naïve child she must seem to him. She'd run back home after graduation, while Mike had gone all the way across the country for college, then settled there. "Yeah, it's not too exciting going back home after college." She shrugged and stared down at the tabletop. "I planned on starting my career here to get some experience and then going someplace else. I guess I'm not as courageous as you were, going to California."

Mike grimaced and looked at his hands. "It wasn't really courage. I just felt like I was ready for a new life somewhere else."

"It didn't bother you, going there alone?"

His dark eyes lifted, nearly piercing hers for a moment. "I've been alone for a long time, Nikki." His statement weighed heavy in the air. Words eluded her so she sat in silence.

In a bright voice that seemed forced, Mike said, "I'm trying to picture you getting tough with a group of teenagers. You must be stronger than you look. I still imagine you as a little kid."

"No, I'm not that little girl anymore," Nikki said firmly, adjusting to his abrupt change of topic. "See, I'm all grown up." She framed her face playfully with both hands. She *had* to redraw the lines of their relationship.

"Yeah, I see that." He grinned. "Now I want to hear how you came to know the Lord. Tell me everything."

The waitress arrived again, placing two plates of steaming oily breakfast food before them. She poured more coffee and disappeared again.

Nikki sliced into her stack of pancakes. "You know I grew up Catholic, but in our family, it was mostly a label, nothing more. My friend Elaine invited me to a campus ministry meeting. The meetings were fun, and I met new people. And I got curious about God. I'd never thought much about Him before, but when I knew it was possible to know Him, I really *wanted* to. So, Elaine and I began to study the Bible together every week. At the end of my junior year, I gave my heart to Jesus."

Mike's expression softened. "That's great. I was so happy to hear you're a believer."

"What about you?"

Mike's brow creased. "My story is, uh, different. Difficult. God must have known it would take a crisis of some kind for me to turn my attention toward Him." He thrust one hand through his hair. "My crisis was Stephanie."

Nikki watched his face. "Your fiancé?"

Mike nodded. "We weren't actually engaged yet. I met Stephanie the spring after my last Christmas visit. We started dating and a few months later, I moved in with her. She'd gotten interested in Christianity through a colleague at work, so she and I started visiting churches together. That got me interested too. I pictured us together on this journey of spiritual discovery."

He paused. Nikki thought she saw his eyes glisten for a moment before he blinked and continued. "That lasted a few months, then one day she tells me she's in love with someone else. I was on the verge of proposing to her, planned on spending my life with her, and she falls for another guy, right under my nose."

Nikki leaned forward. It was as though the distance they'd gathered over the silent years fell away, as his honesty lay bare before her. How could any woman walk away from him, hurt him so deeply? "How awful. You must have been so hurt."

"Devastated is more like it." Mike's voice held a gravelly edge. He shook his head, frowning. "I've never felt that kind of pain in my life. I'd never had my heart broken before."

He leaned back and pushed his half-empty plate away. "But afterward the interest in God stuck with me. I hurt so bad, I was running to Him for answers. Didn't know what else to do. I went back to the church and one day after the service I met with the pastor. Told him my story. He led me to Christ then put me in touch with a guy at the church who was looking for a roommate." He finally smiled and the previous gloom seeped away from his face. "I felt less alone, like I had a family and a father."

"I was so happy to hear about it, I couldn't wait to email you."

"Your email made my day too. Both of us now believers. As kids, didn't it seem like our hearts were already going in the same direction?"

Nikki nodded, sensing he'd read her mind. Hearing about his pain and his burgeoning faith clutched at her heart with breathtaking force. *I have always loved you. I will always love you, Michael Branagan.*

His voice broke into her thoughts. "What are you doing the rest of the day?"

"Uh, nothing. I'm free all day," she said in a casual tone, though his question caused a joyful flutter inside. She hoped he hadn't seen the silent confession on her face.

"I have to return Jim's car, but if you follow me in yours, we can still hang out."

"That would be great. Why don't we drive over to the reservoir and stir up some old memories?" She watched his face.

He laughed. "Got lots of those."

Nikki followed him in her car to Grandpa Jim and Catherine's house, at each stoplight shoving papers and trash under the seats. When they arrived, Mike parked and slipped into her passenger seat. Minutes later they arrived at the reservoir, a natural park area between the towns of Greenbrier and Adams Bridge. Nikki's car sat alone in the parking lot. The reservoir glistened glassy gray, hemmed by spindly bare trees reaching upward on every side. Layered sheaths of milky clouds hung as if ready to fall into the water with a splash.

They walked together toward the edge of the reservoir. A breeze reached chilly fingers under Nikki's scarf and scattered ripples across the water's surface. "Remember the path over there that goes all the way around one side of the lake?"

"I'll race you." Mike's eyes held mischief and they both took off running.

He ran ahead along the worn path that followed the embankment as their feet pounded the nearly frozen dirt. Once they were partway around the lake, Mike slowed down and finally stopped, gulping air. "Here it is." Puffs of vapor spouted upward with his breath. He stepped gingerly over some large boulders, and reached back to guide Nikki. They treaded on a few more rocks and settled into a familiar place, a cove where they used to sit as children to talk or hide.

Nikki looked around with wonder. "It's been so long, I'm not sure I would've known how to find this place again."

"I come to this spot every time I'm back in New York." He encircled one bent knee with his clasped hands.

"Oh? I thought you didn't like coming back at all."

"I don't, really. I come back mostly to see Jim and Catherine. And of course, you and Danny and Marie." He smiled. "I don't hate it here. I just feel that in California I can be myself."

"Sometimes I want to do that too, live somewhere else." Nikki shivered. "Why do you come here to the reservoir when you're visiting?"

"My life out west is so removed from the past, you know, with my parents, then my years with your family. When I'm back for a visit I come here to sort of reassemble the pieces of myself."

"*That's* deep."

They both laughed. He shrugged. "Some would call it brooding, I guess. Though it still hurts some, I think about my parents. Sometimes I remember the good memories from my childhood."

"For example?" She baited him with a smile and raised eyebrows.

He paused in reflection then grinned broadly. "Like the time we sneaked out here to swim, remember? You, me, and Danny. And we didn't tell Laura because she would have ratted us out."

Nikki laughed. "I remember. We tried to hide the fact that we were all wet. Laura saw us dripping on the floor and went yelling, 'I know what you did!' She was the tattle, but you were the ringleader, getting us into trouble."

"Yeah, sorry about that. Once I tried to get you out of trouble with Frank, but it just made him madder at both of us. He's hard to soften once he makes up his mind."

Nikki sobered at the mention of her father. "Are things any better between you and him?"

He shot her a frown.

"Maybe you should talk one of these days."

Mike's face closed. "I think he resents my presence in your family. He always has. He didn't like the fact that I went to live with Jim and Catherine after my parents died."

"Are you sure?"

He nodded, crossing his arms. "I have no idea why he never accepted me like everyone else in the family. Danny was like the brother I never had. You, Danny, your mom—you were like my own family. But not Frank. And that wild phase I went through right after my parents died . . ."

"Dad lost *his* mother at about the same age. I would expect that to bring you together. You know, mutual understanding from a similar loss."

Mike nodded solemnly and stared down into the dark, half-frozen water. "You would think. Maybe it brings back bad memories for him." A small smile lifted a corner of his mouth. "But Nikki, I'll never forget how you were there for me."

Nikki swallowed, remembering the phone call. She and the other kids had been eating watermelon around the kitchen table at the Big House. Ever since that night, the scent of watermelon evoked a mental snapshot of shock around the table, the frozen paleness of Mike's face. Jim and Catherine had insisted Mike come and stay with them.

A moment of brooding silence passed. "Nikki, it's so great to be with you again. I'm sorry for deserting you when I was a teenager. I guess I reached an age where it wasn't cool to hang around with younger kids, and I was tired of feeling like a barnacle in your family. I got my little band of friends instead. I'm sorry we never made it back."

"Until now." Nikki's voice was quiet. "Of course, you wanted to be with your buddies. I see this in my students. Their peer group is all-important." She wouldn't tell him that she'd cried for months, or about the agony she'd lived through waiting for him to come by the house, which he'd done less and less.

21

She reached out and touched his shoulder. "It's okay. As long as we rebuild from right now."

His gaze locked with hers for a long moment, his breath pushing clouds into the cold. Warmth rose up her neck into her face, in spite of the low temperatures. Was there something behind his gaze? Still holding eye contact, he softly said, "We will, Nikki."

The warm flush was soon smothered by an icy wind. Though she'd tried to ignore the cold seeping into her bones, Nikki finally gave up. "I'm freezing. Can we go sit in the car? With the heat on?"

He grinned and caught her arm as she nearly slipped from a smooth boulder. "You *are* a pretty shade of blue. Race again?"

Before she could respond he ran ahead of her toward the car. Once inside she turned on the motor and the heat full blast, rubbing her hands in front of the vent. "It s-seemed w-warmer when we first got here." She shivered.

Mike took her gloved hands in his and rubbed them briskly. "Better?" She nodded and smiled gratefully at him. "Much."

The heater fan spilled out white noise and gradually warmth filled the car. Nikki turned the heat down a notch. "It's like all those years between didn't matter. We don't waste any time on the superficial stuff, do we?" She cocked her head at him.

He met her gaze. "No, we never have. Like old times."

"Yeah, only new and improved." She smiled and cradled her arms. "We're adults now."

He smiled peacefully, leaning back against the headrest. "I like it."

Nikki silently absorbed the heat. Would Mike be shocked if he knew her feelings for him, that she'd never been able to cast aside her childhood infatuation? Would he welcome the news or keep a platonic distance? Could he feel the intensity of the emotional and physical chemistry that she did at that moment, as he sat only inches away in her car?

The melody of Nikki's cell phone jangled sharply through the silence. She decreased the heater fan and answered.

"Hi, Nikki." Her mother's voice chimed through the phone. "What time do you think you'll get here?"

"Uh, not sure, Mom. I'm with Mike, but we should be home pretty soon."

"If you can, I need you to pick up some light cream, mascarpone cheese, and a dozen eggs for me."

"Sure, we can pop by the grocery store on the way. See you soon." She hung up and turned to him. "You got that, I guess?"

Mike nodded. "To the grocery store, then?"


Nikki and Mike arrived at the Big House in the late afternoon, having spent nearly the whole day together. For her, it had been heavenly. As she crossed the threshold, her mother immediately recruited her to help make tiramisu. Mike went to the den where her father was watching the news, perhaps to attempt a conversation with him. Nevertheless, Nikki felt that an invisible bond had been forged that afternoon.

Twenty minutes later a horn outside summoned them. Outside, Nikki's brother, Danny, and her sister-in-law, Cheryl, were climbing out of the car, pulling baggage and baby paraphernalia out behind them. She hugged each one in turn. Eighteen-month-old Cameron clambered out as soon as he was liberated from his car seat and ran into the waiting arms of his grandmother.

A gentle wave of contentment filled Nikki as she watched the crowd on the front lawn swell, with fresh rounds of greetings and hugs. Everyone shuffled inside and the noise level increased, occasionally pierced by Cameron's infant babble. Laura and Trey arrived and joined everyone in the den, where the fireplace was already sputtering a welcome.

The spruce Christmas tree dominated one corner of the cozy room. Colorful lights wrapped each branch, interspersed with ornaments that had been collected over several decades. The lights and greenery that Nikki had arranged on the mantle continued the colorful theme.

Her mother beamed as she served hors d'oeuvres and eggnog. "Try this, you'll love it," she said, proffering the tray to each family member.

"Great to see you, Sis." Danny squeezed Nikki with a side hug. "We've been so busy selling out everything before the end of the year, I haven't been able to make it for a visit in a while."

"Yes, I noticed." Nikki exaggerated a grimace then bumped his shoulder with hers.

Again, her mother appeared in the doorway calling, "Dinner's ready, everyone. Christmas Eve tradition: fish."

A few voices in the room cheered. Laura said, "Again?"

Dinner was noisy and festive. Despite the hidden family tensions and her own growing wanderlust, Nikki enjoyed the meal around rosemary mullet and roasted potatoes. Her unforgettable day with Mike was at the root of her contentment, but the holiday atmosphere was an additional treat. She participated in the dinner conversation, feeling like her old self again.

Empty dessert plates covered the table. Frank swiped his mouth with his napkin and said, "I'll be leaving for Mass at eleven-twenty. Any takers?"

Cheryl, Mike, and Nikki agreed together. Frank looked quizzically at Nikki. "You, the Protestant, going to midnight Mass?"

Nikki cocked her head to one side, smiling. "Oh, Dad. It's the same Jesus. Let's just go focus on Him."

To her surprise he chuckled. "You're right. Let's go."

Seated in the church between her father and Mike, Nikki closed her eyes and breathed deeply of incense. Although she normally attended a Protestant service, she loved Christmas Mass, as she savored the tradition and ceremony of her childhood. The candles and dimly lit arched spaces formed a protective cover, like a cupped hand overhead. She glanced toward Mike. His eyes were closed. She basked silently in their spiritual bond.

After the Mass, people hugged one another. Nikki hugged her father, then Cheryl, careful of her rounded belly, then Mike. He held onto her for a long moment. She felt his lips brush lightly against her forehead as she closed her eyes, buried in his sweater, his arms wrapped around her shoulders.

When she opened her eyes, they were misty. "Merry Christmas," she whispered breathlessly, face tilted up toward his.

His dark eyes caressed hers. "Merry Christmas, Nikki."

# Chapter Three

"This is the last moment of peace and quiet you'll have for the next four hours," Nikki warned Mike as they ambled toward the Big House after a long walk around the neighborhood.

"I'm sure you're right about that."

When the first round of Christmas activity waned, they'd headed outside for some calm shortly before ten more guests were due to arrive. Being cold was a small price to pay to get distance from holiday noise and especially to be alone with Mike. Over one shoulder hung her new camera, a Christmas gift from her parents.

"Getting everyone together is the great thing about holidays," Mike said. "At least for everyday life we each have our best friend as a roommate. My friend, Jeff, is like a big brother to me."

Nikki took a deep breath, chilly air filling her lungs. "Elaine is the same for me." Dry leaves crunched under her boots as she consciously slowed her pace. "Is it harder to live your faith in a big city? I feel like my life here in a small town is so. . .easy."

He looked down at her with warm brown eyes. "I don't think it makes much difference where you are. Just depends on your focus." He walked in a slow shuffle, occasionally brushing his shoulder against hers. "In a city you're thrown together with a bigger variety of people. There are just more of them, so you get a little bit of everything. But it's so lively, there's always noise and constant activity. You see loads of diversity in nationalities and ways of life. A few weird people too. It's fascinating."

It sounded scary to Nikki, but she didn't say anything. What different worlds they lived in. Could she ever fit into his world? And could she have done what he did, gone across the country with no one waiting on the other side, settling into a large metropolis?

She treasured and savored each instant she could spend with him now, no matter how small. Too soon, it would be over, and he'd be back in California. Far, so far from her.

"I didn't tell you about my families. I mean, my tenants," Mike said. "A few of them have become friends. I got interested in urban housing projects through some volunteer work I did. Later, I bought a few run-down houses with the inheritance I got from my parents, and fixed them up."

"Sounds like you gave a lot to those families." A flood of emotion swelled inside her as she pictured Mike helping needy families.

"Believe me, they've given a lot to me too."

Bare trees arched over the deserted road, sheltering it in silence. At each home in the neighborhood, more cars than usual filled the driveways and lined the streets.

"Stand by that tree and I'll take your picture." Nikki stopped walking and pointed to a birch tree.

"I guess you like your new Christmas gift." Mike flashed a grin and stood still in front of the tree.

"I've wanted to start a photography hobby for a while, so this is the perfect gift." She stared through the viewfinder and framed him, his dark hair in bold relief against the gunmetal sky and white bark of the birch trees. Nikki snapped a photo, then another. She'd attach his photo to her mirror and every day she'd see him as he was right now.

Despite his ready smile, a haunted sadness dwelt in his eyes, captured in her photo. How she would love someday to erase the echo of tragedy that still hung in his gaze after so many years.

The previous day, as they were leaving the restaurant, his phone had rung. He'd stared at it for a moment as it continued to ring, then silenced it. He'd said only, "Just a friend. I'll call him later." The burdened look deepened, but he'd said no more.

Mike and Nikki rounded a curve in the road. The bulky outline of the Big House rose in view through a network of naked trees. She wasn't ready to go back, but her mother would soon need her help. And the humid New York cold had soaked through several layers of clothing.

"Should be good and noisy over dinner with twenty of us," Mike said.

"Are you glad? I mean, glad to be here, to be part of our family?"

He paused. "Yeah, I am. Over the years, I've wondered if everyone wishes I'd go get my own family." He smiled, but a shade of melancholy flickered in his eyes. "Sometimes I've wished it *were* my real family. But I'm thankful too. I'd be all alone otherwise, and I really do care about all you guys."

"Everyone's glad you came this year, Mike." She squeezed his elbow, eager to convince him. She didn't speak only for herself. "You've always been wanted and welcome, and always will be. I hope you believe that."

Too quickly, he said, "What about you, are you glad to have a big Italian family?"

Nikki nodded. She couldn't force him to talk more about feeling like an outsider. "Yes, it's fun, especially at holidays."

"I wouldn't necessarily want to live around it all the time."

Nikki considered his statement. What would it be like to live somewhere else, and not be able to drop by the Big House whenever she wanted to? Her feelings often swung between gratitude for her parents' nearness, and restlessness for a more exotic life. But that would mean being alone, depending completely on herself. A thought she didn't relish.

A car rumbled past, then slowed in front of the Big House driveway. It was Aunt Trudie, her husband Dave, and their son Drew with his girlfriend. They piled out of the car, yelling, "Merry Christmas!"

Within thirty minutes, Aunt Grace and her family also arrived, followed by Nikki's other grandparents. The group was then complete, and chaos ensued. Fortunately, the house was large enough to absorb everyone and keep them from tripping over one another.

"I brought my famous zeppole, my own recipe," said Grace proudly, patting the covered top of her casserole dish. "I only make it at Christmas."

After a flurry of foot traffic in and out of the kitchen, the buffet table was covered with plates of roast lamb, baked ham, fennel gratin, stuffed artichokes, walnut ricotta cake, amaretti cookies, and several kinds of pasta, polenta, and salads. Noise and laughter kept pace with the multiple round trips to the buffet table, as everyone filled and refilled their plates.

A spark flickered inside Nikki each time she caught a smile from Mike across the table. She watched as he leaned toward little Cameron to carefully cut his meat into tiny pieces. A gush of emotion gathered in her throat.

After the meal, the aunts surveyed the platters, bowls, and casseroles on the kitchen table, hands perched firmly on their hips. Trudie groaned, "Looks like a massacre! We'll have enough leftovers for two more Christmas dinners."

Nikki's mother appeared in the doorway, but Grace shooed her away. "After all the work you've done, Marie, leave the cleanup to us," she said. "You too, Nikki."

"I'd rather help than collapse on the couch like a beached whale." Nikki continued rinsing plates at the sink. "Assembly line. Who wants to put the rinsed plates in the dishwasher?" Grace took the cue, and the women chatted as they worked.

After the kitchen was clean, the relatives gradually said their goodbyes, family by family. Nikki took her time in the kitchen, savoring the increasing quiet that settled over the house. Finally, alone, she hummed to herself as she hand-dried the silverware.

"Still in the kitchen?" A voice laced with amusement came from the doorway. "The guys just leave the women to do everything. At least I showed up once everything was done." Mike offered a sheepish grin, then reached for a towel and wet serving spoon.

"That's the way it's always been. Mom usually doesn't even ask for help. She didn't have a choice this time. She had an army of helpers."

"Mild-Mannered-Marie, we used to call her. Remember?" He chuckled.

"Yes, I remember." Nikki smiled and rubbed a crystal serving bowl with a towel. "That's one reason I help so much, because she doesn't usually ask. And it's our special time, talking together as we work."

"That's nice." Mike reached across the sink for another spoon, enveloping it in the moist tea towel.

Nikki peered out the window over the sink, past the frost that had gathered in silvery triangles on the panes. Moonlight bathed the backyard in light, casting shadows in every corner. "Would you look at that?" she said in awe. "It must be a full moon. It's lighting up the backyard like daytime."

Mike stepped alongside her and leaned forward. "How beautiful. We're about done here, so why don't we go out to the porch and get a better look?"

They grabbed their coats and slipped out the kitchen door to the screened-in porch. Plastic sheets shrouded the patio furniture, forlorn in winter abandonment. Nikki shivered slightly as she stepped toward the dusty louvered windows. "It's so beautiful and so bright."

Mike stood beside her and slipped one arm around her shoulder. "Better?"

She nodded and turned to slip both her arms around his waist over his leather coat. She settled her head on his chest, feeling his chin just above her head, hearing his breath. It felt so natural, so comfortable. Nikki sighed in contentment. They stood for several minutes in silence, gazing out at the looming shapes of trees and shrubs, distorted in the moonlight.

Nikki turned her face upward, about to say something to him, but froze. He stared down at her, his face shadowy planes and hollows in the murky light. She could feel his breath on her cheeks. She didn't speak.

"Nikki. . ." The word came like a sigh. He leaned toward her then and gently pressed his lips against hers. He slipped his other arm around her shoulder, turning her gently, and pulled her close. His lips were soft, yet insistent. Nikki tightened her arms around his waist and responded eagerly, leaning into him. Her mind was spinning, unable to believe what was happening. It must be a dream, the dream she'd had for so many years. The doubt about his feelings, which had haunted her for days, melted away. Fiercely, then tenderly, he kissed her, as if he were hungry for her.

A sudden light streamed through the kitchen window, slicing through the darkness of the porch. Mike pulled back from her and fixed his gaze ahead through the porch windows. Neither of them spoke. Clouds of breath pierced rhythmically through the cold air. Nikki heard a muffled voice, her grandfather in the kitchen. "I don't see it, Marie." Then, "Oh, here it is. I have it." The light went out and his footsteps shuffled away. Again, inky darkness engulfed them.

Should she speak? What would she say? Before she could decide, Mike's lips found hers again. His hand left her shoulder to brush her cheek. He wove his fingers through her hair. She could smell the light scent of his cologne, feel the rough scrape of stubble as his jaw moved against hers. A soft sound escaped from deep inside her. Finally, he pulled back from her and said in a throaty murmur, "Oh, Nikki. I guess I crossed a big line."

"No, no, you didn't," Nikki protested, wanting to say so much more, wanting to shout for joy, but Mike's face was sober.

With his arm around her shoulders, he gently drew her toward the back door to the house. "Let's go in." Once inside, he turned and helped her out of her coat. "We need to talk, but now isn't the best time. I promise we will, okay?"

She nodded, still staring at him. He led her into the den where her parents, her grandfather, and Catherine were watching a movie on the wide-screen television. Mike and Nikki sat beside each other on the couch, not touching.

Nikki stared ahead at the screen, unseeing. What had just happened? And what was Mike thinking now? She could still feel his face and lips against hers. Joy and confusion spun around together in her mind as her heart continued thumping. Something had definitely changed, and there was no turning back. But what did it mean to Mike?

Grandpa Jim was snoring quietly in the overstuffed chair. He abruptly opened his eyes and jerked his head. "I'm about to fall asleep after all this food."

"You *were* asleep!" Catherine laughed.

He turned to his wife with groggy eyes. "Ready to call it a day, my dear? A Christmas day?" She nodded and dragged herself out of the recliner. Mike stood up to leave with them. For a moment, he stared at Nikki as if to speak, then pressed his lips together in a guilty half-smile.

Nikki left the couch and went to where Mike stood in the doorway. "Why don't you come to my apartment tomorrow for brunch and we can talk, okay?" She kept her voice low.

He nodded. "That's a good idea. Ten?"

"Ten is perfect. I'll text you my address. You know the Pineview Apartments?"

He nodded.

"Second floor."

"See you tomorrow," he said softly, meeting her eyes before turning to leave.

&#8475;   &#8475;   &#8475;

Frank leaned back in the leather chair in his office next to the den. He laced his fingers behind his head, savoring the silence. It was like a symphony after the bustle of the holiday. Danny and Cheryl had gone up to the guest room over an hour ago and Jim's gang had just left. It was a good day, tiring and noisy, but good, even with all twenty of them at once. He was looking forward to using his new golf clubs.

Mike and Nikki seemed to spend a lot of time together that year, more than in the past. Maybe it was their religious affinity that gave them a new bond. True, almost everyone else seemed paired up. It was natural that they gravitate to one another. And they *had* been close as children. He sighed heavily. Yes, maybe that's all it was.

Yet he had an uneasy twinge inside, call it intuition or just good observation, which told him it might be more. Mike's presence brought it all back, those tense months following the deaths of his parents. In all these years, had Mike ever learned about the investigation following the accident that took his parents? How could he? All the adults in the family, wanting to put it all behind them, had sworn silence.

Branagan had purchased his car used at Mancini Motors only months before the accident. Police and mechanics alike found nothing unusual in the brake pads or cylinders themselves that might have pointed to faulty work. Frank had confidence in his mechanics, but there was always that slight chance that something had been overlooked.

Something that could have taken the lives of two innocent people whose son was nearly a member of his own family.

Mike didn't appear to know anything about it. It was all water under the bridge, anyway. Just an uncomfortable memory that lodged inside, like indigestion.

A gentle tap on the door caused Frank's head to jerk up from his reverie. Marie's face appeared in the darkened space. "Are you coming up, Frank?"

"Yes, soon. I was just enjoying the quiet."

"Nice, isn't it? You know I enjoy all the company and the noise, but it's pleasant when it quiets down too." Marie's dark hair blended with the shadows behind her, nearly swallowing her from view.

Frank rubbed his chin in several slow strokes, an old habit when he wanted to choose his words carefully. "I was just thinking, seems Mike and Nikki have been spending a lot of time together during this holiday. I guess now that Danny's married, things change between the boys. They aren't as close."

"Mike and Nikki were close too." Marie's voice held a slightly defensive edge. "I don't know, seems kind of normal to me for them to get back together."

"Maybe. Nikki spent half her childhood infatuated with him. Seemed to get over it, and then after that he came around so seldom. I hope she doesn't wind up getting hurt."

"I think it's nice for them." Marie's voice was quiet, but with a touch of insistence. "They're having a good time, Frank."

"I guess you're right. Probably nothing more than that. Well, I'll be up soon. Don't wait for me." He smiled up at her.

Marie pulled the door closed. Frank sighed. He knew he worried too much about Nikki, maybe because she wasn't settled yet. As a child, Laura had been more fearful, but now seemed to have found her way, working as a physical therapist, and nearly engaged to Trey. Frank had always felt more protective of Nikki, as if she were fragile, even though he'd seen her stubborn, scrappy side many times. When he looked at her, he often saw his mother, who'd had the same gray eyes, the same slightly pointed chin.

At the thought of his mother, a surprising pain stabbed at him. It seemed some things never completely healed. She would have enjoyed this Christmas. She should have been here, watching her grandchildren all grown up. Instead, she'd left the earth as a young woman while he'd watched her life ebb away, helpless to do anything. He'd made up his mind he wouldn't be helpless again, and to some degree, he'd succeeded. With the small empire he'd built, he provided for his family. If there were any way to help his loved ones avoid the kind of injustice, the agony his mother had endured, he would find it.

Mike also knew pain as a child, losing not one, but both his parents at the same time. Even before the accident, he'd encrusted himself into Frank's family, since his own parents were too busy for him. Then he landed on Dad's doorstep, burdening an aging man with a teenager. Frank had never appreciated that, although Mike's trust fund had helped with expenses, and his dad and Catherine didn't seem to mind. On the contrary. Catherine had the son she'd always longed for, and Mike had continued attending the same high school.

"Branagans shoulda thanked us all for raising their son," Frank muttered into the darkness.

Despite his hardships, Mike seemed to lack depth and substance. No wonder he sailed in and out of Adams Bridge every few years as the golden boy, lapping up everyone's interest and admiration, including Nikki's.

He hoped she wouldn't fall for the charm just as he disappeared for another three years. Frank wanted more for Nikki. She and Mike were likely just catching up while they could, so Frank probably had no worries about them.

He nodded in satisfied relief and leaned to turn out the lamp.

# Chapter Four

Mike stuck the key into the ignition and shivered as cold air gushed from the heater. "Got a breakfast appointment, but I should be back by noonish," he'd told Jim on his way out. Not the day for explanations. His head was too crowded with whirling clouds of guilt, desire, and confusion. With a grimace, he wondered which one would win out.

The kiss with Nikki had taken him by surprise, though he wasn't surprised about his feelings, which had been building for the last three days. Just surprised he'd acted on them. He thought he'd developed more self-control than that since finding faith. It seemed natural. But the next morning, he wasn't so sure.

Nikki's clear longing for him had shone undiminished in her eyes, even before responding to his kisses. He wasn't sure if that made matters simpler or more complicated. He shook his head. *Definitely* more complicated.

He had more baggage in his life than Nikki could possibly know, and some of it involved her own father. Did she know about the investigation into Mancini Motors at the time of the accident? He himself hadn't known it until Ely told him years later, right before he left to go to college in California. If Nikki knew about it, she didn't let on. She might have forgotten the whole matter.

His was about the only car on the road that morning. The landscapes, subdivisions, and strip-malls stood faded and lonely in winter whitewash. So quiet. He'd grown to dislike sleepy suburban America. No noise, no bustle.

The Pineview Apartments resembled so many other complexes in Greenbrier, with gray siding and identical white wooden balconies. He found Nikki's apartment and rapped on the door next to a wreath sporting a cheerful Santa frog.

When Nikki opened the door, he slipped in without hugging her. He already fought the feeling of guilt and exposure. She looked casual, yet elegant in a fuzzy pink sweater. Around her neck was the silver necklace from the famous Helen, Jim's first wife. Why did she have to wear that all the time?

"Want some coffee?" Nikki already had a mug set out for him.

He trailed behind her and stood by the counter. "Nikki, I just want to say I'm sorry—"

"No, Mike." She turned toward him. Her gray eyes pleaded and invited him at the same time. "Please don't be sorry. Please."

He felt a few ounces of the heavy weight inside fall away.

"It was wonderful," she said softly. "I have some things I want to tell you. We can be open with each other, you know, cards on the table. But first let's eat. Okay?"

Mike nodded hesitantly. He wasn't sure he liked the "cards on the table" idea, but he couldn't very well passionately kiss her, then pretend nothing had happened.

"I'm making omelets. Do you want mushroom, cheese, green onions, or avocado?"

"All the above would be fine." Mike watched her as she cut the vegetables. Either she was confidently calm or tightly controlled. Why did he feel cornered?

He looked around the apartment, tasteful in blues and beiges. Watercolor prints on the walls and a tall potted Ficus tree near the window made it peaceful and serene. He swallowed and forced a slow, deep breath, consciously relaxing his shoulders.

Several minutes later, Nikki placed the omelets on the table alongside a plate of toasted English muffins. Mike busied himself pouring orange juice and trying to stay busy until the meal was ready.

They sat down at the small kitchen table. "I'll pray for us." Mike took her hand. "Lord, thank you for this meal. Please guide us in our, uh, friendship, in ways that are pleasing to You. Amen." He looked up and saw her smiling at him. "I figured we needed some help." He finally felt able to grin back at her.

Nikki paused, appearing to gather her thoughts. "Okay. I'll talk first."

"You can finish eating."

"I don't think I can." For a moment, Nikki stared down at the table, as if rallying her thoughts. Then her eyes met his, and she took a breath. "Okay, here goes. You know I had a crush on you when I was a child. Everyone thought it was cute. Maybe you did too. I always felt close to you, like I understood your heart. But there was more than that. As I got older, my feelings never totally disappeared, even when you got involved with your other friends and then left for college."

She looked down at her steaming plate, which she hadn't touched. Her words tumbled out quickly. "Then when I became a Christian, and you weren't, I knew I needed to move on. And there was Stephanie. Stephanie didn't work out and then you became a Christian, so. . ." She paused and looked back up at him. "I'm rambling. Sorry. When I knew you were coming for Christmas, I was afraid that all those feelings I tried so hard to get rid of would come back again." In a whisper she added, "And they did, more than ever." She looked directly at him then, almost apologetically. "Mike, I love you. I always have. Ever since I was a child. The closeness we had in the past and the faith we share only increase my love for you." She sat quietly and waited for his response.

Mike shifted in his chair and swallowed. He'd known about her feelings as a child, but had pushed it aside as a childhood infatuation, as had other family members. After that, she must have hidden it well. Until last night, when she'd laid her heart bare to him, hiding nothing.

He felt like a heel. He'd opened her wounds, her emotions, and instilled hope he wasn't sure he could fulfill. All with a kiss that felt as natural as breathing.

"Thanks for your honesty, Nikki. I didn't know you felt that way all these years." She'd loved him for a *long* time. How could he respond to that? He felt humbled, yet struggled to breathe. If only there was some way to turn back the clock. Instead of fleeing his old life, he was sinking deeper into it. "I guess it's my turn, huh?"

"Don't feel pressure, Mike. Just say what you feel."

He pursed his lips, mentally trying out various phrases. He didn't want to hurt her, nor deny the attraction simmering under the surface. What a mess. "You know I've always cared for you like a sister, ever since we were kids." Her face fell just slightly, though she held a small smile tightly in place. "But during the last Christmas visit three years ago, I thought, wow. You were all grown up and really cute. I was attracted to you, I admit. But I'm almost like family."

"But *not* family."

"No, not quite. After that, I avoided you some." He paused and savored a faint memory which drifted into his mind. "Except for that one evening when we were eating dessert together at the kitchen table. You wiped some crumbs off my face, and we just stared at each other, remember?"

Nikki nodded, a secretive smile spreading across her face. "Oh, yes. It was magic."

He chuckled. "It was for me too. Then I left New York, met Stephanie, and it was all a nice memory. Then this year—" He shrugged and dropped his gaze down at his plate. How to slow it all down? When he lifted his eyes, her face seemed pale, though the conciliatory smile remained. "I'll be honest with you, Nikki. You've had these feelings for over fifteen years, but this is all new for me. I mean, I enjoy being with you and I'm attracted to you, that's true. But I need time to figure it all out." He watched her face for a sign of understanding.

"Do you feel weird because you've known my family for so long?"

"Yeah, a little." But that was only a small piece of his hesitation.

"Having grown up together gives us a deeper basis of friendship. We really understand each other."

She was so logical. Why, then, wasn't the cramp in his stomach easing? "It seems like we *can* talk about anything." He looked at her with a sideways smile. "I shouldn't have kissed you last night. Don't get me wrong. I *really* enjoyed kissing you." His face grew warm, whether from embarrassment or the memory of it, he wasn't sure. "Okay, this is getting awkward, so why don't we eat our omelets?"

They both laughed, breaking the tension. "This is really a good omelet. Did you invent it?"

She shrugged. "Omelets are a single girl's best friend. That and quiche. So easy and versatile."

Mike finished his omelet quickly, thankful for some release to the heavy conversation. "You don't take after Gourmet Marie?"

"Is that her new nickname? I guess I don't, not yet. Want some more coffee? We can sit on the couch."

Settled on the couch with a second steaming mug, Mike relaxed, feeling a slight escape from the intensity. Maybe they could take the relationship slowly. It might be okay. But when he glanced over at Nikki's face as she gazed at him adoringly, he knew his relief was premature.

"Um, what do you say we just take it a day at a time? We can talk on the phone and, uh, continue to get to know each other, as adults, I mean."

Nikki nodded. "That's a good idea. We don't have to rush anything, or even tell anyone." A slight edge of insistence in her voice belied her words. "I'm okay with that. I'm just glad we talked."

Mike leaned back against the couch, feeling her nearness, inhaling her mellowed perfume. He looked up at the ceiling and reviewed the conversation that had just happened. She'd agreed to take it slowly. That was good. Might give him time to figure things out. He thought about Frank. He'd have apoplexy.

He turned to Nikki. "What about your dad?"

She shrugged. "What about him?" Her eyes darted away from his.

"Come on, Nikki. Don't tell me you think he'll accept it nicely and congratulate us. He dislikes me and you're his prized treasure.

How do you think it'll go over if he knows we're, um—" He finished with a shake of his head. How to describe their new status?

"Yeah, I see your point. But it's my life. I've loved you my whole life and I won't let Dad influence me about you. I don't know why he has this grudge, but it's his problem." She crossed her arms emphatically.

Mike could see an edge of surprising stubbornness emerging. "You say that now, but you and he are close." She wasn't ready to hear that she was under Frank's thumb without even knowing it. "He's very protective of you," he said instead. "I'm sure he'll have a lot to say." He drained back the last of his coffee. He'd probably need more of it. Lots more.

Family disapproval would be harder on Nikki than it would be for him, and she'd be unprepared for it. He'd broken that hold long ago. *Unless he hurt her.* Then there'd be trouble—loads of it— with the only family he had. He'd quickly be on the Mancini dirt list. And on the Mike Branagan dirt list as well.

He turned his head to look directly at her as she sat next to him on the couch. Soft black curls lay across her shoulders and smooth olive skin surrounded thick, dark lashes. Beyond her through the picture window, the snow had begun, drifting downward in large, wet flakes. "It's snowing," he said softly. "Reminds me of that time when the snow was up to our knees in the woods behind the Big House. Remember?"

Nikki nodded as a gentle smile spread. "It was too deep for me, and I kept falling on my face." She turned her head to glance at the flakes that swirled faster now, then back to him. She rested her head on the back of the couch, eyes level with his. "It's so beautiful." Her voice sounded almost like a purr. "I'm glad to be here with you on a snowy morning."

Then that clutch inside, infused with heat, bubbled up and filled him. In silence, they stared at each other for several seconds. Desire roared in his head and her gray eyes seemed to swallow him whole.

"I knew the couch was a bad idea. . ." Mike whispered hoarsely, then leaned toward her. He gently drew her chin upward with one hand and tilted his head slightly to kiss her. Nikki reached her arms around his neck, responding hungrily, leaning her weight into him as he enclosed her in his arms. Her soft lips tasted of coffee and cinnamon. Time seemed suspended while the snow fell in silence just outside the picture window. How many minutes passed? Too many.

Gently and reluctantly, Mike drew away from her. "We should be careful, Nikki."

"That won't be hard once you're back in California." Her voice was glum, her face a mask of sadness.

He reached up and caressed her silky cheek. She turned her head and burrowed her face in his palm, kissing it lightly. He'd told her he needed time. Yet the urgency to hold her invaded him. He let out a long breath and pulled back.

Mike suddenly glanced down at his watch. Nikki's head bolted up. "Do you have an appointment?"

He nodded. "At one I'm getting together with an old friend who I've neglected in favor of you." He shot her a twisted smile. "Then I have a few other people to meet with, so I won't see you until tomorrow late afternoon. I'll stop by after that. Will you be at the Big House?"

Nikki nodded. "I'll be over there a lot in the next few days, since Elaine is gone, and I don't want to stay here alone. I should be there whenever you come." She seemed to withdraw into herself in an almost protective gesture.

"Are you okay?"

"It's going by so fast." Her voice broke. "And you'll be leaving so soon. I don't know when I'll see you again."

"We'll stay in touch, Nikki. I promise."

As Mike gently closed the apartment door behind him, he stopped on the landing and looked out at the flakes, now swirling in a white cloud. He murmured aloud, "What have I done?"

CR   CR   CR

Nikki leaned against the door after Mike left. She had no concrete reason to feel uneasy. He said he was attracted to her, but needed time to figure it out. That was reasonable, wasn't it? She would rather him feel the same intensity she did, but she understood the newness for him. Why did she feel like he'd sent mixed messages, one minute saying he was unsure and the next, ardently kissing her?

She rummaged in the purse on her bedroom floor for her cell phone and called Elaine.

"Hi, Nikki. Did you have a good Christmas?" she asked cheerfully.

"Hi Elaine, it was great. I have big news about Mike."

"Oh, do tell!"

Nikki summarized the previous few days. "I don't know if that means we're together, or just checking it out. It's exciting, but doesn't feel very, um, established, I guess."

"Nikki, that's great. You sound kind of stressed out about it, though."

"I *feel* stressed. I've been fixated on him for so long that now I'll probably scare him off."

Elaine paused. "Yes, Nikki. You might very well do that. Just give him some space and try to relax about it."

"Do you think I should have acted more distant instead of telling him everything?" Nikki's tone climbed to a squeak.

"I don't know. Given the fact that he seemed surprised—"

"Oh no, I knew it," Nikki nearly wailed. "I went too far." If only she could tamp down the anxiety rising inside, the *need* for Mike to respond in the same way. Of course, it was obsessive. Imbalanced. It always had been. But she couldn't help herself.

"Not necessarily, Nikki." Elaine's voice was calm and even. "At least you've talked openly. Just see where it goes from here." Elaine would likely have held back more than Nikki had. Wise Elaine. Impulsive Nikki. A small groan escaped her throat.

"Nikki, don't worry so much. Just enjoy it, okay?"

"Okay, I'll try." Nikki consciously relaxed her shoulders and stared out her bedroom window out at the whirling snowflakes.

Elaine was doing her best to rein Nikki back, but she hadn't seen the way Mike had kissed her. It *had* to mean something to him.

Nikki couldn't remember a time in her life when she didn't love Mike Branagan. She'd always known he was her destiny.

After a few more minutes of catching up about the holidays, Nikki hung up. She lay down on her bed and stared up at the ceiling for a long time.

CR   CR   CR

Mike scanned the booths and bar seats of the crowded sandwich shop for Ely's wiry black hair. It took him a moment to realize that in the three years since he'd last seen his father's friend, the black hair had turned mostly gray. Ely's gaze warmed with recognition behind wire-rimmed glasses.

Mike slipped into the booth and stuck his hand across the table. Ely grasped it tightly. "You're right on time," the older man said with a grin. "You're looking good, Mike. I guess the West Coast agrees with you."

Mike nodded and smiled back. "You could say that. How is Allison? How was your Christmas?"

Ely signaled for the waitress, who arrived and slipped two menus on the table. "She's fine, thanks. We had a nice day. I have two new grandsons since I last saw you. I'm just going to order a sandwich. You hungry?"

"No, I just had a big breakfast. I'll get a Coke."

"I guess you've been wondering about what I told you." A shade of solemn sincerity fell over Ely's face. "I wasn't trying to be mysterious, but felt it was better to talk in person."

Mike was relieved that Ely wasted no time in preamble. For a month he'd been eaten up with nagging curiosity. "Yeah, after all these years, I was shocked," he said.

After ordering a Reuben sandwich and a beer, Ely leaned forward slightly and lowered his voice. "I don't know how much local news you've heard since you've been here. There is a company called Hamilton Industrial. Your father was doing an external audit there just before he died. This company just went under about two months ago. They discovered that the books had been cooked for at least the last fifteen years. Their lead accountant has gone missing."

"Did the accountant know my father?"

"Yes, they knew each other. Your dad worked for this company for a little while. Their bylaws required an external audit, but I remember your dad met a lot of resistance. When all of this broke out in the news, I recalled him telling me there was something fishy going on. He said he had a feeling it went really deep. Before he could find out what it was, he was dead."

Mike fell back against his chair. Words jumbled in his mind, but nothing came out of his mouth. He swallowed, took a breath. Finally, he said, "Someone wanted to keep him from finding out something?"

Ely's dark eyes met Mike's. "That was my conclusion as well. It raises the question, in any case. He was working late at Hamilton one evening. Afterwards, he got in his car and had the accident."

"My mother met him after work that day because they had to leave town for something. I don't remember what." The lead weight in Mike's stomach became heavier. Suddenly the sounds of voices and clanging cutlery were deafening.

Ely took a bite of his sandwich. After a gulp of beer, he said, "I called the police, not expecting much cooperation. Of course, I didn't get it, not for a thirteen-year-old case that was never even prosecuted. But they recommended that a family member come to the station to make an inquiry."

Mike nodded slowly and let out the breath he'd been holding. "I see. I can ask about it while I'm here. Would they even consider it after so many years?"

Ely shrugged. "Probably not, but it's worth a try."

"If it was foul play, it would rule out any kind of mechanical error by Mancini mechanics."

"Oh, that question was resolved years ago. I don't think it was that."

"I've always wondered, though. They've never talked to me about the investigation, but it always stayed in the back of my mind. This might settle the whole thing. Of course, I want to know. But it would also help since I'm involved with the family. And now with Frank's daughter—"

Ely's his eyes widened. "Are you? Involved with Frank's daughter?"

Mike grimaced. "I think I am now. I mean, it kind of just started." He hadn't meant to say anything about Nikki, though she hovered on the edges of his thoughts.

"Does she know about the investigation with her dad's company years ago?"

"I don't think so unless she's forgotten or is hiding it. We haven't had much time together."

"Enough time for romantic sparks to fly, I guess." The older man grinned, despite the severity of his tone. "Just be careful, Mike."

"A warning too late." Mike returned a wry smile, then sipped his Coke. "It just adds more complications to the New York chapter of my life."

"The one you've tried to run away from, you mean?"

Mike's gaze darted to Ely's. He said nothing. Not ready to go there.

"Don't think I was blind to what you were doing, running off as soon as you turned eighteen. I'm not judging you, by the way. But you need to embrace the past, Mike. Make peace with it. Nothing you can do to change it."

Mike's gaze panned across the room, just past Ely's intense stare. It was after two, and the dining room was sparse with customers. May as well tell him. "This was going to be my last trip."

"Not so fast. You have some unfinished business here."

Mike snorted. "You have *no* idea." He thrust several fingers through his hair. Nikki's face rose in his mind.

"You should file a request before you leave." Ely pushed his plate away from him and rubbed his fingers delicately on a napkin before dabbing it on his lips.

"I leave in two days. Tomorrow I'm booked solid, so I'll need to do it now."

"Okay, let's go."

The Adam's Bridge police station loomed sadly against a cloudy backdrop. Mike and Ely approached the gray brick building and went inside. Florescent light flooded the room and counter. Keyboards chattered in the background. Who would have thought they'd be standing here after all these years? Would anyone take them seriously?

Drab white walls matched the dull exterior of the building. Several uniformed officers spoke on phones or radios and hunched over desks. At the counter, Mike cleared his throat. A pleasant-faced officer approached the counter. "Can I help you?" He appeared to be a few years older than Mike.

"Um, I have a question regarding the case with Hamilton Industrial—" Mike felt gratified when the officer's green eyes widened under arched brows. A good start. "My father was working as an external auditor for that company thirteen years ago. He noticed the accounting didn't look right, but before he had the chance to find out anything, he died in a car crash, along with my mother. I have reason to believe there may have been foul play."

The officer stared at Mike for a moment, his brows furrowed. "Was an investigation done then? I wasn't with the force thirteen years ago."

Ely spoke up. "There was an investigation into the brakes, and into the company who sold the car to the victim. No brake fluid was found on the ground, and nothing was proven, so the case was closed. Foul play wasn't brought up at that time. That is, the possibility of a murder wasn't mentioned. But now, with the allegations involving the missing accountant of that company, we know there may have been a motive. Maybe with all the new forensic methods, fresh evidence will show up."

Mike flinched when Ely pronounced the word *murder*. His parents may have been murdered. His mind and emotions felt frozen, though a stream of stale pain slipped through like a splinter of light through a dirty window.

The officer looked at Mike. "How old were you?" His voice was gentle.

"Fourteen."

His face sobered. "My kid is fourteen. I'm sorry for your loss."

"Thank you," Mike mumbled. Maybe this guy would help him, be willing to pry open the long-closed lid of a cold case. Talking about the deaths of his parents after all these years had jerked his emotions out of the frozen storage where he'd kept them sealed. Discreetly, he grabbed the edge of the counter as his knees weakened.

"Tell you what," the officer said, reaching under the counter for a sheet of blank paper. "Put your name here, and the names of your parents, along with your contact information. My name is Officer Garner. Todd Garner. Here's my number. I'll see if we have anything from the accident still in the property and evidence room. I won't promise anything, but I'll let you know what I find."

Mike smiled with gratitude. "Thank you, Officer Garner. I appreciate anything you can do."

Mike and Ely left the building. As they approached the car, Ely turned to Mike. "I'm glad we did that, Mike. It's all you can do for now. Go and enjoy the rest of your visit, okay?"

"If I can."

# Chapter Five

There was no point in knocking on the large black doors of the Big House. Mike had practically grown up there. He let himself in and tossed his leather jacket on the bench in the hallway. Maybe Nikki was in the den. He glanced in the den but found only Ginger, curled into a furry ball on a small, braided rug by the glowing fireplace. A slice of light streamed from Frank's office.

"Mike, is that you? Mind coming in here a minute?" Frank must have seen him drive up. What could he want, a moment of catching up? Mike doubted it.

Frank was leaning back in the black leather chair, looking like an employer or school principal with bad news. "Close the door behind you, would you?"

Mike raised his eyebrows, but complied. He turned to Frank and perched on the stool as if he wasn't planning to stay long. "Somehow, this doesn't look like a friendly chat." His tone barely hid his wariness.

Frank waved the air absently. His face didn't invite or reassure Mike. "I wanted to talk to you a minute about Nikki." He swiveled his chair around to face Mike. "I noticed you two spending more time together. It's good that you can catch up on old times, and I'm sure it's nice for Nikki to have someone to hang around with over the holidays."

Mike eyed him suspiciously. So, this was about Nikki. He could predict what Frank would say next.

Frank leaned back. His chair squeaked into the silence. "I'm sure you know Nikki has always been very fond of you." He smiled, as if recalling a tender memory of her childhood. Then he turned a hard gaze back to Mike. "Nikki hasn't had the same life you have. She's less, shall I say, worldly, less experienced in life. Given her previous feelings for you, she might easily misinterpret the attention you've paid to her during this holiday."

"You make her sound like a child, Frank. She isn't a child anymore." Mike knew his voice sounded sullen.

"I didn't say she was a child," Frank snapped. "I said she lacked worldly experience. It's not the same thing. She'd easily believe anything she hears you say or wants you to say. I don't want her to be hurt, Mike. That's what this is about. I don't want Nikki hurt."

Mike bristled at Frank's words. As if he would treat Nikki carelessly. A stab of discomfort gnawed inside. Is that what he had done? He weighed his words. "I wouldn't hurt Nikki for anything. She's important to me too."

Frank's eyebrows lifted almost imperceptibly. "So, you admit you are attracted to her?"

Now he felt cornered. Maybe it was best that Frank knew. Certain things, at any rate. "Is that impossible for you to believe?" Mike braced himself.

"Of course not. She's lovely. She's full of life, she's smart. But don't you find that somewhat inappropriate? You grew up together."

"It's not like we're siblings, or even cousins. We're childhood friends. And if you think she's naïve or overprotected, you have only yourself to blame for that." He shouldn't have said that, but it had boiled up in his throat for years.

Frank drew his shoulders up, as if to assert his authority. "I didn't call you here to discuss my parenting." His voice was as cold as a stone tomb. "I want to make it clear that Nikki is not like one of your many girlfriends. She's—"

"I know. She's innocent. Sheltered. I get your point. I know how much you care about her, Frank. I'll keep that in mind."

Before Frank could lecture Mike about his past behavior or question his morality, he stood up and left the room. What he wanted to do was shout, "One conversation every three years and you only warn me to stay away from your daughter." Anger trailed by hurt boiled up into his throat. Frank would never change.

Mike had to find Nikki, but Frank was the last person he would ask. When he'd taken off his coat, he'd noticed the back door was slightly ajar. Maybe she'd gone out to look at the moon. He glanced through the frosted glass and saw her silhouette against the pale lawn. The cold moon overhead beamed a frigid glow onto the backyard, though it had melted down since the night they'd looked at it together, the night he kissed her.

He grabbed his coat and slipped out the door.

"Thought I'd find you here," he said gently behind her shoulder.

She turned in surprise. Despite the ready smile on her lips, her eyes brimmed with melancholy. "Did you have a good time with your friends?"

"Sure. It was almost like old times. My friend Leo is engaged now. My group from high school shrinks every year. They keep scattering and will probably disappear before very long." He glanced over his shoulder and saw Frank's outline at the back door. Mike stepped behind a copse of trees and drew Nikki into its shadow. His relationship with Nikki was none of Frank's business.

"Do you want me to drive you to the airport tomorrow?" she asked dully.

"That would be great. We could spend more time together, but it would help Jim out too. He doesn't like making the drive. Says it makes him nervous."

"He's getting old for the traffic and noise all the way to JFK," she agreed, then fell silent.

Mike scraped the frozen ground with his heel. "No sign of the pool anymore. No trace of all those summers we spent here."

She nodded silently.

He stood beside her in silence for several minutes. Should he tell her what he'd learned about his parents? No, not just before leaving again. The cold isolation he'd felt for so many years contained a new ingredient. Anger. Someone might have deliberately taken the lives of his parents, robbing him of his childhood. Quiet fury swirled inside, threatening to choke him. He needed time to process it by himself. He pushed it down.

They stood quietly, looking out at the moonlit yard that still bore small tufts of snow. "You seem unhappy, Nikki."

She turned to him and encircled his waist with her arms. He wrapped his arms around her shoulders as she laid her head on his chest. "I'm going to miss you," she murmured into his coat. "We're just beginning in a new place. Seems kind of unfair."

"I know." His eagerness to return to San Francisco wrestled vigorously with his desire to stay with her. "I'll miss you too. We'll take one day at a time, okay? I promise I'll stay in touch. I'll call you after I get to San Francisco."

"And we'll always stay friends, right? No matter what happens with. . .with *us*?" She looked up and searched his face for reassurance.

Mike looked down at her upturned face. He couldn't bear risking the friendship they'd rediscovered. He leaned forward and brushed her lips softly with his. The second time they clung together longer, with exquisite gentleness. He pulled back and whispered, "We'll always be friends. I promise, Nikki."

ᘓ   ᘓ   ᘓ

After a final hug at the gate at John F. Kennedy Airport, the hollow chasm in Nikki's stomach radiated into an ache. Mike's form became smaller and smaller as he threaded through security and moved farther away from her. She barely saw him turn and wave the last time.

On the drive to the airport, she'd tried to recover the camaraderie they'd shared on Christmas Eve. She chatted about school, her goals for the New Year, but something seemed different. Could a few kisses destroy their friendship? Was she the one letting it happen with her excessive love for him? Maybe she was just imagining his distance.

As she returned to the parking deck, she glumly wondered if Elaine was right. She was holding on too tightly and Mike didn't know if he should run or not. She'd seen hesitation in his eyes. Yet she couldn't hide her sadness. When would she see him again?

But another impression nibbled at her mind. Mike represented something beyond Adams Bridge and Greenbrier. He was like an open door to another world. Curiosity about his life and about other places piqued her appetite. Was *that* door closing as well as he passed through the checkpoint? Was *her* limited world drawing back in on her?

As for them as a couple, everything seemed up in the air. They'd crossed a line, a good one, she was sure. But everything surrounding that change seemed muddy and uncertain. She couldn't stop the tears that flowed down her cheeks as she drove back to Greenbrier.

ଓ ଓ ଓ

"Marie, can you get some more bread while you're up?" Frank called toward the kitchen.

They were down to three at the dining room table, Nikki and her parents. Nikki pulled the last biscuit from the wicker breadbasket. "Why are we still eating in the dining room instead of the kitchen? This is depressing."

"Thanks very much," said her mother with a sniff as she placed more dinner rolls next to Frank.

Nikki grinned and shrugged an apology. "I didn't mean I don't love your company. After twenty people, though, this huge table looks downright lonely."

Her father sent a long, knowing look in her direction without speaking. He then reached for the rolls, shaking his head. She didn't dare ask him what he was thinking.

As Nikki pushed her chair away from the table, he said, "Nikki, let your mother do the dishes. Why don't you come visit me in my office? We can have a chat."

Nikki eyed him. "Am I in trouble, Dad?"

Frank laughed, the large, warm sound echoing in the hallway as he walked toward his office. "My Nikki? Never. Just want to talk with my little girl. Anything wrong with that?"

"It's just that your office has a sort of, well, association. Every time one of us kids was in trouble, you called us into your office."

Frank laughed again, closing the door behind her. "I guess next time I'll have to serve tea and watch silly movies on the computer. Will that change your associations?"

Nikki sat still on the soft chair beside his desk, waiting for her father to make his point.

He turned his chair toward her and wrapped his large, dark hands around hers. "You know how much I love you and don't want to see you hurt, don't you?"

She nodded, a prickling sensation beginning on her scalp, as she suddenly understood why she was there. She looked past his head at the half-circles of frost on the mullioned windows and braced herself.

"I know Mike means a lot to you. Maybe you still feel. . ." he seemed to grope for words, though Nikki was sure he was only straining for diplomacy. "Attracted to him. You don't have to answer that, of course. That's your business. I just want to let you know something about Mike that you may not already know."

Nikki tensed. Maybe he'd finally admit the cause of his long-standing grudge against Mike.

"Our family has known Mike for years. He's had many girlfriends over that time, starting when he was quite young. I always thought he went through these women rather quickly and easily, and I didn't approve of that. It wasn't the way I raised you kids. But when he got into high school, I guess he was more influenced by his peers." He paused and frowned. Was he building up to something that would shock her?

"When Mike was about seventeen, he got involved with the daughter of a close friend and client of mine, who was a judge and a very prominent man in the community. His daughter became pregnant by Mike, or so we thought." Nikki watched her father's troubled face as he paused. "The girl was two months along when she finally told her father. He was heartbroken, as well as furious with Mike. I was furious too. I thought Mike was irresponsible, and I told him so. Thankfully, the girl wasn't pregnant after all, only late with her cycle, but it gave us all a big scare."

"I didn't know about that." Nikki's voice sounded small in her own ears.

"I tried my best to patch it up with the judge, since Mike was almost part of our family, living with Dad and all. We all did our best to keep this quiet, which is why you knew nothing about it. Probably Mike has never told you that story, but it may give an indication of his character."

She didn't speak as she considered her father's words. It didn't sound like the Mike she knew. Yet he himself had admitted to being *wild* as a teenager. What else had happened during that blank period when they'd lost touch? A needle of jealousy stabbed at her.

But what did that have to do with today? He was a new believer, after all. Didn't that erase the past? Might he still be tempted to follow old impulses?

"Dad." She cocked her head. "That was ten years ago. And teenage guys do mess around. It's not good, but it happens."

Skepticism etched her father's face as he merely sighed. "And you should know," she continued. "Mike made a commitment to faith in Jesus. That makes a big difference, don't you think? He's a new person with new values and priorities. I mean, he helps needy families with housing. Don't you think that shows a new heart?"

"I hope you're right, Nikki. I only wanted to warn you to spare you pain. You might think you're in love, but you never know if he's still playing the field."

Nikki felt exposed. Had he been watching them? Did her father know Mike had kissed her? "Is that why you seem to, um, dislike Mike, because of what happened ten years ago?"

Her question seemed to catch him off guard. "I don't dislike Mike. We don't have a lot in common and we're many years apart in age. Anyway, that's in the past." He waved a dismissal, despite the intensity of his previous words.

"But you haven't let it go." She leaned forward on the edge of her chair. "Guys do these things when they're seventeen. That doesn't make them womanizers forever."

Her father let out an exasperated sigh. "I'm not calling him a womanizer, Nikki. All I'm saying is be *careful* with your feelings. *Guard* them. Maybe you should meet someone who's not so close to the family. And someone who lives closer to you." Frank thrummed his fingers on the desk.

Nikki didn't regret her comment. She'd finally been able to gently confront her father about his attitude toward Mike. But she didn't feel any wiser for having done so. "Okay, Dad. Thanks for the talk. I know you're just worried about me." She leaned over to kiss him on the cheek, then pulled back. "Just remember, though, I'm not a kid. You don't always need to protect me."

At this, he smiled sadly, as if he alone saw dangers to which she was oblivious. A thread of irritation darted through her, but the conversation had left behind a remnant of discomfort as well.

# Chapter Six

Mike collapsed into the window seat of the commuter train for the trek from the San Francisco airport to his apartment downtown. Almost home. He changed his watch to late-afternoon West Coast time and leaned back. Napping on the flight had been futile, thanks to the whirring tornado in his mind. He propped his head against the vinyl headrest and watched the gray city pass by through the steamy window.

It was an understatement to say it wasn't the usual Christmas visit. The possibility of someone having murdered his parents, for starters. Yet it was only that, a possibility. Perhaps nothing would come of it after thirteen years. As Ely had said, Mike had done what he could, which felt like absolutely nothing. Maybe Officer Garner would make the case his personal crusade. That would be Mike's only hope. As long as the head accountant of Hamilton Industrial was on the run, he was hamstrung.

And then there was Nikki, who filled his thoughts ever since he left her looking forlorn that morning at JFK Airport. He'd felt empty too, as he walked away from her, especially after their closeness over the holidays. Seemed they'd recovered their neglected friendship, and more. "Huh," Mike muttered, then swallowed a dry lump in his throat. *So* much more, after the smoldering attraction had burst into a bonfire. Then he went and gave Nikki hope before knowing how much he could commit.

Depending on the moment, he regretted his impulsive kiss, though there was also relief that they'd openly declared their feelings. And kissing her was a delicious memory that haunted his unsettled mind. The train window reflected the wily smile that crept across his face.

What *did* he feel for Nikki? More than a casual attraction, undergirded by a friendship. A bond that trailed back for years, and comfortable, open communication. Was the recently renewed friendship in jeopardy now? If only he hadn't kissed her, he could have plodded forward in the relationship at whatever pace would have allowed him more certainty.

A middle-aged man with two young children settled into the seats facing Mike. The little girl stared at him for a moment. Her large blue eyes peered out of her ruddy round face, framed by unruly coils of blond hair. "Merry Christmas, Mister. Even though it's over."

"Shh, Amanda," whispered the man. "Don't bother the gentleman."

Mike smiled at her. "Merry Christmas to you, too."

*Even though it's over.* It was only the beginning. The beginning of a possible mess.

Frank's attitude only made things worse. He simply wouldn't let Nikki be an adult. Though that was obvious to Mike, he wasn't completely unaffected by Frank's words.

And that was the snag. True, he and Nikki could talk about nearly anything, and the chemistry between them was undeniable. A shared faith was something he'd had with no other woman. There were so many good signs. But Nikki deferred to her father and didn't seem to realize to what extent she lived under his protection and guidance. In returning to Adams Bridge, she'd returned to the shadow of her overpowering father. Even if Frank liked and accepted Mike, his influence over Nikki raised a red flag.

If all that was not enough to slow him down, Nikki seemed excessively—or obsessively—in love with him. He'd always been highly allergic to clingy, overly dependent women, a fact confirmed by his last two attempted relationships. Maybe his attraction to Nikki wasn't enough to outweigh the mounting obstacles.

His new life in California came with a clean record and a fresh identity. He'd been determined to create his life on his own, without the Mancini family bolstering him up. Nikki would tie him to the past and all the tragic memories he'd tried so hard to escape.

Mike sighed deeply, stamping a circle of vapor on the window.

Despite his hesitations—memories of conversations, stares, gestures, the way Nikki fit in his arms like a glove—a wave of giddy warmth filled him.

"Oh, Lord." He pressed his forehead against the cold window. "Please help me sort all this out. I'm making mistakes, but maybe You ordained all this. Or maybe not, I have no idea. I hope You'll guide the way and help me not hurt Nikki in the process. I give You the case with my parents too. You're the only one who can bring the truth to light."

Having shared his heaviness, a trace of optimism crept back. He glanced over and the little girl was staring at him again, as if to say, "That man there is talking to himself." Mike smiled at her.

Finally, he unlocked the door to his apartment and eased his luggage over the threshold. Every surface was coated with a layer of dust and littered with magazines, socks, and yesterday's toast. His roommate Chad's disorderly habits had reigned unchallenged all week. At least Mike's tropical fish were still alive.

He dropped his carryon bag next to his suitcase and fell backward onto his bed, glancing around his room. His gaze flitted to the wall where some of his most recent sketches of the Golden Gate Bridge dangled from thumbtacks. He slipped out of his shoes and let out a sigh. Home. His relief was tempered by the realization that he was alone again.

Later that evening when Chad came in from work, he peeked into Mike's room. "Hey, welcome back, dude."

Mike was transferring Christmas photos from his phone to his computer. "Thanks, Chad. Hope you had a good holiday."

He peered at Mike's photos over his shoulder and whistled. "Who's *that*?" He continued chewing on a piece of cold pizza. They both observed Nikki in her pink cashmere sweater, her gray eyes inviting with a hint of mystery.

"This is Nikki." Mike offered no further explanation. He advanced the photo to Nikki laughing on Christmas day, her teeth and eyes sparkling like a cover model. The next photo, which he'd taken with the self-timer of her new camera, showed the two of them in a tight hug.

"*Very* nice," Chad murmured, peering closer at the screen. A morsel of mushroom dropped onto Mike's desk. "Pretty quick work, Branagan. You were gone for, what, less than a week?"

Mike laughed. "I've known Nikki my whole life. We were just friends."

"Were? And what are you *now*?" Chad lifted his eyebrows mischievously and grinned. "You dog! You played hide and seek together as kids?"

"I was best friends with her brother. After my parents died, I went to live with her grandparents. Her family unofficially adopted me."

Chad stilled. "So, you guys, like, grew up together? Is she like a sister or something? 'Cause that would be weird. Don't you think?"

"No, she's—she *was* kind of like a little sister when we were young. But not anymore." No one would kiss his sister like he had kissed Nikki. "I hadn't seen her in three years."

Chad chewed and squinted at the screen. "You know, you guys kind of look alike. Sure she's not your sister?"

Mike clicked to another photo and glared at Chad. "She's an old friend. If we look alike, it's pure coincidence. Anyway, we're not an item, just. . .yet." He ran one palm over his jaws, willing Chad to leave him alone.

"Weird." Chad shook his head and shuffled from the room, dropping crumbs in his wake.

Mike grimaced. *Was* it weird to suddenly be attracted to someone he'd known almost his whole life? Maybe distance from Adams Bridge would straighten his perspective and protect the fragile remains of his heart.

Suddenly he felt a crushing aloneness. He longed to talk things over with Jeff, his third roommate and best friend. But Jeff wasn't due home for two more days. Maybe he'd call Harriet, one of his tenants, but more like a motherly friend, to wish her a Merry Christmas. No, on second thought, he'd let her enjoy her holiday with her family.

He grabbed his phone and dialed Ely's number. "Hey, just wanted to let you know I got here safely," he said to Ely's recorded message. "Uh, keep me posted if you hear anything. I'm sure you will. I'll do the same. It was good to see you. Okay, bye."

He frowned. Babbling on the phone wasn't his style. Maybe the struggles erupting in his life were already taking a toll. Truthfully, he was deeply disappointed that Ely hadn't answered. At that moment, he really needed a thread between his past and present worlds.

ℂ ℂ ℂ

"How does this look, Nikki?" Elaine swept her curly blond hair from her shoulders with one hand. Her gesture revealed a necklace scattered with pink stones and fresh-water pearls on a delicate chain. It filled the half-circle of creamy white skin above her fuchsia bodice.

"Just perfect. Did you get that for Christmas?"

Elaine stood before the full-length mirror, turning one way then the other, to admire the full effect. "I got the dress for Christmas, then I absolutely had to find the perfect necklace for it. That was my gift to myself." She giggled and let her hair fall. "What better time to wear it than New Year's Eve?"

"You'll probably meet your man tonight, looking like that." Nikki stood beside her in front of the mirror.

Elaine shrugged and stepped away. "I'm okay with God's timing. I'm having fun, so I can wait."

Nikki braced against a stab of envy. She craved Elaine's ability to live peacefully in the moment. She'd hoped her friend's serenity would rub off on her, but so far, it hadn't.

"Okay, what about me?" Nikki pouted theatrically and fluttered her eyelashes. She'd bought a black crepe dress that fell above the knee—completely unlike her usual style. A gently draping cowl bodice rippled down toward her narrow waist. Diamond dangle earrings and an up-swept hairstyle completed the daring, sophisticated look. She'd wanted to shake off the child-like image Mike must have of her. Instead of being elegant and mature, she felt like she was disguised for Halloween.

"You're a knockout. Too bad Mike can't see you now."

Nikki offered a half-smile she didn't feel. "Yeah. Why don't you take a picture of me, and I'll send it to him? Maybe he'll invite me to visit during my spring break."

"There's my phone. Better still, where's your new camera?"

Elaine's calm presence balanced Nikki's doubts about Mike and reminded her to take things slowly. He had called once to let her know he'd arrived safely and to tell her again how good it was to see her. He seemed sincere enough, but what would happen next?

As if in response to her thoughts, the phone rang. "Hi, Nikki. Happy New Year," Mike said. "What are you guys up to?" Just hearing his voice on the phone made her insides weak.

"Hi, Mike. Elaine and I are getting ready for a party with the singles' group at our friend Bart's house. How about you?" Nikki sank onto the soft couch, meeting Elaine's gaze with wide eyes.

"My roommates and I are going to a neighbor's party down the hall. At least I don't live too far if I need to sneak out early. I don't know what they get into after midnight." His laugh sounded uncomfortable to her. Maybe he thought she'd disapprove.

"That sounds fun. It's great that you know your neighbors. I don't know many of mine."

After several minutes of catching up on the week's activities and work news, they hung up. Elaine hovered in the kitchen. "So, did that go well?"

Nikki sighed. "I guess so. He's making an effort. I sense something holding him back, like he's not in it one hundred percent."

Elaine sat on the chair opposite the couch and chewed on a carrot. "He didn't blow you off after Christmas, like you feared. Isn't that something?"

"Yes, it is." Nikki's voice faltered. "I just wish. . ." She pressed her lips together and her eyes met Elaine's. "I want to be *pursued*. I feel like I'm the one running after him like I always have, in fact. He's just doing what he thinks I expect."

"It's a legitimate desire, Nikki, being pursued."

"I want to be cool about everything, and let it develop, but it's so hard for me, when I was obsessed with him for most of my life." Nikki let out a laugh. "When I was thirteen, I even followed him a couple of times to see what he was doing and if he was with a new girl. Is that psycho, or what?" A hot flush crept up Nikki's neck.

Elaine chuckled and shook her head. "Almost nothing is psycho when you're thirteen and in love." Her voice softened. "Try to relax, though. Act glad to hear from him, but not obsessed. And one more thing." She lifted her eyebrows. "This may sound like a cliché, but trust *God* with Mike. *Entrust* him to God. That doesn't mean you'll lose him. Or get him, in fact. Either way, I'm sure you want what God wants, right?"

Nikki nodded solemnly. Elaine was right. Her whole life had revolved around Mike Branagan or getting over him. Now she was on the threshold of finding her dream, but what if it wasn't right for her?

An icy trickle of apprehension slipped through her. She tried to shake it off. Of course, it had to be God's plan. She'd waited so long, and Mike was a Christian now. It *had* to be right.

# Chapter Seven

The afternoon bell clanged. Twenty students erupted from their seats and scrambled, scuffing and shouting, to the door. The last one disappeared, and Nikki found herself alone. Wearily, she erased the chalkboard, not sure if her lessons had seeped into the students' restless minds. Or maybe only hers was restless.

Outside the smudged windows, the mid-January landscape was awash with sadness and hibernation. The room felt clammy and smelled of sweat, cold, and outdoors. Colorful posters, photos, and French decorations on the walls did little to boost her heavy spirits. Instead of savoring her Christmas memories, her joy was tamped down by the formless certainty that things weren't going well in her relationship with Mike.

"Oh, Miss Mancini." Jeremy, a tenth grader in second period English class, poked his head around the door frame. "I forgot to tell you I won't be here tomorrow. So, uh, can I do the British poetry quiz the next day at lunch?"

She stared with little mercy at his gelled spikes of hair. "Do you have an approved reason to miss class tomorrow, Jeremy?"

"Um . . . I'll bring a note when I come for the quiz, okay?"

He vanished before she could think of a suitable response. Since returning from Christmas break two weeks earlier, the students had been unruly and distracted. She had less patience than usual to deal with them, especially Torrie the Terror, who Nikki had sent to the principal's office the previous day. Earlier that day, another student had accused her of being less fun than she had been before Christmas. What was happening to her?

Nikki's nerves felt exposed and ready to short-circuit. She needed to pull herself together.

Mike had called only once since New Year's. Nikki had called him once and left a message, not sure how much initiative she should take. He'd responded with a one-line email that read more like a choppy telegram: "Big deadlines at work; will call you soon."

The waiting-for-Mike game might last a long time. Nikki knew she should focus on her own life, but she ached for an unmistakable sign of interest from him. At the end of the school day, she stopped by the office to check her mailbox. Faculty chaperones were needed for the senior trip, field trips, and dances. Maybe volunteering would take her mind off Mike. Nikki signed up for all of them. She would prove to herself and anyone else that she had a life of her own.

Nikki snorted at the irony of it. She was truly pathetic.

As she drove toward Greenbrier, she prayed aloud, "Father, I'm having trouble keeping things in perspective. I want to trust you and not hold on too tight. But I'm failing at that. Please give me more strength." As she passed the Pancake Palace, tears broke free and trickled down her cheeks.

ᑫ   ᑫ   ᑫ

Mike wrapped one hand around a hot ceramic mug and reached for a menu. Those seeking a Saturday morning treat or catch-up with friends filled up the restaurant, and the clamor kept pace. The decor was more edgy by decades than the rundown, homey charm of the Pancake Palace. The memory of that day at the Palace brought a breeze of wistful sadness that nearly engulfed him.

"Wow, you look like a lost soul." Jeff looked up from his menu in time to catch the expression Mike had hoped to hide.

Mike gave his friend a wry, mirthless smile. "Just thinking of. . . everything. Of Nikki. It was like we'd never been apart. We really connected." He gazed sadly into his coffee.

"You make it sound like it's already over."

"It's not over. It's just confusing." Mike thrust his fingers through his hair. "There's so much that works, but loads of red flags too. I need to talk to her soon, and I don't know how. So, I've avoided calling her for over a week. I'm sure she's thinking the worst."

"Yeah, you need to talk to her," Jeff agreed. "But if you guys are really close, she'll understand, right?"

Mike shook his head. "I'm not so sure. The things I have to say, I don't think any woman wants to hear."

"Such as?"

Mike sighed. "She's sheltered. She lives only a couple miles away from her parents. Her dad is a real strong influence in her life. He's never liked me. He's already given me a warning about her."

Jeff whistled softly. "I see."

The server hovered patiently near the table.

"Here, maybe we should order." Mike lifted his gaze to the woman without consulting the menu. "Good morning. I'll take Eggs Benedict and orange juice."

After she left, Mike looked back at Jeff across the imitation wood grain table. "I was entwined in their family for years. That's one reason I came out here. I needed to be on my own. Nikki hasn't ever separated from her family."

Jeff nodded, his blue eyes compassionate behind wire-rim glasses.

"I can't very well tell her to call me when she's more grown up, can I?"

"That could come with time, don't you think?"

"Maybe. But can she even wait for that? I mean, she's madly in love with me and it blocks me from taking a normal course in the relationship."

"You're right, it is complicated. But you really like her, right?"

Mike nodded. "But does that mean we automatically belong together?" Mike gazed over Jeff's head for an instant. "I like a woman who knows she's an equal, not someone who puts me on a pedestal or depends on me for her happiness."

Jeff crossed his arms behind his head, staring thoughtfully down at the tabletop. "I totally get that. Do you remember my friend Greg? When he started his business, he had so many obstacles. But he just kept plugging away, and in the end, it was worth it all. So, I wonder, is Nikki worth all the trouble? She *could* be." He grinned and his voice lightened. "Or maybe you should find yourself a nice girl whose dad likes you."

"Gee, thanks, Jeff. Your wisdom astounds me." Mike frowned as the food arrived. "I think at this point I need to tell her what I'm thinking. She won't like it, but she's imagining the worst anyway."

"Then again, maybe it's the right thing but the wrong time."

Mike stilled at Jeff's words and let them sink in. "That's quite possible. When you add to that all the issues going on with my parents' death, I'm so distracted I can hardly think straight."

"Does Nikki know about the current investigation into your parents' accident?"

Mike shook his head. "No, I want to tell her, but my head's been spinning from it all. I wasn't ready. I need to handle this alone for now." When the server offered a refill on coffee, he nodded and turned back to Jeff. "I probably shouldn't do that refill. I'm already not sleeping very well."

Jeff smiled in sympathy. "Maybe one day things will work with Nikki. There's always the future."

Mike grimaced. "With everything that's happening, this definitely seems to be the wrong time." A hollow thud hit the pit of Mike's stomach.

෨   ෨   ෨

Nikki slid sliced tomatoes into a bowl of torn lettuce leaves. The front door opened, and she smiled. "Hi, Elaine. I made salad and grilled cheese. Want some?"

Elaine dropped the stack of files she carried onto the coffee table and slipped out of her knee-length wool coat. "Love some, thanks." Her curly, blond hair was windblown, and framed cheeks flushed with cold. "It's only late January, but Christmas break seems *so* long ago."

The truth of her statement struck Nikki daily, especially as she started each day.

Elaine disappeared into the back of the apartment and returned wearing her favorite pink sweats. "Oh, comfort! Couldn't wait to get out of those heels and panty hose." She plopped down into the dining room chair as Nikki served them both.

"Anything new?" Elaine sliced her sandwich through the center and gingerly picked up one half.

Nikki frowned, staring down at her lettuce leaves, glossy with olive oil. "Actually, I got an email from Mike this afternoon. He said he'll call tonight. He wants to talk to me about something." She moved her lettuce around with her fork, then met Elaine's gaze.

Elaine had just taken a large bite of her sandwich. Her mouth was still full when she mumbled, "Uh-oh."

"Yeah, that's what I said too," Nikki said glumly. "If he ends it—"

"Nikki, maybe he just wants to clear the air. Don't expect the worst."

"You're right." She should relax. Let *go*. That was what Mike wanted too. She needed to trust God more, as Elaine kept telling her.

After Elaine went to her bedroom, Nikki graded papers on the couch. Her phone sat on the end table. Her hands felt moist and clammy. What could he want to talk to her about? A weight pulled downward inside her stomach.

By the time the phone rang at nine thirty, Nikki's nerves were in such a state she wanted to get it over with. She forced her most relaxed voice. "Hi, Mike. Thanks for your email. Is your deadline finished?"

"Yeah, turned everything in this morning. How have you been?" His voice sounded strained.

"It's been hard to get back into the rhythm I had before the holidays. My students are rowdy, like they can't get back their groove either. My mind's been preoccupied—" Idiot! Why did she gush everything that was on her mind?

There was a long pause on the other end of the phone. "Nikki, I want to share some thoughts with you, and I hope you'll be open. First, know that I really care about you. I want to be honest with you too, though."

Nikki braced herself, then leaned back against the couch. "What is it, Mike? I know there's something bothering you."

He hesitated, then said, "I. . .kind of wanted things to be more relaxed between us. It feels, well, pressured. I'm not blaming you. Maybe the fact that we only have the phone now makes it harder to be more natural. Take things slowly, like we said."

"Yes, it's a shame we can't just hang out together. I'm sorry if I've put pressure on you. I don't mean to. There's no pressure from me, Mike. Really." She so wanted to change, to let go. She hoped he would believe her.

"There's another thing. I have trouble explaining this, so bear with me. Sometimes it seems to me like we live in two different worlds, you know, with different life experiences. You've mostly been with your family."

Nikki was silent. She understood what he was saying, but a sliver of defensiveness crept upward from her gut and filled her chest. "I. . . do want more experiences in my life, but haven't had a chance just yet. I've been to France twice. And there's time. I'm still young, and there's a lot I'd like to do." She felt confused. "Is there something else?"

"Yes, or rather, part of the same thing."

Oh no, there was more. Nikki felt like a rock crushed her chest as she heard his tortured breath on the line.

He said, "You seem, well, dependent on your family. I know you're close with your dad, and he seems to have a lot of influence on you. I'm not sure I'm explaining this very well, Nikki."

Nikki felt punched in the stomach. She knew she'd been too zealous in her feelings for Mike, but too close to her family? "It's a problem that I'm close to my family? What does that have to do with *our* relationship?"

"Of course, there's nothing wrong with being close to your family. I...I guess I wouldn't want to become a replacement for your father."

Her mouth dropped open. "Are you kidding?" she sputtered. "Do you think I'm a *child* who needs another father?" Her voice trembled.

Mike sighed loudly. "No, no, that's not what I'm saying. You are a grown woman, but if you don't make choices that are your own, find your own independence . . ." He sighed in frustration. "I'm not saying what I want to say. You've misunderstood."

"So, I guess I'm okay for a make-out session, but for something more serious, I'm too immature. Is that what you're saying?" She heard the edge in her own voice but couldn't rein it in.

He made a sound in his throat. "No, Nikki." He began more gently, "That's *not* what I'm saying. I never said you're immature. You're sheltered. I'm used to women who are more independent, less sheltered. I just think, as much as I care about you, it might not be the best timing for us."

Nikki forced a calm breath as she pressed her lips together. "I see." Then her emotions caught up with her mind like a wave crashing to shore. "Let me get the list straight. I'm too immature for you and I love you too much and am pressuring you. That's what I understood. Are you sure that's all?"

"No, no, you distorted what I said—"

"So, it's *my* fault? I wonder if you just used me at Christmas, if you had any intention—"

"Stop, Nikki. I didn't use you nor intend to mislead you. I keep telling you I really *care* about you. You're not hearing me. You're only hearing my hesitations. I'm trying to be honest with you so we can look at this *together*."

The tidal wave kept coming at her, engulfing all her hopes. "So, is that like, 'we'll keep your application on file'?" Her words spurted out in a bitter splash.

"Maybe we should take some time, and talk about it again later," he finally said. When she didn't answer, he added, "Don't hold on too tight, Nikki. What is supposed to happen will happen."

Despite her greatest efforts to hide her emotions, Nikki sniffed. She didn't want him to hear her crying, to know he'd broken her heart. "I understand perfectly." She kept her voice level. "You're not ready, I'm not ready. So, it was nice while it lasted, I guess. Goodbye, Mike."

Quietly, she hung up the phone, then leaped up from the couch and ran into the bathroom. Amidst sobs, her stomach lurched, and her grilled cheese came hurtling up. Through a mist of horror, she vaguely heard the phone ringing, ringing. As she continued to cry and cough, she heard a sleepy voice, "Nikki? What's wrong, Nikki? Is it Mike?"

She couldn't answer, but nodded. Elaine, sleepy eyed, stood in the doorway to the bathroom. She whispered, "Oh, Nikki. I'm so sorry. Here, let me help you." She led her from the toilet to the sink, where she rinsed her face with a moist cloth. Nikki rinsed out her mouth, continuing to cry, her voice breaking into another sob.

When she could speak again, Nikki gave Elaine a tearful summary of her conversation with Mike. Elaine listened quietly, then wrapped her arms around Nikki's shoulders. She cradled her tightly for several minutes, gently rocking her like a small child. "Shhhh," she whispered, as Nikki began sobbing afresh.

"I don't think he was saying no, never, Nikki. Just let go and if it's supposed to happen, it will."

"Yeah, that's what he said too," Nikki muttered. She grabbed two tissues. "And meanwhile he'll meet someone, and that will be that. I know I need to let go. It's just not meant to be."

# Chapter Eight

In the art department of the software company where Mike worked, eight desks linked to one another with partitions and file cabinets. He stared glumly out the window at sheets of winter rain sliding down the glass. Everything beyond it shimmered in misty tones of gray. The frequent splashes from cars driving by blended with honking horns. New deadlines and pressures flooded into his morning. For once he was thankful for them, since they kept his thoughts from being sucked down into a black hole.

Each time he relived the conversation with Nikki three days earlier, he cringed with a visceral ache. He'd never intended to end it with her. He'd only wanted time and space.

The conversation had definitely gone wrong. Maybe she considered his words, "Not the right time", as code for, "It's over." No wonder she'd refused his phone calls and emails. He'd stumbled through the confrontation with the grace and sensitivity of an elephant walking backward. At this rate, he wouldn't even be able to salvage the friendship.

He could always leave a phone message saying he hadn't given up on them. But he'd likely find himself in the same place, with her expecting too much too soon, or adapting her behavior to please him. That wouldn't resolve anything.

He ought to be relieved. One less complication in his life. If he were smart, he'd leave things as they were, and keep his new, carefully crafted life intact, hermetically sealed off from anything connected to Adams Bridge. That would be easiest, in light of his aversion to mixing the present with the past. But with the investigation into his parents' death, he didn't have that choice anymore.

The depth of his emptiness following his call with Nikki took him off guard. In a short amount of time, emotional threads had woven together. What he felt for her was *real*. If he let it all go, would it be a convenient, cowardly way out of an emotional puzzle? To abandon everything, just because he had an open door to do it?

A burst of laughter followed by bantering conversation cut through the silence. Overhead, a florescent lamp flickered. He sighed and clicked to open a photo treatment software program, though he didn't really see the screen past his distraction.

His cell phone sounded. "Hello, Harriet," he said to the familiar voice of his favorite tenant. "I hope you had a nice holiday."

Her elderly voice crackled. "Yes it was, and I hope the same for you. I hate to bother you, Mike, but we have a leak under the sink in the kitchen. Joe tried to fix it, but he doesn't have the right tools."

"I'll stop by and have a look after work today." Good, at Harriet's house, he'd have a distraction from his thoughts, not to mention a smiling face and a hot cup of tea.

His mind swept back to Nikki. If she *was* worth fighting for, as Jeff said, what could he do now? He could keep calling until one day she picked up the phone. At the moment, he couldn't think of anything he could do or say that wouldn't just make things worse.

&#x0512; &#x0512; &#x0512;

February slunk by in a hazy mist of drizzle and broken dreams. Each morning as Nikki awakened, the memories flooded back—the afternoon at the reservoir, the Christmas kisses, that awful final phone call—

It all crushed on her until she had to catch her breath. When she could put it off no longer, she'd slip from the bed, hating February and hating her life. The aching, barren place inside her didn't allow her any hopes except for the end of the day. It took all her strength to push thoughts of Mike from her mind. Then no energy remained to thrust away the sadness. Her students seemed aware of something horribly wrong, as they curbed their misbehavior and spoke in hushed voices.

Each evening Nikki holed up in her bedroom, blocking with music or talk radio any thoughts or memories likely to unleash a new flood of tears. With time, she cried less, but the aching cavern was a constant companion.

During the fourth week, a question grazed the top layer of her misery. Could Mike be right? She tried to look at herself objectively, the way Mike or even others might, and a slow throb of shame unfurled. Spoiled, selfish, dependent . . .words and images floated into conscious thought. At first, she objected, then flinched. Finally, the sobs came in fresh waves and were less about Mike Branagan and more about her. It was true. She lived her fears within the safety and suffocation of her father.


Nikki pulled another steaming piece of pizza from the plate. "Feed a heartache," she mumbled, then blew on the hot melted cheese.

"Nothing like pizza on a cold March night, is there?" Elaine said as they watched tiny snowflakes swirl gently and ricochet off the plate-glass window of the restaurant. She reached for another piece of pizza. "Are you doing better, Nikki? It's been a tough month."

Nikki shrugged and slurped her diet drink. "I understand better Mike's point of view. Trying to see it from his shoes. I *am* limited in life experience compared to him. I get that. I'm not his type, as much as he might like me in other ways. It's not his fault. I'm not angry anymore, but I'm still really sad." Her voice softened to a whisper, though the disappointment throbbed through her words. "I have no more illusions that things can work out for us. This was my one shot with Mike Branagan, and now it's over."

Elaine was quiet for a moment as Nikki's words hung in the air. "I know it hurts a lot," she said gently. "It might seem like you'll never stop crying. You *will* feel better one day, Nikki. You'll meet someone else, and you'll wonder why you thought Mike was the only guy for you."

"Do you really think there's anyone like Mike for me? I can't even imagine that. I feel humiliated about the whole thing. How am I ever going to face him again, after this? At least ignoring his frantic phone messages gives me my dignity back."

Elaine laughed. "If he's leaving frantic messages, maybe you mean something to him after all."

"Maybe," Nikki said. "He promised, we both promised, that whatever happened we'd stay friends. Maybe that's what the calls are about. I hope we can be friends again, but I'm not ready yet."

"Who knows, maybe God is protecting you from something. Or it could just be timing."

Nikki nodded. "He was too important for me, for too many years. I've been mad at God for taking away my lifelong idol. All this time I thought it was Mike's issue, his self-protection and fear of commitment. I think he has some of that, but I have to look at myself too." She had to be honest with herself. Being needy and dependent had sent Mike running.

Elaine reached across the table and squeezed Nikki's arm, empathy in her smile.

"Be honest with me." Nikki stared back at her friend. "Do you think Mike is right about me being too protected by my dad. Is it true?"

After a long pause Elaine said, "Uh, I've noticed that you seem to care a lot, maybe too much, what your dad thinks." Her eyes crinkled apologetically. "There may be a bit of truth. If you want my loving opinion, I think you could benefit from more independence from your family."

Nikki leaned forward on her laced fingers. "Some people can handle being near family more than others. In my case, it was always easy to be the youngest and the favorite, easy to be smothered. I never even noticed. That was just the way it was. But Mike saw it. No wonder he's afraid I'll transfer my dependence from my dad to him." She swallowed and her eyes became moist. "Maybe I would have."

Elaine's face was unsmiling, her eyes intense. "If that's what you've learned through all this, Mike's done you a service. A painful one, of course."

"Maybe that was the whole purpose." Nikki blinked once, twice. "I've started to see a few things, and I guess I have some work to do in my own life."

Her own life. Although she'd spent much of it getting over Mike, she'd have to do it one last time. She could no longer build her future tied to what her father thought and did. Nor could she plan it in view of either hoping for or getting over Mike. She'd get over him. She'd do whatever it took.

ભ ભ ભ

"Please be quiet. Now." Nikki paced the front of her classroom and waited for the room to hush. "We still have ten more minutes. For those ten minutes I'm going to give you a phrase in passé composé, and I want you to respond in the imperfect. For example, I'll say *J'ai habité à Paris'*, and you'll respond, *J'habitais à Paris*. Does everyone understand?" A chorus of student voices chimed, "*Oui*".

She spun out phrases and students from around the room responded. For the most part, they understood. "Good job, class! I think you've got it! Joanne, this one's a bit harder, but I think you can do it. *J'ai connu le voisin*."

Joanne squinted in concentration. "Um . . . *Je . . . connaissais le voisin?*"

"Excellent. Beautiful job, Joanne." Joanne's freckled face widened into a broad grin. A beam of encouragement sliced through Nikki's gray mist.

The bell finally rang, and chaos erupted. Nikki shouted, "Everyone, please read chapter ten and do the exercises on page one forty-five before Friday. See you tomorrow." She sighed. One more class over. Three to go. Her head was pounding already.

She sank wearily back into her desk chair. Her spirits sagged when Torrie approached her desk. Strands of flaxen hair hung over half of the girl's face. She chewed on a bright pink pen.

"Miss Mancini, um, what's the difference between *J'ai parlé* and *je parlais*? Are they different tenses?" Her voice was dull, though not insolent, as it usually was.

Mustering a tight smile, Nikki said, "Yes, that's right. Good, Torrie. This is the passé composé," she pointed to the phrase in the book, "and this is the imperfect, which we've been learning about this week." She half expected Torrie to complain about the class then flounce out of the room, but instead she stood rooted beside Nikki's desk.

"Is there something else on your mind?" Nikki asked gently.

Torrie's large pale blue eyes were somber. "Um, Miss Mancini, it's just that you seem really sad."

Nikki tried to hide her surprise. She leaned back in her chair. "I am, Torrie. I had some hard things happen lately."

Torrie tilted her head. Gone was the sardonic glare Nikki had seen nearly every day since September. In its place could only be described as compassion. "Oh, Miss Mancini, I know what that's like to have hard things."

She reached for a chair near the wall, pulled it close to Nikki's desk, and flopped down, straddling it backwards. Her backpack plopped onto the floor. "Last fall I was so hurt I wanted to disappear. Ross Goldman broke up with me just before third period and I couldn't even finish my classes. I went out to the bleachers and just cried and cried."

Nikki smiled sadly. "What a terrible way to start the school year. Maybe that's why we had trouble getting along back then, huh?"

Torrie's smiled and lowered her gaze. She flipped her straight hair over one shoulder. "Maybe that was part of it. I was in a bad mood for months. And it always seemed like to me you had everything, a rich dad, a nice house. Seems you never had a bad day in your life. That's probably not true, but seemed like it."

Nikki's mouth dropped open in surprise. "Really? Of course, I've had bad days and broken hearts. Failures, mistakes. People aren't always how they appear."

Torrie nodded, giving Nikki a lopsided grin for the first time all year. "Yeah, I guess so. I shouldn't have compared your life to mine. I can't stand it at my house. We're always fighting, and there's never any money. Dad's only there once in a while. Mom has her boyfriend on the side, who I'm not supposed to know about. I stay away as much as I can." She paused and looked at the floor then back at Nikki. "I'm sorry you're having a hard time. But in a way, it gives us something in common."

Nikki nodded. "Yes, it does. We understand each other better now."

Torrie stood up, smiling. "Well, thanks for talking. I hope you feel better soon." As she left the room, a warm trickle nudged Nikki's despair aside. So, Torrie the Terror was simply Torrie the hurting teenager, envying what she thought Nikki had. Nikki had overlooked needs right in front of her while lost in her depression. Time to stop her obsession. Time to turn the page.

# Chapter Nine

A two-inch stack of English essays weighed on Nikki's lap as she sat on her couch after dinner. Teaching honors English had seemed an exciting challenge at first, but no one had warned her about all the papers she'd have to grade. This batch might take until midnight, but at least she had a quiet evening alone to concentrate, while the wind grumbled outside.

March days were longer, the cold less biting. Slowly Nikki emerged from the cocoon of despair that had surrounded her days for the previous month. There would be life after Mike Branagan. She would make sure of it.

At nine-forty the phone rang. Nikki checked her phone and her pulse surged. It was Mike. He hadn't tried to call for over two weeks and she thought that he'd given up. She braced herself and shifted the stack of English papers to the couch beside her, then reached for the phone. "Hi, Mike."

"Hi, Nikki. I'm glad you answered." Warmth coated his voice.

Her stomach tightened, and perspiration moistened her back. She swallowed, keeping her voice calm and nonchalant. "Yeah, sorry I haven't taken your calls. I, uh, I needed some time. I hope you understand."

"I do. We left a lot of loose ends the last time we talked. I never said things were over between us, only that it might not be the right time."

That phrase again. *Not the right time.* As if that was supposed to give her hope. "That's okay," she said. "I'm sorry for the things I said. I was hurt and it came out wrong. It wasn't your fault."

"Don't take the blame, now. I didn't express myself in the best way, either. I want to apologize for that." He spoke hesitantly, and against her will she felt warmed. "In fact, I really blew it. It must have sounded like I thought you had no mind of your own. That's *not* at all what I meant. In fact, I've seen your convictions for different things, like teaching. You have such a heart for your students, and I love that about you." He paused. "I've missed talking to you, Nikki. I miss our friendship."

So, *that's* why he was so persistent. He'd made a promise and intended to keep it. At least he was a man of his word, when it would have been easy for him to simply stop calling. "Me too," she said. "We promised we'd always be friends, didn't we?"

"We did. I hope we will, no matter what."

"I'll try not to get so upset when you're only trying to be honest," Nikki added. "I'll be a better listener."

"And I'll try not to say stupid things and exaggerate minor problems." Mike chuckled and Nikki joined him. Though their conversation seemed forced, a few threads of relief wove through her tension.

In any case, it was a first step.

ର    ର    ର

Mike frowned. He'd talked to Nikki for about twenty minutes. When they hung up, a faint wave of disappointment baited him. She clearly didn't believe he still wanted to explore a romantic relationship with her, albeit slowly. To her, it was a line, nothing more. She'd also taken the blame, which closed the door to any further discussion. It had been agonizing to wait over a month to talk to her again, wondering if he ever would. When he did, he felt empty.

Then again, if she were willing to be friends again, he could build the relationship with her gradually and without pressure. The way he *should* have from the beginning. It was a chance to start over. That would be his new strategy with Nikki. He'd win back her friendship and trust, and along the way, see if there could be more.

Cozy lamplight bathed the small urban bedroom. Mike flipped on his computer and scrolled to the photos, viewing them one at a time. Each photo triggered a specific memory. Nikki with a relaxed grin, surrounded by multicolored Christmas paper. Looking over her shoulder at him as she helped Marie in the kitchen. Nikki, gorgeous and chic in that black New Year's Eve dress.

On an impulse, he leaned down toward the bottom of his bookshelf and drew out a photo album he hadn't looked at in years. He turned to a page of photos when Nikki was a child of six, shortly after he'd gotten to know Danny. He grinned at the image of the three of them playing together in the pool, and another one, at ages seven and ten, in front of a Christmas tree. Nikki's dark bangs hung nearly into her eyes, but hadn't hidden the mischief sparkling there.

The past conjured up such a complex mixture of joy and pain. Many of his best memories were at the Big House with his borrowed family. All told, he'd had a decent childhood. He'd coped the best way he could with his parents' deaths, which had hurtled him into a dark, painful tunnel. The aloneness he'd felt for years afterwards had been worse than the event itself. But the Mancinis—Jim, Catherine, Nikki, Danny, and Marie—had been there to soften his fall.

He turned back several pages and stared at a vacation photo with his parents. Their faces smiled out at him from a long, cloudy distance. He touched the photo through the plastic cover, a hollow pang filling him.

A soft tap interrupted his memories. Jeff's face appeared behind the door. "Want some frozen pizza?"

"No thanks. Hey, Jeff—" Mike called as Jeff left.

"What's up, Bro?" He returned into the room and sat on the bed.

"Just a thought. I wonder if my interest in Nikki might be tied to my attachment to her family. I mean, they were like *my* family. Maybe it's just nostalgic residue, or something."

A wide grin split Jeff's normally serious face. "Nostalgic *residue*?" He laughed aloud then for several seconds. "You're funny. Residue. With her family, without her family, I think you *like* this girl, and you're in denial. She could be an orphan and you'd still be stuck on her."

Mike frowned. "You think? Everything would be simpler if she were."

Jeff laughed again, then his face sobered. "Do you have any news from that police officer yet?"

"No. I called the station about a month ago. They didn't want to start a new inquiry until they caught the suspect."

"I guess they have their hands full with current cases. Something may turn up later. Don't lose hope." He stood and left the room.

Mike closed the album and slipped it back into its forgotten place. Drawn back to the computer screen, he met Nikki's gray eyes. Jeff was right. Nikki had gotten under his skin. She'd broken through the surface of his protective shell in a way that not even Stephanie had. He and Nikki had always understood each other, at times with only an exchanged glance. So why was it going so wrong now?

A new thought stabbed him broadside. What if, in the last month, she realized she didn't really love him after all? If reality hadn't measured up to the fantasy she'd had of him all these years. What if, despite hurt feelings, she was now relieved?

If that were the case, then it really was over. But how could he know if she wouldn't tell him? The answer seemed to be the same: time.

ത    ത    ത

Temperatures touched the mid-sixties on a Saturday afternoon in April. Outside the windows, small bouquets of lime green leaves hung delicately on the tips of the branches.

Elaine pushed the windows all the way open and inhaled the earthy fragrance of spring. "Doesn't it make a difference to have sunshine and warmth after a long winter? I feel like a new woman." She threw up her arms in a burst of childlike joy. "Maybe we should clean off the balcony." Instead, she grabbed a cloth and began dusting the furniture.

Nikki looked up from her journal, where she'd been writing furiously for several minutes. "Yeah, it's great. Sorry, I'm distracted, Elaine."

"Hope it's good stuff." She grinned the nodded toward the journal, then sat down on the couch next to her.

Nikki leaned back on the couch and shut the small, cloth-bound book. "I'm just writing some prayers. Mostly telling God how sorry I am for being a brat." She gave Elaine a lopsided grin and shrugged. "I wanted Mike, but that didn't automatically make him God's will for me. My father loves me and tries to give me whatever I want, but God loves me enough to *not* give me whatever I want. God treated me like an adult who could handle hearing 'no.' I sort of *like* that. My father almost never denies me anything. I'm always his little girl. It made me feel special for a long time, but now I'm resenting it."

Elaine leaned forward on her knees. "Your dad probably thought he was being loving." They both fell quiet for a few moments, then Elaine softly added, "Sounds like Mike had a lot of insight into your relationship with your dad."

Nikki's eyes stung. She squeezed them shut for a moment. "I think that's why I've always felt like such a child, not quite ready for real life. My dad thought he was showing love by intercepting problems for me, protecting me. Protecting me from *life*. Sometimes I almost feel handicapped, like I can never live alone or make it by myself. I need to get away somewhere, to be my own person, and learn the hard way how to be an adult." She mustered a small smile. "Maybe I'll hitchhike across the country."

Elaine laughed. "Yeah, I hear the rebellion now. I think you're getting over Mike, too."

Nikki didn't answer. Pushing him from her conscious mind with dozens of activities didn't mean she was getting over him. If she was, it was a very slow process.

How she desperately wanted to change, to own her life, develop her true self, increase her courage, and not always defer to her father. She wanted to learn to follow God's leading through her own instincts instead. What would it take? Yet she knew she'd begun the process, even though it would likely be a long and painful one.

CR  CR  CR

Following an animated discussion about the authors and stories in American literature, the serenity of the empty classroom was music to Nikki's ears. She'd slogged through a bleak, unhappy winter and finally felt more like herself. Confident again in the classroom, like an adult with something to impart. In less than two months, school would be out for the summer. She'd have to look for a part-time job to keep her hands and mind busy.

Nikki straightened the books, paperweight, stacks of papers, and pens on her desk. Under the blotter she peeked again at a sketch Mike had given her at Christmas, of Ginger sleeping beside the Christmas tree. She'd been unable to look at it for weeks. Now she studied it in minute detail. He had talent.

She smiled, remembering her phone call with him the previous evening. They'd spoken like they had that day at the reservoir. No issues, just friendship. Felt good to finally get it back. They'd laughed together about a funny experience he'd had in his neighborhood. He told her all about spring in San Francisco, festivals that were going on, the weather, the rhythm of the city. She'd felt intrigued, drawn by his world. Too bad she'd never be a part of it. Those kinds of conversations would drag her backward, yet she couldn't help herself. As soon as she heard his voice, nothing else mattered. Her protests hung in the back of her mind, then quietly floated away. He was an addiction for her. Soon she'd have to do something radical, otherwise the getting-over-Mike cycle would never end.

Nikki locked the classroom door behind her. Over one shoulder hung her canvas sack full of papers. A balmy breeze playfully fingered her hair. The afternoon was warm enough to wear a light cardigan while she drove with the car windows down.

At a long stop light near the edge of Greenbrier, Nikki thumbed through a teacher's magazine a colleague had loaned her. Her eyes fell to a half-page ad that read, *Teach English in Paris*. She stared at it for a moment too long, for the car behind her blasted his horn.

"Okay, okay," Nikki murmured. She drove toward her apartment while her mind raced. Paris. France.

As soon as she unlocked the apartment door, she turned on her laptop and found the website she'd seen in the ad. She skimmed the page twice then read the details aloud. "Teacher's Assistant Program in Paris, sponsored by the French government. Assistants work in public school English classes to help with conversation and teaching." It started in late September and lasted until the following May. Some French was required, some teaching experience desired. So far, she was qualified.

A spark of exhilaration flickered inside her. This might be the opportunity she needed, to fill her summer, develop her independence, and perhaps get over Mike. That was radical, no doubt about it.

With dismay, she noticed that the application deadline was well past. She'd apply anyway. If she was supposed to go, she would. Nikki completed the online application and pushed *send* before her fears could drag her away. Then she leaned back in her chair and breathed. "Whatever you want, Lord," she whispered.

Nikki blinked and sat up in her chair. "What did I just *do*?" She gasped at her own impulsivity, then calmed herself, knowing they'd never accept her. Still, it was fun to think of the prospect of living in Paris for a year. When she'd been an exchange student, she'd lived in Dijon and had seen Paris only briefly. During her trip last year with her students, they'd visited the key tourist sites of Paris.

Living there would be completely different.

Nikki thought about her French friend, Aurélie, who lived in Paris. Aurélie had been a foreign exchange student at Nikki's college, and Nikki had befriended her. Later, they'd seen each other during each of her visits to France. At least Nikki wouldn't be alone if she went to Paris.

She picked up the phone to call her, then put it back on her desk. One thing at a time. First, she had to be accepted, and that was not a sure thing. Suddenly, Nikki felt an urgency to live abroad alone, to develop as her own person, far from Adams Bridge, her family, and Mike. If that didn't work out, she'd find something else, spend the summer working on a fishing boat in Florida, or on a farm in the Midwest, or at a vineyard in New England.

She would break out one way or another.

# Chapter Ten

Nikki didn't have much of an appetite as she looked down at the baked ham and scalloped potatoes on her plate. Around the dining room table sat her father, her mother, Laura, and Trey, all oblivious to the hummingbirds flitting around in her stomach. She fingered the embroidered design on the linen tablecloth. That evening during dinner, she planned to announce to her parents that she was moving to Paris.

A few days after sending her hurried online application, instead of being refused, Nikki was surprised to be put on a waiting list. Two days later she was told that because of a cancellation, they were short one teacher for the high school level. Her experience as a high school teacher gave her priority. She was on her way to Paris.

In the few days that followed her surprise acceptance, Nikki found herself in a whirlwind of preparations. She called Aurélie, who was overjoyed. Aurélie convinced Nikki to come to Paris early so she could enjoy the summer there. It seemed a much better idea than getting a part-time job in Greenbrier, New York, so Nikki decided on a late-June departure. That would give her time to finish the school year and pack.

Nikki also applied for a French visa and turned in a one-year leave-of-absence request to her department head. The woman assured her that teaching for a year in France would increase her value as a French teacher.

Nikki's panic swelled as time passed. It was the biggest decision she'd ever made in her life. Whenever she pictured herself alone in Paris and felt her pulse go into overdrive, she pushed her anxiety down. Keeping busy with her long to-do list helped smother her sheer terror, but at odd moments, a voice shrieked in her mind, "Are you *really* doing this? It's not too late to change your mind! Going overseas? Alone?"

Yet, since the day she saw the ad in the magazine, going to Paris became less about getting over Mike and more about her own need for independence and adventure. She'd prove to herself she could make it on her own, and in a foreign country, no less. Of course, she could have chosen something easier to strengthen her character. But it was too late now. She was on her way.

That evening, as she prepared to go to the Big House for dinner, Nikki had practiced in front of the mirror. "Mom, Dad, what do you think if I go live in Paris for a year?" She shook her head. No more asking permission. She'd simply tell them her decision, like any adult would. "I've decided to teach in Paris for a year and I'm leaving in a month." Sounded better.

She'd made a point to notify Aurélie, accept the position with the French officials, and apply for a French visa before telling her parents. That way, her father couldn't talk her out of it. There was no turning back now.

Why was she nervous telling her parents of her decision? It only confirmed her need to go away, to be an adult. This need had taken on crusade proportions, despite her growing apprehension. Mike had been right.

 Nikki looked up around the table at her father, her mother, Laura, and Trey. *Get it over with, Nikki. Then you can enjoy your dinner.* She cleared her throat. "I have an announcement to make, everyone." No one seemed to hear her voice, which felt like dry fibers about to split. She waited several minutes for another break in the conversation.

Louder this time. "I have an announcement to make, everyone." Conversation stopped, forks hung in midair, and everyone stared at Nikki. Her father's face paled. She could guess the news he expected to hear.

"I have a wonderful opportunity in the coming year." She gathered her courage to not only inform them, but mark a line within herself at the same time. "I have decided to move to Paris to teach English for a year. I'll be leaving at the end of the month." She looked around the room. No one spoke.

"What's all this about?" Her father's bushy black eyebrows shot up, as though he hadn't heard her correctly, or simply couldn't believe his ears.

Nikki took a deep breath. "I've been accepted to teach English for a year in a French high school. The program is offered by the French government. It places native English-speaking teachers in French high school English classes. That helps students learn conversation from a native speaker."

She glanced around the table at blank, uncomprehending faces. "I just learned about my acceptance a few days ago." She'd expected a chorus of objections, telling her it was a hare-brained idea. The clock ticked from the wall, battering the silence.

Finally, Frank spoke. "Are you sure, Nikki? It's awfully far away. And for a whole year."

"Yes, I'm sure. I've already sent them my acceptance." She closed her ears against the words "far" and "a year", thankful she couldn't turn back. Her heart pounded.

After a moment's pause, her father said, "That sounds like an exciting opportunity for you, Sweetie."

Nikki's mouth dropped open, then closed. Was he really accepting it so easily? Or was he merely relieved she hadn't announced she was eloping with Mike? "You really think so? I'm so glad. Of course, I'll miss you all, but I need an experience like this." She relaxed. This was going better than she expected.

"Wow. Cool," murmured Trey in his laconic style, as he flipped his shaggy blond hair over one shoulder. "Paris." He nodded. "Cool."

Even Laura said, "Sounds great, Nikki. It'll really improve your French, too."

"Where will you live over there?" Her mother's brow furrowed.

"I'll find an apartment when I get there. Remember my friend, Aurélie? You met her when she visited here a couple of years ago.

She lives in Paris and will help me get settled. I've started looking for some places online."

Nikki was finally calm enough to eat a forkful of potatoes. She chewed slowly and scanned the faces of her family and the familiar dining room, the chairs, wallpaper, colorful curtains. A ripple of melancholy formed and snaked through her. She would need to store up memories like this one for the year to come.

"I'm so glad you'll have someone there to help you." Marie leaned back against her chair, relief on her face. "It'll be difficult enough to move by yourself to a new country. But. . .what will I do without you? Who will I talk to while I do the dishes?" Her dark eyes glistened behind her glasses.

"What about me?" Frank asked with a chuckle, nudging her. "I'll talk to you. I'll still be here."

"You're too busy, Frank," she murmured.

Frank's eyes grew wide. He blustered, "Aw, not true." He turned his attention back to Nikki. "How about the salary, Nikki? Can you live in Paris on what they'll pay you?"

"I'll be honest, the salary is pretty low," Nikki admitted. "But when I told Aurélie about it, she said it was possible. Not easy, but possible. She'll show me the tricks to discount living. I want to support myself and not have any help from, um, anyone."

Frank frowned and rubbed his jowls. "No help from your old man? Come on, Nikki. I'm always glad to fill in when you need it."

"I know, Dad, and I'm grateful for what you've done. For help with car repairs, trips, taxes. But I really want to do this on my own now. I *need* to. I have savings, so I can travel a little while I'm there, but for daily living, I'll make do on whatever I earn. There will be a way, and I'll find it."

When Nikki had seen the salary offered, she almost backed out. No way could she survive in Paris on the monthly pay proposed by the French government. But she realized this was her chance to see how other people it did, without help from a wealthy, generous father.

Frank chuckled. "My stubborn Nikki. Okay, have it your way. I'll make a deal with you. What if I take care of your flight and you can take care of the rest? And, of course, if you ever get into any trouble while you're there that you can't handle yourself, you can just call. Deal?"

Nikki nodded, grinning back at him. "Deal." She looked around the table at them and smiled.

The meal ended, and Nikki helped her mother with the dishes. Marie said, "Nikki, I think it's a wonderful opportunity for you. I'm so glad you're doing this."

"Really, Mom? Are you okay with it?"

Her mother nodded. "I'll miss you, and it will be sad for me. A whole year without seeing you. I won't lie, it'll be really hard. But you need this. You've needed it for a long time."

"Thanks, Mom." Nikki felt flooded with emotion. Her mother had always understood Nikki's struggle and conveyed that insight without words. She threw her arms around her mother for a long, tight hug. When she pulled away, their eyes spilled over with tears. A wave of sadness swept over Nikki as she looked at her mother then around at the cozy warmth of the kitchen where they'd spent so much time together. She'd be leaving them both for a year.

A year. Nikki swallowed and pressed her lips together. Her face was wet with tears. She tried to grasp how long a year would feel, living in a foreign country, in a new situation. Even when she'd been in college, she came home to visit at least every other month. She'd always considered herself a homebody, a Daddy's girl.

Now she was going to be her own girl.

CR    CR    CR

Two weeks later, Nikki's bedroom looked like a disaster zone. Large suitcases gaped open, and piles of clothing littered the room on every surface. How to choose what to pack for a full year? She'd decided to mail two cardboard boxes of winter clothes to Aurélie's parents' address. Whatever she needed before then, she'd somehow fit into two suitcases.

"You can't take your whole wardrobe, Nikki. Just take your favorites. Maybe you can do some shopping there." Elaine crossed her arms and surveyed the clutter.

"On my salary, I'll be doing well to eat every day."

"Oh, it won't be that bad." Elaine snickered. "Aurélie told you it was do-able. And you're probably taking more clothes than most people have in their entire closet. You'll be fine."

Nikki lifted an eyebrow of warning and continued folding cotton pants and skirts, stacking them into tight piles in the suitcase. Elaine just laughed, flopping down in the wicker chair next to a mounting pile of coat hangers. "Are you feeling more excited, less nervous?"

"Depends on the minute, I guess. I am both excited and nervous all the time." Nikki leaned back on her heels. "I know some people go overseas without a second thought. But I've barely been out of New York. I'm *sooo* glad Aurélie will be there to help me. I'm not sure if I'd have the courage otherwise."

This once-in-a-lifetime opportunity sometimes appeared to be a year-long feat of endurance. She had to do it, for her own sake. And it was Paris, not Siberia.

"Will you be able to find a church there? It would be good to have some fellowship."

"I have no idea." Nikki shook her head. "I guess I'll have to see once I get there. Aurélie isn't a Christian, so she won't be of help in that department. I'm eager to get to know God in a new way, though, apart from props. Just me and Him. I bought extra journals." Nikki grinned and held up a pastel book. "But I hope to find a church too. I've gotten the impression from Aurélie that there aren't many practicing Christians in France. Maybe God can use me there this year."

"I hope so. Have you told Mike?"

Nikki frowned, a stab of regret cutting her breath. "I didn't want him thinking I was doing this so he'd approve of me. In the beginning, I wanted to go to Paris because I thought getting far away would help me get over him. Then I realized I needed to go for my own growth. *Wanted* to go. The French schools have lots of vacation time, so I'll be able to travel in Europe, which is something I've always wanted to do."

"Like you said, Nikki, it's Paris. I think lots of people would love to be in your shoes."

It was true. Everyone she'd told was ecstatic for her. A whole year in a place many people only dream of visiting. But it was a foreign country. And a city. Two million people inside the city limits, with another ten million in the nearby suburbs. Nikki gulped. From Greenbrier to Paris.

The phone rang. Nikki was glad for the break from the mind-boggling process of packing, but when she saw Mike's name on the screen, her heart flipped over.

"Hey, Nikki. I'm surprised to catch you home on a Saturday afternoon, but thought I'd give you a try."

"Hi, Mike." Nikki felt weak and sank down into the bed pillows as Elaine quietly slipped out of the room.

"With summer on its way, I had an idea." Mike's tone was warm and energetic. "I'd love to spend some time with you this summer. We kind of got off on the wrong foot before, and I thought if I came east this summer, we could hang around together. We could go to the Jersey Shore, down to Manhattan, to the Catskill Mountains, whatever you want. I have a bit of vacation time. What do you think?"

Nikki's throat felt dry. He wanted to see her, to try again. Regret, uncertainty, and joy interlaced inside her in a confused tangle. What was he saying? Whatever it was, it was too late.

"That sounds like a wonderful idea, uh, but I won't be here this summer. I'm moving to Paris for a year. I'll be teaching English there."

The truth spilled out of her mouth and the lengthy silence that followed pounded against her ears. For a moment, she thought the phone had disconnected. Finally, Mike cleared his throat. "Paris? Really? Have you. . .have you been planning this for very long?"

"No. I just heard about it a month ago. It wasn't sure I'd be accepted since it was past the deadline. I didn't tell you before because. . .um, I guess I didn't want you to think I did it for your sake, you know, to have more life experiences." Her voice was just above a whisper. "I mean, I didn't do it for that reason."

She heard a heavy sigh on the line. "Oh, Nikki. I said a lot of stupid things to you on the phone a few months ago. Please forget them. I wasn't trusting God or the natural process very much." His voice sounded unguarded, gentle, and it drew her. For a moment, she considered canceling everything to be with him. In the next instant, she knew she couldn't.

"No, Mike, you were completely right," she said softly as she fiddled with a tassel on the pillow sham. "Everything you said was true, but I couldn't see it yet. Thank you for your honesty. I knew I was sheltered and inexperienced, and too protected by my parents. I didn't realize it at the time, but that's *not* what I want for myself. This year in Paris is the perfect opportunity to break out."

"I'm happy for you. Really, I am. It'll be a great experience. Will you have any time before you go? Maybe I can come for a few days."

How could this be happening now? She felt as though a knife was slicing through her, taking her breath away. "I leave in two weeks. I have to close out my grades and finish packing before then. I don't think I'll have time. I'm sorry."

His voice was quiet. "I know you'll have a lot to do. But let's keep in touch, okay?"

"Yes, absolutely. We can talk before I leave, and of course I'll keep in touch once I get there."

After she hung up, Nikki sat silently on the bed, staring at the window, where the spring breeze gently filled the curtains. Tears slid down her cheeks. Not only because of the week she wouldn't spend with Mike that summer. Was he trying to say something different to her? If he were merely bolstering their friendship, would he have offered to come for an unscheduled visit? Why wouldn't he tell her if his feelings had changed?

Maybe they hadn't.

Elaine appeared in the doorway. "Did you tell him? How did he take it?"

"When I told him, he seemed shocked," Nikki said dully, leaning her head in frustration back against the headboard. She turned her face, cool with tears, toward her friend. "He wanted to come this summer for a visit. Said we'd gotten off on the wrong foot. What do you think *that* means? Does he want to start over? Is he pursuing me, or is he just being friends? Why won't guys say what they mean?"

"I don't know what he meant." Elaine gave her a sympathetic smile. "It's possible that he wants to keep the door open without making promises. And he doesn't know how *you* feel anymore."

Nikki sighed. "I can't tell him how I feel. I did that last Christmas. The ball is in his court and the last time we spoke about it, he was perfectly clear. Before he left New York at Christmas, we promised each other that no matter what, we'd stay friends. I think he's trying to honor that commitment. Maybe it goes no further than that. But his voice sounded different."

Elaine sat down at the foot of the bed. She thrust a spoon into a carton of yogurt. "Maybe the summer trip he suggested was to help him decide how he felt about you."

"If that's the case, then I'm losing that opportunity. Why didn't this happen a month ago?" Nikki couldn't stop her voice from rising as her tears continued to trickle.

Elaine moved closer to Nikki on the bed and laid a hand on her arm. "Nikki, I think you *need* this year in Paris, regardless of what happens with Mike. Just go. Go and don't have regrets. If it's supposed to work out with Mike, it *will*. Remember who's in control?" She tilted her head with a smile.

"I should know that by heart by this time. It's *so* hard to let go." Nikki sighed deeply and swiped at a tear that traced a path down her cheek.

Elaine leaned forward and hugged her. "I know it is," she whispered against Nikki's ear then pulled back. "It's hard to entrust something that means so much to you to a God you can't see. You don't have guarantees, except knowing that He knows what's best." Elaine's curly blond hair had become slightly frizzy in the humidity, giving her an angelic appearance.

Nikki nodded. "I'm really going to miss you, Elaine. You'll always be my best friend." Nikki threw her arms around Elaine again and squeezed her for a long moment. When she pulled away, more tears flowed down her cheeks.

"Don't you get me started." Elaine smiled as her own tears began. They both cried quietly until Elaine grabbed a box of tissues on the floor next to the bed. She threw some toward Nikki and took one herself.

"You really stood by me through all my depression over Mike. I'll never forget that."

"I'm going to come see you, maybe in the fall." Elaine's face was pink and shiny from tears, and her blue eyes glistened.

The doorbell rang, and they both jumped. "Good, a break from the tears and sadness." Nikki sniffed and ran to the front door. She returned to the bedroom, holding an envelope in her hands.

"What is it?"

"My tickets. I'm really going to Paris!"

# Chapter Eleven

Nikki shuffled through a throng of passengers toward passport control at Charles de Gaulle Airport in Paris. After only two hours of sleep on the overnight flight, she was thankful to be alert enough to follow the signs. The previous day, she'd said a tearful goodbye at the airport to her parents and Elaine.

As she moved along in the crowd, her emotional tension from the previous weeks settled into a quiet spirit of observation and a tingle of excitement. The fatigue would surely hit her full force in a few hours. For now, she was crossing the threshold into a new life.

With luggage and customs accomplished, her cart now heaved under two large suitcases and a carry-on backpack full of books. She emerged to the waiting area and scanned for Aurélie. Instead, she saw a sea of faces of every color. Faces with turbans, Muslim veils, African headscarves with matching print dresses, and many western European faces. Finally, Aurélie's familiar smile came into view, along with her hands, which she waved over her head. Her willowy height and dark blond ponytail were easy to spot in the crowd. Nikki wove her way through the crowd with painstaking determination until she reached her friend.

"*Enfin, tu es là.* You're finally here, Nikki." Aurélie reached out to Nikki and pulled her into a tight American hug, followed by a French greeting, a light kiss on each cheek.

"It's so wonderful to see you." Breathless with excitement, Nikki squeezed Aurélie's arm as they advanced toward the parking deck.

"This year will be so perfect. We'll do so many things together. First, I can help you get. . . uh, installed. Is that the word?"

Nikki grinned. "You mean get *settled*?"

Aurélie laughed. "I haven't practiced my English in a long time. You can help me."

"You're so modest, Aurélie. Your English has always been good. I'll need far more help than you will, and I want you to correct me. Eventually, I'll speak to you only in French."

Soon, Aurélie's tiny Renault hurtled down the highway as she navigated the beltway around Paris. Nikki watched the change in landscape, billboards in French, towering apartment buildings on the outskirts of the city, and tiny European cars zipping along the multiple lanes of the autoroute. Gradually they merged into another road. The traffic came nearly to a halt several times.

"Welcome to Paris, including traffic jams." Aurélie adjusted her dark sunglasses. Perched on her smooth complexion, she looked like a movie star. "This road is the beltway around Paris. It's called the *periphérique,* and is almost always crowded. We will drive to the western suburbs where my parents live and have lunch with them. Then we will take your boxes and go to my apartment in Paris. You can rest after that. Tomorrow, we look for an apartment for you."

"Sounds like an excellent program," murmured Nikki. Her eyes grew heavy as she settled into the comfortable seat. Through her leather purse, she felt the outline of her camera, a valuable necessity for the coming year. Her trigger finger was ready to capture anything remotely interesting or beautiful.

"I've already looked up a few apartments online and printed out some that looked promising."

"I made several appointments to see apartments tomorrow afternoon, some from the ones you sent me last week," Aurélie said. "We'll get you a phone and a bank account too, if we have time."

"You're such a huge help. This is the scariest thing I've ever done, but you are making it much easier for me."

Aurélie waved a dismissive hand. "Don't forget, you did the same for me a few years ago. I didn't know anyone in America. You became my first friend. I know what it's like to move to a new country. I want to make it easier for you too."

Thirty minutes and a few traffic jams later, Aurélie veered off the highway. Soon they were driving through an attractive smaller town. Floral baskets swung over brick sidewalks and botanical displays artfully graced each intersection. Above shops sat several layers of apartments, many with geraniums tumbling from balcony boxes.

"This is the town where my parents live," Aurélie told her. "It's called Saint Germain-en-Laye. It's a suburb on the west side."

The downtown opened to a residential area. Stone walls and gates surrounded sprawling homes with meticulous landscaping. Finally, Aurélie pulled into a driveway framed by wrought-iron gates on either side. Nikki had met Aurélie's parents when she was in France for her college exchange program, but had never been to their home. It would be Nikki's first time in *any* French home since she'd always stayed in either a dorm room or a hotel room. Soon she would have her own French home.

As the two of them stepped into the dimly lit front corridor, Nikki recognized the distinguished woman in her late fifties who came toward them. "Nicole!" She pulled Nikki forward for a heartfelt kiss on each cheek and immediately began chattering in French.

"Bonjour, Madame Dominique," Nikki murmured, hoping she'd be able to keep up.

"Call me Brigitte, please." She followed her slow request in English with a broad smile. Like an older version of Aurélie, Brigitte exuded the same classic beauty.

"You have been practicing your English." Nikki enunciated, not sure what the older woman understood.

Brigitte reverted to staccato French in short phrases. "I don't speak much English. You must be tired, Nicole. We will have lunch in a few minutes. You can stay the night if you like. Claude can help you with the boxes later."

Aurélie's father, Claude, appeared several minutes later, his eyes dancing with warmth as he greeted Nikki. His English was better than his wife's and Nikki promised him, as she had Aurélie, that with time they could address her only in French. Aurélie asked, "Would you like to call your family to let them know you arrived safely?"

"Oh, yes, thank you for reminding me." Nikki closed the door to a small office behind her and punched the number at the Big House. Relief washed over her when she heard her mother's voice. It was eight in the morning in New York.

"I'm so glad you called, Nikki," her mother said. "I was just headed to work. How was your flight?" A stab of melancholy peaked, then faded. *It'll be okay. Life is going on.*

"Everything went smoothly. Aurélie met me at the airport, and we just arrived at her parents' house. We're about to have lunch. And my boxes arrived safely."

The sound of her mother's voice brought a wave of comfort. The relief that she heard reassured Nikki that it went both ways.

By the time Aurélie, her parents, and Nikki settled around the long dining room table, Nikki was ravenous. The light breakfast she'd eaten so many hours ago on the plane was gone. Two hours later, after several leisurely spaced courses, Nikki fought drowsiness. She attempted to hold her eyes open.

A well of satisfaction and a sense of accomplishment puddled inside. The enormity of this first step buoyed her spirits, despite her building fatigue. There was life, an exciting one, after Greenbrier, New York. And there was life after Mike Branagan.

ଔ   ଔ   ଔ

Mike dashed across the noisy intersection and joined the river of pedestrians on the opposite sidewalk. It was a sunny Saturday morning, and a temperate breeze stroked the back of his neck. Stacked neatly in the stiff envelope under his arm were ten sketches he'd done over the previous months. A year earlier, he'd begun sketching San Francisco scenes. He had a sizeable collection of drawings flowing out of two manila folders in his desk drawer.

As summer began, he felt his life had stalled and puttered like an old jalopy. Nikki's decision to move to France had slammed a door in his face, just when he thought he was making progress. The case with his parents was frozen, and perhaps forgotten by law enforcement, until the suspect could be located. Every direction he turned, a concrete wall blocked him. May as well try to do something productive.

It had been three months since the day he'd looked at sketches on his bedroom wall and wondered if he might sell some of them. Worth a try. How courageous Nikki had been to move across the world, though she'd always lived a small-town life of comfort and certainty. If she could face her fears and make such a risky decision, he could too.

He had targeted several shops, the kind that sold touristy kitsch of the city, where he showed his sketches. He hoped to sell them on note cards. After two negative replies, three others expressed an interest in buying some.

Four more shops to go. A tiny bell tinkled as he pushed open the door to Frisco City Gifts. "May I speak to the owner or manager of the store?" he asked a college-age employee behind the counter.

Every shelf of the small shop bore gaudy paperweights, miniature cable cars, watercolor prints of the famous Painted Ladies, a colorful row of iconic Victorian homes, and stacks of folded t-shirts in a multitude of colors. Vertical metal racks filled with post cards stood like columns at the entrance of the shop.

"Can I help you?" An overweight man with a large, gray mustache and serious eyes appeared in an office doorway.

"Morning, sir." Mike drew up to his full height. "If you have a few minutes, I'd like to show you some sketches I've done of well-known landmarks in the city. I'm accepting orders from shops for note cards and postcards. Many people like to buy artists' renderings of the city's beauty." Mike had rehearsed his speech several times before leaving that morning.

"Lemme see." The man leaned forward.

Mike opened the folder and the man leafed through the drawings. Lombard Street, the buffalo at Golden Gate Park, the seals at the wharf, the Golden Gate Bridge. The man was silent, except for a few grunts deep in his throat. Mike didn't know if that meant approval or indigestion.

"You do nice work." The man peered down at each drawing. "Of course, I'd rather see them already in postcard format, but this gives me a good idea. A few years back, I had something like this in my shop, but the artist disappeared."

"Thank you. I can sell you a pack of ten cards for ten dollars, and you can resell them for more. We can do a trial delivery and you can see how they sell." Mike would barely cover costs, but it was a start. If it caught on, he could create a website for his sketches and other projects he hoped to do. Maybe an oil painting one day.

"Tell you what. I'll take, say, ten packs of cards. When can they be delivered?"

"It'll take about two weeks for printing. Will that work for you?"

"Sure. Give me your information."

As Mike emerged from the cluttered shop to the balmy summer afternoon, he breathed deeply, feeling lighter. He'd done it. He'd accomplished a small dream that had tickled his mind for several months, only a fragment of what Nikki had done.

"Mike, is that you?" A familiar voice cut through his musings and left a cold trail. Couldn't be. It had been nearly three years. He slowly turned, hoping he'd been mistaken.

Stephanie. Several feet away from him, she stood still, surprise and a broad smile lighting her face. Aside from a new hairstyle and a suntan, she looked the same. Thick blonde hair clasped in an elegant bow, and she wore the same style blazer he remembered, cuffed loosely above the wrist.

"Stephanie, what a surprise." His voice sounded wooden, forced. What could he say to her?

"I hardly ever come down this street, so this must be fate. Do you have time for a cup of coffee?"

Mike hesitated. One voice told him to run as if in a high-speed chase. The other said it had been long enough, nursing the bitterness and hurt. "Okay," he said. "There's a place across the street."

"Are you still working at the same firm?" she asked him as they hurried across the pedestrian crossing amidst a storm of horns and road noise. A sidewalk vendor filled the air with the tang of bratwurst as they sizzled on a tiny grill in his food cart.

"Yeah, no changes there." He wished he had more exciting news to report after three years. His new faith certainly wouldn't interest her, and his involvement with Nikki didn't really exist. "You?"

"Oh, here's a table free." She slipped into a seat at a small round table and adjusted her sunglasses up on top of her head. A brightly colored parasol muted the direct sun that baked the sidewalk. "I started working for a new company about a year ago. And. . ." she held up her left hand where a sizeable diamond glinted in the sun.

"You're engaged. Congratulations. Any date yet?" He kept his voice low, though a dry thud deepened in his stomach. It was as if he were one of Stephanie's girlfriends, instead of the guy she'd cheated on and dumped. Had she forgotten all that?

Her smile faded slightly. "No, it'll be sometime next year." Her voice softened. "Mike, you must think I'm really insensitive. I wasn't thinking when I showed you the ring. Look, I know I hurt you back then. I've always wanted to talk to you about it. That's why I said fate brought us together today, because it's stayed in the back of my mind all this time."

"What did? That you were living with me and in love with him all along?" It just slipped out. He'd meant to play cold, indifferent.

Surprisingly, he saw unshed tears glisten in her eyes. "I guess I deserved that." Her voice broke. "You need to know it wasn't planned. Probably never is. I told you as soon as I knew I was in love with Steve. I loved you too if that makes any sense." She bowed her head for a moment, then lifted her gaze to his. "Oh, Mike. It's just that there was this huge part of your heart you walled off to me. I could never break through. I wanted to, and thought I could, with time. When Steve came along, I saw the difference. It clicked with him, and he didn't have all those barriers." She shrugged and looked away from him. "Maybe it's from your past losses, but I was afraid I'd *never* be able to break through. I just gave up."

Mike stared at her as a claw of discomfort began to scratch at him inside and work its way up. She'd said so many times that she couldn't reach him, and she wanted to. Like an old reel of film, the memories and discussions circled back, flooding his mind. He'd been deaf to her words until that moment.

He was silent so long that she leaned forward, concern knitting her brow. "Are you okay? Say something, Mike."

"I'm. . .sorry, Stephanie." He never thought he'd say those words to Stephanie. He'd considered himself fully invested in the relationship at the time. And when it ended, he'd considered himself fully the victim, cheated on and abandoned. But just then he saw how he'd hidden himself behind galvanized layers of metal, incapable of intimacy. Had anything changed since then?

"No, Mike." She placed her hand on his forearm. "It is *I* who am sorry, really sorry. I wronged you and I hope you'll forgive me."

Mike stared directly into her clear blue eyes and gave her a small smile of resignation. "I forgive you, Stephanie. I don't understand it all, I'll be honest. But I get it, more right now than I did back when the hurt was so raw. I know that at least some of it was my fault. My own barriers. I didn't really see them before." He leaned back in the rattan chair, feeling a gentle wave of lightness course through him. "By the way, I continued attending that church we went to. I guess you could say my faith helped me recover."

"That's great. You know, I continued searching for God, too, but at a different church. I don't go regularly, but it's helped me too."

They exchanged smiles of understanding, of closure. One short conversation that didn't cover nearly enough ground, but in that moment, it was enough.

ભ   ભ   ભ

A warm stream of morning sunlight awakened Nikki. It took her a moment to emerge from sleepy cobwebs and realize that she was on Aurélie's sofa-bed. In France. Scenes from the previous day flashed across her mind. She'd done it. She'd actually moved to France. Though her face was still buried in a feather pillow, she heard Aurélie humming softly in the kitchen. Nikki lifted her head just enough to glance at her watch. Four o'clock? She hadn't changed it since her arrival.

"You're awake. How about some breakfast?" Aurélie smiled down at her and returned to the kitchen, which was in the same room. "I've been up for a while, so I went to the *boulangerie* to buy some baguettes and croissants. I let you sleep until ten, but we have a lot to do today, *mon amie.*"

"Ten? I never sleep that late at home." Nikki pulled herself up, baited by the smell of fresh coffee. "Must be the jet lag." And the lack of sleep the previous night on the flight.

The kitchen table was perched in a small but tastefully decorated nook of the one-room apartment. A bath of full sunlight streamed from the window. Outside, the whoosh of cars and buses driving by and occasionally honking rose to the window, along with the chatter of women and children on the street below. The sounds of the city greeted her.

"These croissants are fabulous. I've never tasted anything like this in New York." Nikki savored the buttery flavor and flaky texture and the nutty aroma of coffee. She peered through the window and observed the crowded street six floors below.

"I hope you slept well. Our first appointment isn't until two this afternoon, so we'll have time to get a phone for you, and maybe a bank account." Aurélie placed a few dried dishes into the cupboard and reached for the carafe of coffee. "For the apartments, I can tell you what you need to look for, and what things you can't do without." She poured dark coffee into Nikki's mug. "I got these American coffee cups for you, since you need more space in your cup than this." Aurélie held up a tiny demitasse for espresso and grinned.

Nikki cradled the mug gratefully and savored the smooth European brew. "I have all my documents." She wiped butter from her chin. "My summer salary from my previous teaching job will prove I have income now. I had the option to spread it over the summer rather than taking it all at once. Then my *miniature* French salary will start in the fall. I have that document too. And of course, my residence permit."

"You'll need these for your apartment and bank account too. You probably cannot qualify for a decent apartment with your salary, so my parents have agreed to co-sign for you."

"Really? That's incredibly generous of them."

Aurélie laughed. "When I told them what you would earn with your teaching job, they were worried you would have to live in a ghetto. They are very fond of you. Some apartments require your salary to be three or even four times the rent."

Nikki's eyes widened. Surely, without Aurélie, she wouldn't be there. She silently prayed her thanks and gratitude and asked for the apartment search to be fruitful. Already she felt God nearby, paving the way for her new life. Maybe He would work in Aurélie's life as well.

Once Nikki had eaten and showered, she felt ready for the day. All the appointments were scattered on the east side of the city, close to the school where she'd teach in September.

She quickly crossed the first two apartments off the list. One was poorly maintained and had little sunlight brightening the dingy corners. The second was noisy in the halls before they even looked inside, and the furnishings were ugly and outdated.

The third apartment had potential. It was in a building from the early nineteen hundreds, with ornate black wrought-iron railings on each tall window. Mature plane trees lined either side of the street. A few blocks away stood the Place de la Bastille, where the French Revolution had begun.

They bypassed a minuscule elevator in favor of the staircase to see the next one on the list. The owner, Madame Lancret, waited for them in the hall, a fistful of keys in her hands.

The one-room apartment was small compared to what Nikki was used to. The kitchen filled a corner of the room, as in Aurélie's apartment, but had a small bar providing extra counter space. One wall had a built-in bookshelf and the other a large armoire. With a few plants and colorful accents, the apartment could be attractive. Best of all, full sunlight streamed through tall double windows, lighting the entire space with a cheerful swath of warmth.

"This lady is a private owner, so you wouldn't have to pay any agency fees," whispered Aurélie before asking the woman a new series of questions about the amenities and the neighborhood. "The heat is included, which makes it a bargain," she added, still in a low voice. "And there's an underground storage cellar, called a *cave*, for each resident. That's a must, for suitcases and things you want to store."

Nikki could easily live in that apartment for one year, even though the whole thing looked smaller than her bedroom at the Big House. It would take over half her monthly salary to pay the rent, but she was determined to get by.

Before leaving the apartment, Nikki completed the paperwork to apply for the apartment and gave all the necessary photocopies. Madame Lancret, a quiet, plain-faced woman in her fifties, promised to call her back within a week. Nikki tried to hide her disappointment. She'd hoped for a more immediate response, even though Aurélie had told her not to count on it.

As they gingerly walked down the winding, carpeted staircase, Nikki said, "We've accomplished a lot today."

"Yes, and it's now time for a French café." Aurélie led Nikki to a café on the same street. A bright green awning overshadowed the front entrance. Tiny round tables, several filled with relaxed customers reading a newspaper or chatting with friends, were scattered three deep in front of the window. Overhead, streaks of sunlight spilled through the tall trees, casting a dappled design on the sidewalk.

A wave of contentment swept over Nikki as she grasped her steaming café au lait, which she learned Parisians called *un crème*. She loved the neighborhood, with its leafy canopies and narrow, quiet roads, and silently prayed she would be approved for the apartment.

"You told me you were looking for a job, Aurélie," Nikki said. "How is that going?"

Aurélie shrugged. "Not much this summer. I have been looking since my last temporary position ended last March. I've had one interview all summer. But it's good that I have time to spend with you now. And I don't have a boyfriend, so I have lots of time."

"Is there anyone you're interested in?"

Aurélie looked bashful for a moment. "Yes, there's someone I like named Sébastien. He's a drummer in a struggling band and has a government job during the day. We are only friends and go out with a group sometimes. What about you? You told me about a relationship that didn't work out."

Nikki frowned. "Mike, a longtime family friend. Gee, I haven't thought about him since I got here. A whole day." They both laughed. She gave Aurélie a sketchy summary of her previous six months. Aurélie listened quietly, her expression sympathetic. "Since last Christmas, we've kept in touch by phone. He isn't ready for anything more, so we're just friends." She kept her voice nonchalant. It got easier as the pain slowly faded.

"I see in your eyes that you still love him," Aurélie said softly. "You did the right thing coming to Paris. We'll have so much fun together that you won't think of Mike. We should go on a trip before I interview again. Have you been to Switzerland and Italy?"

"I haven't been anywhere except France. When should we go?" Nikki was relieved to get past the subject of Mike. She didn't have the strength to talk or think about him anymore.

"You should move in first. After that, we'll decide."

Nikki sent Aurélie a grateful and contented smile, then squinted up at the sun through the trees.

# Chapter Twelve

The speaker was winding down his last point. No, there were still two more. Mike glanced at his watch then around the cavernous multi-purpose room of the church. He regretted coming to the church singles group. This type of event wasn't really his cup of tea, but Jeff thought it might perk him up. Get him *out there*.

Why did church singles groups often have sermons and seminars? Why not parties and socials? No, that would be worse, having to socialize with strangers, making small-talk, and ignoring attempts at flirting.

He had to admit, the speaker *was* interesting, but his mind still flitted around, refusing to light anywhere. His knees still ached from installing flooring all morning in one of the rentals he'd recently acquired. Like a man on a mission, he'd worked out his regrets and new revelations. His doubts about Nikki were evaporating by degrees, like clouds clearing from a gust of wind. Last December, he'd had legitimate reasons not to pursue her, despite his attraction. The reasons he'd explained to Jeff. It seemed so long ago.

Following his encounter with Stephanie, he understood another element, the subconscious wall he'd maintained for years. Fleeing Adams Bridge and anything associated had been a handy strategy. Or so he thought.

Though it was too late to undo Nikki's decision to cross the ocean, he could at least complete something beautiful and functional right where he was. Hardwood flooring had many purposes.

She'd been in Paris for over a week. He hadn't heard from her yet. She likely had a lot to do, getting settled in a new country, a new apartment, a new job. He liked picturing her there, walking along the Seine, sitting at a French café, far from her family, on her own.

What was she thinking? Did she still have even a small hope for them as a couple? He hadn't given her specific encouragement other than the summer trip he'd suggested—too late.

Mike sighed. Any way he looked at the relationship, he'd botched it. With a taste of bitterness, he had to admit that he'd allowed Frank to influence him. What he'd said about Nikki's naiveté had lodged a doubt, which had festered. Hopefully he'd have another stab at the whole thing at Christmas, when Nikki came back for her winter break. He wasn't ready to go east this soon, but he'd make an exception for her.

Finally, the speaker said a closing prayer. Mike stood and quickly headed for the door, but was blocked by two women, grinning like a toothpaste ad. They were attractive, though he noticed in the same way he'd notice a flashy car or a nice building.

"Hello, you must be new. We haven't seen you here before. My name is Bethany," said the tall blond.

"I'm Susanne. What's your name?" The other woman had Nikki's Italian coloring.

"Mike." He stuck out his hand to shake each of theirs. "Nice to meet you. I'm sorry, I can't stay. I have an . . . appointment." An appointment with his computer, with his tropical fish. The women looked disappointed but promised to chat with him the next time.

As Mike approached his car, his cell phone rang. Ely. "Hey, Ely. What's up?"

"Mike, the CPA that was wanted for questioning has been caught. They found him in Florida and have extradited him back to New York."

"That's great. Now maybe we can get somewhere."

"Just wanted to let you know. We should probably give the police department a couple weeks to focus on the original case. He's wanted for embezzlement. Then while they have him, maybe they can see about the charges involving your parents."

"Thanks, Ely. I guess we still have to sit tight, but at least something's moving forward." Mike leaned back in the car seat and relaxed his shoulders.

"How are you doing with all this, Mike?"

Mike warmed to the concern in Ely's voice. "It's a little raw, still, to be honest. I'm surprised by your news. I never thought this would go anywhere."

"Don't get your hopes too high. It still might not. It's been a long time, and there was never even a criminal investigation to start with. That's the biggest obstacle, in my view."

"Yeah, I know. I want justice for my parents, but in some ways, I wish it would all go away."

"I understand." Ely's tone was quiet. "But we've started this thing, and we should see it through."

"Yes, I will."

After hanging up Mike sat still in the car for a moment and stared through the darkened windshield. Would this investigation occupy his attention the rest of the summer, then lead to nothing? It was a chance he'd have to take. For now, he could only wait.

He got home and noticed an email from Nikki on his phone. His spirits lifted. He got himself a snack and settled in his room to read her message on his laptop.

*Hi, Mike! I guess you know I made it here safely. Aurélie has been taking me all over town looking at apartments and helping me get set up. Don't know what I'd do without her. It's exciting being in Paris. The apartment-hunt took longer than I expected. We must have seen a dozen. I finally moved in the day before yesterday. Here are some photos of my new apartment and one of Aurélie and her family. I hope you're having a good summer. I have an internet connection now, so I'll be easier to reach, that is, when I'm not traveling, which I plan to do soon. Keep you posted! Love, Nikki.*

Mike smiled at the energy and warmth that flowed through her words, and braced against the ache of knowing he wouldn't see her for a long time. He thought he'd been pretty smart trying to deepen the friendship without committing to anything more. Too late, he realized he'd given her no reason to stay. If only he'd told her sooner of his growing feelings, she might not have gone to Paris. But he wouldn't have wanted her to miss out on it either.

He scanned through the photos she'd sent. She stood next to an older, distinguished-looking couple and a tall, cute blond, who he guessed was Aurélie. He'd hardly ever seen Nikki in summer clothes since his visits were always in the dead of winter. She was dressed in an above knee-length white skirt, white sandals, and colorful sleeveless top. He noted she had pretty legs.

In the next photo, he saw the front of a regal, centuries-old-looking building with curlicues of black ironwork halfway up every window. Her final photo was the inside of her apartment. He had to agree with her. It was tiny, like an oversized dorm room.

He was glad for her, despite the events that had taken her there. The year would probably go slowly for him, but she'd be full of memories and stories by the time he saw her again. They'd have a lot to talk about. His current strategy was to call regularly and deepen their friendship until it became crystal clear for both of them. Was it meant to be, or not?

In the meantime, he lived through the daily tug of war between his wayward heart and his commitment to protecting it.

Mike jotted an email back to her, thanking her for the photos, hoping to sound warm and friendly. "Do you have a local phone number yet? Or can I call on your US phone?" he wrote. "I'd love to talk to you. It's been too long."

Should he come right out and tell her his feelings were changing? Growing? What was the point since they couldn't see each other for six more months?

Then again, what if she met a Pierre or François in the meantime? Was Mike taking a chance on losing her? Was she even his to lose?

℘   ℘   ℘

Colorful bell-shaped lanterns suspended from the café awning bobbed gently in the evening breeze. A low mumble of conversation and laughter tumbled out from the terrace to the street. Nikki stood near the entrance of the restaurant and scanned the clusters of people who walked by, looking for Aurélie's face.

After just two days in Paris Nikki had been able to master the métro—the Paris subway system—and use her purse-sized map book of Paris neighborhoods. Piece of cake. She knew it wasn't a huge accomplishment, since the métro was easy to use and she'd been to Paris twice before. A greater test faced her that evening in a social setting with seven young adults, all speaking French at lightning speed over dinner.

Although she'd spoken beginner and intermediate French with her students for the last two years, it required a strenuous mental effort to do it all day and as her only way to communicate. *And* at a native, adult level. Each night she fell into the sofa bed of her new apartment, exhausted. Her senses and brain were overloaded at every moment. Each day brimmed with incidents ranging from simple embarrassments to irritations over simple things that were different from back home. Stores and banks closed at lunchtime and all-day Monday, church bells bonged at odd hours in the morning, and she still hadn't found cheddar cheese among the more than three hundred varieties that France boasted. But at this early stage, culture stress was an interesting and tolerable novelty.

After a ten-day wait, Nikki received her approval as a renter, and spent the next two days scraping together enough money for the security deposit. Next, she set about giving it a more personal touch. At the local discount store, she bought a tablecloth, a coffee table runner, and curtains in beige and plum. Once a few houseplants and several inexpensive framed prints were in place, it began to look like a home. The kitchen was already stocked with a few dishes and two frying pans, and Aurélie's mother was happy to loan Nikki some of her unused kitchen utensils. Within a week, Nikki was already attached to her tiny nest in the midst of the city.

Each morning she flung open the windows to greet the Parisian sunshine, which cast a bright puddle onto the wood flooring of her small room. Her street contained six-story apartment buildings in various styles and from different periods, some dark pink brick with gray trim, others plain concrete but with elaborate grillwork or plain white shutters. Many buildings were like hers, with curved concrete cantilevers under their balconies or sculpted cherub heads or coats of armor over each window. At the top of every building, a slate mansard roof descended a full story, with small inset windows peeking out. Shops and small offices occupied the street level, as well as a bakery, a florist, a photocopy shop, a small grocery store, and several small cafés.

Nikki quickly became accustomed to her new street, Rue St. Sébastien. She and Aurélie had accomplished a lot in two weeks. That evening, maybe she would make some new friends. Nikki looked up and saw Aurélie hurrying down the sidewalk, her blond hair swinging like golden ribbons. She stopped and greeted a young woman with a kiss on each cheek, then noticed Nikki and waved her over.

"Nikki, this is Sophie," she said in French. Sophie leaned forward and kissed Nikki on each cheek, though they'd only just met. The three women entered the restaurant and settled around a long row of small tables. One by one, Aurélie's friends—Sébastien, Jean-Christophe, Olivier, Céline, and Franck—arrived. Each one greeted Nikki the same way, kissing her on both cheeks, as if they'd known her for a long time. With each introduction Aurélie explained, "This is my friend from America. She's here for a year to teach English."

Several of Aurélie's friends attempted speaking English with Nikki during the course of the evening, some fluent, others broken, and most apologetic. "I haven't spoken English since high school," was the frequent lament. Several times Nikki told them, "I speak some French," wanting to practice, and especially wanting to fit in. As the evening wore on, most of them reverted to French, so she had all the practice that she wanted, however mind-numbing.

Seated beside her was Jean-Christophe, shoulder-length blond hair chopped straight and pulled back in a ponytail. He was coolly handsome, in an artistic way, his blue gaze intense as he said, "Nicole, you are brave to come for a year to France."

"Brave? Why? Are the French mean to visitors?" she teased. She had no desire to be timid, here on the cusp of a new life.

Jean-Christophe let out a hearty laugh. "No, Chérie, you are brave because it is not an easy thing to do, to live in a foreign country far away from your home." He pulled his chair a bit closer to her. "We actually like Americans, but are sometimes shy."

She looked surprised. "You don't seem very shy to me." She was enjoying the light-hearted, flirtatious banter. "In fact, many Americans think French people don't like them."

Jean-Christophe's eyebrows shot up. "Really? That's silly. We love America. Look at all the movies and music, fashion, everything. We like the people too. Not always the politics, but that's another subject. Me, I like to see people as individuals. Not everyone does that." He shrugged, and Nikki noticed that his shrug went all the way to his face in an expression of practiced nonchalance.

The waiter appeared, a long white apron nearly covering his black pants and down to his shoes. With a solemn, dutiful countenance, he took each person's order, then nodded and disappeared. Nikki felt daring on several levels, beginning with her order—baked quail with an appetizer of garlic and parsley snails. Just wait till she told Mike about this. She caught herself. She needed to stop making constant mental references to Mike. She still thought of him as a close friend, so it would be a hard habit to break.

Nikki asked the waiter to take a picture of her new friends as they all squeezed together around the table. Mostly a souvenir for her, but she'd probably send Mike a copy.

The conversation strolled easily from movies to politics to the difficulty finding a job. By the end of the evening Nikki not only had excellent practice for her French, but had indeed made new friends. She'd connected especially well with Céline, Sophie, and Jean-Christophe, who had been very attentive all evening. They all exchanged phone numbers before leaving the restaurant.

She still smiled from the memory of her pleasant evening as she unlocked the four deadbolts on the door of her third-floor apartment. Light flooded into the tiny space, her little *chez moi*. She turned on her laptop computer, which occupied a side table next to the foldout couch. She'd send the photos and a brief greeting to her parents first.

Nikki saw Mike's name pop up and she sighed gratefully. He had written a few lines in response to the photos she'd sent a few days earlier and filled in some details about his summer so far. He finished with the lines, "I *really* miss you." She smiled, and a flicker of warmth stirred inside. His words seemed clear, though she was unsure of what lay behind them. He was a mystery. A delicious, dangerous, haunting. . . and aggravating mystery.

He'd asked again if he could call her. How would she ever get over him if they kept talking? But they were friends, weren't they? Nikki jotted a note to him, attaching the photo of her social evening. In the photo, Jean-Christophe was leaning close to her, his shoulder pressed against hers. Let Mike think whatever he will. She told him she had only a French cell phone and it might be expensive for him to call from the States unless he had an international plan. But she didn't include her French number. That wouldn't likely fend him off for long.

Against her better judgment, Nikki scrolled over to where her photos were stored. Slowly, she looked at each photo from last Christmas as a hollow ache formed inside her. Mike's dark, penetrating eyes looked out at her, a mischievous sparkle, long dimples, straight teeth, sensuous lips. She memorized his face, even the shaggy length of his hair below his ears. The *vacation look*, he'd said with a chuckle. She reached up and touched the screen, wishing it were his real face in front of her, and briefly closed her eyes, remembering.

Her spirits sagged, after the earlier buoyancy of her evening. As soon as she realized, she snapped her computer shut. "No, that's not going to happen," she muttered. As long as she straddled her old and new lives, she'd never appreciate the present. She'd never grow, never become herself. Guarding her heart was essential. How to do that was another matter entirely. If coming to Paris wasn't enough, what was?

# Chapter Thirteen

"Bonjour, Madame Noiret. Vous allez bien?" Nikki called a cheery greeting to the *gardienne,* who sorted the mail, cleaned the hallways, and kept the humble building looking respectable and smelling like citrus soap. Always in a blue and white smock, the stern-faced woman in her fifties mopped and dusted, while her frisky Yorkshire terrier, Max, frolicked around her feet, letting out an occasional bark.

Nikki made efforts to converse with her at a basic level, to greet her and pet Max each time she came into the building. Eventually, Madame Noiret unwound enough to smile and correct Nikki's grammar mistakes.

"Bonjour, Mademoiselle." Madame Noiret was mopping the entryway near the mailboxes while Max scampered back and forth, chasing her mop, and growling at it. She muttered to him in a grumpy voice, but then bent down to scratch his head.

"You love Max, even if he bothers your work," Nikki said, smiling.

Madame Noiret gently nudged Max out of her way with the mop. "He makes tracks after I mop, but I'm glad he's here, since my husband died." It was the longest phrase Nikki had ever heard her speak.

"When was that, Madame Noiret?"

"About five years ago." She leaned against her mop and wiped perspiration from her forehead. "I've only had Max for three, but my friends told me I needed a dog. I finally gave in and don't regret it."

"Your friends were right. Look at how much joy he brings you."

"Your French is getting much better, Mademoiselle."

A wave of pleasure coursed through her. It was the first time someone had recognized her progress, and she'd been working at it so hard. "Merci, Madame. *Je travaille beaucoup.*"

The woman smiled and continued mopping. *"Bonne journée."*

Nikki slipped out the heavy wrought-iron clad door to the warm sidewalk on Rue St. Sébastien. She passed the florist and gazed longingly at the bursts of color—red carnations, orange-yellow zinnias, creamy pink peonies—and sniffed their delicate fragrance. Flower shops adorned many corners in Paris, their displays splashing color onto the bland sidewalk. A pastel bouquet would brighten up her apartment. Maybe on the way home.

Three weeks in Paris felt like three months, so different from Greenbrier, New York, was Nikki's life and routine. Each day she calmly talked herself through each moment. She simply had to conquer her fears. Getting to France was only the first step. Now she had to live, to integrate, to thrive.

Her days brimmed with simple urban tasks, done in an old-world way. She selected fruits and vegetables at the open market, dropped bottles into the large recycling bin on the street corner, and bought baguettes and croissants from the *boulangerie* on the ground floor of her building. Everything she did was deliberate, hesitant. But day by day the terror diminished in droplets, as she forced herself into each new experience. Gradually she mustered the courage to ask questions of bystanders and chat with storekeepers to practice her French. She often had to request they speak slowly. She was frequently surprised by the warmth and friendliness of their responses. Before long she felt like a local, especially when they greeted her with a smile of recognition.

Initially, she sounded like a five-year-old child, since that was the extent of her vocabulary. Later, when she'd been able to learn and reinforce her French, she hoped she'd be able to project her personality and sense of humor. In other words, be herself.

*Just be brave, Nikki. Keep on task, God is with you,* was her daily mantra. With time, her fear melted and city life, like an unaccustomed meal, began to grow on her.

Her apartment sat a few blocks north of the Bastille area, with its wide, crowded roundabout surrounding the monument. The Bastille neighborhood bubbled with energy all day and evening with tourists and young people frequenting its many clubs and restaurants, or the imposing mirrored Opéra de Bastille. Often there were concerts and outdoor art, or craft exhibits in the square. Fortunately, the noise didn't reach her tiny street, tucked in a maze of small connecting roads and tree-flocked avenues.

Bargain-hunting became routine for the first time in Nikki's life. She visited the local discount store and open market regularly. The canvas bag on wheels, standard equipment for most Parisians, enabled her to grocery shop without having to lug too much at one time or make multiple trips per week.

That day Aurélie was tied up in job interviews, so Nikki planned to explore by herself, to stroll through the open market and absorb the energy there, then scour the side streets, crossroads, and alleys of her neighborhood.

The *Marché* covered several city blocks, with makeshift stalls of canvas on poles that had been erected the previous evening by city employees. Spread out before her was a visual tapestry of colorful fruits and vegetables, fish, bread, clothing, shoes, and even rugs and jewelry. She took several pictures of the crowded scene, then one of rainbow-colored spices displayed in small burlap sacks. The exotic aromas blended with those of cheese, fresh baked breads, and falafel from the Lebanese cuisine booth. Sounds of shoppers murmuring and merchants shouting special prices filled the air.

A bit further, she browsed the jewelry table, but with an objective in mind. Two days earlier as she dressed, Nikki reached, out of habit, for her silver necklace from her grandmother Helen. She stopped herself. She stared down at it and frowned. She'd never particularly liked it, but had worn it to please her father. *A shrine to*

*Grandmother Helen, who I've never met.* From that day, she decided to wear a necklace that *she* chose and liked.

That day she scanned the silver necklaces, some ornate with pearls, semi-precious stones, or braided chains. She saw a simple chain with a silver geometric pendant. After looking at it on herself with a hand-held mirror proffered by the smiling woman behind the table, she decided to buy it.

Her next target of discovery was the Lycée Jeanne d'Arc, the high school where she would spend the better part of her days. She walked uphill on an uneven sidewalk for twenty-five minutes as cars clogged the nearby street. She glanced frequently at her map and wiped perspiration from her forehead. Once school started, of course, she'd take the métro.

Finally, Nikki stood in front of the four-story high school building that would be her second home for the next year. It was more modern than some of the other schools she'd seen in France, which was only to say it might have been built in the sixties, instead of the previous century. It was early July, and the schoolyard was quiet, with no clusters of chatting teenagers crowding the front doors or courtyard.

As she observed the solemn emptiness of the school and street, she wondered if it had been a good idea to come to France nearly three months before her job began. How would she fill her time? The immediate future was taken care of. The following week she'd leave with Aurélie for ten days in Italy and Switzerland.

Nikki kept her camera handy, always in her purse or around her neck. Her journal too, which she rarely left at home. As she wandered along Rue Beaumarchais, she stopped at a wooden bench and jotted her thoughts in her journal, then continued walking, drinking in all she saw, murmuring prayers along the way.

She hadn't yet found a church, but knew God was with her even when she had no contact with other believers. "It's just You and me, Lord," she whispered with a secret smile, aware of his presence more than before.

A grumbling in her stomach signaled the morning's end. Time had slipped away as she soaked in the images of narrow, picturesque streets, appearing as if from another century, pastel blossoms cascading from window boxes, and ornate carvings over each door and window.

She spotted a sidewalk crêpe vendor. France's answer to fast food. Smiling at her observation, she approached the stand. A man with a large mustache swirled a thin layer of crêpe batter onto a hot griddle. With a long spatula he flipped the paper-thin disc to the other side and placed the fillings on top. With a flourish, he handed her the crêpe in a paper wrapper, like an ice cream cone.

Continuing her stroll, crêpe in hand, Nikki passed several restaurants where noisy customers spilled out at sidewalk tables, their cutlery clinking against the plates, enticing smells floating in the air. She glanced at more storefront windows, until the words 'Église Evangélique' caught her attention.

A church. Nikki stopped and peered into a window encased in metal security bars. In the small, darkened room she could barely distinguish some chairs and bookshelves, though not much more.

If it *were* a church, it likely wouldn't hold more than twenty-five people. Nikki backed up from the plate glass window and read the information painted there. Ten-thirty service on Sunday. Bible study and prayer on Thursday evening. She took a photo of the information so she could pay a visit after her trip with Aurélie.

When she'd lived in New York, Nikki was rarely all by herself. She and Elaine spent their evenings together, sometimes doing different activities, but still at home at the same time. Other times she was with friends or dropped by the Big House. Now she was truly alone, and in a foreign country, no less. At times she felt like she'd been plucked out of her normal life and at any moment would wake up in Greenbrier.

Her phone rang. The number of the Big House appeared on the screen, as if summoned by her earlier thoughts of home.

"Nikki, I'm glad I got you." Her mother's voice filled the phone.

"Hi, Mom. Is everything okay?" Tension prickled inside, since her mother didn't usually call her cell during the day.

"Sure, honey. I. . .I just missed you, is all. I felt so lonely here at the house and thinking of you all the way over there made me sad. I'm happy you're there and having a good time, though. I just wanted to hear your voice."

Nikki and her mom talked for a few minutes. When she hung up a wave of sadness for her mother nudged her. There was something forlorn in her voice, though she hadn't admitted anything was wrong. She prayed for her mother then spotted a métro station.

Seated on the métro, Nikki scribbled in her journal thoughts that had been pinging on her mind all afternoon. After only three weeks, she knew something she couldn't doubt. She'd never go back to the same lifestyle as before. Never be satisfied with those limits again. Her perspective had already expanded like a balloon, so it encompassed the whole world.

Her gaze wandered around the train compartment at the other passengers—French, African, Chinese, Indian, North African, and tourists from a half-dozen countries.

Several minutes later, Nikki changed from the métro to the urban train so she could cross the city to the western side. She had at least a few minutes before her stop and began to write again in her journal. Her thoughts wandered to her father, and with a pang, she realized she hadn't missed him as much as she expected, even though at first, he'd called often. Maybe it was because her days brimmed with new experiences. She was surprised how emancipated she felt. Was she betraying her parents by not missing them more? She felt a twinge of guilt as she remembered her mother's phone call. And yet, it was past time to be on her own.

Maybe when she returned home in a year, she'd enjoy her parents like an adult who understood who she was. An adult who made her own decisions, rather than deferring, following, and anticipating like a child. She sat up, startled. "Just like Mike said," she murmured aloud. He'd been right.

Mike. A smile curled her lips. At least he was making an effort to stay in touch, whatever his reasons. Maybe he noticed her struggling to break free and it knocked down a few of his reservations about her. That would be excellent, though it wasn't the main purpose of her French adventure.

After a long, reflective sigh, Nikki looked up again through the train window. Instead of the blackness of the underground tunnel, she saw wide sunlit spaces filled with graffiti-covered buildings. These were gradually replaced by homes and more shops, similar to the town where Aurélie's parents lived.

She wasn't in Paris anymore and had no idea where she was.

A wave of panic rose quickly inside her as she struggled to recognize something, anything, in her surroundings. Finally, the train screeched to a stop and several people got out. She strained to read the sign. Epinay-sur-Seine. *Where in the world am I? Besides alone in a foreign country lost in a strange city?* If she'd missed her stop, staying on the train wouldn't help matters.

Nikki grabbed her purse and notebook and scrambled off the train. Her eyes darted around the platform, and she spied a woman just about to pass her ticket and slip through the turnstile.

"Madame! S'il vous plait—" Nikki's voice faded, and her uplifted hand dropped as the woman disappeared from view. The other passengers scurried off in every direction and she was left alone on the platform. How easy it was to turn to someone and ask for help before trying to find her own solution. Nothing wrong with asking for help, but for her, it was a default response. This time she'd find her own solution. Now, she had no choice.

When she turned, she faced a tall sign with a map of the train and métro routes. Forcing herself to relax, she stepped forward to study the map. The train had four different branches and she'd taken the wrong one. *Just go back the way you came.* If she crossed to the other side she could simply go in the other direction, couldn't she?

She spotted the exit sign and followed the underground tunnel to the other side of the platform. She made sure the sign read *Paris* and stayed on the platform until the next train arrived.

When her alarm had subsided and she was again headed in the right direction, she embraced a wave of relief, and a bit of pride in herself. She'd navigated her first small difficulty alone. All alone. Once she saw the familiarity of Rue St. Sébastien, she breathed a sigh. Home.

The florist shop was still open. Nikki chose a bouquet of fist-sized dahlias in dusty rose, and bought a colorful ceramic vase to put them in. She arranged her flowers in the vase and placed them on her tiny coffee table.

The following week she took her first electric bill to a local branch of the electric company and stood in line behind two customers. Once at the window she slowly explained, "Can you please help me? I am a foreigner, and this is my first—" she held up the statement, groping through her limited vocabulary.

"Your *facture*. Your bill." The clerk's bored-looking gaze rose over Nikki's head as she muttered her response.

"Yes, my *facture*," Nikki repeated. "Thank you. Do I have to pay this part or the whole thing?" She pointed to the paper. Nikki glanced behind her and saw a long line of customers.

"This is your deposit, since it is a new account, and this is what you have consumed so far. So, you pay the whole thing."

"I just have one last question." Nikki hesitated. She felt like a moron. "Can you show me how to fill out the check?"

The woman stared at Nikki with large, glassy eyes. Nikki's neck began to feel hot, as eight strangers stared back at her. Why hadn't she asked Aurélie how to fill out a French check? Her other apartment bills were drafted from her account automatically, but this one included her deposit.

"The amount goes here on this line," the woman said.

Nikki wrote the check as quickly as she could, murmured a sheepish *merci* to the clerk, then crept out of the office, avoiding the gaze of the waiting customers.

The following day on the way to the *Marché*, she was reading a text message that Aurélie had sent, when she heard a scuffling noise behind her. Suddenly she was surrounded by three tall teenage boys. One of them grabbed the phone from her hands and they all ran away, as Nikki yelled, "Stop, come back!" Seconds later she realized she'd cried out in English.

Helplessly, she watched as they disappeared around the corner. If she'd been able to outrun them, what could she have done to get her phone back?

Nikki collapsed on a nearby bench and moaned, "My phone— my numbers—" as she fought tears stinging her eyes.

When she woke up the next day, she stayed in her pajamas, not ready to venture outside for anything. The events of the last few days would look minor in a week or two. Was it culture shock, or just a buildup of frustrations? Felt the same to her. She'd replace her phone soon, but for that day she'd treat herself to lounging and brooding.

For the first time since her arrival in Paris, she missed Adams Bridge.

# Chapter Fourteen

Mike pulled his head and shoulders out of the darkened cabinet. "Got it, I think." He unfurled his cramped body, straightened up, and shot a grin at Harriet.

She stood in her usual garb, a colorful block-print housedress. Clasping both hands in front of her, she grinned with uneven teeth. The wrinkles in her face deepened, a halo of woolly gray hair puffed around her head. "That's my boy, I knew you could do it."

"On the second try. Guess I'm not gifted as a handyman." Mike ran a hand through his moist hair. Must look like a drowned rat.

"You're soaked, Mike." She handed him a clean tea towel then pulled out a chair for him. "Sit down and I'll make you some tea. And some of my cinnamon muffins I made this morning. I put pecans in them. I remember you like pecans."

Mike didn't argue. He needed Harriet's loving smile and grandmotherly insistence. Moisture had seeped through his t-shirt and the waistband of his pants before he got the leak under control. Sure, he could have called a plumber and paid through the nose. He had a budget for repairs and general maintenance of his rentals, but when he had time, he preferred to do it himself. It gave him more contact with the tenants, and cinnamon muffins weren't the only advantage. At Thanksgiving, he'd taken a full dinner to each of his four tenant families. It was the most fun he'd had in years, seeing their eyes grow round and smiles stretch end to end. One of the families had insisted he join them for the holiday. Another borrowed family, but that holiday would stay warmly inlaid in his memory.

He sat across from Harriet at the kitchen table and sipped hot tea from faded ceramic mugs. Of all his tenants, Mike was closest to Harriet and her husband, Joe. A hard life and seventy-three years had given Harriet a deep-rooted wisdom, which she dispensed sparingly and gently when she saw the need.

"Mike, you must have a girlfriend, a nice boy like you." Her raspy voice scratched out, but the sound was a comfort to him.

"Hmm, how much time have you got?" He lifted his eyebrows, glad she'd asked, since he wouldn't have brought it up himself. He started talking, painting the broad lines of his involvement with the Mancini family over the years and his reunion with Nikki at Christmas. He declined to mention his terror of giving his heart, a fact that had wound in dizzying circles in his mind ever since his conversation with Stephanie.

The low ticking of the wall clock pierced the long silence while, Mike guessed, Harriet pondered a wise response. Cheerful yellow curtains billowed by the window over the sink.

Harriet set down her half-empty cup. She cocked her head to one side. "I wonder if all those years you were looking for some kind of father figure in Frank."

Mike's head jerked back. "Frank? A father? We can hardly be in the same room together."

"You said that rather quickly. Maybe that's why his response disappointed you. Might be good one day to talk with him about your feelings of rejection."

"I don't have anything to say to Frank, except to ask why he never gave me a chance." A thread of sullenness had crept in before Mike could check himself. "I won't beg for his acceptance." It was Frank's place to make a gesture, after all these years.

But Mike was the Christian. He shifted his weight in the chair and averted his eyes from Harriet's penetrating view.

She shrugged and said, "At least think about why his acceptance is so important to you. Otherwise, it may always cloud your relationship with Nikki."

129

Mike frowned. "Nikki's a homebody, and still lives in Frank's shadow." He paused and met Harriet's gaze. "No, that's not true anymore. She did a courageous thing and moved overseas."

That said volumes for Nikki. Her *courage* to overcome what she knew was a need in her own life. His throat tightened as he pictured her, terrified, getting on the plane. Going far from her family, committing to being a foreigner for a full year, just to grow and mature. Harriet observed him with keen interest, likely wondering why he'd almost wept out of sudden respect and admiration for Nikki.

He cleared his throat. "I like Nikki a lot. But sometimes I'm afraid I'll get sucked back into that world, that sad place full of memories, and the dependent, needy position I was in before. Alone with no family."

"I understand." Harriet patted his arm. "But there's nothing wrong with being needy if that's where life has placed you at the time. There's no shame in having tragedy in your life and suffering loss, and there's certainly no shame in receiving help and comfort from others. There's a good side to independence, Michael, being responsible for yourself and your choices. But there's a bad side too, which comes from pride. Could be both." She reached for the teapot. "More?"

Mike shook his head. Hot needles of shame tingled against his stomach. Was it all a matter of his pride and a quest to no longer be dependent on anyone, his headstrong flight from the Mancinis and his determination to go it alone? Was this also at the root of the barriers he'd constructed to keep Stephanie from knowing his heart and penetrating his soul? Harriet was right, there was a good side *and* a bad side to independence. He suspected he was carrying both. And one weighed him down like a sack of old regrets.

"I suggest you accept Frank as he is." Harriet sipped her tea. "But don't base any decisions about Nikki on *his* attitude. You wouldn't want to lose her over all this, now, would you?" After a silent pause she added, "And you don't want to lose her family, either. They were there when you needed them. In fact, you still need them. Just accept it. They love you, and you're lucky to have them." She grinned. "They wouldn't have put up with you this long if they didn't consider you one of theirs."

One of theirs. A small flame licked his insides with warmth. Harriet's intense gaze was followed by a burst of gravelly laughter that filled the kitchen as she reached over and squeezed his wrist. "Have another muffin."

∝    ∝    ∝

The indistinct call of train departures through the intercom blended with the sounds of many languages floating through the Luzern train station. Smells of soot and cigar smoke, along with the tang of fried pastry and sausage hung in the air.

Nikki leaned against her backpack, and though her rear was sore and cold against the concrete floor, she barely noticed as she wrote in her journal. Striving to capture all she'd seen in the last ten days, her hand was unable to keep pace with her thoughts. The pristine Swiss Alps, covered with snow or goats, centuries-old walls surrounding the town of Luzern, the colorful Renaissance bustle of Florence, and the enchanting water world of Venice. . .

Aurélie napped against her backpack, her lips slightly parted. Nikki sighed in contented fatigue as she and Aurélie waited for their train from Luzern to Zurich. Tomorrow the Zurich train would carry them back to Paris. Before leaving, they had decided several days in fewer cities was preferable to rushing across both countries and seeing little besides the inside of trains. They'd still covered a lot of ground. But Nikki felt ready to be back in her apartment in Paris.

Aurélie's eyes fluttered open. She yawned. "What are you always writing, Nikki?" She groaned and stretched her arms up. "Are you writing a book that will embarrass both of us?"

"No. Only you." Nikki grinned at her. Over the previous days, they'd shared secrets, minor disagreements, and hopes for the future. Nikki felt closer to her friend than when she'd first arrived. "I'm writing memories from our trip. I write short prayers too." Nikki snapped her journal shut.

"You write prayers? Like the Our Father?"

"No, more like a conversation, whatever comes to my mind. Remember when I told you that God is like a friend for me, and I talk to Him at different times during the day? Sometimes I write to Him too. It helps me when I read back over what I wrote."

"I like that idea. I'm glad for you."

Nikki had spoken several times to Aurélie about her faith, and usually Aurélie had politely listened, seeming unsure of its relevance in her daily life. "Everyone can have that friendship, you know." Nikki kept her voice soft, not wanting to appear pushy, yet deeply wanting Aurélie to understand. "It's not just for religious people, but for anyone."

Aurélie appeared to reflect on that a moment. "French people don't talk about that very much. I like the way you describe it, though. Makes me want to think about it more."

Nikki smiled at her, tamping down a rush of hope. "We can talk about it anytime you want."

"Tomorrow, we go back to Paris. It's sad."

Nikki knew she had to leave the subject alone, and let God work in Aurélie's heart. "But you'll see Sébastien again."

"Oh, yes." Aurélie grinned and leaned against her backpack again. "There's something I didn't tell you." Nikki perked to attention. Aurélie's clear blue gaze was shuttered with sudden shyness. "Sébastien and I are together now. We're a couple."

"You were just friends the last time we spoke." The evening she'd first met Aurélie's group of friends, Sébastien had spoken the least.

"Well, things change, sometimes quickly." Aurélie giggled. "I told him that you and I were leaving on vacation for ten days and he said he'd miss me and that I was becoming more than a friend."

*More than a friend.* A sudden stab of barrenness took Nikki by surprise. Envy? Or sadness and loss. From a friend to something more . . . *It would have been nice.* Yet she was happy for Aurélie.

Aurélie lifted an uncertain gaze at Nikki. "I wanted to tell you sooner, but I didn't want to cause pain, you know, because of Mike."

Nikki reached out and grasped Aurélie's hand. "Oh, Aurélie. You're sweet. Don't worry about me. I'm truly happy for you. You've liked him for a while, and my turn will come someday, with someone."

They fell into a comfortable silence. Nikki looked back down at her journal. A wave of comfort flowed gently across her like a breeze. She'd believed her words, that God would bring her together with someone one day. It wouldn't be Mike, but someone else, the right person at the right time. She suddenly understood Elaine's confidence and acceptance. Nikki wasn't quite there yet, but she'd made progress in the last two months.

She turned to Aurélie. "I forgot to tell you, I was exploring the other day and I got on the wrong train. I ended up in Epinay-sur-Seine. I figured it out, though."

Aurélie's eyes widened. "You're so adventurous, Nikki. I don't think I would have gone exploring alone while I was in the States."

Adventurous? Nikki laughed aloud. Her faith was an essential element to her forced courage, but she'd already said enough for one day. "My personal transformation program must be working, like in the movie *Sabrina*. Audrey Hepburn goes to Paris and gains self-confidence and sophistication. That's just what I'm hoping for myself."

Aurélie nodded with a smile. "I can see it's starting to work. But don't change who you are on the inside, Nikki. Your heart needs to stay the same. I like the way you are."

Warmth trickled through Nikki at Aurelie's comment. But her friend hadn't seen her fear and insecurity when she arrived in Paris only two months earlier, or how much she'd needed to stretch her emotional and spiritual boundaries. She didn't have time to waste. The following day marked a new chapter. "Tomorrow is my birthday." She suddenly felt shy.

"*C'est vrai?* Happy birthday!" Aurelie exclaimed. "We should celebrate when we get home."

Nikki leaned back on her backpack and smiled. The event of her birthday was different this year. Of course, she was spending it in

Paris, remarkable in itself, but it also felt like a turning point inside her.

The last six months had taken her life in a completely different direction, one she'd never have anticipated a year ago. If things could change so quickly in less than a year, what would the next year hold for her?

ଔ    ଔ    ଔ

"Why the long face, Marie?" Frank asked as he served himself a second helping of mashed potatoes. He reached for the butter. Marie gently touched his hand.

"Watch your saturated fat, Frank. You've put on weight since Christmas." She added quietly, "I miss Nikki. I find myself looking out the window half-expecting her to drop in, you know, like she used to on Saturday mornings."

Frank leaned against his elbows and nodded. "I miss her too. I worry sometimes. She doesn't keep in touch as much as I thought she would. Of course, it's only been a couple months." Frank hesitated, staring at the butter dish before reaching for it again.

"I envy her," Marie said. "I always thought when the kids got older you and I would travel more."

Frank grimaced. "Marie, the dealership—"

"I know, I know. It's your life, your wife. What am I?" Marie pushed away from the table. She stood then and stared at him. "Is this what you want, Frank? For this business to be your whole life? You have four dealerships and competent people to run them. You could give yourself a bit of time off. You want to control everything, and you don't trust anyone."

"Marie!" He'd never heard her speak this way.

"Wasn't that the gist of your last conflict with Danny?" Her voice rose. She leaned over and began to clear the table, clanging plates as she went.

Frank sat still before his still-full plate, pinched his lips into a tight cord.

"He's thirty years old, Frank," she said. "He needs to know you trust him and are proud of him."

"I *am* proud of him. He wouldn't be working there if I weren't."

"He needs to *hear* it. Laura needs to hear it. Nikki and I need to hear it. We all need to know that we're more than just planets in your solar system."

Abruptly, Marie left the room. Frank's mouth hung open for several seconds as he listened to loud clattering from the kitchen.

ぐ    ぐ    ぐ

Frustrated, Mike pressed disconnect on his cell phone. Officer Garner must be overwhelmed with the embezzlement case against the captured accountant from Hamilton. Either that, or he'd decided Mike was becoming a nuisance. In any case, the walls surrounding this investigation were impossible to scale. Granted, the police and investigators had their hands full with the unruly suspect, who reportedly was refusing to talk. How could Mike ever go past the current case into the past, if no one was talking to him?

For the umpteenth time that summer, Mike felt like his hands were tied behind his back. Maybe if he went to New York, his physical presence would remind the police force that there was a possible murder investigation to unravel. Common sense told him they'd just consider him to be in the way, but an insistent voice inside shouted that it might be worth a try.

Was that voice from God? Maybe it was his own compulsion to feel he was doing all he could, even if it meant crossing the country.

He didn't know whose voice was prodding him, but he had to do *something*. He'd only take a few days over a long weekend. It wasn't much, but he had to try.

# Chapter Fifteen

"Four avocados for only two euros! Fresh nectarines and melons! Dates from Tunisia!" Noisy *Marché* hawkers filled the air with shouts. All over the country the same scene, the bustle of the *Marché*, was replayed in cities and villages at least once per week, often on Sunday mornings.

Nikki didn't need produce that day, but rather cut across the festive outdoor market on her way to visit the tiny storefront church she'd seen nearly a month earlier.

"Mademoiselle—" A vendor she saw frequently during her weekly shopping held up a head of lettuce. "Un euro. Two for one fifty." She shook her head and waved at him as she walked.

Weaving her way through the tiny, one-lane streets, the noise of the *Marché* ebbed away, replaced by hollow silence. On Sunday mornings, most neighborhoods in Paris were quiet. In August they were like a tomb, since many residents left on three or four-week vacations, though the city center still overflowed with tourists. The calm would shift within a few weeks, when the new school year burst back onto the city scene, like blazing streetlights after a blackout.

Through her canvas handbag strapped across her chest, Nikki could feel the outlines of one of her birthday gifts from Mike, a blank journal covered in turquoise paisley fabric. She smiled to herself. He remembered she liked to journal. Inscribed inside the front cover was a hand-printed Psalm. Along with the journal, he'd sent a book on French bloopers. "In case you haven't made enough on your own," he'd written in the card. He'd wrapped both books in humorous gift paper. Whatever the motivation, she was touched he even knew the date of her birthday.

The sky overhead was a cloudless velvet blue, contrasting sharply with the bright green summer leaves. Once Nikki was on the street where the small church was located, she double-checked the address, which she researched online after her phone had been stolen.

She recognized the storefront, its glass doors opened wide as a couple stepped through the doorway. When she entered, the couple greeted her with a smile, and continued murmuring together in French. There were two young men about her age, one Asian, one African, tuning guitars in the front of the tiny room. Folding wooden chairs sat in neat rows. She sat in the second row from the back.

A door near the side wall opened and a wiry man with a ruddy face and tight red curls came through, followed by two small children. The little girl, about four years old and wearing a ruffled green print dress, skipped in. The boy looked slightly older.

"Go sit with Magali," the man whispered to them with a British accent. The children scrambled to the front row where an older woman sat. She addressed them in French and pulled the little girl onto her lap.

"Bonjour." The man approached Nikki and extended his hand. "Is this your first time with us?"

She shook his hand. "Yes, I'm visiting today. I passed your church a few weeks ago. I'm Nikki."

"My name is Andrew Calvert. I'm the pastor here. Are you new in town?"

"I'll be in Paris for a year teaching English at Jeanne d'Arc High School. I'm from the States."

"We're happy to have you, Nikki. You're welcome to join our church family as long as you're in France."

She surveyed the room as several more people, mostly college-aged, came in and sat down near her. "Thank you. It's nice to finally find a church."

"We're pretty typical of evangelical churches in France."
Andrew leaned against a column. "The population at large isn't
interested in God or Christ, so most Protestant churches are filled
with foreigners. Of course, we have a few French people as well." He
smiled. "And it's growing, albeit slowly."

"How many people usually come?"

Andrew chewed on his lip a moment as he thought. "I'd say up
to thirty. But in August, we won't have half that many. We get some
tourists, some Bible school students and exchange students. It can
be transient. Our core is about eighteen or twenty."

Nikki's eyes widened. Such a small congregation, more like a
home Bible study. "Is that typical?"

Andrew shrugged. "I'm afraid so. Nowadays we see a few
churches in Paris that have several hundred, but most of the time
they run about fifty or less." He grinned. "I'll bet that's a surprise
for you, coming from the United States. I hear many of the churches
there are enormous."

"Yeah, I guess a lot of them are, in the bigger cities. I've made
some French friends here, and they don't feel the need for God."

"That's one of our biggest challenges." Andrew cast a pensive
glance at the floor. "People aren't hostile, just indifferent. And their
religious history is tragic, so you can see reasons for some
resistance. It's God's work, though, to help people to see. We just
make ourselves available."

"How long have you been here in France?" Behind her, Nikki
heard the scrape of chairs as new arrivals settled into the back row.

"My wife and I arrived about six years ago from England,
studied French for a year, and began this church with just three
people. It's been slow, but God is working."

She took so many things for granted back home. Andrew and
his family had left everything behind. "Thanks, Andrew, for all you
are doing here."

He smiled then looked up at the growing group. "Well, we have
to start now." He took his place in front of the room near the
musicians and greeted everyone in French. By the time the service

began there were seventeen people. Given the size of the room, it was nearly filled. Everyone began singing praise songs, some which Nikki recognized as French versions of songs she sang in her church in Greenbrier. She was able to follow the sermon for the most part, reading along in her French New Testament, and jotting new vocabulary words into her notepad.

After the service, snacks and drinks were served in the small room, which quickly filled with noise. Several people introduced themselves to Nikki, Elodia from Spain, Rolf from Germany, Madeleine and Ruben from the Ivory Coast, and three French people, Magalie, the older lady, Séverine, and Philippe, who looked close to her age. She also met Penny, Andrew's wife, who spent most of her time hissing admonishments to her young son, Peter.

"Where are you from in America?" A cultured French accent grazed Nikki's ears as she reached for another coconut cookie from the snack table. She looked up and smiled at Philippe, who stood nearly a head taller than her.

"I grew up just outside of New York City," she told him. "Do you live here in Paris?"

He reached for a handful of almonds from the plastic tray. The room spilled over with noise, and he raised his voice slightly. "I was raised in Alsace, a region in the east of France. Do you know Colmar?"

She nodded. "I know the name. It's near Strasbourg, right? Close to the German border?"

Philippe nodded and smiled. His light green eyes reflected the sun streaming from the plate glass window. "It's not far from Strasbourg, about a half hour by train. Many people think Colmar is more beautiful than Strasbourg. We have canals, and the half-timbered houses you see in many German towns."

"You seem to like it a lot."

"Yes, I love it there. You should see it someday. I think you would like it. I just got a job in Paris, so I'll be moving here in a couple of weeks. I came early to find an apartment, and of course, wanted to find a church too."

"Do you belong to a church in Alsace?"

"Yes, I was raised in a Christian family. Alsace is like the French Bible Belt. We are fortunate. When I knew I'd be moving to Paris, I did some research to find a church. Would you like to sit?"

Nikki nodded and sat in one of the folding chairs across from him. "You're the first French person I've met who was raised in a Christian family. Seems there aren't many of you."

"Sadly, it's true. Many French children go to catechism, then do their first Communion. After that, nothing. They leave the church forever, possibly returning only to get married, or baptize their children."

"I wonder why they leave."

Philippe shrugged. "I guess many of them decide the church stories they heard were just fables to make people behave. They think it's manmade, unfortunately."

Nikki gave an understanding nod. "It's sad. So many mistakes have been made in the name of God, so it's no wonder people think they don't need Him."

"The younger people frequently think this way. They're empty for something, but they don't want the church. They've had it pushed on them and think they need something else."

Nikki chewed thoughtfully on her carrot stick. She was hearing the same thing repeatedly, from Jean-Christophe, from Pastor Andrew, and now from Philippe. This indifference was part of a world she didn't often think about, but her awareness of it was growing every day.

"Didn't mean to depress you, Nikki," Philippe said with a wide grin. "You look so sad. Let's change the subject. You said you came all the way from New York to teach English? That's a big step."

"And a great opportunity. I've learned so much already. And of course, Paris is a wonderful place to live. Are you looking forward to settling here?"

Philippe cocked his head to one side and gave Nikki a bold stare. "I think I am now."

A warm flush crept up her neck as she just grinned back at him.

It was close to one-thirty in the afternoon when Nikki finally arrived at her apartment building on Rue St. Sébastien. She was encouraged to have found a church family early in her visit. For sure she'd had divine help. Talking to Philippe, she hadn't seen the time pass. Maybe she'd see him again once he moved to Paris. It would be nice to meet the other members of the fellowship as well. She'd plan to attend the weekly Bible study next Thursday.

After a light lunch alone in her sunlit apartment, Nikki turned on her computer, which she hadn't checked in several days. Her heart jumped when she saw Mike's name pop up. Maybe his deadline was finished now, and he'd had time to write some news. She looked forward to telling him all about her new church and the people she'd met there.

Trying to discipline herself, she read her parents' email, then one from Elaine. She'd met a new guy, Eric, from church and was interested in him. Before leaving in June, Nikki had given her email address to Torrie the Terror, and had received a note from her that she had registered for French Three for the coming school year.

She saved Mike's email for last, but with disappointment saw that it was brief. "I'm a bit swamped now, but will write when I can. Hope you're having a good summer. Love, Mike".

A good summer? She frowned. Did that mean he wasn't planning to write to her again? Was his cryptic phrase equivalent to *have a nice life?* The tone held nothing of his previous warmth, especially his last email and his birthday note. It didn't even sound like him. Maybe one of his roommates or colleagues had written in his place, as a practical joke.

She shook her head. That would be stretching it. More likely, he realized he was starting to sound like he actually liked her, and got terrified of having sent the wrong message. He was backpedaling, just so she understood, so she wouldn't jump to conclusions about his intentions. Only friends. Nothing more.

Nikki swallowed hard, her eyes stinging. She'd heard his message loud and clear.

CR  CR  CR

Mike pushed through the glass doors of the JFK airport where exhaust fumes and bleating horns welcomed him to the city.   He scanned the curb where Ely said he'd be waiting. No sign of the older man yet. Another five minutes and a familiar gray sedan came into view. Mike slid into the passenger seat. He stuck out his hand and Ely grasped it in a warm shake.

"Had to circle around. They're getting strict about people parking too long." Ely grinned across the darkness in the car. "Twice in one year, Mike. This is a record."

"Sure is. No one knows I'm here in New York, not even Jim and Catherine. They don't know what's going on, so it'll save me a lot of explanation."

"Up to you. I'm sure they'd understand, but I know you're tired of thinking and talking about it."

Mike stared ahead where a stream of red taillights lit up the horizon. "I sure am. I don't know if this trip will do any good, but I felt like it was better than doing nothing. Probably be a wasted trip."

The snag of cars ahead began to move. "Good, go on," Ely muttered and eased on the gas pedal. "I won't make any promises, Mike. It's all unknown territory, but it can't hurt."

Mike nodded and stayed silent. He knew in his gut it was futile to have come to New York, but he couldn't stay paralyzed on the West Coast while all this was going on.

With a wave of guilt, he thought of Nikki. He hadn't wanted to explain what was happening yet, but had to have contact with her before leaving for New York. In retrospect, he realized his email had been too abrupt and had likely hurt her feelings. As soon as he got back to California, he'd explain everything to her. She'd understand. Right now, his mind could only deal with one tangle at a time.

After a quick lunch at Ely's favorite diner, they headed to the police station. Officer Todd Garner was out of the office. Officer Bailey, a tired-looking woman at the front desk, stared at Mike in a way that silently asked him why he was wasting her time. "There is no murder investigation, to my knowledge. Never has been one. This man is wanted for embezzlement, and that's the active investigation that's being done. I'm sorry, nothing more I can tell you."

Mike sighed, deflated. Had he come to New York for nothing? Ely pulled his arm aside. "Don't give up, Mike. We'll come back tomorrow and ask to speak to someone else. In the meantime, call Officer Garner and tell him you're in town. You've had a long day already, with the flight and all. Come back to the house. Amanda's expecting us for dinner."

No surprise. Stonewalled on the West Coast, blocked on the East Coast. Why had God brought him back to New York, if in fact, He had?

Mike and Ely entered Ely's two-story colonial style house and were immediately engulfed by mouth-watering smells. Mike felt the strain cascade from his tense muscles once inside the simple but neatly decorated home.

"Mike, how long has it been?" Amanda, Ely's wife, came toward him and enfolded him tightly in her arms. She also showed signs of age since the last time he'd seen her, but her bright intelligent eyes were the same, engaging his, speaking of history and friendship.

"I can't remember, maybe four or five years, at least."

"Dinner's almost ready, so why don't you get settled upstairs? Ely will show you your room."

After the meal, which left Mike feeling satisfied and loved, Amanda served slices of hot apple pie and vanilla ice cream. "Mike, I keep expecting each time you come that you'll be married or engaged. Are you being too picky?" Amanda grinned at him as she slid a wedge of pie onto his plate, and topped it with a dollop of ice cream.

The state of single adults was always fair game for discussion, it seemed. Mike gave her a sheepish shrug. "I, uh. . ."

"Mike has his eye on a young lady who is currently in Paris. Mancini's daughter," Ely told her. He turned to Mike and added, "Hope it was okay that I told. It's just between us."

"Sure, sure. There's nothing much to tell, except that she's in Paris for a year and we stay in touch by email. She's been traveling a lot this summer and otherwise avoiding phone calls."

"Why is that, Mike?" Amanda licked drops of melted vanilla ice cream from her fingers and settled back into her seat. "She'd be nuts to avoid you."

"That's nice of you, Amanda, but it's pretty much my fault. She likes me but believes I only want to be friends. I haven't told her otherwise because, frankly, I have too much on my plate now, with all this going on." There was more to it than that, of course, but he didn't want to unwrap his whole series of gaffes.

"Do you like *her*?" Amanda's gaze and tone were direct. Mike wanted to squirm.

"I'm starting to, more and more. I just thought it would be good to take things slowly."

He saw Amanda and Ely exchange a knowing glance. "What?" he asked.

"Slowly? And she doesn't know how you feel? You might end up losing her."

Mike stared down at his pie. They were right. Why was he so paralyzed? Was it just the investigation that had him overwhelmed, or was it simply a convenient excuse? He'd already lost Nikki once when she left for Paris. He could have stopped her, and he didn't. But he *had* rebuilt the friendship. Didn't that count for something?

"We talk regularly on email. I stay on her radar."

Amanda smiled warmly and placed a motherly hand on his arm, much like Harriet had done two weeks earlier. Suddenly he felt like a small boy. "Women like to know what a guy is thinking, Mike. You like her but she doesn't know it. Not telling you what to do, but just think it over. I'm saying this as a friend."

"A pushy friend, eh, Mike?" Ely chuckled.

"Pushy match-making friends, but friends who care," Mike grumbled, but cast a smile through a mouthful of apple pie.

# Chapter Sixteen

The first hazy, sunbaked days of August strolled in with a lethargic pace, seeking to savor the last moments of summer. Green enamel-painted chairs surrounded the flowerbeds and fountain of the Luxembourg Gardens. The fountain spurted glistening drops high into the air. They splashed down in a pattering chorus, while miniature sailboats glided aimlessly across the water's smooth surface.

Nikki leaned back and pushed her sunglasses up on her nose. The warm sun gently melted into her skin. She closed her journal and slipped her pen behind her ear as her eyes swept over the artful expanse of begonias, dahlias, and dozens of other flowers in coordinated pinks and purples.

In the previous two weeks Aurélie began working full-time and was otherwise occupied with Sébastien. Nikki's new friends, Sophie and Céline, also worked during the day, as did everyone else she knew. She'd started attending the church Bible study, but that was only one night per week. Nikki kept herself busy by visiting unknown or far-flung corners of Paris, walking for miles along tree-lined streets, exploring monuments, museums, and parks, reading along the banks of the Seine River, or on one of its islands, Ile de Saint Louis and Ile de la Cité.

It was a strange contrast, unlimited time in the world's most beautiful city, while carrying a weight of solitude and lack of purpose. Some days Nikki awakened eager to discover new sights to treasure in this incomparable place. At other times, the need to fill a full day alone felt like a coat of bronze pulling her emotions downward. At times the old question nagged at her. Could she make it alone? Did she have what it took?

Daily she filled her camera with anything her eyes found interesting, beautiful, or memorable, and each evening transferred photos to her computer to catalogue and label. This tedious activity was a comfort on still summer evenings in her tiny apartment, as the sounds of voices and cars drifted up through open windows.

She kept a running list of her favorite streets, museums, parks, restaurants, and neighborhoods, knowing she'd be too busy for such luxuries in just over a month.

In small increments, however, her tolerance for her own company grew. And in a month the new job would fill her days with lesson plans and noisy, spontaneous teenagers.

No word from Mike in nearly two weeks, the longest lapse apart from her travels since she'd been in France. Maybe he'd changed his mind even about friendship. That thought was as painful as the self-reproach she hurled at herself for still holding out hope. "Okay, Lord. I just can't seem to let go, can I?" she murmured, gazing down with apathy at her tanned legs. "Please, help me let go."

She squeezed her eyes shut and clenched her fists. There had to be a way to do this, short of cutting off all communication with him. She didn't want to do that. After all, his friendship remained a tiny consolation for her. Yet she knew she needed to move on, and soon.

Nikki let her whole body relax and whispered, "I give it to You, all of it. On the altar, I place Mike, my feelings, all the past." With her eyes closed, a slight breeze of peaceful release fluttered through her. She sat like that for several minutes before opening her eyes again, feeling lighter. She'd probably have to fight this battle a few more times, though it might become easier.

Nikki leaned over the arm of her metal chair into her canvas tote bag and pulled out her Daring Things Notebook, a small spiral-bound journal. There she recorded her varied attempts to conquer her fears and become more adventurous. The idea had germinated a few weeks earlier, as she realized that living abroad afforded her an ideal opportunity to become braver.

The first entry in the Daring Things Notebook chronicled her participation in a demonstration. It hadn't been difficult to find one since demonstrations and strikes were frequent in Paris. One day when she set out to explore, she encountered a noisy throng clustered around the Place de la Bastille, not far from her apartment. Under a makeshift bandstand, a man in a colorful coat was shouting about something. As Nikki listened more closely, she understood he was speaking about the plight of illegal immigrants, that many were forced onto planes and sent back to a dangerous situation in their home countries.

She nodded thoughtfully and decided to join in. Not only was it a good cause, but she could also add it to her Daring Things journal. Though the demonstration turned into a street party, she was glad to have eased gently into her bold goal of conquering fear.

Her most terrifying challenge by far had been going with Sophie to a karaoke club. With trembling knees and a faltering voice, she stumbled through an Eagles song in English to the applause of a roomful of half-drunk French young people. Afterwards, she decided there should be limits to the terror she'd endure for a growth experience.

Nikki's cell phone jangled in her purse. "Allo?"

"Hello, Nikki. It's Céline," said a female voice in French. "*Ça va?*"

"Hi, Céline. I'm fine, thanks."

"Good. Sophie and I were talking about visiting England and Ireland later this month. Would you like to come? It would be fun to go together, and maybe you can translate some for us."

A tingle began to lift her glum mood. Could this be an answer to her prayer? A bit of distraction? "That sounds fun, and I had planned to go sometime. When do you want to leave, and for how long?"

"We can leave next week, if you are free. We'll take the Eurostar across the Channel, visit London, and find a cheap flight to Ireland. How does that sound?"

"Wonderful," Nikki said, shooting her other hand up in a joyful fist, as she murmured a prayer of thanks.

"Okay, I'll tell Sophie. It'll be great."

"Au revoir." Nikki slipped her phone back into her bag. Mental pictures of rugged ruins, rolling green hills, and Windsor Castle sprang into her mind, providing a welcome shift of focus. She couldn't have chosen a better distraction for herself.

CR  CR  CR

Mike hoped this would be his last time at the Adams Bridge Police Station. He'd called Todd the previous evening after dinner and had to leave yet another message on his phone. At least the officer knew Mike was in New York and would be coming to see him. He hoped the man would have something, anything, hopeful to tell him.

Mike shifted his weight as he stood at the familiar gray counter waiting for Officer Garner to appear. He was grateful Ely stood beside him.

Officer Garner appeared through a far doorway, a solemn expression on his face. Mike hoped that had nothing to do with his inquiry because it didn't look optimistic. "Hello, gentlemen. I received your message yesterday, and the one from last week. I was unable to call back."

Ely stepped forward. "We'd like to request that a full murder investigation be made on this case." His voice was laden with authority. "You now have the suspect in custody. He can be questioned, and the evidence can be reexamined."

Officer Garner leveled a gaze at the older man. "I wish that were the case, Sir. You see, the murder charge isn't a case now because it never *was* a case. It was ruled an accident thirteen years ago. If it had been ruled a homicide or even a possible homicide back then, we'd have more to work with today. At this point, the only way we can go anywhere is if our suspect makes a confession. That isn't looking likely at this point. He isn't even talking about the current charges." He paused and looked from Ely to Mike. "I wish I had different news to give you. I've looked at every angle, but there's only so much that can be done. I'm sorry."

Mike took a breath. "Thank you for your efforts, Officer," he said quietly. The heaviness of defeat began to ooze through his torso and limbs until he could barely move. "Would it be possible for me to speak with the suspect? You never know what he might say, since he knew my father."

Todd's pinched lips communicated regret and a negative response. "I'm afraid he isn't here at this facility. He's upstate in a prison and can't have any visits until after his sentencing if he's found guilty. It could be a long time before that happens, depending on how the evidence unfolds. If it's any consolation, though, if he's convicted, he'll be there for a while."

Ely and Mike exchanged a look. Mike wondered if his friend would try a new angle, push a little harder. But there was nothing else to say. "Thank you again, Officer Garner. You have my number if ever anything changes."

"Sure thing. Again, I'm very sorry."

Mike and Ely walked to the car in heavy silence. Once seated in the passenger seat Mike turned and said, "Ely, would you mind dropping me off at the cemetery? I'll take a bus back to your place."

Ely's eyes were etched with compassion. The grooves down his weathered cheeks seemed to have grown deeper since the previous day. "I'm sorry, Mike. You can have the satisfaction of knowing you tried, and now the police are aware of the possible connection between the current allegations and your parents' deaths. If we'd said nothing, it would always be considered just an accident."

Mike nodded. "That's a good point. They might not have thought about it, and now maybe they will. We may hear something years from now."

As he slipped out of Ely's car, he stuck up a hand in a static wave and turned toward the tall wrought iron gates of the cemetery.

The scent of freshly mowed grass, moist with dew, surrounded him. Wet splotches soon appeared on his shoes as he trudged across a familiar trail to the place where his parents lay. A thick stillness that was nearly physical pressed Mike on every side. A distant mower hummed into the silence.

Finally, he stood before two worn stones. Carl Branagan. Joyce Branagan. The first dates were several years apart, but the second dates, identical. They were taken at once, gone from the earth, gone from his life. Gone. In one moment.

A slight throb began in his throat and became an ache. Mike breathed deeply, and despite the freshness in the air, almost choked. He gasped and knelt on one knee before the stones. "Mom, Dad," he whispered. His eyes began to sting. He blinked, blinked again. "I tried. I really did. Maybe there was more I could have done. Maybe if I'd been a different kind of kid, you wouldn't have traveled as much. Especially that last day. I'm sorry.

Two hot tears squeezed out of his eyes, then two more. He didn't attempt to stop the flow. "I miss you guys. I missed having parents to grow up with. I missed being normal, with parents. I wish you could have been there."

His voice broke and a sob erupted, leading to a quiet, shuddering river. For the next several moments of anguish, he couldn't see, couldn't think. He wasn't in the present, but touched the depths of that first agony, which had left a hollow cavern ever since.

Minutes passed. Slowly his sobs subsided. He pulled a tissue from his pocket and mopped his face, feeling a calm settle upon him and through him, like a cloud. He sat still and quiet for a long time. When he finally spoke, a web of peace surrounded him. "You weren't there for me, with me, but you couldn't help it. God provided other people for me. And He was there watching me too. So, it's okay. I'm okay."

Mike knelt quietly beside the headstones for several more minutes, not caring about the moist grass that was leaving streaks on his knees and hands. Then slowly he stood, turned, and walked toward the gate.

He left the cemetery and strode along the busy road, cut through a neighborhood, and kept walking. Finally, he reached a bus stop that would take him to Ely's house. As he waited, he thought about Nikki and longed to talk to her. Ached to tell her everything that had happened, how the investigation came up, then fizzled to nothing, but how God used it to nudge him closer to where he needed to be. . .to acceptance.

Startled, Mike realized that he wanted to open his heart to Nikki, but hadn't had that same desire with any other woman. Physical closeness had always taken the place of emotional transparency, as he tried to fill the void, up until the time he became a Christian. His desire to talk to Nikki, to be with her, to see her, went beyond friendship. Mike's face broke into a wide grin. Why didn't he finally admit to himself that he was in love with her? He was in love with Nikki Mancini.

As the bus rumbled toward Ely's neighborhood, Mike watched the green, flowering city roll by. It seemed to be a new place he'd never seen before, yet was vaguely familiar. It was part of his past, part of his life. He no longer wished to rub out the memory of this city, that life.

For the second time that day, Mike smiled.

"You're offering seconds on dessert? Are you trying to get me fat, Amanda?" Mike teased Amanda as she slipped another walnut brownie onto his plate. "Or maybe just preparing me for a woman's touch?"

Amanda's eyes grew large, but she said nothing.

"I'm glad you're feeling better, Mike," Ely said. "At least you appear to feel better. In fact, you appear downright relaxed and happy. Is that possible?"

Mike nodded as his fork pierced one corner of the moist, dark brownie. He leaned forward and inhaled deeply. "Mmm. You just baked these today, didn't you?" He turned to Ely and said slowly, quietly, "I think I was supposed to come here this week, not to get someone to open my parents' case, but to. . .how do I put it? To heal. I've been running, as you yourself said. I had to come back to face everything so I could see it was okay. It was okay to have the past I had, even though it hurt."

Mike suddenly noticed that Ely and Amanda had stopped eating and stared at him. Amanda's eyes glistened with tears. "Oh, Mike, that's wonderful." Her voice broke. "You've been burdened for so long. I used to wonder if you'd spend your whole life that way, and never be happy." Several tears had slipped down her cheeks, but joy filled her eyes.

"Time to embrace the past, but move on to the future." Ely's voice was gruff, Mike knew, to hide the fact that he, too, was moved. He knew the older man's depth of compassion. He'd seen it many times over the years.

"Yeah, I'm ready for that."

"And ready for that woman's touch too?" Ely smiled broadly.

"Yes, I believe I am. That'll be my second step." Mike wiped chocolate crumbs from his mouth, then reached for another brownie. "I have one more thing to do first while I'm still here. I'm going to call Jim and Catherine and try to see them before I leave. They're my other parents, the ones God gave me."

# Chapter Seventeen

With a hollow thud, the backpack slid from Nikki's shoulders and fell to the wooden floor. She let out a long sigh. It felt good to be home from her third trip in two months, as much as she enjoyed them. That would be it for a while.

The flower vase on the small dining room table held only the shriveled colorless remains of baby carnations she'd bought several days before leaving for Germany. She pulled open the tall windows and unhooked the metal shutters. Light flooded into the dark room and the crisp, September air gently flowed in, ferrying out the stuffiness.

Her week in England and Ireland had been full of contrasts, the lively pace of London, with Westminster Cathedral, the changing of the guard at Buckingham Palace, a cruise up the Thames, the serene hillsides and rugged cliffs of Ireland. Bouts of utter exhaustion from speaking French so much assailed Nikki from time to time, but her language level took a sharp turn upward. A working vacation, though memorable, the last trip before school.

Or so she thought.

Impulse led Nikki to Germany barely two weeks after returning from England and Ireland. Soon she'd have neither time nor money for travel and Germany had been on her *must visit* list. Having no one to go with, she decided to go by herself. The old Nikki would have never visited a foreign country alone. The old Nikki didn't even like going to a fast-food restaurant alone. The new Nikki was determined to go, despite her dread. She'd been fearful, not for her safety, but of loneliness. But it ended up being one of her favorite trips, alone with herself and God.

During quiet moments in the evening Nikki thought about how much she'd changed, expanded her horizons, in just two months. Could she really return to the quiet routine of Greenbrier, New York? Her appetite had been whetted for a bigger world.

Nikki emptied her backpack into the laundry basket and made a late-afternoon snack of sliced apples, brie, and crackers. She glanced across the room at her computer. Maybe it had been mean, or merely self-protective, but she hadn't responded to Mike's emails before or after her trip to England. She'd sent two lines just before leaving for Germany. As a friend, she probably ought to respond. Was she playing a game, or fooling herself?

She finally turned on her laptop. He'd sent two messages before her trip to England, one while she was gone, and another one after, as if making up for the silent two weeks. In the most recent message, he asked a second time for her French phone number.

Nikki sat comfortably on the couch, laptop on her knees, and began to write, as to a casual friend. Time had flown. Didn't have time to write. So much to tell. Giving him the highlights of England, Ireland, and Germany would distance her from what her heart still murmured, either loudly or quietly.

She attached photos, several from each country. After staring at the screen another few seconds, she typed her cell phone number, including instructions on how to dial overseas, though he probably already knew. If he checked the message the same day, he might call that evening.

During the next several hours, she distracted herself. He might not call for several days. And when he did, she'd be a friend, with no hopes, no more girlish panting for him.

She'd try, anyway.


Later that evening, the small coffee table bore a stack of English as Second Language books. No more goofing off all over Europe.

Time to buckle down in preparation for her new job, which wasn't very far in the future.

Nikki left a message for Aurélie, then made a light supper. She settled on the couch with a fat ESL textbook open on her lap and ate as she read.

An hour later her cell phone rang. Her heart accelerated, though she knew it could be Aurélie calling back.

"Boy, it's good to hear your voice." Mike's warm exclamation touched her like a balmy breeze, caressing her thirsty soul. She closed her eyes for a moment, loving the sound of his voice, the fact that she was hearing it again for the first time since arriving in Europe. She squeezed her lips together with both regret and longing.

"Hello, Mike. It's good to hear you, too. What's it been, two months?" *Be friendly, but not overly enthusiastic.*

"More. Seems like two years to me." He added softly, "Thanks for letting me call. Have you been mad at me?"

"No, not at all. I was gone, just taking advantage of being in Europe."

"Sounded fantastic in your email. I'd do the same thing if I had the chance."

"How has your summer been?"

He sighed. "Really hard and boring, compared to yours. I didn't take any fun vacations and had loads of work to make up for those who did. Basically, I got punished for sticking around." He gave a light laugh, as if it didn't bother him at all. Or maybe he was hiding something. "I'm not complaining, though. The weather was pretty good this summer. Not too much fog."

"Fog in summer? That's strange."

"Not in San Francisco, it's not. Our real summer hits around September and October." There was a brief silence. "I need to tell you about something else that happened."

Nikki tensed. What could explain his cryptic email followed by two weeks of silence?

"I'll summarize. I just don't want to think about this anymore, but you have a right to know, since I was distracted. The company my dad was doing an audit for just before he died recently went under, and they discovered the accounting had been tampered with for years. The accountant went missing, and this led Ely and me— Ely was my dad's friend—to think that maybe my dad knew about it, and had been killed because of that."

Nikki's relief was mixed with alarm for Mike. "Oh, Mike, that's a lot to have on your mind. Do you think someone killed your parents to keep your dad from talking about what he knew?"

"That's what we thought. And it's very possible, but unfortunately, difficult to prove after so many years. We dealt with the police in Adam's Bridge over the phone and in person, but they couldn't do anything. I went back to New York last week, which is why you didn't hear from me for a while. Maybe you didn't notice."

Nikki bit her lip. Fat chance she wouldn't notice, but at least there was an explanation that had nothing to do with her. "I wish you'd told me, so I could support you through this."

Mike sighed on the phone. "I wanted to, you don't know how much. It was pretty overwhelming for me, but I felt like I had to go through it alone. I know better now. The whole trip helped me to let go of a lot of baggage, though, get some things clear in my head."

"Thanks for telling me, Mike." With surprise, Nikki noticed that compassion swelled in the place where pining and romantic frustration had always dwelt concerning Mike. "I'm still your friend, and I care about you." It felt good to speak the truth without double meanings or attempts at persuasion.

"I know, Nikki. That means a lot." His voice was quiet. After a pause he said, "I wish I could see you. We still have a lot of things to talk about, you and I."

Nikki's heart started to hammer. "What do you mean?"

"I don't know if the trips just got in the way, or if you wanted to put distance between us this summer," he said softly. "If so, I don't blame you. I'm sorry for the part I've played in that. I hope I can make it up to you."

Nikki heard regret, but wasn't sure. Her throat felt parched. Did he want an honest response? She wanted to insist that he explain exactly what he meant. Instead, she murmured, "I haven't been good at keeping in touch, but it *was* really a crazy summer. You can certainly make it up to me, though." She pushed out a chuckle. What might that look like? She wouldn't get her hopes up.

For the next twenty minutes Mike plied Nikki with questions about her trips and about her new job. "You went to Germany all alone?" An edge of worry crept into his voice. "Is it safe for you to travel alone?"

Nikki laughed. Was he now the homebody, afraid of foreign adventure? "It's pretty safe in European cities, more than in the States. It was fun. I just hung out with God, and we saw all the sights together. I think my relationship with God has gotten deeper since I've been here. Just Him and me walking around in Munich and Rothenburg. That's the medieval city with a wall all around it. You'd like it."

"Sounds great. I'd love to do that sometime, a trip with just Him. Then maybe another one with you. Someplace you haven't already been, though it might be tough to find one."

There it was again, this unaccustomed. . .flirting. Nikki swallowed. It didn't necessarily mean anything. "I'd like that too. And there are plenty of places still on my list that I haven't seen yet." Why couldn't she just ask him what he was thinking? After her conversation with Mike the previous January, she wasn't ready to stick out her neck.

"This call must be costing you a fortune," she said. "We've been talking for a while."

Mike laughed. "Don't worry. I got an international plan. Not that a phone bill would stop me, be sure of that."

"An international plan is a good idea." Maybe to call frequently?

After they ended the call, a warm tingle continued in her stomach for several minutes. He hadn't come across either indifferent or platonic. More like pursuing her again, though with subtlety. Why didn't he just tell her clearly, instead of touching on the topic then scuttling away? Was he still unsure of his feelings, yet hoping to keep the doors open? She'd have to accept that, since it wasn't likely get any clearer until she returned to the States. And that was another nine months away.

Once again, she'd have to tuck her questions and hopes into the cupboard of her mind. Three days later was the orientation meeting for all the new teacher's assistants. Now with her new job less than two weeks away, she'd have her plate too full to spend much time wondering about Mike Branagan.

‘ ‘ ‘

Marie Mancini stacked her reports into a neat pile, watching the clock for the ten-thirty break. Her mind needed a rest from contracts and premium quotes. From her peripheral vision she saw a man's silhouette approach. A tiny flutter came unbidden inside her and her face grew warm.

"Why don't you come down to the break room? They have donuts." The deep voice of her new colleague and department manager, Doug, filled her cubicle. For the last two months his buoyant humor and light-hearted manner lifted her spirits, even when she was stressed with deadlines. She enjoyed the innocent flirtation, and was glad she could be a friendly face for him as he adjusted to his new position in the department.

"I was just waiting for a good stopping point so I could take a break. This file is giving me a headache." She rolled her eyes in exaggerated frustration before her lips widened into a grin.

Doug stepped aside as Marie stood up. His eyes cascaded down her and she flushed with pleasure. She was wearing a new dress with a scoop neck and uneven hemline in muted fall colors, along with a suede vest and matching suede boots. It was a far cry from the housewife clothes she usually wore at home and on weekends, and she reveled in being pretty again. And the look Doug gave her was a far cry from the indifference she got at home. He even treated her like she had a brain in her head, as though she could do more than cook for clients and family members. His compliments were a superficial pleasure, but she liked them. Would it hurt anything to enjoy the attention of a man, for the first time in years? It wouldn't go anywhere.

"Don't let this go to your head, Marie, but. . . wow! You look stunning. Any special occasion, or just run-of-the-mill class?"

She laughed lightly. "Oh, I'm full of class. Everyone knows that." She kept smiling and fell into step beside him, listening to the latest joke he'd heard, and giggling all the way to the break room.

℞   ℞   ℞

The subway platform swarmed with more passengers than Nikki had ever seen in her life. They were dressed for purpose and career, wearing suits, blazers, skirts, scarves, and ties, more formally than those who traveled later in the day. They wore four-inch heels, leather jackets, smelled of cologne. They had hair freshly gelled or sprayed. Some carried briefcases. Others had backpacks or large art portfolios slung over one shoulder. Many listened to music on tiny earphones or fiddled with their cell phones, or read one of the free daily newspapers distributed at métro entrances.

Nikki wove slowly through the narrow platform to find a small space to stand. When the subway train rumbled down the track and stopped in front of the platform, it seemed that there was already a huge crowd inside. Where would they all fit?

The doors slid open, and a few people got out. In the tiny remaining space, dozens of travelers filed on, squeezing into every available cranny, pressed body to body inside the small subway car.

Amazingly, most of them were able to get on. No one made eye contact or spoke, which might have been possible had they been able to breathe. Three stops later, Nikki sighed when she stepped out of the hot crowd and walked to the exit.

Her relief didn't last long, as she approached the four-story gray building where she would spend the next nine months. She identified with Dorothy approaching the Emerald City after a tiring trek across Oz. She was excited. She was intimidated. She wondered what she was doing there. Slowly mounting the wide staircase, Nikki was immensely glad to have had the summer to break into the culture before teaching English to French teenagers.

At the orientation class she had attended two weeks earlier, she learned she would have to develop games and activities to help students practice their English conversation skills. She would rotate among nine different classes but could use the same lessons with the different groups, which was a relief. Otherwise, she'd spend every spare moment preparing and wouldn't do anything else, including sleep.

Nikki wouldn't receive her first paycheck for several weeks, and had begun stashing her summer reserves like a nervous squirrel facing winter. Her larger New York teacher's salary had been enough to provide for her needs that summer as well as put a little aside. She'd make it. She was determined. While some people's lives were financially precarious all the time, with nothing to fall back on, her frugal year in Paris was only temporary. Besides that, she had savings, a wealthy father, and a job waiting for her in New York. For this year, she'd pretend she had none of those things.

As she passed through the doorway bearing the same number from her orientation sheet, several pairs of adolescent eyes looked up at her in unabashed curiosity. She smiled and nodded at them. She'd already met one of the English teachers, Mademoiselle Anne-Laure Genaille, at the orientation. She would have five classes with her and four classes with Madame Rashida Mahmoudi.

The room was plain, with none of the colorful bulletin board decorations or posters and flags Nikki put up each semester. Gray and white walls stared back at her next to a row of smudged windows overlooking a parking lot. The students, dressed in jeans, t-shirts, leather jackets, and sweatshirts, sat in rows of wooden chairs with desktops attached.

Anne-Laure glanced up from her desk and smiled at Nikki. She appeared to be in her early thirties. Her clear blue eyes were almond-shaped and sparkled with determination behind wide rectangular glasses. Thick brown hair was pulled back into a bun, with tendrils already escaping on both sides, even though it was early morning. "Bonjour, Nicole. You can sit over here." She gestured to a desk alongside her larger desk.

"Bonjour," Nikki responded with a smile. She watched as more students filed into the class and took their seats. Anne-Laure had already briefed her on each group's level, and she'd come prepared with an introductory exercise.

Anne-Laure leaned toward Nikki and said in a low voice, "You won't have to do any teaching today, since it's your first day, but you'll start tomorrow. I'll introduce you then orient the class to the new school year."

Nikki felt a wave of relief. Observing, she could handle. But with twenty students staring at her, even that seemed a challenge. What were they thinking? She smiled at them with a guarded level of friendliness.

Anne-Laure stood. "Good morning, class. This is Mademoiselle Mancini. She is from the United States, and she'll be helping you with your English this year. Does anyone have any questions for Mademoiselle Mancini? Please say your name first."

Several hands lifted in the air, mostly girls. "My name is Berangère. Where do you come from in the States?"

Nikki nodded at the dark-eyed teenager, her brunette hair in a high-flung ponytail, bordered on either side with large hoop earrings. "Hello, Berangère. I am from New York, just north of Manhattan."

"I'm Samira. How old are you?" Dark eyes peered shyly from behind folded hands.

"Hi, Samira. I'm twenty-five."

"My name is Bertrand. Have you been to France before?" Bertrand's face looked almost surly until he spoke, when his eyes lit up and his frown widened to an open grin.

"Yes, twice. I love your country, especially Paris." An honest compliment, which seemed to please the students.

"My name is Véronique," said a thin blond with large, pale eyes. "Do you have a French boyfriend?" A titter rippled through the class.

Nikki grinned. Jean-Christophe had become a casual friend, though nothing more. "No, I don't. I do have some French friends, though."

Fortunately, the interrogation didn't last long before Mademoiselle Genaille got down to business. Nikki would certainly learn a lot that year from experienced teachers. Throughout the rest of the class some of the students continued to eye her with curiosity. Maybe she was their first American. French teenagers didn't seem all that different from American ones.

Later that afternoon Nikki stumbled exhausted into her apartment. She'd made it through her first day with six of her nine classes. The other teacher, Rashida Mahmoudi, was warmer than Anne-Laure Genaille had been, yet just as professional. Nikki would spend more time in her classes the following day, then the schedule would rotate back again.

Nikki breathed deeply, smiling in satisfaction. Back in the classroom. Regardless of country, back where she belonged.

# Chapter Eighteen

The cell phone felt warm in Mike's hand as he swiveled absently in his desk chair. Most of his colleagues had left for lunch. After more than two months, hearing Nikki's voice was a gulp of fresh air. Yet he knew he hadn't succeeded in being clear with her about his feelings. Had she picked up his change in attitude toward her? Once they were together again, he would be able to tell her. The phone didn't measure up for that purpose.

Had he ever been this clumsy with a woman?

He shuffled the hard copies for the web site he was working on to one side, restless. The late September sun splashed onto his desk and highlighted the dust that spun slowly through the air in his cubical.

There was no question in his mind. He wanted to tell Nikki in person that he was in love with her, so he'd have to go to New York at Christmas. He'd call Marie at the Big House to find out what day Nikki was arriving, so he wouldn't lose any time. It was a good time to call, since she'd likely be home.

The phone rang two, three times. "Mancini residence." Frank's voice on the line. Mike's heart sank.

"Hi, Frank. It's Mike. I didn't expect you to be home this early." Too bad Frank would know why he'd called.

"I had a doctor's appointment, so I took the rest of the afternoon off. Maybe I'll get a little rest while I have the house to myself." His tone was relaxed. Perhaps the conversation wouldn't be difficult.

"Sounds like a good plan," Mike said, then braced himself. "I'm calling to see if you know what date Nikki is flying in for Christmas this year. I might try to come." He tried to sound casual, as if talking about a normal family visit. Considering how their last conversation about Nikki had gone, Mike doubted that Frank would be cooperative.

"But it hasn't been three years yet."

Irritation rose in Mike's throat. "I come whenever I want, Frank."

"Nikki won't be coming home this year. She said she wanted to stay in France for the holidays. I even told her we'd pay for her ticket, but she wants to stay there. You know, Paris at Christmas."

The news splashed into a deep pool of disappointment. Why hadn't it occurred to him that she wouldn't come home?

Frank interrupted his thoughts. "Are you still in touch with her?"

"Yes, we keep in touch some. I thought it might be nice to see her again at Christmas. Too bad she isn't coming."

"You could have asked her yourself, if you're in touch."

"I wanted to surprise her. She wouldn't have expected me two years in a row."

"No, I guess not. Will you come this year anyway? If so, I'll let Dad know."

"Probably not." Mike traced a line in the dust with his finger.

"I thought not." Frank's tone was dry. "I should tell you, I warned Nikki about you last year after you left. Thought it was for the best."

Irritation spurted through him. "*Warned* her? What am I, a predator, that you have to *warn* Nikki? About what, exactly?"

"I just told her that you had more worldly life experiences than she did, and that she should bear that in mind," Frank said crisply.

Control, Mike told himself. He glanced quickly around his work area, keeping his voice low. "Either you don't think she's mature enough to make her own decisions, or it's me you don't trust. You're still condemning me for events in the past. You must think I haven't changed in the last ten years." Mike collapsed back in his chair, realizing he'd spoken like a well-oiled machine gun, too fast, too defensive.

Frank sighed. "Maybe you have changed, Mike. What do I know, as little as you come around? I didn't want Nikki getting hurt. Maybe I interfered—"

"Yes, you did," Mike said. "You have no right. Nikki is an adult. She and I can navigate our own relationship."

"I was acting in Nikki's best interest."

"I understand how much you worry about Nikki and care about her. But letting her grow up and make her own decisions would be in her best interest."

"I'll do anything I have to do to protect Nikki from pain. And I was right, you did cause her pain in a very short amount of time."

Mike winced. "We would have done just fine without your meddling. And by the way, we *are* doing just fine."

His voice lost its combative edge as his words slowed. "You know, Frank, when I was seventeen, I had no parents to give me guidance. I might have accepted it from you, but you always seemed to want me to disappear and never come back. You're the only one in the family who has ever treated me that way, and it's always been a mystery to me." Mike forced a softer tone. "You never took time to get to know me when I was a child, even though we had similar tragedies in our lives. Instead, you just watched with disapproval and hated me for no reason." Maybe he'd gone too far. But the pain and bewilderment had festered inside him for nearly twenty years.

He stopped and breathed heavily. Finally, he'd told him. There was a pause on the other end of the phone. For a moment Mike thought Frank had hung up. Then Mike heard him clear his throat.

"I never hated you, Mike. I'm sorry if it seemed that way to you." His voice was quieter than Mike had ever heard him. He didn't speak, hoping Frank would continue to explain himself. Silence.

"It did seem that way, for many years," Mike said. "I wasn't a perfect adolescent, as you know. I probably brought grief to Jim and Catherine, and you likely resented that. But you know what it's like to lose a parent. Your world ends. I'm not excusing anything, but I was young. I hope you'll relate to me now as an adult. Especially now." He almost said, "because I'm in love with your daughter", but caught himself. "If you have anything specific to reproach me for, you are free to tell me. I'll listen and take it to heart."

Another silence. Mike braced himself for what would come, but nothing did. He debated bringing up another taboo and decided to try. "And Frank, I know about the investigation into your company after my parents died. That may be a forgotten issue for you, but just in case it isn't, I wanted to mention it, to get it into the open."

"You know about that? How did you find out?" Surprise leaped into Frank's voice. Had he struck a nerve?

Mike deliberately kept his voice calm and soothing. "My father's estate executor told me when I was eighteen, just before I left for California. I know they cleared your mechanics of any negligence. I just wanted to tell you that it isn't an issue for me."

"I'm glad. You never said a thing."

"No, there wasn't a need, until now. I just wanted to clear the air in case that was what you had against me."

"Thank you for saying it now. It was very difficult for me to have my company brought into question. And I don't hold that against you. That would be ridiculous. You were a child, and had nothing to do with it."

"I don't hold anything against you either, Frank."

After hanging up, Mike stared at the cell phone for a long time. He felt emotionally drained. His back and underarms were moist, but a buoyancy nearly lifted him off his chair. Frank had finally heard Mike's perspective after all these years. He hadn't really apologized, but had come close enough. There was a chance for healing now, a second chance at a relationship.

Harriet had said he'd sought a father in Frank. Maybe he had, but no more. He saw the possibility of a friend. Maybe one day.

Mike's father void had always been a dry wound in his heart, a painful echo of what could have been. He'd crossed the country, had claimed he didn't need a father. His own father had been distant and busy, then had abruptly died. Frank had been disinterested, hostile. Yet only one Father had followed him everywhere he went. God had been with him, and also provided other people, Jeff, Harriet, Ely, Jim, and Catherine, to fill his gaps. Mike was rich with loving relationships that he'd never fully appreciated.

For several moments he allowed that fact to flow over him like a warm current. He tightly closed his stinging eyes, then leaned back in his desk chair. Only a muffled phone conversation across the room cut the silence. A quiet whisper of peace stole over him.

Mike reached again for the phone and dialed the three-digit extension of his boss, Ralph. "Hey, Ralph. I know you're just getting ready to leave for lunch, but I wanted to tell you that I need to reserve a couple weeks' vacation at Christmas. I didn't take any last summer—"

"Take as much time as you need." Ralph's voice crackled warmly. "I appreciate the way you held the fort this past summer. How long you want?"

"Twelve days ought to be enough. I need to go to Paris to see a certain young lady."

"Oh, in that case, by all means! You can uphold Paris' reputation." Ralph guffawed and Mike couldn't help smiling. He hoped so.

"Thanks. I'll send a post card."

Next Mike dialed Penny, his travel agent. She'd get it done quicker than he could on the internet. "I need a flight to Paris, a few days before Christmas. And a hotel, somewhere between—wait a minute . . ." he shuffled through some notes he'd jotted from one of Nikki's emails. "Get me a reasonable hotel somewhere between Bastille and Republic. Please give me a call back to let me know what you find."

Penny's voice was cheerful. "Paris? Well, *that'll* be a great Christmas. Be sure to see the lights on the Champs Elysées. I don't know what flights are running, since it's holiday time, but I'll get one as low as I can."

"Thanks, Penny." Mike hung up the phone and leaned back in his chair, feeling strangely light. He'd finally had the dreaded blowout with Frank, and it had led to a conversation he'd never expected. Old roots of bitterness were crumbling, he sensed, on both sides.

Now Nikki was his focus. All other tragedies, apprehensions, and double mindedness were swept away. It was all perfectly clear.

ଔ ଔ ଔ

The month of October arrived quickly. The days darkened earlier, laced with chill, as the trees lining the broad avenues shed their leaves in brown and orange patches that swirled daily to the sidewalk below.

Nikki pushed the chilled glass door to the florist shop. Maybe she'd try something different this time, pink roses, or dahlias in fall colors. Browsing through the tapestry of color relaxed her after teaching.

The days passed in such a blur that she could hardly distinguish one from another. Each week consisted of a strand of activities in predictable order: rushing to the métro to join the breathless squeeze of bodies and repeating games and activities in English five times per day. She grew more comfortable at the high school and was relieved that her typical good rapport with teenagers had continued with young Parisians.

This routine was followed by grocery shopping or other errands and a short evening of preparing for the following day. Sometimes on weekends she went out with Aurélie and her friends, some fellow teaching assistants, or new acquaintances from her church.

At the end of October would be Nikki's first school holiday, La Toussaint, or All Saints. For once she wouldn't travel. Instead, Elaine would arrive on the first of November and stay a week. Nikki wasn't aware how much she missed Elaine until she began planning for her visit, even though they'd kept up by phone and computer.

It was nearly dark when Nikki emerged from the florist shop with a bunch of purple asters tucked under one arm. On the other arm, her canvas bag weighed heavy with a cylinder of goat cheese and a slab of garlic boursin from the cheese shop, along with some oranges, tomatoes, lettuce, and bananas from the produce stand nearby. She shifted the heavy bag further up her shoulder just as she heard a voice call, "Nikki, hello."

Startled, she looked up and saw Philippe coming toward her. "I was across the street, and I thought I recognized you." He flashed a warm smile, dimples lengthening.

"Hi, Philippe. I didn't know you'd arrived in Paris. Have you started your new job?" The day she met him at church two months earlier he claimed to be starting his job in two weeks. For some reason he hadn't returned to the church, and she'd guessed she wouldn't see him again.

"I feel embarrassed. I started over a month ago, but I've been so *débordé*—how do you say, "swamped"?"

Nikki laughed. "Yes, swamped. I guess they teach you that in advanced English."

"My new job is busy, and there's so much to learn. I haven't even made time to come back to the church. Can I walk with you? I'll carry this." Before Nikki could protest, he'd slipped the heavy bag of cheese and produce from her arm.

"Where did you find an apartment?" she asked him. "I think you were looking for one the last time I saw you." Nikki fell into step beside him, aware of his height overshadowing hers.

"It took me a while, but I have a small flat over in the twelfth. I like that district. It's very green. We have a nice park and walking paths. How about you? I guess you have stayed busy with your new job too?"

She hurried to keep step with his long stride, pleased to have run into him again. "Yes, it's really busy. And I try to see exhibits or other sites in Paris when I have time."

Philippe shook his head and frowned. "I haven't had time to do any of that, but I think it will change soon. Have you done anything interesting lately?"

Nikki searched her mind. "Have you heard of Nuit Blanche? Once a year in early October lots of museums and temporary outside exhibits are open all night. I'd heard about it but couldn't find anyone to go with me, so I went alone." It had been the perfect candidate for the Daring Things Notebook since she'd never have dreamed of going alone six months earlier. "The only hard thing was when the métro stopped running and I had to walk for an hour to get home."

Philippe's eyes rounded with alarm. "Nikki, you should be very careful. It is unsafe, not to mention unpleasant to be stuck with no métro in the middle of the night."

When they reached Nikki's apartment she said, "Here's where I live. Thank you for carrying my bag. It was nice to see you again."

Philippe gave her the canvas bag but didn't move, his eyes fixed on her. "Nikki, if you're free later this evening, may I take you to dinner?"

She smiled with surprise. "Oh, yes, that would be nice. We could meet in a couple of hours if you don't live too far."

"That's perfect. It's direct on the line nine. I'll be waiting right here at seven-thirty, okay? I have a special place to take you."

Nikki waved goodbye to him and punched the code in the front door to her building. The day she'd met Philippe, she'd found him attractive, with laughing eyes and tousled blond hair. She'd wondered if she'd see him again, then gave up hope.

She checked her mailbox and waved to Madame Noiret. As the tiny elevator rose, she smiled in anticipation of her evening with Philippe.

After putting the cheese into the tiny half refrigerator, Nikki arranged her teaching materials into a carefully labeled folder. That day at school Nikki had introduced a new activity, which had been so popular with the students, she decided to try it again in a few weeks. In two weeks, Elaine would be bringing her some Thanksgiving decorations, for a lesson she planned to do around the holiday the French had only heard about but didn't practice.

Nikki glanced at her watch. She had just over an hour and a half before her appointment with Philippe. She opened her computer and Mike's name caught her eye. After her last conversation with him, his words chugged through her mind over and over like a train on a circular track. They had a lot to talk about, he'd said. What else could he be referring to, except their romantic relationship? That is, if there was one. It didn't seem as though he'd closed the subject, yet he didn't seem eager to discuss it either. And he wanted to take a trip with her. *That* didn't sound platonic. Was she complicating her life by going out with Philippe? Yet Mike hadn't declared himself. For all she knew, he was still aiming for pure friendship, nothing more.

The inbox held a note from Elaine asking about the weather so that she could begin packing, and a recipe that her mother had promised, apologizing because it required an oven much larger than Nikki's. She glanced over her shoulder at her dwarf-sized oven.

Nikki clicked on Mike's email, which she'd saved for last. It was brief. "Hi, Nick, do you have a camera on your computer? Can we Skype either tomorrow or the next night? Big screen is better than the phone. Mike."

She reread the message as a wave of warmth flowed through her. Was it a good idea to see his face? A month or so ago, she wouldn't have been ready. Was she now?

In her return message she wrote, "Hi Mike, let's Skype on Thursday at nine o'clock, my time." In two days, she'd see him for the first time in ten months. She hoped she'd be ready.

But for tonight, she'd focus on Philippe.

# Chapter Nineteen

"Do you have a few minutes before your tutoring session, Nicole?" Anne-Laure glanced up from her desk at Nikki, who was erasing the chalkboard. "I'd like to talk to you about something." The noisy chatter faded to a peaceful silence as the students left the room, except for Berangère, who awaited Nikki for extra tutoring.

She turned expectantly toward her supervisor, hoping there would be no critique or reprimand from her.

Anne-Laure leaned back in her chair, more relaxed than Nikki had seen her all year. "Nicole, I wanted to let you know of an opportunity that may interest you. English is very important in the corporate world, and there's a lot of demand for teachers. I know of a company in need of English teachers to go into companies to teach the employees. If you are interested in a position like this after your year with us, I'd be happy to recommend you. You'd have a better salary and professional working conditions."

Nikki sank down on a chair alongside Anne-Laure's desk. "What a surprise and an honor. Thank you for your willingness to recommend me."

Anne-Laure smiled, her almond eyes engaging Nikki's. "I've been happy with your work and I'm sure you'd do a good job in a French company."

"I don't know what to say. I'd have to think about it, of course, and decide whether I want to stay in Paris longer after this year."

"I'll give you the information and you can let me know what you decide about the reference."

After Nikki's tutoring session with Berangère, she walked home instead of taking the métro. Her mind was spinning as she considered the prospect of staying in Paris another year. She could get a bigger apartment, have a better salary, and live like a young urban professional, instead of scraping centimes together at the end of each month. She'd done reasonably well with her limited salary, but it would be nice to be able to enjoy more of what Paris offered.

If she stayed, she could be more involved in her church and with her new friends. She could see more countries of Europe. And she'd have the chance to get to know Philippe better. Anne-Laure's statement about the high demand for English teachers in France didn't surprise Nikki. She'd heard the same thing elsewhere. That being the case, she could stay in Paris as long as she wanted, another year, or even longer.

In another year, she'd have ample time to get over Mike.

Two days earlier she'd spent a delightful evening with Philippe. They'd talked easily for hours, discovering several things they had in common. She felt drawn and attracted to him, as different as he was from Mike. His wavy blond bangs nearly touched his mischievous green eyes, contrasting with Mike's dark hair and eyes.

Maybe that was an advantage. With time, she might fall in love again. Was this her golden chance to stay in Paris another year, and fully develop her new self, her new life? A thrill of excitement shimmered through her.

Her phone rang. "*Salut, Aurélie. Tu vas bien?*" She'd begun speaking only in French with Aurélie. It had been awkward at first, but became easier, like breaking in new shoes. She wouldn't tell her just yet about the job opportunity, since her friend would hardly be objective. Besides that, Nikki needed time to process the enormity of it herself.

After they'd caught up on the news, she said, "Aurelie, I've met someone. A Frenchman named Philippe. He's originally from Alsace. I met him two months ago at church, but then ran into him again this week." Before her phrase was complete, her friend had already squealed a response.

"*C'est super*! Let me know how it goes. I hope I can meet him sometime."

"We can double date one day soon. I'll keep you posted."

"Are you still in touch with Mike? How is that going?"

"We've been talking by phone but tonight, I have a Skype appointment with him for the first time. He sounds different on the phone now, like he's considering becoming interested." She laughed. "One day he might make up his mind."

At Aurelie's laughter, Nikki felt a stab of guilt. She shouldn't criticize Mike to her friend, even if he was the source of never-ending confusion. It would likely end one day, and a bit of confusion was better than nothing. Maybe Philippe would change her perspective and whisk away any need to think about Mike anymore. One day they'd laugh together about how infatuated she'd been with Mike all her life, how childish. One day.

ೞ   ೞ   ೞ

Everything was going wrong. Frank's sigh was belly deep as he steered his Mercedes toward his favored shortcut through back roads. An unusual amount of traffic brought him to a standstill. Flipping on the radio, he learned the cause. An eighteen-wheeler that had jackknifed, causing a twenty-car pileup. Many vehicles had escaped the blockade by flooding into back roads, clogging them for miles. It would be a long ride home. Just what he needed, adding to his load of worries.

He'd kept his medical appointment a secret from Marie. No need to worry her. Just the mention of chest pains and she'd probably become hysterical. Not that they talked very much anymore. He felt a stab inside. He'd neglected the relationship for a few years as the business had grown, but he thought she'd understood. His increased success benefited her, after all.

But he missed her.

The recent drop in car sales was disconcerting. Dark possibilities invaded his thoughts when he awoke during the night, delaying falling back to sleep. Maybe that's why the chest pains had started in the first place.

The car rolled forward, inches at a time. Frank sighed with relief when it seemed the bottleneck broke, and he sped up to twenty miles per hour. Then he came again to a full stop, red taillights inflaming the bleak October dusk.

He missed Nikki. Sometimes the ache inside gripped him without mercy. Over the summer, he'd worried about her daily, especially when she didn't keep in touch for two or three weeks at a time, other than a brief email. Seems she was sowing all the wild oats she'd never dreamed of in her previous twenty-five years. He hoped she was being wise. She was out of his reach now. If only she were coming at Christmas, he'd have something to look forward to.

Let Nikki grow up, Mike had said. Had Frank smothered her? Had he overreacted in his effort to protect her from Mike? A slab of regret lay deep in his stomach ever since his terse conversation with him a month earlier. Why had he always treated Mike like a reprobate, as though his teenage indiscretion had been an unforgivable sin? Even before that, he'd ignored Mike for the most part. Yet, as Mike himself had said, Frank could have been like a fatherly or at least brotherly influence during those difficult years. Especially given his loss. Why hadn't he?

Perhaps his very presence triggered Frank's own painful memories of loss.

He'd been unreasonably nasty to Mike at the beginning of their phone call. Frank never knew Mike even wanted a relationship with him. Strangely, the thought touched him. They had muddled through some kind of understanding by the end of the conversation. A bit of weight had fallen away from his conscience, but he knew much more needed to be said. He was uneasy with emotional things, like apologies and explanations. When he thought about Mike, shame sent uncomfortable pricks into his chest, not unlike the pains he'd been having.

His thoughts returned to Marie, layering on added guilt. Marie was his wife, but he'd let Nikki be his joy all these years. His sweet little girl, who took so much after his mother. Marie had understood, never acted jealous. Though Marie deserved more, he knew. But lately she'd been finding her nerve and her voice, and he wasn't sure how to handle that.

If he hadn't let this chasm develop, he could talk to Marie about his pressures. He could try to talk to her more, share with her like he used to so long ago. It might be tough to get started after all these years. Maybe with a small step. . .

Frank caught his breath as an invisible fist seemed to grab his chest. He shook his head. His health, his marriage, Nikki, Mike, the business. What else? Oh, and he'd had a blowout with Danny just the other day on the phone. Danny had called him an insufferable dictator. His own son had called him a dictator! These relationship problems were hurtling at him from all directions. No wonder he was having chest pains.

ᘓ   ᘓ   ᘓ

At nine o'clock that evening, Nikki typed her password into the computer and wrote, "Are you there?—Nikki." Her heart pounded. She hoped she was prepared to see Mike's face for the first time in months.

He responded, "I'll be ready in about five minutes. Just finishing up a meeting."

With annoyance, she noticed she was perspiring. She ran to the bathroom mirror to check her face and hair. A bit of loose powder would get rid of her tired, shiny look, though she didn't want him to think she'd fixed herself up for the call. When she slipped back into the chair, she caught her breath. His face already filled the screen.

Something clutched inside as she permitted her eyes to roam around his face, since he wasn't yet looking at the screen. He was wearing a short-sleeved dark gray polo shirt that stretched across his broad shoulders. Several dark chest hairs peered above the top button. A spark of heat fanned through her chest.

"There you are." He gave her a welcoming grin. "I don't know why I didn't think about this before. It's free, too. No more worries about the cost of phone calls."

She smiled back at the screen. "It's a great idea. I have the app on my phone, but prefer the larger screen. I'm behind the times. Most of my friends have used it for years, or some other platform."

He smiled and stared at the screen less discreetly than she had done, while a pregnant silence hung between them. In the background florescent office lights glared. "I'm just enjoying looking at you," he said lazily. "It's been too long, Nikki. You look great. Paris seems to agree with you."

Nikki leaned back in the dining room chair, wishing she'd changed out of her shapeless sweatshirt. "I probably look tired. You haven't changed at all. I know I always say that, but you don't ever change."

His face widened into a smile, and he shook his head. "Yes ma'am, I do. I even have a few gray hairs, which you probably can't see. I think I've changed on the inside in some ways, which I'll be happy to tell you about some time."

Was that an invitation she was meant to pursue? "Whenever you want." She'd lob that ball into *his* court.

"Some time," he repeated. "How is the teaching going? Are you adjusted to everything now?" He leaned forward on his elbows and his face approached the screen.

Back onto safe ground. "I really enjoy it," she said. "Teenagers are similar all over the world. You know, they listen to the same music, wear the same kinds of clothes that my students did back in Greenbrier. They're pretty cute."

"I love that about you, your love for the kids. Not everyone can relate to teenagers, but you always have. You get where they're at, and they sense it."

"Thanks for saying that." His words touched her. "I guess I'm meant to be there to walk with them through that piece of their lives. I feel like I can give them something, friendship, understanding, a bit of strictness when they need it. I'm only starting with these kids, but I feel acceptance from them, maybe even a little fascination."

Mike laughed. "You're their American specimen. You can give them the low-down on everything they've always wondered about America."

"And boy, do they ask. I don't even know all the musicians they listen to, but they think it's cool that I'm from New York. It's not as though I lived right in Times Square." A warm layer of friendship slid over her previous jitters. "Oh, guess what? Elaine is coming in two weeks."

"That's great. I know you've missed her."

"It'll be so much fun to show her around Paris."

"You'll have a great time together. What are your plans for Christmas?"

"Well, for the first time in my life, I'm not going to be with my family. I'm actually looking forward to staying right here. I'll have Christmas dinner with Aurélie and her parents, but otherwise I'm going to relax and catch up with friends if anyone is still around."

"No trips, then. That should be relaxing." Was there a strange undercurrent in his words? Nikki couldn't put her finger on it. Maybe he was simply surprised that she wasn't going to travel during her Christmas break.

"And I guess you won't be going back to New York, since you went last year," she said.

"No, not this year. Especially not with you gone." A small smile crept onto his lips. "Nothing could match last Christmas, kissing you under the moonlight."

Nikki's face heated as she struggled to find words. "I, uh, still don't know what to make of last Christmas."

"Don't worry, it's coming," was all he said. Then, "Is that a new necklace you're wearing? What happened to the Treasure of Saint Helen?"

She rubbed her temples in exasperation at his abrupt change of topic. "Yes, it is. I never really liked Helen's necklace, but I didn't realize it." She shrugged. "I think I did it for my dad. It meant a lot to him, but then I decided it was time to wear something *I* liked."

"Good for you." He looked silently at Nikki for a moment. "Can you do me a favor? Just for a few seconds, can you lean closer to the screen? That way, I can see your eyes better. Then I'll have to go."

Nikki complied, but wondered if he'd see the undiminished love which she'd tried for months to extinguish, shining through her eyes. She heard him murmur, "Nikki, it's so good to see your eyes. Your beautiful eyes. I've missed them."

She looked down, smiling bashfully. "Okay. Your turn, before you go." Nikki looked at him expectantly with a half grin. He leaned forward and looked into the camera, as she had done. His direct gaze almost took her breath away. She had to stop herself from reaching up to touch the computer screen. His dark eyes seemed to stare into her soul, though she knew he saw only the camera.

He dropped his gaze and said, "I'm sorry our visit is so short today. I have yet another deadline. Keeps me on my toes, though. Can we do this again soon?"

Nikki just nodded. "Sure. Bye, Mike."

"Good-night."

After the screen went blank, Nikki stared into the empty room. He'd done it *again*. Dropped little hints, began conversations he was unwilling to finish. Made her go crazy. Was he just teasing her, still unable to commit to a real emotion? Annoyance but also enchantment. It was too soon to see him. She needed more time to attach to Philippe, so she'd have immunity to Mike's face.

Nikki dropped her head down onto her crossed arms. In the past ten months, after all of her efforts to erase or at least dilute him from her mind, even after crossing the globe. . .she hadn't gotten over Mike Branagan one drop.

# Chapter Twenty

Nikki's eyes filled up when she saw Elaine's familiar face through the doorway of baggage claim at the Charles De Gaulle Airport. They leaped into a hug and clung to each other tightly for several seconds.

She linked her arm into Elaine's. "How was your flight? We have so much to see and do and talk about." They started to chatter as they headed through the double glass doors toward the commuter train that would take them into the center of Paris. They continued all the way to Nikki's stop, almost missing it.

"Just four months ago, I was terrified here in a foreign country." Nikki shifted Elaine's carry-on to her other shoulder. They reached her apartment building. "And now I feel like the experienced expat, ready to show you around."

Elaine giggled. "It's just so good to see you, no matter what we do. Is this your apartment?" Elaine looked straight up at the regal stone building, shadowing her eyes with one hand.

"This is it. The palace. Wait till you see the size. It's kind of like my room at our apartment, only with a kitchen stuck on one side."

"Don't tell me. I want to see it for myself." They could barely wheel Elaine's suitcase into the elevator. "Ooh, this elevator is really small. Is it safe?"

"I had the same thought when I moved in. It's no good for moving furniture, but you can stack three people back-to-back. It was put in after the building was here, so they didn't have much space to work with." The elevator lurched, and the bell rang as they arrived at the third floor. Metal doors squealed open.

An hour and a half later, Nikki and Elaine were comfortably settled in a crêpe restaurant near Rue Sébastien, looking out at the gray early November sky from a cozy dining room. "You *have* to have crêpes in France," Nikki said. "Might as well experience this delicacy on your very first day."

Her gaze panned over Elaine. There right across from her, after almost six months, was her best friend. Elaine looked the same as always, her fluffy blond hair curling in wisps around her fair complexion.

Nikki slid her chair closer to the table. "So, tell me about Eric. Anything new since the last time we talked?" She giggled. "I get right to the heart of things, don't I?"

Elaine's eyes crinkled with laughter and her face pinkened. "I'd say things are moving along well. *Very* well. I need to tell you, there's a possibility you won't have a roommate when you get back to New York."

Nikki's eyebrows lifted. "Really?"

Elaine smiled coyly. "I don't want to predict anything too soon, but it's possible by next spring we'll be engaged."

"Please don't get married until I'm back in the States."

"Of course not." Elaine squeezed Nikki's hand.

A bearded waiter in a long, starched apron appeared at their table to take their order. "I'll translate for you," Nikki told her. Elaine looked duly impressed as Nikki explained in French what they both wanted.

She turned back to Elaine. "I ordered us some cider, which is a traditional drink to go with crêpes. It's more like sweet beer than our apple cider, though, so don't be surprised by the taste."

"Food and drink are all part of the experience."

Nikki placed her elbows on the edge of the table and leaned forward. "Elaine, I need to tell you something. I've decided not to go back to New York once this school year ends." She smiled at Elaine's look of surprise. "I can't go back to Greenbrier. I'll start sending resumes in the spring for bigger cities and see where I end up." The previous week she'd gotten an email greeting from her department head back in Greenbrier. When she thought about going back to teach in the same school in the same town, she knew she just couldn't. "That is, if I don't stay here for another year."

Elaine's eyes widened and her mouth dropped open. "What? You may stay in Paris? Are they extending your position?"

"I could stay at my school another year if I wanted to, but there's another position available. I can teach English to professional people in big companies. It would be a real job with a real salary. I could stay in France for. . . well, for years if I want."

"Oh, Nikki." Elaine fell silent as she considered Nikki's words. Her gaze rose to Nikki's. "Could you do it? I mean, you were so afraid of coming to France, and now you're talking about not leaving."

"I know." Nikki's voice was quiet. "I've changed so much in just a few months. Maybe I'll stay one more year, and then just take it a year at a time after that. My supervisor only recently told me about this opportunity. I'm still thinking and praying about it. You're the first person I've told."

"Would you come back for visits?"

"Of course. Our friendship won't ever change, Elaine. For sure, I'd come back to see you and my family. I haven't decided yet. But if I don't stay in France, I'll definitely go somewhere else."

Elaine seemed to recover herself. "I completely understand your desire to change scenery. And Paris is so exciting and beautiful. I've only been with you for a couple of hours, and it seems like you've really adapted here. After this year, you'll need something more cosmopolitan than Greenbrier."

Nikki squeezed Elaine's wrist. "I knew you'd understand. I'm ready to move on. I told you on the phone about Philippe. He's really sweet and funny, and we have a good time together. Believe it or not, he thinks I'm adventurous."

Nikki laughed at the impression she must have given him. If only he'd seen her before. "Staying another year would give me a chance to see where that relationship will go."

Over the last two weeks, she and Philippe had spent hours on the phone, or walking under autumn leaves, talking and laughing together. She planned to visit him at his parents' home in Colmar the following weekend.

The waiter placed colorful ceramic plates in front of them. Crispy wafer-thin crepes steamed from the plate, appetizing fillings scenting the air.

"I thought crêpes were rolled up like a cigar." Elaine looked down at her artfully arranged crêpe folded in a square. Melted cheese and sausage peered out from the steaming hole in the middle. "Which one did you get?"

"Mushroom and spinach with cheese." Nikki blew on the hot cheese mixture.

"I'll have to try one of those next time." Elaine gently carved the crispy edges of her crepe and took a bite. "Mmm."

As they ate, Elaine asked, "Anything new on the Mike scene since we last talked about him?"

Nikki frowned. "That's always a hard question. As of recently, he seems interested without really saying so. I wonder if he's waiting until we can see each other again to declare himself." One way or the other. Although there were positive signs. "We've started to Skype, and it's almost like being together. I'd love to ask him directly what his thoughts are, but I don't dare, after what happened last year."

Elaine chewed thoughtfully on her crêpe. She took a hesitant sip of cider. "I guess he doesn't know you're in a relationship. But he hasn't seen you in a while, so maybe that's why he hesitates to dive in."

"I don't blame him since we only saw each other for five days nearly a year ago. But I'm the one in limbo. I'm getting tired of it. I guess that's why I was open to Philippe."

"Do you think you'll give up on Mike, or is it still a contest between Mike and Philippe?"

Nikki was silent and slowly smiled.

Elaine laughed aloud. "I guess that answers my question."

CR   CR   CR

Marie sat alone at her steering wheel. She watched dully as each car in the insurance company parking lot roared to life and its owner drove away. Only when her car was the only one left in the expanse of asphalt did two hot tears tumble onto her cheeks. Others followed until a sobbing torrent shook her shoulders, her entire being.

What had she been thinking? Had she naively thought nothing would happen when Doug invited her for lunch to see his new house? Or had she known what was on his mind, on both their minds, what had been building between them for months? Had they been taken by surprise? Or had they just pretended to be blindsided by the sudden passion that had overtaken them? She was truly stupid. Naïve and stupid. Or lonely. She wasn't sure which. What would she do now?

Marie had already told Doug this could *not* happen again. She even thought of resigning from the company, just to make sure. Should she tell Frank, even though it was just one slip? Marie shuddered and a new flood of tears began. How could she live with the guilt? Lately, she would describe their marriage as dull but stable. Could anyone blame her for being resentful? And lonely?

Frank was a human body that ate at the table, lumbered around the house, and cloistered himself in his office. She didn't have a husband.

Yet, she did. And she had to tell him about Doug, sooner or later.

She didn't want to leave Frank for Doug. She wasn't in love with Doug and didn't picture a future with him. What if Frank didn't forgive her? Tears pulsed again from her tired eyes. What would she do? *What would she do?*

Marie clenched her fists on either side of her head as she leaned forward onto the steering wheel, wretched with regret. An unbearably heavy weight pressed down inside her. She looked up just as three crisp November leaves danced across the windshield.

November. She couldn't possibly tell Frank before Christmas. The Christmas holidays would be difficult enough without Nikki. She couldn't add this burden. Not for Frank and not for herself. She'd tell him after Christmas. And try to live with herself between now and then.

ભ  ભ  ભ

Stone farmhouses dotted the gentle green hills as the French countryside sped by. Nikki leaned toward the window, frosted with vapor, trying to glimpse each village and white church spire, so different from Paris. Travelers filled every seat of the TGV high-speed train, most likely getting away for the Toussaint holiday.

An open book lay on Nikki's lap, but she spent most of the two-hour trip gazing at the scenery and kneading through the basket of thoughts crowding her brain.

The week before, she and Elaine had scurried across Paris, chatting for hours in cafés or brasseries. They visited Notre Dame, Montmartre, the Eiffel Tower, the Seine River banks, and many lesser-known corners of ancient charm Nikki had discovered since her arrival.

One day, they impulsively got the same trendy French haircut, did some clothes shopping, and finished the afternoon with luscious hot chocolate from Angelina's on the Rue de Rivoli. On Sunday, Nikki took Elaine to her little French church. Despite being a tiny congregation in a huge, indifferent city, the pure, fervent spirit charmed Elaine.

Each night they fell asleep exhausted, after talking until late hours. Nikki told Elaine about her spiritual turning point in Germany, when God became more of a friend and constant companion than a distant idea. They prayed together for their futures, and for Nikki's French friends, who still stood at a distance from faith.

Nikki's throat throbbed with emotion as she remembered their goodbye at the airport. "I'll never forget this week. It's been fabulous." Despite Elaine's enthusiastic tone, sadness had lingered in her eyes as she stood with Nikki before boarding.

Pain clutched Nikki's throat, much like the one she'd felt months earlier as they'd said goodbye in New York. "This goodbye thing is always so hard." Tears filled her eyes and traced a path down her cheeks. "I'm going to miss you. It'll be our last time. . ."

Elaine threw her arms around Nikki's shoulders and squeezed her tightly. "No, Nikki. It won't be the last time. We might not be roommates anymore, but we'll *always* be best friends. We may even live on different sides of the country, or world. One day, we'll both be married, but we'll always be close. I'm sure of it. Some things are that strong."

Nikki had smiled through her tears. "What was it we used to say back in Greenbrier? Men come and go, but girlfriends are forever."

Several new tears slipped down her cheeks, reflecting back through the train window. The next time she saw Elaine might be just before her wedding. Some things in their friendship would never be the same.

Nikki glanced at her watch. Her first stop was Strasbourg, near the German border. She'd board another train to Colmar, where she'd spend the weekend with Philippe and his parents.

Was his invitation simply a desire to see her over the holiday? It seemed too soon to meet his parents, despite the many hours she'd spent with Philippe over the last three weeks. Often, she imagined herself staying in Paris and getting to know him gradually over the coming year. Were his thoughts moving much more quickly than hers? An uncomfortable twinge told her they were.

It didn't help that she was talking to—and seeing—Mike almost every week, sometimes more often. He'd given her no concrete reason to think things had changed, so she felt justified in continuing to date Philippe. However, every time she hung up with Mike, her confusion deepened.

A question flitted frequently through her mind, though she brushed it off like an insect, as if afraid it would sting. She had to stare it bravely in the face. What if she *did* fall in love with Philippe? Was she prepared to stay in France permanently if she married him? To become French, raise French children, take an international flight to go see her parents? Was she ready for that?

Nikki swallowed hard. She wasn't ready yet, but maybe sometime next year it might seem normal. Might seem a natural decision, an exciting one. At least she didn't have to decide right away.

She looked again at her watch. The next task was to meet Philippe's parents and spend the weekend in Colmar. Not a lifetime, just a weekend.

# Chapter Twenty-One

Philippe's blond head was visible above the milling throng on the train platform in Colmar. He caught sight of Nikki through the train window and waved. A grin stretched across his handsome face. As she stepped off the metal steps onto the platform, he was right beside her. He whisked her suitcase from her with one hand and threw his free arm around her shoulder for a hug and a kiss on both cheeks.

"Chérie, you're here. My dad suggested coming to the train to meet you, but my mom talked him out of it." He winked and continued chattering as he led her through clusters of passengers out of the station. He seemed more talkative than he had in Paris, but was perhaps excited to see her on his home turf. "You must be hungry. My mom made some snacks for us, and we'll have dinner a bit after that. Did you have a good trip?"

"Yes, it was quick. I enjoy train travel." Nikki dodged several people who hurried to the platform. "The scenery is beautiful here in the east. Well, all of France is beautiful, but this is my first time in Alsace. I saw rolling hills and vineyards everywhere."

He grinned down at her. "You'll love Colmar. We'll go into the Old Town tomorrow and visit everything. You'll see the German influence, but the mixture is unique to this area, neither fully German nor fully French."

Philippe's Renault wound through picturesque villages and continued on a country road. Nikki leaned toward the window, taking in the fresh sights, so spread out, so green compared to the big city.

Finally, he pulled into a driveway in front of a long white fence that stretched out as far as Nikki could see. Behind the fence sat an imposing stone house, surrounded by fields and forests. An ancient-looking stone stable big enough for a dozen horses flanked the left side of the property near a riding ring, linked to more pastures. Philippe had rarely talked about his childhood home. His family appeared to be quite wealthy.

As they entered the spacious foyer, Nikki saw a serene blend of beige and burgundy brocade curtains and marble flooring. A marble table adorned with a vase of fresh chrysanthemums dominated the entrance. "Your parents have a beautiful home. Is your mother an interior designer?"

Philippe laughed. "I'm sure she'd take that as a high compliment. She has a wonderful touch with colors and décor. It's her hobby."

"You must be Nicole." The warm greeting echoed in the hall first. Nikki looked up and saw a tall woman with a stylish cut of graying hair emerge from another room and come toward her. Following close behind her was a slightly shorter, mustached man with glasses and a full head of graying blond hair.

Philippe's mother enfolded Nikki and planted a kiss on each cheek. "I am Françoise, and this is my husband, Frédéric. We are so happy to meet you. Philippe has told us about you."

Nikki couldn't help but wonder what Philippe had told them. She returned the welcoming smiles and responded in French.

"He has told me about you also. Thank you for inviting me to your lovely home."

"Mother, I'll show Nikki to her room then we'll be right back."

"The pink guest room, Philippe. The green one is messy with my sewing projects for the moment."

They'd just finished a light snack when Françoise served a significant dinner around a massive mahogany table in a formal dining room. Nikki's head was already throbbing with the unaccustomed quantity of rapid-fire French. While in Paris with Philippe, they usually spoke in English together.

"Your French is quite good, as Philippe said." Françoise slid a bowl of green beans across the table. "That's why I haven't spoken more slowly."

"Mother, maybe you should," Philippe said and winked at Nikki.

"I think I'm doing okay, though it's a bit more than I'm used to." Nikki tilted her head toward Philippe with an apologetic half-smile. And the weekend was only beginning. She'd have to pace herself.

"I told you both how daring Nikki is, first by coming all the way to France for the year. She teaches English at the high school. She enjoys a good challenge. That's an inspiration to me." Philippe passed a bowl of browned potatoes with parsley. Daring? As if it were natural for Nikki, as if she'd been running toward adventure all her life. She almost laughed.

Frédéric finally spoke up. "Philippe has also told us that you're a Christian. We're very glad he's met a Christian girl. We raised him in the church and in the faith, and he has stuck with it."

Nikki nodded and smiled. She seemed to have their complete approval so far. It might be nice to have Christian parents-in-law. She caught herself and pushed away the thought. No need to burden the weekend with expectation too early.

After dinner, Philippe took Nikki's arm and led her to a cozy den, just as she was about to offer to help Françoise with the dishes. He sat close to her on the couch in front of a sputtering fireplace with a massive stone mantle. Firelight reflected off the wood paneling and cast dancing shadows on the picture frames.

Philippe tucked Nikki's hand into his and snuggled against her shoulder as they gazed into the fireplace. "I really missed you this week, Nikki. I know we've gone a week before without seeing each other, but it seemed long this time. I'm so glad you were able to see Elaine."

"I'm happy you weren't jealous." Nikki chuckled. He'd have no reason to be.

"No, Chérie. Maybe I'll meet her one day in the States."

Nikki's brow furrowed. At least Philippe couldn't see her face. What should she make of his statement? Was he assuming they'd stay together and be married in the United States, or that they'd even move there together?

"Would you like to visit the States one day?" she ventured, knowing he might misinterpret her question.

"Sure, one day. I've always wanted to go on a trip there, but I'd love to do it with you."

Nikki fell silent. For several moments, neither one spoke as Philippe rubbed her hand with his thumb. Then he turned to her and stared unblinking into her eyes. He leaned toward her and gently tipped her chin upward to kiss her. His lips moved tentatively at first, then more boldly. Nikki encircled his neck with her arms, enjoying his kiss while trying not to compare him with Mike. As if to force Mike from her mind, she pulled closer to Philippe, which made him increase his ardor. "Oh, Nikki. Mon amour," he whispered against her ear.

My love? What did he mean? It had been a perfect evening. *Don't ruin the moment with useless questions.* She wouldn't. She relaxed into him and let him envelop her in his arms.

Nikki awoke abruptly and threw off the heavy down comforter. It took a moment to remember she was in the guest room at Philippe's parents' home.

She suffocated with so many layers weighing down on her. Without moving, she stared at the moonlight painting pale streaks on the thick carpet and spilling onto the bedclothes. The house was silent, except for ticking from the grandfather clock in the hall.

What was wrong with her? Philippe was being romantic and charming. He seemed increasingly committed to her. His parents were wonderful. It was clear they'd accepted her easily, especially since she was a Christian. It might even outweigh her other flaws, which they'd discover in time.

Was it simply going too fast, or was something else amiss? She must be too difficult to please, too idealistic. What did she want?

She'd grown in the last several months, but needed to grow up in the romantic realm as well. It was as though she was trying to think of ways to sabotage her perfect weekend.

Nikki rolled over with an exasperated sigh. She'd do everything to enjoy her time, enjoy Philippe, and be open to this relationship and its future possibilities, whatever they might be. She had a good shot at loving again. Philippe was a good man, handsome, a strong Christian, and seemed to love her. This might be her chance.

She forced herself to relax, and sometime later fell back to sleep.

ᘓ  ᘓ  ᘓ

Nikki glanced at her watch, then back at the row of heads in front of her. The supermarket checkout line seemed at a standstill. A customer had some kind of hang-up with pricing. Her grocery basket became heavy in her arms. If the grocery line didn't move soon, she wouldn't have enough time to make a light dinner before Philippe came over at six-thirty.

She knew he wouldn't care if dinner wasn't ready when he got there. It was *her* agitation gnawing at her. In fact, that tension had trailed around with her all day. Though it had shadowed her for the last few days, it arrived full-blown after she woke up from a dream in the early hours of the morning.

In the dream, she'd stood at the rail of a large ship that was pulling away from the American shoreline. Standing on the dock were her parents, her brother and sister, Elaine, and several of her friends. Even college acquaintances she hadn't thought about in years were there in the crowd. Everyone waved and wept. She also wept uncontrollably, sobbing and clutching the rail as the ship slowly eased into motion. She'd awakened with a jolt and a cool sweat, still gripped by the grief she'd felt in the dream.

The memory of grief had haunted her throughout the day. What did the dream mean? Was it a symbol of her previous dependence on her family? Or was she simply unprepared for the idea of staying in France, whether to pursue a job, become more serious about Philippe, or both? She'd gotten the reference from Anne-Laure for the teaching job, but hadn't sent her résumé yet. Adding further anxiety, Philippe told her the previous day he wanted to talk to her about something important. She could guess what it was.

In the month that had passed since she'd visited his family, they'd seen each other often and had fallen into the routine of a serious couple. She hadn't known how to slow things down, or if she should, and even her feeble attempts to do so met with his resistance.

Nikki managed to calm her emotions enough to make broiled salmon with rice and a small salad by the time Philippe arrived. When he thrust a bouquet of roses into her hands, she feigned delight and tried not to think about their significance. He'd dressed carefully and looked more handsome than she'd ever seen him. Over dinner, he talked about his day, a train strike that was predicted, and Christmas festivities coming up in the next weeks. She tried to mask her tension throughout the meal, but wondered if he sensed it, anyway.

Afterwards, she made him a demitasse of black coffee and settled next to him on the couch, expectantly.

He turned to her and grasped both of her hands, locking his gaze into hers. "Nikki, you might have predicted what I'm about to say. When I met you that day last summer, there was an immediate spark. I don't know if you felt it too. With time, it's only been confirmed to me that we are meant to be together."

She drew back slightly and pressed her lips together, juggling words in her mind for an adequate response. "Philippe, I like you a lot, and I've enjoyed getting to know you. But it's only been two months. Can't we just keep spending time together without guessing or planning what will happen next?"

He frowned. "I guess we could do that. But we shouldn't deny what's happening right in front of us, should we? Why drag it out if we know?"

"I'm not sure *I'd* be ready for it. Maybe I could be, eventually, but I feel like you're rushing me. I want to continue like we have been, but for a while longer." She paused and looked at the scowl painted across his face. She should wait for his full response before bringing up the question that had hung like lead in her mind for a month. At his silence, she spoke softly. "And there's another thing, Philippe." She tightened her lips. "I'm not sure you know the real me yet."

His head jerked up. He eyed her warily.

"You think I'm adventurous. Let me tell you something. I went to college a few hours from my parents and came home for weekends about twice a quarter. After graduation, I got a job a few miles from where I'd grown up, and I visited my parents at least three times a week." Nikki felt her voice trembling slightly, as if confessing a dark secret. "I never did *anything* alone. I was uncomfortable in most situations outside of my habits."

Philippe's eyes widened as he continued to stare at her.

"That's one reason I came to Paris. I knew I needed to change, to grow up, to expand. I was terrified of being alone in a foreign country. All the daring things I do are like medicine for me. I do them because I think it's good for me. But I force myself. It's true that all this has helped me become more confident and braver. I feel more independent now and actually enjoy most of it. But it's still a growing process."

When Nikki stopped speaking, Philippe leaned back against the couch, as if overcome by tension. "I had no idea you were like that," he sputtered. "You come across completely different, and never said otherwise. Why didn't you tell me? You led me to believe—"

"I'm sorry, Philippe. I should have corrected your impression of me sooner. I just thought that with time, you'd get to know me. The real me."

Philippe's gaze had settled on the ceiling, his arms crossed tightly across his chest. Nikki waited for a response. After a moment, he looked back at her. "I don't know what to say. Do I need to start over getting to know you? It's not that being daring is all that important to me. I liked that about you, and I still like you, but I feel I have to go back and start again."

Nikki pulled one knee up and leaned against it. "Maybe that's not such a bad idea. I told you I felt rushed. It's very possible that I could fall in love with you one day, Philippe, but I'm not sure you'll fall in love with the real me."

Philippe's face hardened like a plaster mask.

*Tell, him, Nikki. Tell him the rest.* "And Philippe," she added softly, "The other reason I came to Paris was to get over a broken heart. I was trying to forget someone. I never told you about that."

He turned his head toward her, but his arms remained locked across his chest. "No, all this time you didn't tell me. So, do you still love him?"

Nikki bit her lip. "I'm much better now, um, about that. It doesn't subtract anything I feel for you, Philippe."

Philippe sighed and pulled himself up from the couch. "I wonder what else you haven't told me." He turned away from her and said, "This is a lot to take in. And you might still be in love with this other guy." He stood still for a long moment, then said, "Why don't we take a break for a few weeks? I think I also need some time."

"Okay, if that's what you want." Nikki stood but remained unmoving when Philippe reached for his jacket he'd hung over the back of the couch. Within seconds, he was gone, and she was alone.

Nikki stared at the door that had closed behind him. With a stab that twisted inside, she realized that her childish dependence had driven Philippe away, just as it had Mike. She hung her head, and a heavy weight seemed to descend on her shoulders. She'd tried so hard to change. In fact, she had. A lot. But somehow, it wasn't enough.

She trudged to the table and cleared the dishes as her mind rewound the conversation. She'd expected Philippe to be disappointed, though accepting. She hadn't expected him to walk away. What was she feeling? Sadness, hurt. . . or relief?

As she returned from the sink to wipe the table, her gaze fell on a framed photo of herself and Aurélie in a Swiss hamlet. Their heads were close together and their grins spread wide. Nikki forgot who had taken the photo. She peered at Aurélie's face. Aurélie, her loyal friend. She'd told Nikki not to change on the inside, regardless of how she grew as a person, or how self-assured she became. Essentially, she hadn't changed. She was the same Nikki, though less dependent and fearful. Still growing, still learning. She had more confidence, more faith, more interest in new and exciting situations. Yet at her core, she was still herself, and she was glad. The heaviness lifted and a light peacefulness took its place.

It was enough.

# Chapter Twenty-Two

December arrived with a harsh chill, etching frost crystals on the tall French windows. Nikki kept the curtains closed against the draft and curled herself more deeply into the knit afghan. She reached for a tissue then pulled the entire box into her lap, just as another sneeze exploded. A winter cold had attacked the day before and she'd spent the day at home, napping and catching up on reading.

In her medicated haze, Nikki had almost forgotten Mike was planning to contact her that night. She dreaded him seeing her red nose and puffy eyes, sniffing and sneezing. She hadn't seen Philippe or heard from him in the previous two weeks since their breakup. Was that the end for him? She felt hardly more than a surge of sadness and regret.

As for Mike, their Skype chats continued. The bond of friendship gradually deepened, against her better judgment. Urban events on both sides of the ocean, parades or strikes, festivals, or attitudes about politics, the exchange rate, or Biblical prophecy. . . the range of conversation was wide and seemingly endless. With the notable exception of their relationship. Mike always said he missed her and couldn't wait to see her again. No deeper commitment than that. And there was really no use even saying it, since it would be next summer or next Christmas before they would be in the same city. Would this bland, half-flirtatious non-commitment go on until then?

She knew she must have a high fever when the sight of him failed to stir her more than a flicker. "I'll tell you right off that I'm sick, in case you're wondering if someone hit me in the nose today."

Mike laughed. "Your nose looks fine. A bit red, but cute all the same. Are you feeling bad?"

"Yes, I am. Very bad. I have a fever. I missed work today and probably will tomorrow too. I slept a lot today."

"I'm sorry to hear that. I won't keep you long, then."

Nikki felt a jab of disappointment. "It's okay. I haven't talked to anyone all day. Tell me what's new in your world."

That was an excellent solution, letting him talk about his day, his week, while she quietly rested and listened, occasionally blowing her nose. It sounded like December in San Francisco wasn't as cold and damp as Paris, which was still mild compared to New York.

"I think you'd like it in San Francisco, since you're a city girl now," he told her.

Was he hinting at something? Or was that too much to hope?

"Are you dozing off on me?" he asked with a chuckle.

Nikki's eyes flew open. "No, I'm not. Just resting. I heard everything you said. I like hearing you talk about your life."

His voice softened. "I'm glad we discovered Skype. It makes a big difference being able to see you. I missed you so much this year."

Suddenly Nikki felt irritated. "You did?" Her voice grew sharp. "Why *is* that?"

Mike's eyes widened. "Uh. . . because you're far away?"

"Is it because I *mean* something to you? Or do you just miss your friend, your pal, Nikki? And nothing more? I have the feeling we're never really going to *talk* about our relationship. I just have to make guesses and try to read your mind, with only your innuendos to guide me." She stopped. She'd said too much.

Nikki shut her eyes tightly and rubbed her temples. "I'm sorry, Mike. I'm not feeling well. I'm short-tempered tonight."

"Nikki, you're right." Mike's voice was quiet. He no longer smiled, and his eyes searched hers. "I've been unclear with you. Just—" He hesitated, as if gathering his thoughts. "I want you to know two things. First, that we *will* talk soon. Very soon. I want to. The second thing I want you to know is that I *do* have feelings for you beyond friendship and they are growing. I'm not just toying with you."

She sighed. "Okay. Sounds like you're still not ready. But good old Nikki will always be there, won't she? Unless, of course, someone comes along, like Philippe, for instance. She'll be there waiting until one day. . . she won't. Goodnight, Mike." Nikki clicked the exit button, and the screen went blank.

She took a breath. What an awful way to end a conversation, just when he said he had feelings for her. Was she crazy? But he'd been saying similar things for months. She had friends who heard the phrase, *I'm not ready* year after year. Would she be one of them? Was this better than loving him from afar, as she'd done all her life?

She curled up in her misery, wondering how he would respond to her frustration. What was he waiting for? He offered her clues and promises, but nothing more. Yet they were what she clung to. His feelings were growing, he'd claimed. He seemed to promise one day there *would* be more. And in the meantime, what choice did she have?

It was ten o'clock at night. She had to talk to Elaine. Hopefully, she'd be home from work. Relief flooded Nikki when she heard her friend's voice. "Oh, Elaine, I'm glad you're home. I needed to talk."

"That's perfect timing, Nikki. I got off early today because I was feeling a fever coming on."

"You too? I'm sick right now. I just hung up on Mike. I got so frustrated at his inability to tell me clearly what he's feeling. It hit me all at once, how uncommitted some men can be, or, as with Philippe, too committed. He wanted a relationship, but wasn't willing to take the time to let it develop properly. Sometimes I say to myself, who needs this? I don't need a man! I'm just fine by myself."

Before Nikki finished her tirade, Elaine was laughing.

"Am I rambling?" Nikki asked, then sneezed. "I'm rambling, aren't I?"

Elaine recovered. With a giggle in her voice, she said, "Ranting is more like it. I'm encouraged to see that, to be honest. It's healthy, and you're absolutely right. You do not *need* a man in your life. Especially when they aren't ready for *you*."

Nikki grinned and sank back into the couch cushion. "Yeah, thanks for affirming me. I need to let it all go and live my life, don't I? Maybe that's what God has been saying to me all along. Trust Him and keep moving forward."

"That's all you can do. Take care of your own life. Keep doing what you know you should. And remember you're enough all by yourself, without a man. Of course, when the timing is right, it'll be good. In the meantime, don't worry about it."

"That's always been your philosophy, hasn't it, Elaine? I used to envy your peace. I think I'm about to get some of that myself."

೪ ೪ ೪

Mike frowned at the blank screen. Had he pushed Nikki beyond her patience? She probably thought he was taking her for granted. Well, she'd clearly said it, hadn't she?

Call him a romantic, but he really wanted to tell her in *person* at Christmas. Christmas had become almost symbolic after last year. In fact, for years, the only time he saw Nikki was at Christmas. Once every three years. So, it was fitting that at Christmas he would tell her how much he loved her.

For the past couple months, he'd been nearly bursting to tell Nikki clearly that he was in love with her, and it was increasingly difficult not to do it. He'd nearly told her on the phone that night. Right before she hung up on him. Understandably, she was impatient. But in just two weeks, he'd see her face to face.

Two weeks. A thrill rippled through him.

Knowing he'd see her soon, he'd relied on what she called his *innuendos*, hoping she'd pick up a difference in his attitude. She clearly had little tolerance for indirect communication. Normally, he did as well. That is, when he wasn't completely over his head in emotional quicksand.

He wondered whether her reference to someone named Philippe was merely figurative. Was there a Philippe he had to compete with? Mike hoped her heart still belonged to him. But was he being overconfident? After all, it had been nearly a year since they'd seen each other.

He'd call her a week before his flight to let her know he was coming, so it wouldn't be a total surprise. She could meet him at the airport, or at least be mentally prepared to see him. Maybe she'd forget her frustration when she knew he was coming to Paris to spend Christmas with her.

Paris with Nikki. A slow smile spread across his face.

The day after she'd hung up on him, she'd emailed an apology, though hadn't suggested they talk again.

A week later, Mike emailed her, saying he wanted to Skype that evening. There was no response. At lunch, he tried calling her phone number. Still no answer. Was she still angry? An icy chill swelled through him. What if she'd left town? What if she wouldn't even *be* there when he arrived, since she didn't know he was coming? Although he'd always wanted to see Paris, he didn't relish the idea of spending Christmas there alone.

Mike grimaced, unsure of what to do. Nikki's best friend, Elaine, might know where she was. He waited until six that evening and dialed the number he still remembered.

"Hello, is this Elaine?" he asked tentatively.

"Yes, it is. May I ask who is calling?"

"Um, yes, this is Mike Branagan. Nikki's friend."

"I know who you are," Elaine said coldly. "I'm sure you must know Nikki isn't here."

Mike felt a wintry blast coming from Nikki's best friend— understandable, as he imagined Elaine consoling her during the past year. "I'm trying to reach Nikki, but for several days she hasn't answered her phone or email. I was worried about her and thought you might know if she's okay."

"She's in Spain. I don't think she has email access where she's staying, and she might have turned her phone off."

Mike's heart sank. "She didn't tell me she was traveling again."

"She wasn't planning to." Elaine's tone softened slightly. "A Spanish friend from her church was going home for Christmas and invited her to come along for a few days. Seville, I think. She left the day after her classes ended."

"Do you know when she'll be back in Paris?"

"Yes, she'll be back on December twenty-third. We have a phone date that evening, in fact, so I know she'll be there."

Mike sighed audibly, then added, "I'm so glad she's alright. Thanks for your help."

December twenty-third. He'd arrive in Paris on December twenty-second in the early morning. At least she'd be there the following day and he could finally see her. Of course, he'd have to bounce around Paris alone for a day, but he could handle that. And she'd be totally surprised. He wasn't sure that was a good thing or not, but at this point it couldn't be helped. She'd find out when she saw him.

On impulse, Mike picked up the phone again and tapped Harriet's number.

"What brings me this honor, Mike?" The older lady's warmth seeped through the phone. Mike could hear dishes clanging in the background.

"I wanted you to be the first to know I'm going to Paris for Christmas."

"You rascal!" She hooted with laughter. "That's great news. You go to her and tell her how you feel." He heard her pull away from the phone and yell, "Joe, Mike's going to Paris to see his girl. Yes, he is! Tanya, Jason, Mike's going to Paris!"

*His girl.* Finally, Nikki would be his girl. At least Harriet was deliriously happy. He sure hoped Nikki would be.

# Chapter Twenty-Three

The mob of passengers stalled a few yards from the passport control window. Mike widened his eyes several times, trying to fully awaken while he shuffled in the line. He'd slept poorly on the flight, resting his head alternately on the chilly window and down on the tray table. His frenetic thoughts had bounced all over his skull. He kept wondering if, in the next eleven days, he would succeed in wooing Nikki back in love with him. Either that or he'd reinforce the chain of misunderstandings. During the in-flight movies, he'd prayed. A lot.

"Welcome to France," the uniformed man behind the glass said from a dispassionate face as he stamped Mike's passport. Mike nodded in response. Nikki could explain how to pronounce the courtesy phrases. He knew thank you was *merci*, but hesitated to pronounce it incorrectly. He didn't need someone snickering at his French efforts. Not that day, at any rate.

Baggage was a word he could understand. He stood next to a large carousel waiting for the appearance of his luggage and surveyed the people around him. Several American voices rose above the din, but mostly he heard French mixed with Arabic, Chinese, and languages he couldn't identify. Couples and families or friends waited alongside him as the luggage belt heaved into motion with a groan. Some carried wrapped Christmas presents in paper bags. Likely they were all meeting someone for the holidays, or returning home.

Mike was meeting someone for the holidays too. Someone who didn't know he was there and who had hung up on him the last time they'd spoken.

He retrieved his suitcase. How would he get to Paris from the airport? Penny, his travel agent, has sent a small train ticket, along with his airline ticket. He heard someone speaking in English and matched it with a tall young man with tousled blond hair and a huge backpack. Mike sidled alongside the man. "Excuse me, do you know where I can catch the shuttle to Paris?"

"Sure thing, mate." The young man responded with a wide, white-toothed grin. "We're goin' that way ourselves. Come along, follow us." Mike smiled and followed the friendly blond Australian and his perky surfer-looking friends. They seemed to have gotten plenty of sleep on their flight if their rowdy banter all the way to Paris showed their energy level. It helped him relax and regain his humor.

"Where'r ye headed?" the young man asked Mike, once the train neared the Gare du Nord, in the northern section of Paris.

"My hotel is near Bastille."

"Here, this'll help." The young man pulled a tiny fold-out map from his vest pocket and traced a line with his finger. "Look here. Our group is gettin' off here at the Gare du Nord, but you want to keep going to the next stop after. It's called *Châtelet*. Then you change here to the line one and ye go east. Get off at the Bastille stop, just there." He jabbed an index finger at a place on the small map. "You can keep this map if you want. I have another one."

"Thanks very much." Mike took the map and sighed in relief. He waved goodbye to his travel companions and found himself alone on the crowded train. Out the windows, he saw only darkness, guessing he was underground.

With a loud screech, the train stopped. He saw the word *Châtelet* emblazoned on a large blue sign through the window. He pulled his suitcase behind him and followed the human river to the exit.

Once the escalator reached the street, a cacophony of street noise surrounded him. Cars hurtled in and out of a roundabout. In the intersection was a towering monument topped with a gold statue. It was his first glimpse of Paris, and it made San Francisco look like a village.

Mike observed his surroundings for several minutes, taking it in. The large glass opera house with a wide staircase across the street. Cafés, stores, open markets, street performers, and throngs of people on every corner. Glancing to his left, he could almost make out the reflection of a river under the subway bridge.

He pulled out a more detailed map of the city in search of his hotel. Wide awake now, he dragged his wheeled suitcase toward a smaller street, as the noise behind him diminished. He easily found his hotel, inlaid in a gray block-long building with white shutters.

Once in his miniscule room, the bed seemed to murmur as his eyelids again grew heavy. He ignored the lure of a nap. He planned to locate Nikki's apartment and leave a note in her mailbox as soon as possible. That way, she'd have advance warning of his presence. A note would catch her attention the moment she entered her building. Mike grinned, enjoying the drama. He only hoped it would be a positive, romantic drama instead of a different kind.

He found the métro easy to use. Within minutes, he spied Nikki's street. The quiet of the narrow avenue calmed him after the clamor and crowds of Bastille. Overhead, mature bare trees arched like bony arms shadowing the street. He vaguely recognized the building from the photo Nikki had sent months earlier. He pushed on the massive wooden door with wrought iron grillwork. It didn't budge. Next to the door, he noticed a small keypad made for a code he didn't have.

For several minutes, he stood wondering what to do. Then a twenty-something guy in a black leather jacket stopped at the door and punched in a code. With a click, the door opened easily. He held the door open for Mike, who braved a grateful *merci*. On one wall were rows of shiny silver mailboxes. It didn't take long to spot

*Mancini*, which drew a tired smile from his lips. It was a treasure hunt, and he'd accomplished the first step.

He fished in his pocket for the note he'd written at the hotel. It said, *Welcome home, Nikki. I hope you don't mind that I came to Paris to visit you for Christmas. We have a tradition to uphold! Please call me when you can. Love, Mike.* On the bottom was the number at his hotel, and a smiley face.

That task finished, he was free until the following day, when he'd receive her call. Just twenty-four more hours and he would see her, hold her in his arms. It seemed impossible, after the slow buildup of longing over the last twelve months, after all his missteps and confusion. He'd make up for it. He loved her and he planned to tell her so.

His stomach let out a yowl. The next task was to find a restaurant and navigate a French menu. That would keep him busy for now.

಴   ಴   ಴

Nikki straddled her small suitcase between her knees. Passengers filled every space with travel bags, strollers, and bodies. Her arms encircled a large canvas bag of carefully wrapped treasures. She'd bought ceramic plates for her mother. For Aurélie's parents, a bottle of Spanish olive oil, a few rolls of spicy chorizo, and a few more souvenirs she'd been unable to resist.

It had been another unscheduled whirlwind trip. Christmas itself had triggered this one two weeks earlier. Nikki had invited Aurélie and Jean Christophe to the annual Christmas program at her church. They seemed touched by the service, and she was grateful. Afterwards, as she hugged each one goodbye, a wave of melancholy nearly engulfed her. Alone at Christmas for the first time ever.

Everyone she knew would be with parents, friends, and relatives. Though she had wanted a quiet, restful holiday after a busy semester, two weeks alone seemed frighteningly long.

A few days later, Elodia, a Spanish exchange-student from her church, called Nikki and invited her to visit her home in Seville for the few days before Christmas. Nikki abruptly booked a flight to Seville.

With each trip, it was more difficult for her to rank her favorite place. Seville hovered near the top of the list. Elodia ushered her into the charm of the walled city, gothic cathedrals, and Moorish architecture. Another treasured collection of photos filled Nikki's camera, in constant use since she'd arrived on European soil.

Elodia's large family had welcomed Nikki warmly. Despite the language barrier, their noisy Latin hospitality left her feeling loved and nurtured.

Her thoughts follow the uneven rhythm of the train, bouncing one way, then another. The pleasure of her trip versus the confusing letter she'd received right before leaving Paris.

From Philippe.

She'd taken the letter with her and re-read it several times while she was gone, running his words back and forth in her mind, like marbles in a bowl. She'd set it aside for the last two days, but wanted to read it again. In the outside pocket of her suitcase, the letter waited. She sighed and retrieved it.

*Ma Chère Nicole,*

*The last time I saw you, my dearest, I behaved very badly. I was surprised by what you told me, and believed you had not been honest with me. Now I know that it is not in your nature to be dishonest, but you are trying to overcome your fears. This is courageous and wonderful. I hope you will forgive me.*

*I have an overwhelming desire to love you and relieve your fears. I want you to live in peace and comfort because I will provide everything for you. You will have no reason to be afraid of anything.*

*Please give me another chance, mon amour. As you say, we will begin again, as from the start.*

*Yours,*

*Philippe*

His words caressed a corner deep inside her and gave her a flicker of something light and airy she couldn't yet identify. He understood and had accepted what she'd told him. Exhaustion tumbled over her as she anticipated a quiet holiday at home. She'd still find time to reflect, to pray about Philippe. He was willing to start from zero, as she'd suggested the night of their breakup.

Nikki emerged from the metro in her neighborhood as her mind still churned with thoughts of Philippe. Caution and a stirring of warmth blended uneasily as she pictured them together again. Was this turn of events from God?

She pulled her suitcase behind her and balanced her bag of souvenirs. Still lost in thought, she almost collided with an older couple. "*Excusez-moi.*"

When she reached the front of the Saint Amboise church near her building, she came to an abrupt halt, despite the cold. A phrase from Philippe's letter returned and ricocheted in her mind. *I want you to live in peace and comfort because I will provide everything for you. You will have no reason to be afraid of anything.*

Philippe's vision of marriage and relationship was strikingly similar to her father's. Like a treasured pet, he provided everything and let her stay a child. And Philippe was proposing to do the very same thing.

"No way, Philippe." Her words rang out in the empty churchyard. If they were to be a couple again, she'd have some strong conditions for him. She hadn't come this far to return to a sheltered existence, dwelling in shadowy layers of safety. He'd have to fully know the real Nikki. Her dreams, strengths, weaknesses, and fears, though her fears had already diminished.

Nikki punched her door code and pushed open the heavy wooden door, backing in with her baggage cradled in her arms.

"Mademoiselle, a box came for you." The voice of Madame Noiret reached into the foyer from her tiny office. The older woman shuffled into the hallway, a reserved smile on her face and Max yapping around her ankles.

Undoubtedly, the box was the Christmas package her mother had promised. Her father had told her that her main gift would be a deposit into her account for whatever she needed. "Dad, you're a rascal," was all she'd said. At least his gift could fund one more trip in the spring, or allow her to buy some Parisian outfits during the after-Christmas sales.

"Hello, Madame Noiret. Merry Christmas! I'll have to come back for that box in a few minutes." The woman nodded with a smile and returned to her office. Nikki pulled the few pieces of mail and a few ads from the mailbox and slipped the entire wad under one arm.

Once inside her apartment, she set everything on the couch and lifted her elbow to dump her mail onto the coffee table. After collapsing on the couch, she reread Philippe's letter, which seemed even clearer. Should she even return to him? She'd come too far. *Thank you, Lord, for showing me so clearly.*

She glanced at the stack of mail. A handwritten note drew her attention away from Philippe. She held up the note and read it. Her mouth dropped open. Mike was in Paris? Immediately, her pulse ratcheted up and sweat broke out on her back under two layers of clothing. Was this a joke? Could he *really* be here?

Suddenly she understood the undertones in his voice during their last few conversations, as if he had a secret. He'd planned this for some time. Joy and anger both fought for a place inside her. He *had* been toying with her!

And yet he'd come all the way to Paris. That certainly meant something. But why hadn't he told her sooner, rather than torturing her for months with elusiveness? Had his response also been a ploy to hold her off until he arrived in Paris? How long had he been planning this stunt?

Frustration simmered in her mind as she made a light snack for herself and tried to get her bearings. Mike was in Paris. How should she respond? He'd taken her for granted. Assumed she'd always be there. Maybe she was a fool to love him. She'd be wiser to find someone who clearly said what he meant and followed through.

But here he was. In Paris.

It took Nikki another thirty minutes before she mustered the nerve to call him. She'd try his cell first.

"Hey, Nikki. You're back," he said, as though he'd just seen her the previous week. His voice sounded sleepy.

"Mike. What a surprise. A *huge* surprise."

"Yeah, I'm sorry I didn't tell you. I tried to call you a week ahead, so you'd be prepared, but you were off in Spain. Hope it's okay that I came."

She smiled despite herself. "*Of course,* it's okay. How long will you be here?"

"I got here yesterday. I leave January second."

Nikki gulped. Another ten days. Ten days with Mike Branagan, who'd come to see her, and her alone. "That's great. At least I haven't planned to go anywhere else, though I *do* remember you asking me that question." Her voice scolded lightly.

He laughed. "I wanted to surprise you, but I guess I should have told you sooner. Hope you'll forgive me for that."

"Don't worry. You succeeded in surprising me, that's for sure. Where are you staying?"

"I got a hotel near Bastille, so I'd be close by. Can I take you to dinner tonight?"

"That would be nice. Why don't you come to my apartment at six-forty-five? That'll give me time to get myself together. I just got home. Also, the restaurants here don't open until seven."

"That sounds fine. Six forty-five. In two hours." He sounded disappointed. Maybe he wanted to come over immediately. Well, she wouldn't drop everything just because he'd come to Paris unannounced.

"I should give you the door code." Nikki pulled off her sneakers with one hand. "It's B-4023. When you come into the foyer, push the buzzer by my name."

"Got it. See you in a couple of hours."

In the silence, Nikki remained still on the couch. At any point in the previous year, she'd have only daydreamed about this scenario. But now? She should feel indignant because he'd taken her for granted. But her irritation had faded, and anticipation budded in its place. He was in Paris. And she would see him in two hours.

# Chapter Twenty-Four

Nikki willed herself to stay calm as she stood in front of the bathroom mirror. She checked herself again on all sides. The plum sweater-dress hugged her in flattering lines, accented by black tights, a belt, and short boots. Her silver jewelry and subtle make-up added sophistication. Since getting her hair cut with Elaine, it had grown and now nearly touched her shoulders.

Another long-awaited meeting with Mike. And the same somersaults in her stomach.

"Please, Lord," she whispered. "Please do what You want tonight. Your will." Kind of vague as a prayer, but He knew what to do. She let her shoulders relax and blew out a tense breath.

The buzzer squawked like an injured hen, signaling Mike's arrival. "Coming," she called back into the interphone. Nikki's heart pounded anew, and she took another breath. She locked the four deadbolts behind her and entered the elevator, fidgeting with her purse as the tiny box slowly descended toward earth. When the doors creaked open on the ground floor, she saw the top of his dark head through the mullioned wooden door between her and the foyer. Her mouth went dry.

She pressed the buzzer to open the door and stepped into the tiled hallway, where Mike waited. She stopped. It couldn't be that an entire year had seeped away, or that she had changed continents. She was back in Adams Bridge, staring at him after a long absence. Yet so much had changed.

He stood only a few feet away, wearing a black leather jacket and a bright red scarf, electric against his dark hair and eyes. His disarming smile and direct gaze turned her insides to a pool of jelly.

*He's really here.* For a moment, she struggled to breathe.

"You're really here," she whispered, still frozen in place as they stared at each other.

Mike held out both hands. "I can hardly believe it myself. You look great, Nikki."

He kept his arms stretched, beckoning as he moved toward her. Nikki finally went into his arms, reaching around his waist. His leather coat scrunched as he squeezed her. She kept her head down in case he tried to kiss her. They had too much to discuss first. His arms wrapped around her shoulders for a long moment. She closed her eyes. Was this real? His lips brushed against her forehead. He gripped her as if afraid she'd slip away, as if he planned to never let her go.

Nikki pulled gently away from him, a half-smile on her lips. "I can't believe you're here. I know I already said that. Welcome to Paris. How was your flight? Have I already asked you that?" She knew she was babbling as her heart continued to pound.

She turned to the outer door, pushed another buzzer, and emerged out to the chill of the evening. They strolled along the sidewalk, still surveying each other. Streetlamps cast a vanilla glow on the moist pavement. The sound of Nikki's heels echoed through the empty street.

"My flight was fine, although I didn't sleep much at all. I'm so glad you didn't travel over Christmas." Mike paused and stopped, facing her. He stroked her cheek with one finger. "I still can't believe I'm here with you either. You look gorgeous."

"Really?" A warm flush of pleasure fanned out inside her. "You've never told me *that* before."

He chuckled softly. "Get used to it. You look really fit too. Is that from hiking all over the European continent?"

"Actually, I lost a few pounds after, uh, last spring. And here, I walk everywhere—the post office, the grocery store, the bank. I also just walk because it's beautiful and there's so much to see." She stopped speaking. Was she again giving too many details?

Mike didn't seem to mind. "I've always found you attractive, Nikki, but all I can say now is, wow. . ." His eyes fanned over her with admiration. "I have some important things I want to tell you over dinner. How far is the restaurant?"

Important things. She shivered, pushing down her anticipation. "I thought we could go just around the next corner. I haven't been to that restaurant, but it looks nice." They turned the corner and walked together toward the soft orange glow spilling from the paned windows. She was tempted to pinch herself, to make sure it wasn't a dream. Mike Branagan was in Paris. With her. Just her.

And he seemed different, more focused. Gone was the haunted, distracted look she'd so often seen in his eyes, a specter of pain and stale grief and skittish avoidance. He seemed all there with her, fully in the present moment.

They entered a small dining room, with wide wooden planks on the floor and thick, ancient-looking wood beams jutting from the ceiling. Crisp tablecloths adorned the few round tables. Glowing candles invited hushed confessions and loving glances. A waiter showed them to a table and handed an open menu to each of them.

Nikki's eyes brushed across the intimate dining room and returned to Mike, who still had not vanished into her imagination. Rather, he gazed intently at her. It was almost more than her emotions could handle. She was on a dinner date with Mike in a romantic Parisian restaurant. In her fantasies, she hadn't dared conjure up as much.

"I'll help you with this." She leaned forward over the menu and translated the choices, pointing to each one. "These are appetizers. Here are the main courses. There's chicken with a special Normandy cream sauce, flavored with *Calvados*, that's apple brandy. This is roast duck with garlic potatoes, then salmon with herbs and rice."

She continued explaining, aware that he looked not at the menu, but at her as she spoke. Her face heated with pleasure and embarrassment from his focused attention. Finally, she leaned back. "I'm not sure if you caught all that, but I only translate once."

"I'll take the duck."

Nikki ordered in French for both of them.

When the waiter nodded and left, Mike leaned back against the padded chair. "Very impressive. I don't know what you said, but it sounded fluent to me."

She fought down the hammering inside her rib cage as she stared back at him. She swallowed. "It's your turn, Mike. Time for you to translate what's in your head. I haven't understood very much in the last year. Maybe I just don't speak your language."

"You do, believe me. More than anyone else." Mike crossed his arms on the table. He seemed to weigh his words and carefully select them. "It's my fault you haven't understood me. I haven't been clear with you. At first, there were reasons for that."

Nikki stiffened. Reasons? Did he come all the way to Paris to apologize for leading her on? Was he trying to salve his conscience and cut her loose humanely over candlelight and French cuisine? Maybe she'd misinterpreted his innuendos. He'd probably meant nothing, and she'd simply heard what she wanted to hear.

She looked down at her hands, a faint sting burning her eyes. Her shoulders dropped. She was ready to let all this go, this agonizing, exhausting one-way love for him. If she could.

Through the rising noise in her mind, she heard him say, "I came here because I *had* to see you this Christmas, Nikki. I wanted to tell you face to face that I love you."

Her head jerked up. She stared across the table through a glaze of tears. "What?" It was all she could think of to say. Certainly, she'd heard him wrong and didn't want to make a fool of herself. Again.

His gaze was like warm brown sugar. A faint smile twitched around his mouth and his voice was soft. "I said I'm in love with you, Nikki."

She stared at him, her mouth partly open as his words penetrated like raindrops into parched soil. Her eyes filled. She squeezed them shut and hot tears spilled down her cheeks. *Love.* In love. Not "attracted to" or "there's potential." Mike Branagan of her childhood dreams and adolescent fantasies, said he was *in love* with her.

Couldn't be.

"I'm sorry, but I'm pretty sure I missed something." She swiped her wet face with her napkin, aching to believe his words.

Mike shrugged, looking sheepish. "I'm not surprised. I was confused for a while. Then after that, my parents' investigation weighed on my mind. I admit, it all became a handy excuse to avoid my feelings. I know I sent you mixed signals all year. But in the fall it came clear to me—"

"The fall?" Nikki leaned forward. "It all just *came clear*?" Joy and frustration wrestled in a heated match. "And what about me? Maybe you could have let me in on it at some point."

"I'm sorry it took me so long." His face held a shadow of regret. "I wanted to be able to offer you a real commitment. You don't deserve anything less from me. But I also wanted to keep building something with you. There were so many issues that were my own."

She crossed her arms, wary, but with the trace of a smile hovering on her lips. "So now, even though I've been kept in the dark all year, I'm supposed to throw myself at you?"

"Absolutely!" He grinned for a moment, then sobered. "I didn't come to take advantage of you, Nikki. I won't even touch you unless you want me to. I just want to be clear with you in person and tell you how I feel."

She leaned against the padded chair. Her heart thumped, but slowly, a rising tide of joy seeped into the spaces inside her. She pressed down the flood and returned to a safer plane. "The reasons you spoke about. Were those the ones you brought up last January?"

"Yeah, that—" he shrugged. "Those were sticking point at first for me." He reached for the water carafe and poured a glass for each of them.

*Not that woman anymore.* With or without Mike Branagan. Nikki lifted her shoulders higher and leveled her eyes to his.

"I was changed by our time together last Christmas." Mike returned her gaze. "I wasn't just having fun. I started thinking about you in a new way, as a woman I was attracted to, instead of my friend's sister, or my childhood friend. My feelings were growing, but there were these red flags too. When we had our, uh, difficult discussion in January, I was being honest, but I wasn't ending things. At least in my mind, they weren't over."

Nikki leaned forward on her elbows. "When you talked about timing, of course, I thought the worst. I already saw myself as this. . .this weak, naive little girl who had to be protected by her father. Then, without even knowing about that, you questioned my maturity. It just added coals to the fire. I overreacted." Like the child she'd been, in fact. She smirked. "You weren't wrong."

"I'm sorry. I didn't realize how you felt about yourself. I shouldn't have said anything, and should have let it work itself out." He paused. "You may already know this, but during that Christmas, Frank warned me that you might misinterpret my attention. He told me you were less experienced in relationships. I hate to say it, but his words influenced me at the time."

"As if I'm a baby he has to protect," she spat. "He's one reason I'm in Paris now. He crippled me—" she stopped. "No, that's too harsh. He did it out of love, but he never realized what it did to me. *You* saw it." Nikki's voice, having risen, lowered to a whisper. "As much as it hurt, I needed to hear what you told me. It pushed me out of my little nest. And God used it." She stopped. "Any other issues?"

Mike's eyes darted beyond her head as he sighed. "When I was eighteen, I left the East Coast partly to escape my past. It seemed the perfect solution, to draw a line between Adams Bridge and my new life. But *you* were a link with my past. I struggled with that, I'll be honest. In spite of what I started to feel for you. I didn't want to return to the past. But when you stopped taking my calls, it hit me how much you meant to me. By the time I worked it all out," he paused with a helpless shrug, hands splayed outward. "You were on your way to Paris."

She nodded but didn't speak. Her tight springs of defensiveness unwound a coil at a time. Some of the issues were with him, not her.

Mike took a long sip of water. "Over the summer, you were mostly out of contact. When we finally started talking, I wanted to be clearer about my feelings, but I was too subtle. I was afraid of running too fast and creating a new mess." His chest lifted with a heavy sigh as he fastened his eyes on hers. "Nikki, couldn't you see that my interest in you went further than just friendship? I wanted you to know I was falling for you."

*Falling for you.* She let the words caress her spirit and melt her insides. "I thought you were just trying to bolster the friendship, to keep the promise we'd made to each other last Christmas."

Mike's eyes widened. "Really? I *was* serious about keeping our friendship. But there was more than that. Around September was when I realized I was in love with you. That's when I decided to come to Paris, so I could tell you in person. I thought I was being romantic, I guess, wanting to surprise you."

"Well, one reason *I* came to Paris was to get over you one last time. Did it ever occurred to you in the last six months that I might have succeeded, or even met someone else?"

Mike's face paled in the candlelight. "Did you? Maybe I don't want to know—"

She just smiled. "Last year, your words were a catalyst for me, for my need for independence. I *needed* to come here for myself, with or without you."

"That's the only reason I'm glad I didn't tell you sooner. I'm happy you had this chance. And just for the record, those issues I brought up last year, please forget all of it."

The waiter arrived, steaming plates resting on his forearm. He placed them on the table and discreetly vanished. Nikki said with a wan smile, "I don't have much of an appetite now. This is all pretty intense."

"Me either. But it looks and smells great."

"I like this place." She scanned the room, then returned her gaze to him. "And I'm really glad you came, Mike." Especially after what he'd just told her, which she struggled to fully believe.

He smiled apprehensively and took her hand. "You haven't told me about your process. Last summer I think you were avoiding me, trying to get over me, but you haven't said if you succeeded. Or if you met someone else."

Nikki let her hand rest within his, enjoying the feeling of his skin against hers. "There was someone for a little while, but he's gone." She watched his face relax as his smile returned. "But I'd like to make a request. I don't know if you'll understand this or not. I'm not even sure I do, but I'd like some normal time with you first. I have to get used to you again. Can we just be friends for a few days."

"Does it have to do with trusting me? Trusting my feelings for you?"

"Yes, a little," she admitted. "I'm not sure if I believe all this yet, and I'm afraid of being hurt again. If we just hang out as friends, I'll be ready to talk more about it."

Mike nodded. "Okay, that's fair. We'll enjoy the holidays together. We don't even have to define anything at this point. You can let me know when you're ready to talk."

Nikki smiled gratefully, then looked down at her meal, realizing that she was hungry after all.

After dinner, Mike and Nikki sauntered toward Nikki's apartment building under the black velvet of the December sky. Her stomach felt comfortably full, as did her whole being. Her mind spun and she doubted she'd sleep much that night.

"We have a couple of plans for the holidays," she said as they stopped in front of her building. "Tomorrow, we have a Christmas Eve party hosted by one of the English teachers I know, Thomas from Ireland. There will be English teachers there from lots of different countries. That starts at about four. We'll need to make some food to take. Then on Christmas Day we have dinner with Aurélie's parents. I'll call to let her know you're here. I'm sure it won't be a problem to add a place setting. Tomorrow, we have to grocery shop and go to the Marché. Are you up for all that?"

As they stood in front of the massive wooden doors, his eyes glowed black in the moonlight. "Anything you need to do is fine with me, as long as I can be with you. I'll just tag along and pretend to understand everything, observing you in your world. It's been fun so far." He swept two fingers down her cheek and whispered, "I have a huge admiration for you."

"That's so sweet. Considering our history, it almost means more to me than hearing you think I'm gorgeous. I like that too, but admiration?"

"It's true. Just watching the way you handled this last year. I was wrong about you, Nikki. You have strength I didn't know you had. You *are* beautiful, but seeing your heart and your substance, as well as your love for God—all that made me fall in love with you." He paused, a faint smile pulling the corners of his mouth.

The temptation to let him kiss her long enough to make up for the previous year assailed her, but she pushed it down. Her conditions for him had been fair. Reasonable. Protection for her heart.

"I'll let you get some rest, hopefully dreaming of me." He moved away from her. "What time should I come tomorrow? Ten?"

She nodded, then pushed the door open. With a secret smile, she watched him stroll down the darkened street.

# Chapter Twenty-Five

"Do you desire something else, Monsieur?"

The mustached man who had been behind the reception desk poured hot black coffee into Mike's cup. On the table sat a basket of baguette chunks and croissants, along with a bowl of butter and jam. Mike never knew mere bread could be so tasty. "*Non, merci.*" He smiled at the man.

The breakfast room of the hotel was small, but recently renovated, with a wall of textured stone and a small glowing fireplace at one end. Mike was the only guest.

He waved toward the man. "Monsieur, no breakfast tomorrow. Stay with your family." No reason to get the poor man up on Christmas just to bring Mike bread and coffee. The man understood enough to smile gratefully and nod.

Mike took the ink sketch he'd just made of the stone fireplace and gently tucked it into his backpack. He'd give it to Nikki.

His mind wasn't on the coffee or the crisp baguette that morning. After months of anticipating seeing Nikki, she hadn't responded the way he'd hoped. But he understood. No wonder she was holding back. To her, it seemed out of the blue, though he thought he'd given clues. He had given puzzles instead. Maybe after all these years, Nikki had considered it impossible that he would fall in love with her. Maybe she'd lost hope. Yet, during dinner, she never said she *didn't* love him, only that she needed time.

The sight of her last night was more than he'd prepared himself for. Since they'd been adults, Mike had found Nikki beautiful, but there was something very striking about her now. She looked nearly the same, but exuded more self-confidence, more self-acceptance, and it made her more appealing in spades. Aside from that, he'd just spent twelve months pining for her. She could have worn a garbage bag and seeing her would still have melted him.

He decided a brisk walk from his hotel to Nikki's apartment would awaken him fully and better acquaint him with Paris. His phone read only nine-fifteen. He'd studied the map during breakfast. It didn't look too far.

The cold, damp air bit into his skin as he left the cozy hotel. He shoved his hands deep into his pockets, wishing he'd brought gloves. He rarely used them in San Francisco. At least he wore a heavy sweater, which provided a layer of warmth.

The streets were empty and silent, shadowed in morning tones of gray. Strings of unlit Christmas lights hung with promise across the middle of the street, swinging faintly. Christmas Eve day. A year ago, to the day, he was with Nikki at the Pancake Palace, where it all began. Now he was heading to her apartment in Paris. He shook his head in amazement. So much could happen in a year.

Several sleepy streets later, he spotted her doorway and punched in the code. What would the day bring?

"I'll be right down," she called through the interphone when Mike pushed the buzzer. Several minutes later she emerged from the elevator, looking collegiate in a fluffy sheepskin jacket over faded jeans. Her dark, shoulder-length waves flowed out from under her knit cap. He couldn't stop staring at her. Had she become more beautiful since last year?

"Good morning." She smiled warmly and handed him a round wicker basket. Next to her was a tall canvas sack on wheels. "I'll put you to work, since we have a lot to do today. Did you sleep well?"

She pressed the door release button and it buzzed. Mike pushed open the heavy door and followed closely behind her. She seemed friendly, but brisk. As she said, they had a lot to do.

"I'll just say less badly than the night before. Overall, fine. You?"

She shot him a look.

"Did I give you something to think about all night?" he asked with a grin.

With a coy smile she asked, "Are you flattering yourself just a bit?" She giggled and added, "Yes, you were in my thoughts quite a lot. Are you happy?"

"It's a good start."

She locked eyes with him for a moment, then turned behind him to a red-faced man half-collapsed on the steps. "Bonjour, Marcel. Joyeux Noël."

The man looked up with watery eyes over a red puffy nose. *"Bonjour, vous de même, ma'moselle."*

"Who's that?" Mike asked her as they walked away.

"That's Marcel. I wished him a Merry Christmas. He's a homeless drunk guy. Harmless."

"You know him personally?"

Nikki shrugged. "I say hi and give him food sometimes. He's okay."

Mike laughed. He didn't know what to say to the new Nikki.

She then got down to business. "Our first stop is the supermarket. It may be a zoo because it's the day before Christmas, but we have to go. I have no food. And it'll be a good cultural experience for you."

And it certainly was, though overall, it had a strong resemblance to American grocery stores, only much smaller, with skinnier aisles. Mike enjoyed observing the French before-Christmas rush. Apparently, in every country, people waited until the last minute to shop for Christmas groceries.

Afterwards, Nikki led him toward the open market he'd passed on the way to her apartment. The noise grew as they approached. Vegetable vendors called out their special deals. He was recognizing some words and phrases, such as "deux euros le kilo." He turned to Nikki. "That means two euros per kilo, right?"

She looked impressed. "Very good. You'll probably pick up a lot of French by the time you leave."

"And here I thought I'd only come to pick *you* up." He grinned. "But, why not?"

She returned his grin and lightly punched his arm.

The Marché bustled noisily. Shoppers with grocery carts and children milled around the festive stands of produce, textiles, cheese, fish, and breads. One stand displayed regionally sourced honey, another Persian rugs. Several had Christmas crafts, handmade candles, wood carvings, and shoes. An Indian man filled the air with the fragrance of roasting chestnuts from a makeshift stove in a metal grocery cart.

Mike waited at a distance and watched in admiration as Nikki bought fresh fruit, pointing out what she wanted. She explained and joked in French to the man behind the stall, haggled with the vendor, thrusting an apple back at him, insisting on another one. Unbelievable! Timid Nikki was timid no more. Several minutes later, she had the guy laughing, and he offered her a bunch of parsley. She'd charmed him in the end.

When she returned, she told him, "I have a task for you. I need you to go to that stand over there." She pointed across two rows to an awning identical to the others. "See the guy with the beard? Go to him. I'd like you to get a head of Batavia lettuce and two kilos of carrots. About twelve or so."

"I'm happy to help, Nikki, but I don't speak French."

"I know, but you'll figure it out." She smiled at him sweetly, stuffing a ten euro note into his fist. He tried to pull his hand away, and she shoved it into his coat pocket. "My treat."

"You're taking a risk. I might come back with turnips and chard."

He found the stand she'd shown him and waited behind several fast-talking customers. When it was his turn, a burly Frenchman with a gigantic black beard and a glistening earring looked at him and waited. "Bonjour," Mike began awkwardly. The lettuce was the easy one. He held up one finger and pointed to the lettuce. "Un." So far so good. Now for the carrots. "*Diez*," he said. It was Spanish, but it was sort of close to French. "And *dos kilo*."

Again, he held up his fingers. He realized he'd forgotten to point to the carrots. "Carrots," he said, feeling like it was his first day in kindergarten. The big man grinned, white teeth showing through his dense forest of a beard.

"*Comme ça?*" the man asked, holding up the cluster of carrots.

"*Oui.*" Mike nodded and fished the money from his pocket. Whew, that wasn't too bad. When he saw Nikki, he proudly presented his vegetables.

She smiled with approval and put them into her canvas bag. "Next stop, home. We have some cooking to do before tonight, and we need some lunch too."

Mike appreciated the tiny width of the elevator, since, with the groceries and basket, he was wedged close to Nikki. He could even smell the fragrance of her hair. When he entered her apartment, he let out a low whistle. "This is *small!*" The entire apartment was the size of a medium-size bedroom, only it had a kitchen in the corner. She probably slept on the foldout couch under the window.

"Told you." She slid into the tiny corner kitchen and put her groceries away. "We can eat lunch first, then cook. By the way, since tomorrow is Christmas, why don't you come over for a special breakfast at around nine?"

"Sounds great." Mike smiled, grateful to start Christmas day with her. As they finished their sandwiches, Nikki said, "I guess Mom will cook up a storm today at the Big House."

Mike looked up at her from his empty plate. At the mention of the Big House, a heavy layer coated his stomach. "Are you homesick?" He braced himself for her answer.

She shook her head. "Not as much as I'd expect at Christmas. I might have been if you hadn't come. That's one reason I went to Spain so suddenly."

Mike shifted in his chair. "I never told you about my talk with Frank a few months back."

Nikki stilled, and her eyes grew round. "What happened?"

"I called to find out when you'd be coming to New York for Christmas so I could come see you. Frank was home early that day.

That's when he told me you were staying in Paris. At first, we got into it."

"About what?"

"He told me he'd warned you about me. There was this incident that happened when I was seventeen—"

"I know about it. I told him it was in the past. Now you follow Jesus. You have different values."

Mike smiled. "Thanks for defending me. I'm glad you thought the best of me."

She shook her head and her brows furrowed. "I'm sorry that conversation happened. I know it must have hurt you. I don't know why he can be so sweet most of the time, then mean with you. It isn't fair."

"I had the chance to tell him how hurt I've always been by his behavior toward me. For the first time, he seemed to really hear me. We had sort of an understanding in the end." Mike caught her gaze and held it. He didn't know how much to tell her, but figured that was enough to give her a picture of what he hoped was a new chapter with Frank.

"Oh, Mike. That's wonderful." She cast him a relieved and peaceful smile, as if treasuring a thought, then stood up. "Are you ready to make a lemon nut pie? It's one of Mom's recipes. Then we'll do this hors d'oeuvre I found in my French cookbook. It seems easy."

Mike glanced at the enormous cookbook with photos of delicacies and French words all over the front. "You're learning French cooking?"

"I figured I needed to learn how to cook sooner or later. I've always helped Mom with pastry, but I need to know how to cook real food. I thought this year was as good a time as any." She pulled the mammoth book out of the way and peered down at an index card with handwriting on it.

Mike's task was to chop nuts on one side of the counter while Nikki squeezed lemon juice into a measuring cup. They stood side by side in the minuscule kitchen. Several times they brushed elbows, and his heart sped up. He glanced at Nikki and a faint patch of color bloomed on her cheeks, though she kept her eyes down. Being right next to her and pretending to be just friends was challenging. All he wanted to do was take her in his arms and kiss her for a long time. He had to shut his eyes for a moment to redirect his thoughts. He didn't want to break his promise to her.

"Are you okay?"

He smirked. "You're very distracting. I love being with you, but it's driving me slightly nuts."

Nikki crossed her arms, and a mysterious smile appeared. "I knew I should have had you cut the lemons instead." At this, he laughed and held up a walnut, glad to break some of the tension. She leaned her elbows against the counter and tilted her head. Her tone was soft and full of wonder. "You're for real, aren't you?"

He laid down his knife and turned to her. "Nikki, I'm for real. I hope I'll convince you I love you. I'm not sending codes or innuendos this time. Still, no pressure, but know where I stand, at least."

Her face relaxed with a calm that was so gentle and sincere he thought he'd melt.

"Thanks for going along with me for now," she said. "I'm just enjoying this time with you, focusing on Christmas. I'm getting used to you again in a new way."

He considered her words *in a new way,* and his optimism leaped up.

A few hours later, they stood in front of an apartment door. Mike held the pie in both hands as Nikki pushed the buzzer. The door flew open and a wiry young man with curly blond hair appeared. An ample, toothy grin and mischievous blue eyes offset his pale complexion. Loud music poured into the hallway, and soon the throbbing notes enveloped them.

"There ye are, Nicole." He turned an open gaze to Mike said with a Irish lilt, "Hello, I'm Thomas. You Nikki's man? Welcome, Merry Christmas." He shook Mike's hand vigorously.

Mike didn't correct him. Let everyone in the room think he was Nikki's man, as he hoped soon to be. The room was full of young men and women. Several of them came toward Nikki to kiss her on both cheeks. When she introduced Mike, the women also kissed him, which Nikki had warned would happen. "I thought only French people did that," he whispered to Nikki.

"Yeah, but when in France. . .Besides that, no girl would skip the chance to kiss a handsome guy and get away with it."

He couldn't help but smile. She'd never called him *handsome* before.

The small apartment was colorfully decorated with woven rugs. Posters adorned the walls, and more rugs lay scattered around the floor. A long table already filled with steaming platters, hors d'oeuvres, and an array of beverages lined one side of the room. The guests from England, South Africa, France, Germany, the United States, and Canada talked over the din in a variety of accents. Mike felt like he stood at the crossroads of the entire world.

"Come, have some drinks," said red-haired Fiona, Thomas' girlfriend. Mike was forgetting the names already. "You can put your pie in the kitchen. We'll do desserts after the appetizers."

Quickly he was separated from Nikki, as her friends surrounded her, and various people approached him to introduce themselves.

He observed Nikki covertly from wherever he ended up in the room. Effortlessly, she circulated, seeming at ease with her new friends from around the globe. One minute speaking English, the next, French. Where was the provincial girl he'd grown up with? He chuckled, feeling a surge of pride in her.

"Yeah, she's quite cute, idn't she?" asked Thomas affably.

Mike didn't know he'd been watched. "Quite. Why do you think I came all the way to Paris?"

Thomas laughed. "You known Nicole for a long time?"

"I believe we first met when she was five." Mike grinned at the surprise on Thomas' face. "Her older brother was my best friend."

"And now Nicole is." Thomas' voice had a triumphant ring. He lifted his eyebrows in romantic conspiracy. "'Scuze me, I've got to get the door."

Nikki joined Mike a few minutes later, drawing him to the food table. "How are you doing? Hope it's not too overwhelming for you." She shouted over the racket. It was humorous that *she* was asking *him*. Who could have imagined this scenario a year ago? And he had been worried about how she'd react to wild, eclectic San Francisco.

He shrugged. "I'm fine, but I think I might be an introvert after all."

"We won't stay too long. I wanted you to taste my world, but maybe I'm overdoing it." Her face was apologetic. She put several items from the table on her paper plate.

"Your friends seem nice. But I'll be honest, I'd rather just be with you."

Mike and Nikki stayed at the party through the dessert, then bid an early Merry Christmas to the group. Walking quietly toward her apartment, she slipped her arm through his. *That* was a bit of progress. It warmed him.

"You know," she said, her breath puffing clouds into the chill air. "I think if we'd gotten together a year ago, it might have been a disaster."

He looked at her in surprise. "You think so?" Maybe she was ready to talk about her feelings for the first time.

"Yeah. I was dependent and clingy. And pretty obsessed. I'm sure you noticed. Understandably, you ran away. When you said it wasn't time, it was true. My reaction just proved it wasn't the right thing."

"Not the right thing *then*."

She stopped and leveled a gaze at him that was full of intensity and honesty. "I've learned about myself since then, about my dad's influence on me, and other things. Don't take this the wrong way, but I learned I don't need people in a way that makes them a crutch, a substitute for my own responsible choices. I want to need them in a healthier way, but I wasn't capable before. That's one reason I came here. I think I've learned to trust my ability to make decisions, of course, with God's leading. I've had to. Your comments last year contributed to all this change, and I'm grateful to you. I was unhappy and mad at you then, but it helped me grow."

Mike swallowed, an ache of emotion gripping his throat. "I'm glad you aren't mad at me anymore." He scuffed his shoes against the uneven cobblestone sidewalk, echoing in the quiet street. Nikki didn't respond. His scalp prickled. "Are you?" He held his breath.

She laughed. "No, I'm not." They began walking again, a lazy meandering meant to extend the moment.

He grinned into the darkness. "You know, the lessons I've learned in the last year were the opposite of yours. I'd spent my life running *away* from needing people. When I lost my parents, I never fully recovered. I became like this self-sufficient unit, all coated with bronze. Then last summer, I realized I *do* need people, and it's okay to need them in a healthy way. God even used Stephanie to help me see that."

Nikki stilled. "Stephanie?"

"I ran into her one day in July and we had coffee. She apologized for what happened, but she also told me I had a wall that she couldn't penetrate. I hadn't seen it before then, though she'd told me many times. That day, her statement hit me. Then, with the investigation, I couldn't run from the past anymore. But I realized I didn't have to."

Nikki searched his face. "You *do* seem more peaceful to me. Like you're no longer carrying a heavy burden."

They arrived in front of the huge wooden door of her apartment building. He didn't want the evening to end.

"Well, good night. I'll see you tomorrow at nine?" she asked.

He nodded. "I'll be here."

Nikki leaned toward him and gave him a quick squeeze around his waist, then disappeared into the building.

*One December*

# Chapter Twenty-Six

Outside the long, frosted panes, a feisty wind moaned and rattled the shutters. A strand of colored lights encircling the glass cast cheerful orbs of red, green, and yellow. Two thick candles, one red, one white, glowed on the coffee table.

Nikki arranged the dining room table, which she'd set for breakfast with red Christmas placemats and another cluster of candles. She scanned the small room for the fourth time. Why was she so edgy? Was it because it was Christmas, and all that day meant in her relationship with Mike? Or was she simply excited to spend another full day with him? She smiled as a happy sigh escaped.

The previous day, she'd felt relaxed, though self-protective. No more running after Mike like a newborn foal trying its legs for the first time. Since the moment of Mike's confession of love to her, Nikki's mind hadn't stopped turning, savoring, though still disbelieving. Slowly it sank in, yet she still watched for signs that his feelings would suddenly evaporate, and she'd be hurt all over again. Observing him for a few days before making anything official would give her more peace of mind, more certainty. Like a fragile sculpture, one brusque movement could cause it all to splinter into a thousand tiny shards.

After returning from the restaurant on that first evening, she'd called Elaine and then Aurélie. She'd told them that Mike was in Paris and claimed to be in love with her. Both of her friends giggled with delight and congratulated her. They wouldn't understand the depth of her fears, or her desire to take things slowly.

A knock came on the door. A sudden wave of joy flooded through her, bringing her to the point of tears. Catching her breath, she blinked and unlocked the deadbolts. "Merry Christmas," she said breathlessly, waiting until Mike pulled off his coat and put down his backpack before slipping into his arms for a hug. His arms around her felt heavenly.

"That's a nice, warm holiday greeting." He smiled as he pulled away. His face shone ruddy above a black turtleneck sweater. "Something smells wonderful."

"Breakfast is ready, so we can sit down. Coffee?"

"Of course. I would have brought something to contribute to the meal, but everything is closed."

"I have plenty."

Nikki felt him watching her as she poured his coffee. She'd gotten up early to make a big breakfast—French toast, stuffed omelets, and homemade muffins. She placed the loaded plates onto the red placemats.

"This should hold us until our meal at Aurélie's parents' house this afternoon."

"*This* might hold me until next week." His eyes swept the tabletop. "Looks like you've been cooking all morning." Mike ran his tongue over his lips in exaggerated anticipation, like a cat after a meal, then settled into one of the dining room chairs.

"I'll pray for us on this special day." He reached across the small table, and grasped her hand. His fingers, still cold, entwined hers. A smile twitched his lips then he bowed his head. "Father, I'm full of gratitude for this day. First, the chance to be with Nikki. Thank you for keeping her safe and giving her a great experience here in Paris. Thank you for keeping us in touch through this past year too. We know you'll guide us. And most of all, Lord, thank you for your Son, who came to this earth as a tiny baby, just for us. We're eternally grateful for Jesus. Thank you for your good gifts, including this good food. Amen."

They ate in relaxed conversation as Mike shared his cultural perspectives of the party the previous evening. Nikki couldn't help recalling the last omelet they'd had together, the day of their first relationship talk. It seemed an eternity ago.

"More coffee?" she asked when they'd finished eating. "We can sit on the couch."

"I have a couple of gifts for you." Mike rummaged in his backpack and pulled out two gifts, one small and one larger. He placed them on the coffee table, then fell backwards on the couch. "I'm so full, but that was great."

Nikki gave him another cup of coffee and sat beside him, warm from his nearness. She gestured to the gifts. "You didn't have to do that, Mike."

"It's Christmas. Of course, I wanted to give you something. Don't worry if you don't have anything for me. You didn't know I was coming. Here, open the bigger one first." He handed her a shapeless mound covered by festive paper.

Nikki gave him a crooked smile and ripped into the package. She pulled out a gray hooded sweatshirt and held it up at the shoulder seams. "San Francisco, California," she read. "That's great. Thank you. Looks warm."

"That way, you can't forget that someone in San Francisco is thinking about you." He grinned. "Okay, now the small one."

Nikki took the smaller box with slight hesitation. Looked like it might be jewelry. Something more intimate. She tore off the Christmas print paper and lifted the top of the box up. She caught her breath. In the box lay a short necklace of tiny silver branches interspersed with small pearls. "Oh, Mike, this is gorgeous."

He leaned forward. "Do you want to try it on? I can help you."

She nodded and turned her back toward him. She lifted her hair to one side, her heart pounding as he leaned toward her to fasten the clasp. Her neck and scalp prickled as his hands gently swept her skin and his breath caressed her neck.

"I'll see how it looks." Nikki bolted from the room. She looked at her flushed face in the bathroom mirror and breathed to regain her composure. The necklace sat like a delicate treasure around her throat. It was more than a piece of jewelry. It was a symbol of a new phase in her relationship with Mike. His thoughtfulness deeply moved her. And his physical closeness electrified her.

She returned to the couch and placed two small gifts on the table, which she had hidden behind towels in the bathroom. He looked up at her in surprise. "For me?" She nodded, smiling. "How did you—"

"Remember yesterday at the *Marché* when I sent you on an errand? There was a purpose for that."

Mike laughed. "Very sneaky. Let's see, what's this?" From out of the wrapping paper, he pulled out a charcoal gray scarf with a tiny red line pattern. "Very nice. It's a great color."

"I know you have one, but this one's from France. I think it's handmade, too. See, the weave is looser. Now the other one," she urged.

He opened the other package and pulled out a life-size olive wood carving of two tropical fish, flat and triangular, with pointy fins on top. "Look at that. It's handmade?"

She nodded, pleased by his reaction. "I know you like tropical fish, so when I saw these carvings, I thought you needed one. They're hand-carved by this old man from Senegal who has a stand at the *Marché*."

"This one looks like Simon, my fish at home." He pointed at the larger one. "I love it. Can I give you a Christmas hug?"

"Sure." She leaned into his open arms.

He held her for just a moment, then released her. "Do we have more cooking to do today?"

She nodded. "I told Aurélie I'd bring a pie. We can make the same one we made yesterday."

"Sure, let's get to work."


After spending a festive afternoon with Aurélie, her parents, and her brother and his family, Mike and Nikki walked slowly from the métro through dark uneven streets toward Nikki's apartment.

"Your friends are really sweet," he told her. "And that meal was amazing. I'd never eaten lamb prepared that way before. And what was that stuff we had as an appetizer?"

"Foie gras. It's goose liver pâté. It's a Christmas delicacy in France. They sometimes make it with duck too. Good, wasn't it?"

He nodded. "And your pie, *our* pie, was a hit. Just like last night. I could eat that a few more times." He laughed. "We just kept eating and eating. But it didn't seem like a lot because each course was spread out over so many hours." He groaned and placed both hands on his stomach.

Temperatures had fallen again, and Nikki shivered, but treasured the warmth still curled inside her. "That's the way they do it here. You take your time. You savor the food and the company. No rushing where food is concerned. I like that."

"Me too."

After a moment of companionable silence, she said, "It was nice to call my family while we were there. Christmas wouldn't have been the same without at least talking to them. Dad made a point that I should tell you Merry Christmas. Specifically, to you."

His dark brows lifted. "Well. Christmas miracles do happen. I think we'll be able to work out our differences. We've already started."

She looked up at him. "That would be the best Christmas gift for me, other than your visit. And my mom seemed glad you're here. She's always thought a lot of you." Her mother had clearly expressed her approval, which meant the world to Nikki, even though her voice sounded faraway and sad. Even Danny was in favor, seeming to know full well why Mike was in Paris. They'd all have to get used to it. As soon as she herself did.

Nikki punched the code in and pushed the door. She and Mike stood in the softly lit tile hallway. "I'm kind of tired, so why don't we see each other tomorrow at ten?" she suggested. "We can be tourists together for the first time."

"I'm tired too. Too much digesting. And hearing French all day, even with your translations. Wore my brain out." He smiled at her, then fell silent.

Nikki slipped her arms around his waist, pulling into his chest to bury her face there. He encircled her shoulders with his arms and held her, his cheek against the top of her head. A wave of desire rippled through her body as she stood locked within his grasp. They'd hugged before, but something was different this time. It was as though years of silent communication were radiating through their tightened arms, speaking volumes without a word. She felt his lips close to her forehead, his breath softly moving her bangs. She'd only have to lift her head, and he'd probably kiss her. Was she ready?

Yes, and no. In one way, she swam in transparent clarity. She belonged there in his arms. But tomorrow they'd be together, and the busyness of Christmas day would be behind them. She'd have even more clarity then.

Gently pulling back, she gave him a sleepy smile. "Merry Christmas, Mike."

He stood still with a ghost of a smile and watched her slip through the wooden door. She paused on the other side and glanced back. He'd let himself out of the wrought iron exterior door and was still looking through the smudged panes. Through two sets of doors and the tiled space between them, their eyes fastened together for several suspended seconds. Finally, Nikki turned toward the elevator.

As she reached the third floor, she realized she was grinning. Of course, she loved him, had never stopped. She'd known it all along. That wasn't the issue. Now she knew he loved *her*. She'd once told Elaine she wanted Mike to pursue her. Not merely respond to her infatuation. Coming to Paris fit that description.

The previous months of frustration floated away like dry leaves on a river current. There was no way she could run from Mike Branagan, or protect herself any longer. Neither of them was running now.

# Chapter Twenty-Seven

He couldn't get her out of his mind. He'd awakened several times during the night and thought each time of the vulnerability of her hug. The slow, meaningful capture of her gaze through the double doors. When Mike had first arrived in Paris, he'd found Nikki with a carefully preserved wall. Now, after two full days together, the wall had crumbled, and his commitment to her had grown more solid. He finally knew who Nikki Mancini was and who she'd become. He wasn't disappointed. On the contrary.

It had become his new ritual to ring the buzzer, then shove himself into the miniscule elevator. Like the day before, Nikki greeted him with a warm hug, but that day it lasted just a few seconds longer. He hoped he didn't only imagine it.

Gone was the guarded distance. She seemed relaxed as she smiled and bantered easily with him. A map of Paris covered the dining room table. She poured them each a cup of coffee, then settled next to him at the table.

"I thought we could go to the Eiffel Tower first, if you're interested." She pushed her hair behind her ears and leaned forward to point to the left side of the puzzle of hundreds of tiny streets. "Now that our holiday activities are over, we can just be tourists, or whatever you want." Her eyes danced with invitation.

His whole being stirred, on high romantic alert. While she pointed out monuments and tourist sites on the map, she carelessly brushed his hand or touched his shoulder. Was it deliberate? He smiled at that possibility.

Nearly two hours later, Mike stood crammed into an elevator for a second time. That time he was with Nikki and about fifty other tourists, as the metal box inched up one of the massive legs of the Eiffel Tower. The wait in line had been long, though shorter than in the height of summer.

"It's my first time up the Eiffel Tower," Nikki said. "Even though I've lived in Paris for five months. She had to shout over the din of the grinding gears and the rumble of conversation. "The crowds were always too big for me. With you, I don't mind."

He silently agreed. Whether they were making pies or standing in lines with hundreds of tourists, he simply loved being with her. As the room-sized hydraulic elevator slowly groaned in its ascent, Nikki pressed against him, seeming to enjoy their closeness.

Once on the second floor of the tower, the crowd spilled out to a metal platform where the gray winter landscape of Paris rippled out before them. The brilliant blue winter sky offset the dry chill. Nikki leaned out at the railing and peered in all directions. "See that church up on the hill?" She pointed to a dignified white dome that gleamed against the blue backdrop. "That's Sacré Coeur Basilica. We can go there this afternoon. Back in the day, the surrounding neighborhood was a hangout for artists, like Dali and Picasso. Even today it's known for art, but it's more commercial."

She turned back to the panoramic view and, to Mike's surprise, leaned back against him. He considered that permission enough, so he wrapped his arms around her and pulled her into his chest. Instead of pulling away, she relaxed her weight into him, tilting her head back. He closed his eyes and pressed his cheek against the top of her head. The potent heat inside him churned, scoffing at the winter chill. He had an overwhelming urge to turn her around and kiss her then. A kiss on the Eiffel Tower. That would be romantic, though it may be too soon for her.

By the time they descended the mammoth metal structure, the cold had penetrated their bones. "We were up there too long in the wind. I'm frozen." She pulled the zipper of her down jacket an inch higher. "I thought we might have lunch on the tour boat, just down there by the bank, so I packed us a picnic. The boats are heated, and I have free tickets I got from one of my students whose brother works for the tour company."

Mike shivered. "What helpful connections you have. Let's go warm up."

The tour boat was only half filled, but did the job reheating them and providing a warm place to picnic. As they shared sandwiches, tomatoes and goat cheese à la français, they heard commentary in three languages. The landscape rolled gently by, and a lacy wake fanned out with a whoosh from the boat as it cut through the icy water. Mike only half-listened to the facts about sites and history of Paris, thinking mostly of how much he wanted to kiss Nikki on the tour boat.

Back on dry land, Nikki led him north by way of a crowded métro to Montmartre, the highest natural elevation in Paris. They climbed the steep stairway embedded in the grassy hillside that led to the famous white basilica, the Sacré Coeur. In front of the church steps, a wide platform filled with tourists opened to a panoramic view of the city. Perched near the edge of the terrace, they gazed silently at the Paris skyline of concrete buildings that seemed to be piled one on top of another. Mike slipped one arm around Nikki's shoulder. "Warmer?"

She nodded and turned to slip both arms around his waist, her head pressed against his chest. After a moment, she asked him, "Does this pose remind you of anything?"

"Do you mean last Christmas on the porch?"

"Yes. We stood this same way. It's getting to be a habit." Though he couldn't see her face, her light chuckle lifted his spirits.

"It was under the winter moon," he said, "right before I kissed you."

"The kiss that caused so many problems."

He looked down at her. "Do you regret it?"

"Of course not," she answered without lifting her head. "At least we could break new ground, though it was hard sometimes. And if nothing else, I was no longer just Danny's pesky little sister to you."

"I never thought you were pesky. Next to Danny, you were my best friend. Now you're a lot more." He pressed his lips against her temple.

Finally, she lifted her chin and held his gaze with an evasive smile. "Time for a picture." He grinned as she rummaged in her purse for her camera. "I haven't taken enough pictures since you arrived." If she were planning to dump him, she probably wouldn't be taking pictures of them now. Another good sign.

Nikki took two photos of him alone, with all of Paris rolling out in the background. An older French couple strolled by, and the woman said something to Nikki. "*Oui, merci.*" She handed her camera to the woman and showed her the shutter button.

She slipped her arms around his waist and pressed her cold cheek against his. It was the closest they'd been since his arrival. A mere photography pose? After two more photos, Nikki thanked the woman, who gave her a broad grin as she said something else to her. Nikki returned to the railing where Mike, as usual, had been watching her.

"What did she say? You're blushing."

Nikki's bashful smile nearly melted his heart. "She wanted to know if we're on our honeymoon."

Mike grinned and lifted his eyebrows. "Maybe next time. . ."

Her cheeks colored more deeply. "Now you have me speechless." He simply grinned. He wouldn't be surprised. . .

The remnants of sun hung low in the sky, gently warming the winter air for the rest of the afternoon. That was enough time for them to explore the cobbled pedestrian roads behind the basilica. Rows of cafés and restaurants framed the Place de Tertre, where a few brave artists displayed their work. Mike and Nikki scampered up and down the terraced streets connected by steep, narrow stairways. Finally, clouds slid in, and the afternoon temperatures dropped.

Shivering, she said, "Why don't we go home to clean up and rest, and then we can meet again around seven for dinner? I have a surprise for you." Her eyes were full of promise and mischief.

Maybe her surprise would bring them together once and for all. All day she had seemed more open, touching him in small ways, letting him put his arms around her. She'd said she needed space, but for how long? Maybe that evening she'd tell him.

CR   CR   CR

Nikki settled at the table, covered by a starched linen cloth. Candle-lit tables seemed to float like islands in the dimly lit restaurant. She'd taken extra care with her appearance, and Mike's eyes seemed glued to her. That only stirred the butterflies flying around inside her. Soft music floated through the small restaurant, which didn't yet have other customers.

She gazed across the darkened space where Mike's face glowed in the dancing light of the candle. The perfect place and time to have closure. She hadn't really tested him on purpose, but was relieved when he'd been patient and unwavering. And she felt a need to explain her year to him. It was time.

Nikki translated the menu under his watchful eyes. Then he said, "You mentioned you had a surprise for me. Is it a good one?"

She just smiled. The waiter arrived in the same black uniform and long white apron that she'd grown so accustomed to.

"Let me try," Mike told her with a wink. With painstaking effort, he ordered his meal in French. It surprised Nikki how well he did. She felt proud and impressed with his efforts. The apron-clad waiter gave a slight bow of his head, as if he'd spoken in flawless French. "*Très bien, Monsieur.*"

When the man left, Nikki said, "I want to tell you about my last year."

"Okay." Mike's eyes narrowed, as he was unsure he'd like what she would say. He eased back into the chair and linked his fingers across his waist.

Nikki smoothed an imaginary wrinkle on the tablecloth. "Last Christmas was like a fantasy come true for me, since I'd loved you all my life. Then in the space of a month, everything fell apart. I know I overreacted, but I felt like getting *over* you was my life theme. It's hard to live with one-sided love for so long, so I was determined to finish with it once for all. My coming to Paris was part of that." Her eyes met his, encountering a shadow of concern there.

"I tried to reach you all summer. And it wasn't that easy." His voice held a pleading protest, but a sparkle of humor as well.

"I thought I was pretty smart not giving you my phone number and running all over Europe. Traveling was wonderful, but in a way, I was running from *you*. I was trying to get you out of my system. But each time when I came back to Paris, I knew it hadn't worked." She gave him a tiny shrug.

A relieved smile crept across his lips as he listened to her.

She shot him a look before continuing. "You were so persistent in keeping in touch, I wondered if something had changed for you, but you never said so." Her voice scolded lightly. "I started dating Philippe and tried very hard to fall in love with him."

He leaned forward against the edge of the table. "I'm not sorry it didn't work with Philippe, but I am sorry I caused you so much pain." He reached his hand across the table. Nikki grasped his fingers, warm and dry. His gaze found hers. "The trip I made back to New York in August was clarifying for me. It was a time of emotional healing that I'd needed for a long time. After that, I could admit to myself what I really felt for you, that I was in love with you."

"I wish you'd shared it with me. But you started calling again, so it became impossible to get over you."

"At least I did something right in the last year. Aside from coming here."

A flood of sudden emotion cut off her words for several seconds. Finally, she looked directly into his eyes. "So, what I'm saying is my surprise isn't really a surprise. Mike Branagan, I love you and I always have. I never stopped. Even last summer you were always in the background, though I kept trying to push you out of my thoughts."

He rubbed his thumb across her hand. "That could get tiring. You really should give up on that." His grin spread broadly now. "I was getting worried, Nikki."

"You didn't really think I'd gotten over you, did you?"

"I don't know." He stared into the flickering candle, suddenly solemn. "I've made plenty of mistakes along the way." His eyes lifted to hers. "But I'm glad you hung in there with me." He reached his other hand across the table and grasped both of hers, squeezing gently.

"I can't take any credit, since I was running as fast as I could."

"Should we try again?" Mike's eyes crinkled with humor and something deeper, full of promise.

Nikki just smiled.

As they approached Nikki's apartment, she asked lightly, "Want to come up for a tisane?"

"I'd love to. I can't end this evening with you so soon." His voice was deep, thick with emotion. In the tiny elevator, Nikki leaned back against him and closed her eyes as his arms encircled her. This couldn't be happening, and yet it was. A dream she'd had nearly her whole life. She felt his breath against her neck, inhaled the scent of him as the elevator creaked upwards. Her heart throbbed against her rib cage. They didn't speak.

Her hands trembled slightly as she unlocked the four deadbolts, which seemed more cumbersome than usual. Reaching into the darkened apartment, Nikki turned on the lamp and took off her coat and scarf. "Do you want something to drink?" Her voice sounded miles away in her ears, her casual words out of step with the thrumming in her chest.

Mike had tossed his coat and scarf on the back of the chair and stood several feet from her. "Nikki," he said, his tone like silk. "Can I kiss you now?"

Mutely, she nodded and with one long stride, Mike closed the space between them. He placed his hands on each side of her face and drew her forward, covering her lips with his. Nikki melted into

243

him, slipping both arms around his waist. It was so good, so perfect, to be in his arms. Finally, in his arms. Their lips crushed, groped, with hunger and hurry, lost in wonder and the slow fulfillment of the previous year. A small moan escaped Nikki's throat as her lifetime craving for him overtook her.

Feverish entwining gave way to tender touches and quick, soft kisses. "I love you, Nikki," he whispered against her ear as he bent to kiss her beneath it, then down to her neck. His lips burned her throat with kisses alongside the necklace he had given her.

Finally, with a long sigh, he pulled his head back but kept his arms enfolded tightly around her. Nikki buried her face in his chest. They stood still for several minutes locked together.

When Nikki looked up at him, her eyes brimmed, and a few tears trailed down her cheeks. Mike gently traced their path with his finger. "Don't cry. We're finally together."

"*Finally.*" She smiled. With humor lacing her voice she added, "I've only been waiting since the age of seven."

He let out a deep chuckle and bent his head to kiss her again.

# Chapter Twenty-Eight

"Here comes the waiter. I'll let you order your own, since you speak French now." Nikki smiled and re-wrapped her scarf around her throat as a chilly draft whooshed in through the open door of the café. A French rock song blared from the speakers. At a nearby table, boisterous middle-aged Frenchmen filled the air with laughter, as they exchanged news around beers and lottery tickets.

"*Chocolat chaud* . . . did I pronounce that right?" Mike peered at the menu.

"Perfect." Nikki leaned her elbows on the tiny café table, unconcerned about the heavy gray skies outside. All she wanted was right in front of her.

He looked up and closed his menu after the waiter took their order. "We should talk about the future, Nikki. I could move back to New York—"

"Not on your life." Nikki shook her head vigorously. "You'd never be happy there and I'm dying to leave. I'll come to San Francisco after my school year." She saw his visible relief and laughed. "Thank you for offering. That was very sacrificial of you. I'd already decided a month ago that I was going to move to a bigger city. San Francisco was my first choice for obvious reasons." She lifted her eyebrows playfully.

"Have you broken the news to your folks that you're not planning to go back to Adam's Bridge?"

Nikki squeezed her lips tightly together and sighed. "No. I wish I had. They'd be more mentally prepared for my additional news."

Mike smiled and drew his steaming chocolate closer with cupped hands. "If you have another school break coming up in the spring, maybe you could come to San Francisco. I'll help you with your ticket."

"I was just wondering how I'd survive not seeing you until next summer." Nikki gave him a coy smile. "And I *do* have another break in April."

"You can put out some resumes then and we'll look for housing for you, maybe with some gals from my church. I'll see if anyone is looking for a roommate next summer."

Nikki reached for his hands and held them. His eyes locked with hers, then he leaned across the tiny table. He caressed her lips with his, then deepened the kiss. "I'm glad we're in Paris," he murmured after pulling back. "Kissing in public is so in vogue."

"Ah, you've noticed? It's striking at first, but then you get used to it."

He leaned back with a satisfied smile. "I like picturing you in San Francisco. We can actually date each other, like normal people in love."

"I can't wait. I love talking about apartments and jobs. It's so concrete."

"Have you thought about what the family will say about us?"

"Yes, I've thought about it a lot. My mom loves you, and Danny seems to approve too."

"Jim and Catherine won't have seen it coming, I'm pretty sure. Should be interesting to hear the family gossip."

Nikki sipped her hot chocolate. "Laura will probably say, 'Yet once again Princess Nicole gets everything she wants.'"

"We're avoiding mentioning your dad."

"I know." Nikki frowned. "What's the worst he can do?"

He shrugged. "He probably expects something will happen between us, since he knows I'm here visiting."

"He'll get used to the idea with time." She paused. "The only person who could ever make me change my mind would be you. If you, um, changed *your* mind." Nikki's heart pounded as a tiny shard of fear unexpectedly pierced through her joy.

Mike was already shaking his head. "You don't trust me yet, do you, Nikki? Do you think I'd encourage you to move all the way across the country if I wasn't serious about you? I guess I'll have to convince you somehow." He pressed his lips into her clasped hands. "The question is, are *you* ready for your dad's response?"

"I'll have to be, because I choose you," she said lightly. "Should we tell them together while you're still here?" Maybe that would give her some courage to tell her father.

"I call Jim and Catherine every month, so I'll tell them that we're together and that you're moving to San Francisco. You can tell your parents, then word will travel to the rest of the family."

Nikki bit her lip. She'd have to face her father alone. "Okay, I'll tell them after you leave." In the meantime, she'd think and pray about what to say.

CR  CR  CR

During the rest of Mike's visit, Nikki savored every minute, knowing their time together was ebbing away. Despite the cold, blustery days, they'd visited monuments, museums, and quaint neighborhoods, restaurants, and cafés.

She took him to her French church, where the small congregation greeted him warmly. They talked about their faith and prayed together. Other days, they cooked together at Nikki's apartment and talked through the evening.

Since the day she tearfully clung to him and kissed him goodbye at the airport, images of their ten days together filled her waking moments. Every place they'd gone, every look, every touch. The first two weeks of the New Year crept along through cold, darkened days, though Nikki hardly noticed the chill. She returned to her routine leading French teenagers in English conversation. Bustled through afternoon crowds with her groceries. . . yet nothing was the same.

"You seem so happy, Nikki," Anne-Laure told her. "You must have had a good holiday."

Nikki simply nodded with a wide, knowing smile. Her effervescence flowed out into her English teaching. Her students seemed to absorb her energy, responding with enthusiasm to the activities she planned and led. She'd eventually have to come back down to earth, or the rest of her year in Paris would drift by in a fog of daydreams and romantic memories. But for the moment, she'd savor it like a delicious nectar.

All week Nikki planned to reserve her airline ticket for San Francisco, but found herself swamped with tasks. If she did it later that week, she could probably still get a good rate. Having her ticket in hand would serve as tangible proof that she'd see Mike again and prepare for her future in San Francisco.

She'd talked once with her parents, but they'd seemed in a hurry, so she didn't tell them her big news. She told them that she'd enjoyed Mike's visit, hoping it would spark questions. It didn't. Were they avoiding the topic because of disapproval? Wouldn't they at least be curious? She'd have to bring it up herself, but hadn't yet prepared her words. Was she putting it off? Sometimes she felt torn between impatience to tell the whole world and the dread of telling her father.

A few hours later, she settled comfortably in front of her computer screen, looking at Mike on the other side. It was now an appointment they enjoyed several times a week.

"I talked to Jim and Catherine last night about us." He wore a lazy grin.

"You're smiling. Does that mean it went well? Tell me."

"I said they'd be surprised. Well, Jim was surprised, but happy for us. Catherine said she'd always hoped we'd get together."

"Really? Catherine said that? She never said anything over the years."

"How could she? We were miles apart and didn't show visible interest in each other. But she said she always noticed how well we got along. She guessed you'd be moving here."

"Will she tell Dad? I haven't told them yet."

A startled look passed across Mike's face. "No, I don't think they'll say anything. I told them they shouldn't spoil the surprise." He sank back into his chair, frowning. "Why haven't you told them?"

Nikki cringed as the hurt in his voice scraped her heart. "I was going to, but the last time I talked to them, they were both really distracted. It didn't seem to be the right time. I'll tell them this week when they call. And I'll buy my ticket this Thursday." The guilty ache settled deeper inside her.

"You don't need their approval, Nikki," Mike said quietly. He'd leaned forward and his face loomed with intensity on the screen. "You should get that conversation over with. Draw your line in the sand."

"You're right. I will. This week."

After they hung up, the weight persisted in Nikki's stomach. Maybe she wasn't as independent as she wanted to believe she was. Once the conversation with her father was behind her, she'd feel like she was fully Mike's.

He was able to make decisions easily and expect others to respect them. Why couldn't she do the same? She'd set a new standard in moving to Paris. It had been her declaration of adult independence. Now she understood, with a prickling down her spine, that she'd likely have to make more choices like this one. Independence wasn't going to be a one-time event.

❧ ❧ ❧

Huddled over the kitchen table, Marie sobbed. Her shoulders shook and tears pooled on the wooden surface below her nose. As long as she lived, she'd never forget the look on Frank's face when she told him about Doug. His olive complexion went white, then red. Shocked. Incredulous. Not even livid, though that came later. It was as though he'd heard something impossible to believe until the sickening reality seeped in.

Her tears flowed even before she told him. It had happened just once, unplanned, she'd said. She promised to never see Doug again, to quit her job if necessary. Frank had just stared at her for the longest time, unable to speak. When he whirled on his heel and stomped out the front door, her tears became torrential, and she crumpled into a shuddering heap.

What would become of her? Would Frank tell her to leave? Where would she go? How would she support herself? Might he forgive her? Her friend Sandy had an affair, and eventually her husband forgave her, and they went to counseling.

No one in the family would ever believe it. Mild-mannered Marie, they'd called her for years. Code phrase for doormat. The doormat would never go and have an affair, never be attracted to someone, let alone attract someone.

Maybe no one had to know. It was their problem, after all, hers, and Frank's. She hoped he'd be willing to keep it private. That is, if he agreed to stay married to her.

# Chapter Twenty-Nine

The morning following Nikki's conversation with Mike, she slipped out of bed with a surge of strength and determination. She'd call that very day and tell her father about her relationship with Mike. Nikki glanced down at her watch. She'd have to wait until that evening to call when her parents were home from work.

She'd turned phrases around in her mind after her tense conversation with Mike. The shadow of hurt and withdrawal that filled his eyes kept coming back to her. Was he doubting her again, assuming she was too enmeshed in her family?

Was she?

Nikki practiced statements in front of the mirror. "Dad, I have some news for you," she could start. "Dad, as you know, Mike was here at Christmas, and we became very close." No, he'd jump to conclusions. Rehearsed phrases would come out sounding forced. She simply needed to tell him the truth. She loved Mike and wanted to be with him. Was that so hard?

Usually, her parents would call her the following day, but this couldn't wait. Once she'd told her father about Mike, she'd let Mike know and they'd again be on the same wavelength. She surely didn't want him to think *she* was having doubts. Or that her father's opinion was still important enough to sway her decisions and her heart.

That evening, as Nikki prepared herself to call her father, the phone rang. It might be Mike, afraid he'd pressured her. But it was her father. Her pulse leaped.

"Hi, Dad. I wasn't expecting you until tomorrow. Is everything okay?" Tension roiled in her stomach.

"No, Nikki, everything's *not* okay." Her father's voice was ragged, dull. He almost sounded like a different person. A chill rippled through her as she eased onto the couch.

"Is everyone alright? Mom? Danny? What is it?"

"Yes, everyone is fine, physically, that is. No one's hurt. It's your mother. I don't know how to tell you this, Nikki. I'm only telling you, no one else in the family. Just you, me, and your mother will know."

"What, Dad? You're getting me worried. What happened to Mom?"

"Your mother—" His voice broke. She thought she heard a small sob, which she'd never in her life heard from her father. "Your mother has been unfaithful." His voice went quiet, then he cleared his throat several times as if the emotion strangled him.

Nikki's mouth dropped open. She fell back against the stiff spine of the couch. Words eluded her. It was impossible—her mother? She was the last person on earth Nikki would ever expect to have an affair. "Are. . .are you sure? I just can't believe it."

"That was my reaction too, but she's been crying for two days."

"Who, when?"

"Someone she works with. She said it happened just once and wasn't planned. I guess she thinks that makes it okay." His voice emerged between a sob and a bitter snarl.

"If she's crying all the time, she must feel guilty about it and regret it." Nikki paused. "Dad, how are *you* handling it? Have you and she been able to talk it through?"

"Not yet. I'm too shocked and angry to talk. I wanted to tell you because you're part of this family, even if now you're far away. I really miss my little girl. I need to see you—"

Two separate responses rose within her, tangled together like the thorny stem of a rose. One wanted to deny being a little girl, and the other crumbled at her father's despair. He'd always seemed so strong and powerful.

"We can talk on the computer, Dad. We can see each other that way, until I get home this summer," she said in a small voice, feeling like she was swimming over her head. "Dad, can I talk to Mom? Is she there?"

Seconds later, she heard her mother's voice on the phone. She was crying. "Mom, is it true?"

"I'm afraid so, Nikki. It was so subtle, I didn't realize it was getting dangerous. I'm not in love with Doug. We were just flirting. I thought it was innocent until he invited me to see his new house—"

"Maybe Dad will forgive you. . .don't cry." Something ripped deep inside her. "Mom, I hope you'll be able to talk it out together."

Her mother began to sob and could no longer speak. "Y-yes, okay. I'll talk to you soon, honey."

Frank returned to the phone. "Nikki, if you can visit, it would mean so much. I just need to see your face. I know you have your work, but don't you have a vacation coming up in the spring?"

Nikki felt a deep thud inside her as her throat went dry. Spring break? "Uh, Dad, yeah, I have a break, but that brings up something I wanted to tell you. You know Mike was here over Christmas."

"Yes, I know." He sounded annoyed at the mention of Mike's name. Not a good start.

"We, uh. Well, Dad, I need to tell you that Mike and I are in love with each other. I'm planning to go see him during spring break."

She heard a small silence on the phone. "In love? You sure it goes both ways, Nikki?"

"Yes, Dad. He came all the way to Paris to tell me he was in love with me. I hope you'll accept this and give him a chance."

Frank sighed deeply. "Nikki, I have so much on my mind now. You know how I feel about Mike. At any rate, you were just with him, and you can see him next summer. We are in a state of crisis, and I need you here."

Nikki shut her eyes tightly. She heard the clock ticking, marking the seconds of silence. This wasn't how she imagined her conversation with her father. Her trip—she *had* to see Mike in April. Yet her father was crying on the phone.

Finally, she spoke. "I don't know what to say, Dad. I understand you and Mom are having problems right now, but this is between the two of you, isn't it? I mean, what can I possibly do to help? You need to talk it out together. Maybe you haven't talked enough over the years and things build up—"

"Are you defending what your mother did?"

"No, of course, what she did was wrong. You two need to talk about it when you're able. I don't think I can help—"

"Nikki, we haven't seen you in over six months." Her father's voice was impatient. "We don't expect you to help us with our problems. I just need to *see* you. Mike will understand."

She wasn't sure about that, in light of their last conversation. "Dad, I can't give you an answer right now. Let me think about it, okay?"

Her temples pounded in a merciless rhythm. Like a rope, the strands of her heart felt frayed, splitting between Mike and her parents. As soon as Nikki hung up the phone, she threw herself down on the couch and ground a fist into her forehead. A groan erupted from her tortured throat. Would her parents stay together? She couldn't imagine, didn't want to picture the alternative. And how could her father not ask, but *expect* a visit from her?

Yet his broken voice haunted her. He said he needed her. He needed her support, her presence. How could she ignore his misery and go happily to San Francisco?

As the rope stretched tighter, which side would break first?

CR  CR  CR

Mike stared down into his second mug of coffee. Steam wafted upwards, grazing his face with moisture. He sat only half-dressed on the stool at the kitchen bar, paralyzed. He'd be late to work but couldn't make himself move any faster. It wasn't physical. It went deeper than that.

He was as stunned as Nikki by the news of Marie's affair. She was the last person he'd ever suspect of that. He was more concerned with Nikki, who nearly fell apart as she tearfully told him about it, and of Frank's request.

It hadn't taken long for Frank to pull on Nikki's family loyalty. Mike didn't want to be heartless, or encourage her to be, but it was their problem, Frank and Marie's. What right did they have to drag Nikki into the middle of it?

The way he saw it, Frank had neglected Marie for years. Now that the tree had borne fruit, Frank wanted Nikki to fly in from Paris to soothe his wounds. He needed to face his own marriage, and the mess he'd made of it, by himself.

Of course, Mike hadn't said any of that to Nikki. She needed to make her own decision. Not to mention that any pressure or advice on his part might be used against him. His relationship with Frank had hardly been neutral over the years, and any thawing in recent months was too fragile to risk.

He reached for the phone. "Hey, Ralph. I'll be in a little late. Yeah, I'll be there in time for the meeting at eleven. See you soon." He pushed the phone across the counter and took a sip of lukewarm coffee.

A sigh rose from deep within his belly, soulful and dull. He'd known that sooner or later family expectations would suction Nikki back. He just hadn't expected it to happen this soon. Her fledgling independence was being tested, and she was panicking. He too was in the middle. After the year-long evolution of their relationship, he wanted her to choose him, and not only because he wanted her to visit in April. He hoped she could recognize the difference between appropriate family loyalty and losing herself.

Would Frank always cast a shadow over Mike and Nikki's relationship? Maybe things would get easier once she was firmly planted in San Francisco. Maybe this obstacle would help her grow stronger.

She might end up risking their newly defined relationship. If she did, he had no idea how he should respond.

CR   CR   CR

During English discussion class, Nikki tried in vain to corral her frenetic thoughts. It was useless. Her afternoon teacher, Rashida Mahmoudi, noticed Nikki's distraction. "A family crisis," Nikki had responded to the compassionate inquiry. When the woman suggested Nikki take the rest of the afternoon off, Nikki smiled gratefully. She packed her tote bag and slipped out the front door before the next class began.

Though the air scooped its clammy fingers under her scarf, Nikki walked, breathing puffs of vapor, thinking, praying. In deep concentration, she trudged north from the school toward the Place de la République, then on toward the Saint Martin Canal. She stared down at the dormant locks, which dropped fifteen feet when the water washed through the gateway.

She couldn't imagine her parents not staying together. It seemed impossible. She prayed in a low voice, "Oh, Father. I know this wasn't your will, but you can still turn it around somehow. I pray Dad'll forgive Mom and that their marriage can get better."

Nikki's whisper trailed off as she slumped onto a park bench. She glanced around her and saw the prone sleeping figure of a drunken homeless man on the next bench, his breath puffing clouds into the frosty air. No one strolled through the park that bone-chilling day in January. Nikki sat alone in the mist and shivered.

She still couldn't grasp how her own mother could have an extramarital affair. If her parents' outwardly stable marriage revealed such cracks in the foundation, what hope could anyone have? Could she herself hope for a happily-ever-after future with Mike?

Whatever decision she made about her trip would leave her in trouble with someone. She didn't want to decide on that basis, to avoid conflict. No, she wanted to do what was right, but what *was* the right choice? Love or family loyalty? How could she know? Just because her father had pleaded with her in his pain didn't necessarily make that the right choice.

How would she *ever* make this decision?

Wearily, Nikki began a slow walk back toward her apartment. She felt slightly better moving around in the brisk air, but it did little to inspire her with insight. Her quaint street looked more colorless and dull than it had the day before, the barrenness of winter stark before her. She made herself a cup of tea and cradled its warmth in her cold hands. Suddenly her phone rang but the caller was not identified.

She answered. "Allo?"

"Nikki, I'm glad you're home." It was her father.

She sighed. She wasn't ready to talk to him. "Hi, Dad. I'm surprised to hear from you so soon."

"I hope you've decided to come home. You'll need to make your reservation soon. Lots of people travel at spring break."

"I haven't made my final decision yet." Blood pounded in her head. "I promise I'll call you and let you know."

"Don't forget about your family, Nikki. When there's a need, that's your place. This is a crisis. I thought you'd see it that way." His voice faded.

She swallowed. "Dad, this is really hard for me too. I have a new life with Mike now. We need to be together. I know you think it's selfish—"

"Yes, I do." Her father's tone was icy. Then Nikki heard something else. A muffled sob. She felt like her own heart was about to break.

"Nikki, please. . ."

"Oh, Dad." Hot tears slid down Nikki's cheeks. "Don't cry, Daddy. I'll come."

After she hung up the phone, Nikki stared at it, unseeing, her face still wet. Chill threaded through the room as the winter sun slipped away. She struggled to breathe, as if trapped in a box, pushed against its narrow walls. Would her own father manipulate her? Or was he simply flattened by pain?

And what would Mike say or think? How could she possibly tell him?

# Chapter Thirty

Clanging phones sliced through the busy hum of the travel agency. Nikki waited in a small reception area alongside an open space filled with a row of desks and harried agents who were on the telephone or across from their clients.

She hadn't had the courage to tell Mike her decision, but would call him later when the ticket was in her hands. He'd be disappointed, but as her father said, he'd probably understand. She hoped.

Unbidden, a year-old the memory of her conversation with him slipped into her mind. At the time, he'd questioned whether she'd truly separated her own life from her parents'. Berating herself, she wondered what had brought her to this decision, compassion or spineless weakness?

When the agent called Nikki, she sat facing a thirtyish woman with pale, limp hair over one shoulder. Quickly and efficiently, the bored-looking agent, whose nameplate read "Laticia," recited the flight times for a direct flight to JFK airport and back again to Paris. In a resigned stupor, Nikki confirmed the dates. She questioned herself again. Had God led her, or had it been her sense of guilt and sorrow for her father's tears?

She'd have to find another way to apply for jobs in San Francisco and look for an apartment there, and another way to assuage her heart from missing Mike. Another way of convincing him she *was* really serious about a future with him. Would he *really* understand?

The printer rattled like a machine gun. The phones clanged incessantly, jarring Nikki's frayed nerves. A low murmur of conversation hung in the room as customers planned dream vacations.

It felt so wrong. Where was the peace she should have had in doing the *right* thing? She looked back at the agent, who stared at her and proffered the printed tickets. A perplexed look came over her pale face when Nikki didn't reach out to take them.

"Madame—" Nikki began, her heart drumming. "I may have made a mistake—"

Laticia's eyebrows shot up. "Pardon me? I've just finished your tickets, Miss. There are many people waiting." She jerked her head toward the crowded reception area.

"Please, I have to explain—in English." Nikki reverted to English, and her words gushed out. "You see, I've been in love with someone since I was seven years old, and he just came and spent Christmas and told me he loves me, and when I was planning to visit him in the spring, I had a crisis in my family, and now my father is pressuring me to come there instead, and—" Nikki stopped to breathe.

Laticia had leaned forward, the irritation transformed into what appeared to be sympathy. "*C'est vrai?*" Her blue eyes were round. "Since seven years old? But you love him, *non?*"

"*Oui!* I've waited for him my whole life, and now I won't see him until June or July, unless I go this April. But my father cried and wanted me to come home. I just couldn't take it." Tears flowed down Nikki's cheeks. She rummaged in her purse for a tissue and wiped her eyes. "I just don't know what to do. I can't please everyone."

"No, you can't. You have to live your own life, not everyone else's." Laticia's voice was emphatic. "How about if I go smoke a cigarette while you think it over? I'll come back in a few minutes, and you can tell me if you want this ticket, or another one."

Nikki nodded with a weak smile as Laticia rose from her chair and left the room. Alone at the woman's massive desk, she mentally jogged through the scenario for the fiftieth time, despairing of obtaining a clear answer. The agent's words rang in her ears. "Live my own life," she repeated aloud.

Though her mother's actions had been wrong, her longings were understandable. Nikki's father had neglected and belittled her mother for years. He'd always been the righteous one, critical of Mike and Danny. Was it now Nikki's place to help him feel better? Was she being selfish, as he had accused, by not canceling her plans with Mike in order to go to New York?

Suddenly, the decision seemed clear. Giving in wasn't always the best way to show love. She couldn't continue the pattern of fulfilling assumptions, or of being the princess, her father's baby girl.

Perspiration beaded on Nikki's neck. She didn't want that role with her father anymore. She was his adult daughter, not his little girl. He needed to live *his* own life.

And she desperately needed to live hers.

When Laticia settled back into her chair behind the computer screen, she startled Nikki from her thoughts. "Ready?" the woman asked. Nikki nodded. Without a word, the woman reached across the desk and tore the tickets in two.

"San Francisco, then?"

Nikki paused for a moment. It had been six months, and she wanted to see her parents too, but she couldn't sacrifice her trip to San Francisco. "Would you check on something for me?" she asked Laticia in a voice that no longer sounded like a whine. "Is it possible to do a two-day stopover in New York, then continue on to San Francisco?"

Laticia cocked her head at the idea. "*Peut-être*. Maybe. I'll see." She began tapping madly on the keyboard. Several minutes later, she swiveled the flat monitor around so Nikki could see it. "*Bah, voilà!* I can get a stopover for you in New York, where you can spend two days with your parents. Then you continue on to San Francisco to be with your man. For the return, you'll fly directly back to Paris. It's easy because this flight stops automatically in New York before continuing on to San Francisco. It will only cost forty-five euros more."

Nikki stared at the woman and couldn't stop a smile from stretching her hot, wet cheeks. "Thank you. I think that will work fine."

The woman grinned at Nikki. "Love is important, you know," she said. "I print the tickets?"

"Yes, please."

Once again, tickets chugged out of the noisy printer, sounding less aggressive the second time. The woman presented them to Nikki as if they were made of gold. Nikki looked down at them with wonder and fell back in her chair as if she'd just run a marathon. "Thanks for understanding. And for helping."

Laticia shrugged her thin shoulders. "You found the solution yourself. And me, I like a good love story. But now I really need another cigarette."

Nikki felt a hundred pounds lighter as she walked back to the métro. The tickets were printed and tucked in her purse. It was the best she could do, and everyone would have to accept it. When she arrived home, she called her father at work to break the news to him.

"Mancini Motors. Can I help you?" The receptionist's cool, professional voice filled the phone.

"Frank Mancini, please. It's his daughter, Nikki."

"He's out of the office with clients, Nikki. Would you like his voice mail?"

"Yes, please." It would certainly be easier to leave a message explaining everything. But was it the cowardly way? She sighed. Maybe this time it was the best way.

When the beep sounded on the line, she said, "Hi Dad, it's Nikki. I will come to New York in April, but just for two days. We'll have a quick visit, then I'll go on to San Francisco." She almost added, "Hope that's okay with you", but bit back the words. He'd have to accept her decision. "I'll have a longer visit with you all this summer, okay? After that I'm planning to move to California, so I need to look for an apartment during my spring visit. Hope you understand. Well, I have to go now, Dad. I'll talk to you soon. You and Mom are in my prayers." She hung up, relief washing over her in cool waves. He might not be happy, but he'd know her decision, and he'd have to accept it. She was an adult.

Next, she dialed Mike's number. A sense of urgency to talk to him drove her. If he'd already left, she'd contact him at work. She *had* to talk to him.

"Is everything okay, Nikki?" Worry laced his voice. "Good thing you caught me. I was just walking out the door."

"No, everything is fine. *Really* fine," she said, breathless. "I wanted to talk to you as soon as possible." It felt *so* good to hear his voice. She sank into the couch.

"Last night, Dad called again. I felt so guilty and sad for him, I ended up telling him I'd go to New York. I felt pressured into it, but confused it with compassion. But today, I changed my mind. I have to live *my* life, and my life is with you, Mike. I did get a stopover in New York for just two days, so I could see them. Hope you don't mind."

"Oh, Nikki, that's great. It sounds like a good compromise."

She let out the breath she'd been holding. He didn't begrudge her two days with her parents, and she loved him even more for it.

"That way you can support your parents without leaving me here to cry and miss you by myself."

They laughed. "I'm glad you understand. It would have been too hard to do one or the other. I love you both and was feeling pulled. Not pulled, more like dismembered! But I really need to be with you. And one more thing—"

"Yes?"

"I called my dad at work to let him know. He was out with clients, so I left a voice mail. I told him I'll be moving to San Francisco this summer. Maybe it's better for him to hear it on a phone message, so he can mull it over and get used to the idea. And also, I won't cave in under his pressure."

"At least he'll know your decision. That's the important thing."

"I'm counting the days until I see you again. Less than three months."

"Me too, Nikki. I love you." His voice was a gentle caress.

"I love you, more than I can say. Now go on to work. I don't want to hold you up. Will you be able to call tonight?"

"I can't call until about three my time. Midnight for you. Maybe it's better to wait until tomorrow?"

"No, I'll stay up. We can keep it short, but I need to hear your voice and see you. After this week, I need it."

"Okay," he said. "You can't see me now, but I'm smiling. Can't wait to see your face tonight. *A ce soir, mon amour.* My love."

# Epilogue

The mailman had been late that day. Aunt Trudie wrinkled her nose in mild annoyance at the quantity of paper, mostly junk, stuffed in her mailbox. She pulled out the wad and almost overlooked the cream-colored stationery envelope with embossed printing on the front. It brought a smile to her lips.

The sky already scowled with bumpy, gray clouds. She returned to the house and closed all the windows, since a storm was predicted. A cup of tea would be nice to go along with the mail.

She poured boiling water from the shrieking tea kettle, then settled into the wooden captain's chair in her eat-in kitchen. She shuffled through the pile of ads and bills and found the cream-colored envelope. That would be first.

Inside the foil-lined envelope was a small card. On the front was a photo she recognized right away, a photo from long ago. Mike at age ten and Nikki at age seven, standing shoulder to shoulder in front of the Christmas tree. Maybe they'd been soul mates even back then.

She opened the card and read aloud, "Mike Branagan and Nikki Mancini request the joy of your presence as they become husband and wife on Saturday, June thirtieth. . ." Her smile broadened. "My little niece, getting married."

Not that Trudie had been smiling a year earlier when you could have pushed her over with a feather. Yet, why had she been so surprised? Now it seemed so natural. The previous summer, everyone else in the family was in shock when Nikki returned from Paris and announced she was moving to San Francisco. She and Mike were in love. Months after the fact, she'd learned that Mike had spent Christmas in Paris with Nikki. All of this happening right under her nose. After that, she was determined to have a better pulse on the family goings-on.

True to her word, Nikki packed up and moved to San Francisco. Danny surprised everyone by taking off work to drive her across the country with a rental van full of her furniture and belongings.

Most of the family members seemed to approve and cheer for the young couple. Of course, Frank was the one everyone watched, since he'd always babied Nikki and wanted Superman for her, not Mike, a mere human they'd all known for ages. Everyone but Frank thought Mike was the greatest—thoughtful, funny, smart, handsome. Though Frank was her brother, Trudie admitted he could be obstinate. Why couldn't he see that Mike was perfect for Nikki? It was so clear, once you saw them together as a couple, as she had the previous Christmas when they came east for a few days.

Trudie regretted the distance she had always felt with the younger members of her family, including Mike, who was like family, and soon would *be* family. In the last year she'd started making efforts to call and email both Mike and Nikki more often. It wasn't too late to be close.

Besides that, the family soap opera was so interesting to watch, she couldn't stay distant. Frank had had a close call with a heart problem, so was now on a strict diet. He and Marie spent some time in counseling for some reason, though Trudie wasn't supposed to know about it. Seems to have been effective since they'd scheduled a Caribbean cruise for late summer. *That* was a first.

Frank appeared to be making grudging gestures toward Mike. Maybe he realized he couldn't change anything. If he didn't make nice with Mike sooner or later, he'd lose Nikki. Trudie shrugged. There were some things even Frank Mancini couldn't control.

Outside, the wind had picked up and began howling, tossing remnants of last spring's debris into the air. She peered into the envelope and saw a handwritten note. She'd almost missed it. *Hi Aunt Trudie. Guess you aren't surprised by this news!*

No, she wasn't surprised. Nikki had adapted to San Francisco like a fish to water. Her Paris experience had likely prepared her for city life. And she sure loved being near Mike.

Her job teaching French at a local public high school may have been one reason that she and Mike waited a year before announcing their engagement.

Trudie kept reading. *A few months ago, Mike and I were together on the west shore of the city overlooking the Pacific Ocean. He turned to me and said, 'Marry me, Nikki?'* Trudie sighed happily. So romantic!

She took a sip of her mandarin green tea and glanced down to finish Nikki's note. *We are really happy and I'm glad everyone has accepted it. I hope you'll be able to come for the wedding this summer. Remember, I always told you that one day I was going to marry Mike!*

I hope you enjoyed reading *One December*. If you did, please consider leaving a review at Amazon and/or Goodreads for me. It would help other readers discover my books and be encouraged by their inspiring truths.

You can sign up to receive updates about new books at www.Kyle-Hunter.com. At the same place you can read the first full chapter of my books or order eBooks at a number of online stores including directly from me!

## More romantic stories from Love on the Move

Take a romantic trip to Provence, France, in this 2-book inspirational contemporary romance series. Also available in eBook and eBook box set of both books.

### *Prodigals in Provence*

Bree and Lauren own and run Le Bon Voyage, a travel company specializing in tours to charming Provence, France.

Travis is a TV travel critic accustomed to crossing the globe to film documentaries and write books. But he's been in a spiritual desert ever since losing his marriage and ministry five years earlier.

Between film projects, Travis plans to accompany his elderly mother on a tour to Provence, a long-term dream for her. Bree tries unsuccessfully to block him, sure he's coming to spy on the struggling company for one of his exposé articles.

A diverse group of tourists arrives at the rented villa to spend the week and discover the spectacular villages, vineyards, and history of the Luberon mountain region of Provence. Amidst a series of problems and relational tensions, Bree thinks she has all she can handle . . . until she becomes attracted to Travis.

As Bree and Travis are drawn together, will their hidden wounds drive them apart?

Read an excerpt from Chapter One:

# Prodigals in Provence

# Chapter One

Bree Sorenson's parched throat felt like rough burlap and her face prickled with heat. If she could dive into the carafe of water that beckoned from the podium, she'd do it. She eyed it before returning her attention to her audience.

"For those of you who dream of a Provence cooking tour, we have one scheduled later this fall, where world-class chefs will teach you French recipes in small groups." The microphone gave her voice a strength she didn't feel. The metal felt slick in her hand as she relaxed her grip. She panned a friendly gaze around the ballroom, making eye contact with the scattered few attendees seated in the first four rows. If the Coastal Cove Gracious Retirement Community had given her a smaller room in which to do her presentation, it might not have been so brazenly obvious how few people had shown up.

"Our May trip will be to the magical Luberon mountain region, well-known for having the loveliest villages in France." Rivulets of perspiration traced a path down her spine beneath her spring linen jacket and blouse despite the air conditioning flowing through the room. If only she'd taken the *unseasonably warm* forecast more seriously.

Several wizened residents nodded. Others fidgeted in their chairs, faces blank, probably wondering why she was wasting their time. She took a deep gulp of water and forced the corners of her lips upward, trying to keep her expression enthusiastic. "When you travel with Le Bon Voyage, you'll be part of a small, exclusive group of no more than ten people, for a more personalized experience."

*Stay upbeat! Smile!* The mental reminders flowed countercurrent to the weight pulling inside her. If she didn't fill this trip with a minimum number of travelers, the company's profit would be almost non-existent for the second trip in a row. They have to plunge again into their reserves.

Bree glanced around the room. The elegant five-star details— the carved molding on the coffered ceiling, the plush patterned carpet underfoot, the impressionist-style paintings on the walls— spoke of the financial means of the residents. But that didn't guarantee they'd be open to European travel on short notice.

If anything would convince these would-be travelers to sign up for the nine-day Provence excursion scheduled for the following month, her photos would. They'd plant in her audience a burning need to go. That need had been like breathing for Bree, ever since she first lived in France as a college exchange student. But such a passion was difficult to communicate in a few short minutes to a fidgety crowd whose minds were likely on the dinner menu or tomorrow's bridge game.

She started the slideshow and adjusted the focus. A vibrant purple panorama of lavender fields lit up the screen on the wall behind her, and she was rewarded by ooh and ahhs around the room. The pink-hued buildings of Roussillon, the fountains of Aix-en-Provence surrounded by colorful café awnings, stretches of gnarly grapevines in neat rows, medieval walled villages perched on hilltops. She clicked through the photos, one by one and watched the expressions on the faces of her audience. The final photo of an elevated sun-swept terrace shaded by overhanging grape vines expanded on the screen then faded from view. She loved ending with that one, the most dramatic *and* most likely to trigger a decision to sign up.

"After each day's adventures, you'll return to a private villa where you'll be able to take a swim, then dine on the terrace under the stars." Bree proffered a handful of brochures to each row. Her eyes roved to a clock on the opposite wall of the room. Only ten minutes left to convince them. "The brochure highlights our current trip. We still have space and I'd love to have you among us for our tour. If you can't come in May, be sure to sign up for one in the future."

Thirty minutes later Bree stepped through the sliding glass doors from the cool air onto the baking sidewalk. She trudged away from the main building, which resembled a large Caribbean villa, and passed the smaller patio homes on the way back to her car. Her shoulders sagged from a laptop case on one side and a canvas bag of brochures on the other.

It was late April, and the property was already fully landscaped with cloudbanks of impatiens in red, white, and pink framed by pale green ferns. A balmy breeze, carrying a scent of new plants and fresh mulch tickled her neck and filled her lungs. Spring in northern Virginia never failed to revive her spirits, though that particular day she fought her dark thoughts and what-ifs and their tag-along emotions.

Bree moved her jaws, stiff from an hour of eager smiling. More like pitiful pleading. She may as well have said, "Please, I need another warm body in order to make my bottom line!" Maybe the low numbers were the result of the economy or insufficient marketing. Whatever the case, Le Bon Voyage was in trouble.

Once her tired body slid into the gully of her Honda's hot bucket seat, she sighed and ran her fingers through her hair. How long could she keep doing this? The last-minute tension, the fear that important details would fall apart at the wrong time . . . Sometimes the stress was unbearable. Each trip held the inherent challenges of weaving together an excursion on foreign soil. She always double and triple checked dozens of lists and computer files, as well as stacks of folders and notebooks piled on her office desk, just to make sure she hadn't neglected any detail. Despite this, something could still slip past her obsessively watchful eye. And that didn't even take into account the possibility of random events, such as vendors in Europe who had misplaced requests, gone on strike, or double-booked a service she needed.

The phone beeped in her purse. Maybe it was Lauren, her business partner and best friend. Glancing at the screen, she saw the name Mariah, her friend from church. Bree could use a friendly voice, even as she sweated in the car. Mariah was studying counseling and got a lot of practical experience with Bree. She turned on the ignition and flipped the air conditioner to max before responding. "Hi, Mariah."

"Hey, Bree. How did your presentation go today?"

Bree sighed. "The presentation went well enough, but I'm afraid the timing is too tight for most people. We should have done this kind of promotion months ago, but I kept thinking the trip would fill up."

"Don't you think you'll have enough people?" Mariah's voice held a layer of concern which calmed and reassured Bree. It was good to have a friend who wasn't annoyed by Bree's anxious nature.

"It's hard to tell. We still have six weeks, but usually people reserve months in advance." Bree let out a glum sigh. "It's been three years, Mariah, and Le Bon Voyage still takes two steps forward then one step back. All we need is two more tours that are under-filled and that'll be the end of us. We're just a razor's edge from disaster."

"It might still work out, though." Mariah's voice turned soothing, but Bree knew her friend didn't have answers either. "It takes time to get a business established." That part was proven true daily.

"I know." A message flashed across Bree's phone indicating a call. "Oh, I wonder if I should get that."

"You have another call?"

Bree stuffed down a sigh. "I'll call them back. I might as well tell you and please keep this to yourself. I've quietly made some inquiries into other travel companies just in case—you know. In case we go under. One of them just called back." Maybe she should never have contacted them. Would she be ready for their response if it were positive?

Mariah drew in a quick breath. "Are things that bad?"

"If we have a good summer, we can get back into the black. If not—well, it never hurts to make a plan."

"What about Lauren? What would she do?"

"She's dating Mark and they're pretty serious, so I think she's all set. But I'll have no place to go if the business folds." She couldn't return to her mother in Minnesota. She'd never be content with small-town life. No, Bree would have to fend for herself if everything went up in smoke. So, she prepared for the worst, plotting her leap from the burning building before it caught fire.

"Oh. I see. Don't worry, I won't say a word to Lauren or anyone else. Maybe it will work out. Just take one day at a time."

Sound advice if Bree could only do it. She hung up with Mariah and listened to the voicemail. It was from Horizon Tours, one of the companies where she'd sent her resume.

She listened to the raspy male voice. They didn't need her, not right now. The company's current interest was Asia, although they might expand into Europe within the coming two years. They'd keep her posted.

And in the meantime, she'd pray the bottom would not fall out of her fragile business.

*Read the rest of Chapter One at <u>www.Kyle-Hunter.com</u>*

# The story continues . . .

## *A Promise in Provence*

Lauren is at a turning point. If only she knew *where* to turn. Her long-term relationship with Mark is fading fast. Instead, she feels drawn to Jean-Pierre, an attractive Frenchman she'd met the previous summer. When she's laid off from her job as a chef, she decides to go see him in Provence, France.

Mark can't get Lauren out of his heart, even though it's been close to a year since she asked him to give her space. When she goes to France, he's afraid he'll lose her for good. That is, until he decides to go there, too, as a last-ditch effort to win her back.

At first, Lauren is angry that Mark follows her to France. But a joint desire to help a young refugee boy leads them to work together. Lauren finds herself torn between the two men. Worse, she's confronted with obstacles in helping the boy and even greater obstacles within herself.

Read an excerpt from Chapter One:

# A Promise in Provence

# Chapter One

Lauren Abbott pressed both palms against the cool stainless-steel surface of the dishwasher, savoring the sharp chill against her steamy hands, then snapped it shut and pushed the 'on' button. She lifted the left cuff of her chef jacket and glanced at her watch. Ten fifteen.

A few deep breaths were futile in providing extra strength to finish out a seemingly endless shift. She'd still have to scrub down the metal counters and disinfect them. The appeal of working as a chef in a successful suburban D.C. restaurant had expired months ago. Of course, back then, it hadn't exactly been a choice.

"It's gonna be bad out there," said Bryan, who'd started in the kitchen only a week before. His face tensed as he cast a glance through the kitchen window toward the swirling flakes of snow. "We shoudda left hours ago."

Lauren followed his gaze and silently agreed. How much more white glitter would fall before she made it back into her own bed?

A faint aroma of grilled salmon still laced the air. The kitchen was calmer now as the evening wound down. The familiar voice of Chef Daniel, the owner of the Fins and Feathers Restaurant, rumbled from the dining room. He was shouting again, his complaints unintelligible, apart from the way he emphasized particular words, like *always, customer,* and *waiting.* He was often red-faced, from his bushy black eyebrows down to his white collar, as if in the midst of a colossal catastrophe even when there was none. Even when the customers had left over an hour ago amidst reports of seven inches of snow. By this time, the doors would be locked and the restaurant empty, except for the busboys who blew out candles and pulled the soiled linen cloths off the tables and into a pile.

Christmas Eve, and Chef Daniel's holiday special, flame-broiled surf and turf at prix fixe, had gone over like gangbusters, snowfall or not. No employee had taken a break all evening. Instead, each one did the work of three. Lauren leaned back against a counter as exhaustion rippled through her, down her back and pooled in her legs. A glance outside confirmed a steady swirl, like a cloak of dust in the blackness of the night.

Chef Daniel barged back into the kitchen with a loud bang through the swinging metal doors. Lauren flinched. He appeared more subdued now, though he still growled a few decibels lower about something that had happened at table eight. Lauren straightened and put her rag back into motion. Three other white-clad cooks scurried around the kitchen mopping up and putting food into the large double-door walk-in refrigerator. They tried to stay out of his target range until he returned to the dining room with an impatient stride.

A tap at the window caught Lauren's attention. She glanced up and saw the outline of a man peering in through the steam on the panes and the backdrop of swirling snowflakes. She squinted, then a wave of recognition. Mark, bundled in a parka, a wooly cap encasing his head. What was he doing here on Christmas Eve in the snow?

Lauren shot him a perplexed look with a tilt of her head, but her hands kept moving, changing the circular motion to back and forth strokes. Mark mimed a steering wheel turning as his troubled brown eyes beseeched her. He wanted to drive her home.

She shook her head and mouthed, "Thanks, though," adding a friendly smile. She couldn't. It was too soon. And she had no idea what time she'd be finished for the night. She caught his eyes through the frosty glass and shrugged with her palms up. She pointed to her watch, hoping he'd understand.

His shoulders drooped but he nodded then mouthed back the words, "Be careful." He waved and trudged away.

Her eyes burned for a moment, though no tears followed. Instead, a lump spread in her throat and began to throb. She swallowed. Mark had come out on a snowy night to accompany her home. That was Mark. Part of her wanted to let him, to allow him to navigate the icy roads while she rested against the car seat, entrusting her safety to him.

But she knew she couldn't. They would only start talking again about their relationship and it would all lead nowhere. Again. She wasn't ready because, well, what could she tell him? She didn't know herself, so how could she explain anything to him? Right now, she just needed a break from it all. From this restaurant. And from him.

She swiped the rag over the newly disinfected stainless-steel prep table again and blinked. Why did seeing Mark always do that to her? Fill her with guilt and regret so heavy it felt like she'd swallowed lead?

Finally, she was able to work the buttons down the left side of her white smock, pull the toque off her head, and slip into her down coat. Only one thing would do now, to slide between the sheets of her bed and leave the difficult questions of her life for a few hours. That was her preferred way to spend that particular Christmas Eve.

Read the rest of Chapter One at www.Kyle-Hunter.com

# *Circle Back Around*

## *(A stand-alone women's fiction novel)*

Hailey and her father haven't always seen eye to eye, especially in running the failing family textile mill. Frustrated, Hailey leaves the mill and her hometown in North Carolina to start a new life near her sister in Colorado. Only months later her father calls to ask a special favor. He needs heart surgery and asks Hailey to run the mill in his place.

Moving back would devastate Hailey's sister, Hope. Yet Hailey would have an opportunity to possibly save the mill, and at a time when her father needs her most. And maybe he'd even approve of her for the first time in her life.

Filled with self-doubt, Hailey returns to North Carolina and struggles to make a difference at the mill, facing more challenges than she bargained for. Her attractive neighbor, Alex, is almost enough to outweigh the difficulties, but she doesn't know that in the shadows lurks someone who wants to destroy both her *and* the mill.

Read Chapter One:

# Chapter One

Hailey Anderson closed her office door and collapsed into her cool leather desk chair. She would have savored a leisurely lunch hour instead of a frenzied rush of errands in the July heat of North Carolina. But lately, that was typical, amidst the pressures of her family's textile mill. She sat motionless, allowing herself five minutes to close her eyes and relax her shoulders. Cool air poured with a rattle from a vent in the corner of her office and its icy flow chilled her neck, drying the beads of perspiration.

The phone jangled into the quiet. Her eyes flew open and she glanced at the phone. An inside line. "This is Hailey."

"Did you see the paper today?" The breathless whisper came from Lenore, her longtime secretary.

Hailey leaned back in her chair and peered through the space between the vertical blinds to the area where mill administration was corralled. Her eyes met the worried gaze of Lenore, who clutched the phone to her ear.

"Not yet, Lenore. I haven't had a chance. Bad news, I guess?"

"Another mill is closing. Pristine. It's one of the oldest in North Carolina. They're falling like dominos."

"I knew they were struggling. That's a shame." Hailey swallowed and fingered the loose thread dangling from her skirt. Her hands were moist and tension needled her stomach. "But we're not closing, Lenore. Don't worry."

"Are you sure? Even Cannon, as big as they were. And other mills our size, one right after the other. Why would we be any different?" Panic laced each word.

Hailey bit her lip. How to comfort the woman while her own insides were in similar turmoil? She struggled to think of words that would be reassuring, convincing when, to even her ears, they sounded hollow.

"Just because another mill has closed doesn't mean that we will. People still need fabrics and clothes, don't they, now?"

A long pause hung on the line. "I guess so. Still, that doesn't guarantee . . . I'm sorry, Hailey. I know you and your dad are doing the best you can. I—I just don't know what I'd do if I lost this job. You know, with Jerry out of work and all . . ."

"I know, it's hard. But we're trying to be proactive and creative so we don't join the statistics. Be assured of that."

"Thanks." Lenore's voice lost its edge, but its usual cheerfulness was still missing. "Sorry to bother you."

"No, you haven't bothered me. I'll take a look at that article. Maybe it'll give me some ideas."

Hailey hung up the phone and stared at the newspaper, perched on the edge of her overfilled desk. It taunted her like a cobra about to strike. If only she *could* be proactive and creative. Paul Anderson, her father and owner of the mill, was anything *but*. He seemed to be hunkering down for the final and tragic defeat of Anderson Mill.

If Anderson closed its doors, she'd have to find a new job, like everyone else who worked here. Yet for her, it was more than a job. Even as a child, she'd wandered in and out of the various buildings—the carding department, where the raw wool was cleaned, the spinning room with hundreds of dancing vertical spools, the weaving area with rows of noisy looms—asking dozens of questions about what went on there. Everyone in town knew the Anderson family and their mill. They'd employed hundreds of the residents of Larkspur, North Carolina for four generations. For Hailey, many of those employees had names, faces, histories. And she was part of them, yet felt responsible for them at the same time. Like a good parent.

She pulled the newspaper closer to read the headline and the first few sentences, then shook her head. It had happened again, this time, to a neighboring mill whose owner she'd known for years. She leaned back in her chair and sighed. Her gaze panned the small office, a dingy square closed in by colorless walls. The drawing table, spread with designs and fabric samples, dominated the room. Against the wall her desk grimly shouldered her stacks of unfinished work and her computer, which broadcast bad news almost daily.

A tall window behind her desk overlooked a swatch of land with tall grasses and a few dumpsters, a dreary scene that matched her current life, except for one detail. During most of the day she could hear the faint rumble of dozens of looms one floor below, churning an endless, comforting heartbeat into the quiet.

Hailey glanced back at the newspaper, hesitant. Might be worth a try. She rose and took the paper in one hand. After launching a determined glance at Lenore's frightened one, she strode down the hall toward the presidential office, her mind churning out words and phrases as she went. Maybe she'd luck out and Dad would be receptive.

"Hey, Dad," she ventured as she crossed the threshold of his office. A pleasant smile might pave the way.

Her father swung his chair around and motioned to her with one finger, pulling the phone closer to his ear. Fatigue painted his pale blue eyes, which were surrounded by creases she hadn't noticed before. His gaunt face no longer resembled the ruddy Scotsman he was when she was a child. Every day bad news and criticism rained down on him, yet he only dug deeper into his favorite strategy of "wait and see". Only she was pretty sure he'd wait until there was nothing left to see.

"Yes, Hailey." He let out a gut-deep sigh as he set the telephone back on the cradle, his weary eyes on her.

For a split-second Hailey was more worried about him than frustrated. His withered frame no longer filled the executive chair. She reminded herself why she was there and rallied her arguments.

"Dad, did you hear about Pristine?" She placed the paper onto his desk, with a twinge of guilt for dumping more bad news on her beleaguered father. Yet, he had to see facts. The headline, an ugly black gash, read "Another Mill Falls in Forsythe County." She watched his face as he glanced down at the paper. His frown deepened as bushy white eyebrows furrowed, but he didn't speak.

"It has me worried. We need to be more proactive." Despite wanting to stay calm and professional, she added, "*Please*, let's do something new before we have to lay people off. I know you don't want to do that."

Paul Anderson's gaze hardened on his youngest daughter. That stare used to freeze her in her tracks when she was a child. She knew what he'd say next.

"Hailey, my drama queen, you always were emotional about the mill. We *are* taking action, and that's all you need to know."

She wouldn't let him off that easily, patronizing her as if she were still eight years old. "We have to plan a strategy. I'm afraid we'll shut down if we don't do something different. We—we lost another order to Pakistan, just this morning. The Owens account."

A flash of alarm slid across his face, but he pulled on a mask of calm just as quickly. Hailey schooled her voice, knowing it could easily burst out in staccato notes of panic, just like Lenore's had. *Calm, Hailey.*

"I'm asking you again to leave this to me. You are a designer. That's your role. It's not your job to save the mill. That's *my* job. I have lots of pressure on me. Now please, I have a meeting in ten minutes." He turned his chair slightly away as if to dismiss her. She saw only the shiny bald spot amidst wiry red-gray hair as he bowed his head toward his papers. Deflated, Hailey could only leave the office, as her eyes burned. She'd said what she had to say. But as usual, it hadn't made any impact on the elder Anderson. None.

She lowered her gaze, pretending to scan the newspaper she still clutched in her hands, as she passed Daniel Carlton, the assistant manager. The last thing she needed was for him to see tears in her eyes. He'd find some way to use it, sooner or later. Besides, she wasn't in the mood for greetings, especially his. All she wanted to do was wail. As she passed Lenore's desk, she just shook her head then closed her office behind her.

Six years. She'd tried to make a difference at Anderson Mill for the past six years, tried to reverse the fast leak, and had failed. Whatever she said to her father about any subject—especially the mill—was like talking to the wind. An indifferent, chilly wind. It had always been that way, and it had always stung. An acute and all-too-familiar pain, yet it paled against the threat nearly engulfing her family's business. For some crazy reason she had deep roots in this factory, a place whose employees were closer to a surrogate family for her than her own family. It wasn't merely a job. If only she could make a difference. If only she weren't fated to watch it slowly grind down and go the way so many other mills had gone in the last decade.

Growing up in a textile town, Hailey had always taken for granted the fact that these factories would always be part of her landscape. Textiles had once been the largest industry in North Carolina, but during the eighties and nineties, they rapidly lost their place. Hundreds of jobs vanished and would never return, having been replaced by foreign contracts and automation. The new millennium had shown improvements, but the mills weren't out of danger, even now in 2004. Hailey had watched the trend with interest, then mild panic, as she understood that it could happen to them, too. Especially with the current style of leadership. In response, she'd tried to court new clients on the side, bring suggestions to the presidential office. Nothing made a scratch.

When the long work day ended, Hailey wearily drove toward her townhouse a few miles from the mill. Her languid gaze painted across the familiar buildings . . . the town hall, the park in front of it where the city held an art festival in summer and placed a tall evergreen at Christmas, colorfully lit, towering in the center, gathering townspeople for caroling or New Year's Eve festivities.

On the diagonal corner sat The Scoop, a local ice cream parlor where she and her sister, Hope, went as children, escaping from their preoccupied parents on Saturday afternoons. They'd share secrets while enjoying one of twelve homemade flavors.

How she'd love to be able to sit down with Hope right then, pouring out her fears and anguish, since Hope had always been the one she'd turned to for family warmth. But Hope had never shared Hailey's attachment to Anderson Mill. She'd moved away to Colorado without a twinge for the family business, while Hailey was still anchored and rusting in place.

She could always talk to her best friend, Nina, whose calm manner usually put Hailey's frustrations into perspective. But Nina had recently gotten engaged to Justin. Hailey wouldn't dampen her friend's joy with her own struggles.

Hailey passed the post office, Hank's Auto Repair, the Ace Hardware store. So many memories from a lifetime in a small town that now hemmed her in, narrowing her possibilities, suffocating her.

Tears moistened her lashes and blurred her vision. It was bad enough that things didn't look good for Anderson Mill, in danger of joining all the bleak statistics of textile manufacturing in the previous decade. So many of Anderson's employees were like grandmothers and grandfathers to her. She'd known their children and their grandchildren, had watched them grow up. She saw the dread on their faces as they spoke to her of their fears. It squeezed her gut to see them tied in knots by day and likely losing sleep, as they wondered when they, too, would hear that their jobs were gone.

For some, it was the only work they and their children had ever known. She could only guess what they would do.

Hailey pulled into the numbered space at her condominium complex and, with a deep sigh, left the air-conditioned sanctuary of her car. The sweet fragrance of fresh-cut grass wafted toward her. Up the street, her neighbor, Alex, was shoving something bulky into the dumpster. When the mass finally disappeared into the opening, he stepped back and turned in her direction. Seeing her, he lifted an arm in a static wave then sauntered away toward his condo.

Her hand raised in a weak response as she watched him. For too long. She hadn't seen Alex since the homeowners' meeting a couple of months earlier. That evening they'd had a minor debate, as she objected to the landscaping fees. She'd probably come across as stubborn and hot-tempered. She'd considered dropping by his house to apologize, not for her opinion, but for her tone. That gesture might have smoothed things out instead of reminding him to avoid her.

Hailey let out another long breath from a deep well inside as she locked the car. Friday afternoon. What would her weekend hold? Trying to stay cool and push away dark dread until Monday, when she'd have to face it all over again. She'd forgotten what it was like to feel any other way.

*Kyle Hunter* is the author of ten novels of inspirational romance and women's fiction. Her relatable characters will become like close friends you'll cheer for and learn from as you join them on their journeys. Story settings range from Europe to small town America. As characters face challenges, the insights they gain are always relevant.

Kyle spent thirteen years in France, and she's intrigued by faraway places. Currently, she lives in North Carolina where she writes fiction, non-fiction (under the pen name K. B. Oliver), and the travel blog OliversFrance.com. She also teaches French to adults.

*One December*

*One December*

www.ingramcontent.com/pod-product-compliance
Lightning Source LLC
Chambersburg PA
CBHW070658180626
46817CB00006B/2430